Kimi's Secret
John Hudspith

Published by FeedARead.com Publishing – Arts Council funded

for Ande

nee worries, pet

~}~

'Mousehole, the prettiest village in England.'
Dylan Thomas

'It's in the eyes. Always get the eyes.'
Monster's Chronicles

High on a Cornish moor… twenty-three

ancient stones bent and twisted through time into a haphazard circle, poke from the mist like the gnarled teeth of a sleeping giant. On top of every stone stands a crow, each perfectly still, not a flutter or twitch among them. A whisper of breeze swirls the mist and all at once the crows take flight, charging the circle's middle in a screeching mass of beak and claw. Bones crack, feathers fly and mangled bodies thump to the dewy grass until only a single crow remains. With blood on its head and a small black eye impaled on its beak the triumphant crow alights to the nearest stone, scrapes the eye off, gulps it down, then takes flight once more. It has a message to deliver, and like most ominous creatures it will enjoy sending some little hints that it's on its way…

~ 1 ~

~ NO SERVICE ~

Tucked in a cosy little pocket on Cornwall's south coast is the charming village of Mousehole, where tranquility sparkles on apple-gold water and the peace is about to be rudely shattered.

In the smallest bedroom of number seventeen, which overlooks the harbour, Kimi Nichols is sitting on her bed. She is staring at her left hand and has been for some time. She woke with it numb and the dull buzz of pins and needles. Her left hand is smaller than the right, slightly bent, and she can't part her thumb from her fingers very far. Indentations, like grooves, run diagonally over the thumb and forefinger and again down the little finger. It doesn't hurt or anything just looks a bit odd. Kimi even has a name for it: *Little Hand*. It wouldn't be the first time she'd slept on her hand. I mean, everybody does now and again, right? Problem is, she's been awake for more than hour, but the pins and needles won't go. She gives it a rub and tries to move her fingers.

"KIMI!"

She startles. It's Dad. "Yeah?"

"Your brekkie's ready. Me and Mum are going soon. That meeting…remember?"

Kimi sensed skullduggery where *that meeting* was concerned. It was the way Dad announced it after tea last night – all nervous – like he was hiding a secret.

"KIMI?"

"Be right down." She draws back the curtains and fills the room with yellow, ties her hair back, slips her mobile into the pocket of her penguin-patterned peejays, bids a good day to her animal skull collection which fills almost every shelf, then heads downstairs.

In the dining room, in faded jeans, equally faded green tee-shirt and with his hair gelled into spikes, Dad is dishing up Kimi's favourite: beans on toast with a good blob of Marmite mixed in.

"Thanks," Kimi said, tucking in.

"Hi," Mum said, sat to Kimi's right.

She looked pretty as usual; bright eyes, shiny hair, purple sweater, but she had a weird smile this morning. Probably too much tea. "Hi," Kimi said with her mouth full.

Dad took his seat and flicked open the paper. "Nice?" He nodded to the breakfast.

Kimi swallowed. "Lovely thanks. Erm, what time'll you be back from your erm…*secret* meeting?"

Dad's eyes did a fidgety-flash. He lifted the paper and disappeared behind it. "Shouldn't be too long," he muttered.

"Don't worry, lovely," Mum said. "We'll be back in

plenty time for birthday shopping. Plenty time."

She said all this with the weird smile firmly in place. Kimi couldn't put a finger on it, but it was a smile that didn't belong. "This meeting," Kimi said. "I think I know where you're going, and, well…can I come?"

Dad's eyes peered over the paper. "Still on about the pink limo?"

Tomorrow, Kimi would be eleven. She dearly hoped they had booked the pink limo she'd hinted for at least a trillion times.

"Listen, Kimi," Dad said. "This is a simple business meeting on the golf course and nothing at all to do with pink limousines. If you were getting a pink limo for your birthday, don't you think it would have been booked weeks ago?"

He had a point. But still, he was hiding something. Kimi was sure of it. Little Hand tingled. The pins and needles weren't letting up. She put her knife and fork down and gave it a rub. "Can't you ring up and put it off 'til Monday, Dad? I – I don't want you to go."

"We can't. Haven't got a number. All we got was this note left behind the bar in the clubhouse." He took a piece of paper from his pocket and pushed it across the table.

JACK AND VALERIE NICHOLS
YOUR SOFTWARE EXPERTISE IS URGENTLY REQUIRED
WE PAY GENEROUSLY

BE AT THE FIRST HOLE AT PRECISELY 10 AM ON SATURDAY

PRESCISELY!

(PS: DON'T BRING YOUR KID)

"That's just rude." Kimi pushed the note back.

Mum laid a hand on Kimi's arm. "But you knew we had this meeting."

And there was that weird smile again. What was that film where aliens take over people and make them act all stupid? Kimi shuddered. "I - I don't want you to go. Really, Mum, something doesn't feel right. My hand – it's -"

Mum rose slowly to her feet. "Oooh, I know what you mean," she said, staring at the ceiling. The weird smile had vanished. "I'm getting a vibe. There's something in the air, for sure."

This *was* good news. Something always came of Mum's vibes. One time, the fat bloke next door had a heart attack five minutes after she said he would and she saved his life. Another time, Mum scorched her angel cakes and might have burnt the house down if she hadn't vibed and got out of the bath. She was always sensing things. If Mum said a storm was brewing then a *stor*–

"There's a storm brewing," Mum said. "It's best we stay right here." She sat back down with a determined nod.

Kimi looked hopefully to Dad. His fingers were tapping the table.

"No! It's a weird appointment, I admit. But I've a hunch we'd regret missing it."

Kimi glared at him. "A *hunch*? What about Mum's vibe?"

"Can't I stay here, Jack?" Mum cut in. She had a forlorn look that Kimi thought might do the trick. She was good at forlorn was Mum.

"Nope, sorry, the note asks for us both."

Mum folded her arms. "Well then I'm sorry too, Jack. I've a very bad feeling about this. We're staying put."

Dad appeared flustered. He looked to Kimi then back to Mum, and with piercing eyes said: "Before you know it, we'll be back in a *wiffy*!"

Mum froze like a dummy and Kimi went icy cold. The pins and needles in Little Hand suddenly vanished. It felt like the room had paused for a second. But only for a second. Dad was zipping up his jacket and heading for the hall with the car keys dangling from his hand. Kimi jumped to her feet. "Stop!"

He stopped. "What?"

"What *are* you on about?"

"What?"

"You said `wiffy` - it's *jiffy - back in a jiffy*."

He shrugged. "Wiffy - jiffy - whatever."

"Ahhh, yes," Mum said. "Back in a wiffy, yes." She was wearing the stupid smile again.

"I'm sorry," Kimi said. "But you two are acting bonkers."

Dad glanced at the wall clock. "We need to be going."

Mum sprang to her feet, grinning madly.

"But Mum, what about your vibe?"

She looked puzzled. "What vibe?"

"You're kidding, right?"

"Don't fret," Dad said. "You'll be back in a wiffy!"

"Huh? Me? Don't you mean, *you*? You're not making any sense. And quit with the wiffy thing!"

"Ah, of course, how silly of me - *we'll* be back in a wiffy - your Mum and me, yes."

Kimi couldn't find the words.

Mum came and kissed her on the nose. "Bye, my lovely." She gave her a squeeze.

"But Mum, you said a storm was brewing."

"Stop worrying, Kimi. Slightest sign of a storm and we'll be in the clubhouse." She kissed her again on top of the head.

Dad bustled Mum into the hall and Kimi followed. "Why aren't you listening to Mum's vibe?"

Now he was pushing Mum out the front door.

"There's something you're not telling me," Kimi shouted. "I'm not stupid you know. What's the big secret?"

Dad rushed back inside, pushed the door closed and strode

up to Kimi with purpose. His hands landed on her shoulders and gripped firmly. Their eyes locked. "Let's say there *is* a secret. A blooming great whopper. And in less than thirty minutes *you* will know *all* about it!"

Kimi's breath caught. "Really?"

"Really."

"Is this one of your birthday games?"

"No," he said, his eyes woefully wide.

A feeling of darkness dropped upon Kimi as if a thick, black umbrella had closed over her head. Little Hand gave one almighty throb and the pins and needles returned. The tiny hairs on the nape of her neck bristled and prickled and pulled her in two with a shudder. A scatter of wing beats rushed through her ears then vanished. She swallowed the lump from her throat. "Dad, it's – it's - I think – well, I think I'm having my first vibe. I – I don't know what to do."

He did not even blink. "Trust me, sweetheart. I need you to stay here and figure things out. Can you do that for me?"

"Figure what out? I - I'm meant to be doing my homework and - "

"Forget your homework." His hands slid from her shoulders and gripped her upper arms. "Get this right, and you will never have to do homework *ever* again. Can you do this, Kimi?"

Kimi laughed. A nervous laugh.

"Answer me!" He was shaking her.

"You're scaring me, Dad."

His grip relaxed. He kissed her forehead. "I really must go." He went to the front door, paused, looked back. "You'll get through this," he said, before turning away and stepping outside with what Kimi was certain was a tear in his eye.

"Through what?"

The door pulled shut.

Car doors opened and closed.

The engine hummed to life then faded through Mousehole's narrow streets.

They were gone.

Kimi was cold and shaking. Little Hand felt like a pin cushion. Was this how vibes made you feel? Mum always said that one day *she* might get a sense for these things, too. Kimi returned to the dining room. The radio whined like a cat then crackled with static. Outside, wind surged, throwing leaves and litter at the patio doors. Kimi stepped back. The gulls were growing in number, getting louder. Then she noticed something. The hundreds of gulls that filled the air above the harbour were parting down the middle like a giant zipper. Through the growing V shape to the clear blue sky beyond, a spec of black, moving black, beating wings black, was coming this way.

Vibe - or imagination?

A black dart swooping into the harbour.

She did always get giddy around the time of her birthday.

Seagulls dispersed, an explosion of white.

So maybe that was it.

Raggedy black. Faster, closer.

Or maybe it wasn't.

Coming straight for the patio doors.

Oh crap.

THWUMP!!!

Kimi ran to the doors and crouched. Through the glass, a bundle of black feathers was straightening itself up. It was a crow, looking stunned and kind of rocking on its feet. She reached up and opened a door. "Poor thing. Are you all right?" The crow stared at her. She considered getting it some bread but had no time to act. The crow hissed and leapt forward, wings flapping. She shut the door fast and the crow thumped into the pane for a second time. It clawed at the glass and hammered with its beak. There was blood on its head and nothing but black in its empty eyes. Kimi gripped the door handles and was about to scream for help when the crow backed off. It stared for a moment, gave one final hiss, then turned and fluttered over the lane to the harbour railings where it settled, facing the house. No longer feeling cold, Kimi carefully opened a door and poked her head out.

The crow cawed and ruffled its wings.

Then it spoke…

"One…death…today…"

The words were screechy, but Kimi was certain that's what it had said.

"One…death…today…" the crow repeated, before lifting off backwards and tumbling away over the harbour, diminishing quickly to a black spec over the sea.

Kimi ran up the path trying to keep sight of the crow - but it was gone, and so had the sunshine. Heavy grey clouds were rolling in from nowhere, casting the harbour into shadow. Across the bay in Penzance, clouds as black as night moved in on the headland, right above where the golf course was situated. Kimi hurried back inside, stopping only to pick up a long, black feather. She quickly closed the patio doors behind her.

Thunder rumbled, the room darkened, and rain began spitting on the windows. Outside, a hunched old lady hurried past in a swirl of leaves. Kimi told herself that crows can't talk and that she was probably imagining things. She looked at the stiff feather and bent and crumpled it tight inside her good hand. A barrage of thunder made her shriek. She thought of Mum and Dad. The clock said it was almost ten. The mystery client would be appearing at the first hole. She returned to the patio doors where rain pattered and trickled and leant her head to the glass. The pulse in her temple tapped dully against it. Across the bay, tails of black

18

cloud trailed so low they seemed to touch the headland. Lightning blinked within the clouds and thunder grumbled. She tried to imagine Mum and Dad, safe in the clubhouse, but could not shift her gaze from the blackening sky.

The rain pattered to a stop.

The radio crackled and died.

The hairs on her neck stood to attention.

Little Hand gave one great pounding throb.

And right at the spot she was staring, a brilliant blue lightning bolt ripped from the sky, splitting the blackness into two jagged halves. Kimi screamed and jumped back. A series of massive bangs followed and the house vibrated around her. Windowpanes rattled in their frames and light fittings danced and jangled.

She had to call Dad. Right now!

Stumbling to the table with the lightning bolt imprinted on her retina and her heart booming, Kimi retrieved her mobile from her pocket and shakily hit speed-dial.

She held her breath, waiting for the call to connect...

Then the words `NO SERVICE` blinked on the screen.

———

~ Is it You? ~

With Little Hand throbbing like the time she trapped it in the car door, Kimi went to the patio doors and stepped outside. The sun was back out and the gulls were fewer. Across the bay the headland gleamed wetly in the sunlight. A pair of rainbows curved down into the sea. Calm and peaceful it might now look, but Kimi knew different. In her mind came a faint image of two shadowy figures standing in an open space; a flicker, a bright flash and the image was gone. She tried her phone again.

This time it connected.

`Hi there, um, you're through to Dad - um, Jack Nichols, that is - um, leave me a message after the beep and you'll get back to me in a wiffy!`

BEEEEEEEEP

Kimi breathed hard into the silence. That was not Dad's usual recording. And of course one word stood out. She thought of the talking crow…*one death today*…and considered that Mum or Dad might have been killed by the lightning. But then there was a feeling of something else, something Kimi struggled to understand. It was a feeling of being alone, of being disconnected. Maybe the crow was wrong and both her parents had been struck by the lightning.

Mum had said they would be in the clubhouse if there was a storm, but the storm came in quickly. *Too* quickly. And that lightning bolt was enough to blow the clubhouse apart. She closed her eyes and tried to summon the image of the shadowy figures once more. But nothing came; apart from the realisation that `one death` could mean her own. Of course, that's why the crow had visited *her*. It had nothing to do with Mum and Dad.

No - impossible.

There was no crow.

Just imagination at work.

But the feather? It was still crumpled tight in her hand.

She threw it on the floor where it unfurled like a newborn insect.

Feeling vulnerable in her peejays, she placed her mobile on the table and went to the ironing basket. Her pink tee shirt with the Superman logo, the jeans with a sparkly heart on the backside and an old baggy sweatshirt were snatched from the pile. She dressed quickly and slipped into her trainers.

Dad's words came back to her: *Let's say there is a secret!*

Wind howled and a whole heap of rubbish hit the patio doors. Kimi rushed forward intent on locking the doors when the howl became a roar and the doors blew in and slammed off the walls. Leaves and litter burst into the room, pushing Kimi backwards. Hair blowing wildly around her head, she made a grab for the table. Her chair tipped over and slid into the hall. Soggy debris spun round the room. A polystyrene chip carton came flapping at her face. She yelped and ducked. The room groaned, the walls appeared to waver in and out, and the carpet billowed dreamily. Kimi was finding it difficult to stay on her feet. Then the wind vanished as quickly as it had started. The leaves and rubbish dropped to the carpet all at once. The patio doors relaxed from the walls with a little creak. The radio, now on the floor, gave a hiss and went dead for the second time.

Kimi kept tight hold of the table. A crisp packet dislodged from the curtain rail and dropped to the floor. A wet chestnut leaf peeled from the ceiling and landed on the remains of her breakfast. She reached to remove it but froze. The leaf was lifting itself from the plate of its own accord. It rose in the air until it was in line with Kimi's head where it hovered as if it was inspecting her. Kimi was so frozen that she thought her heart might stop. The leaf did a little jiggle, screwed itself into a soggy ball, then launched itself back to the ceiling where it stuck with a splat. Her breakfast plate was moving, rotating, spinning - faster and faster until the cold beans parted from their sauce and danced in the air like orange fireflies. The plate came to a sudden stop and split into two with a crack. The firefly beans swirled upwards and joined the leaf on the ceiling. Kimi gasped. The beans had spelled out a word.

BOO!

Kimi's eyes rolled upwards and the ceiling fell away to darkness. She dreamed she was in the back of the pink limo watching sparks spraying from its sides as it forced its way through Mousehole's narrow streets. A feeling of excitement was interrupted however when the chauffeur turned around and revealed his huge beak, feathery head and black ball eyes. `*One death today*!` the crow chauffeur said, before breaking into hideous cackling which juddered his shoulders and made his cap fall off.

Kimi's eyes shot open. She was sat at the bottom of the stairs and had no recollection of getting there. Little Hand still buzzed with pins and needles and her chin ached something awful. She must have fainted and banged it on the table and somehow crawled from the dining room to here. She thought about making a cup of tea - that's what Mum would do - but Mum and Dad would be back soon. She'd be safer waiting right here.

She pulled to her feet and peered into the hall mirror to examine the bump on her chin, but only managed to glimpse a purple blotch before the mirror popped off the wall and crashed to the floor at her feet, smashing into pieces. She bounded up the stairs and flew towards her bedroom, arms outstretched, but before she got there the door swung open and invisible hands stuck in her back, propelling her forward. She had to jump onto the bed to avoid cracking her shins. The door slammed shut. She spun around to see her rocking chair slide in front of it. Her chest heaved into sobs and she flung the duvet over her head, wishing more than anything she would hear the car pulling up. Her heart knocked hard in the darkness beneath the duvet. She choked back the sobs and forced herself still.

Then a creak.

The rocking chair.

Back and forth, faster and faster, so fast it started banging off the door and Kimi just *had* to look. She threw the duvet off and gasped as the rocker went crazy, twisting and turning. The rows of shelves on all three walls began to vibrate. Balled up socks fell to the floor, followed by Ollie dog, Ashley the clown, and most of her animal skulls. The rocker stilled and the shelves stopped vibrating, but one shelf, the top one, caught Kimi's eye. Right in the corner, her keepsake box slid slowly along the shelf, pushing dolls and teddy bears. One by one they tipped over the edge and dropped to the floor. Lastly, her keepsake box teetered.

It fell, bounced off the arm of the rocker and spilled its contents on the floor.

Movement. A theatre programme lifted and flopped over. Cinema tickets, foreign coins and old photos scattered themselves as if an invisible hand was sifting through them, and then from their midst her long-forgotten corn dolly rose like a vamp from the grave. A tiny thing, no bigger than her thumb, all dusty and worn and one leg missing. It lifted into the air and floated towards her.

Kimi held out Little Hand. As the dolly settled on her palm she felt the fear, and the pins and needles, slipping away. In a whisper, she said, "Is it you?"

—

~ 3 ~

~ Bentley ~

Silence.

"Please tell me it's you." Kimi didn't want to say his name, just in case it wasn't.

Silence.

Then she caught the smell of bananas. "Bentley!" she said, and immediately the dolly stood up on her palm. The missing leg regenerated and the dusty corn limbs turned golden. "Whoa!" Little Hand closed around the dolly - and she remembered.

She was five. Picnicking on Bodmin Moor where Dad liked to sketch the old standing stones. Hot yellow sun made for bright and inviting corn fields and Dad said not to stray because people had reported seeing big black cats. But Kimi did stray. Mum on the blanket in bikini and sunglasses. Dad in shorts with his head in a sketch pad. Kimi chased the purple butterfly. She liked the way its wings shimmered. When it fluttered over the corn tops, Kimi followed. It was very hot among the stalks. Puffs of dust fell in her face and corn stalks caught her hair as she pushed through. But the butterfly was nowhere to be seen.

Then came a sound like snoring - or purring. She recalled Dad's warning, but still, she adored cats. She followed the sound to a circle of flattened corn. In the middle lay an enormous cat all black and shiny like a giant blob of liquorice. Kimi giggled. The big cat opened one bright yellow eye - then the other, lifted its bulky head and sniffed the air. It pushed to its feet, yawned and stretched.

"Hello," Kimi said.

The big cat slinked towards her. Its whiskery snout nudged her tummy and she fell backwards to the sight of long silvery fangs. Another step and the enormous cat was right over her, blocking out the sun. When its jaws opened wide she saw right down its throat. Kimi screamed and a boy appeared in an instant, a boy all misty and blue. He smacked the cat on the nose. It hissed, lurched away and vanished into the corn.

The blue boy smiled, pulled Kimi to her feet, snatched off a corn head, crumpled it in his fist, then held out his hand. In it sat a tiny corn dolly. "I'm Bentley - at your service," he said.

A cloud of blue mist appeared in the rocker. Kimi smiled as the form took shape, but it was not a boy that appeared. Not Bentley. A man, grinning, and he looked older than Dad. Creases wrinkled a face that was a darker shade of blue. His blue shirt and blue trousers appeared to be woollen. His flecked hair lay in brushed back waves.

"You're not Bentley." Kimi shuffled backwards on

28

the bed.

"Yee gads!" said the apparition. "That was hard work!"

It did sound a little like him. "*Are* you Bentley?"

"Course it's me. Ain't aged that much, have I?" The ghostly figure looked offended. He screwed up his face, gripped the arms of the rocker and began to shudder. The blue man shrank. His features and his clothes smoothed out, and seconds later there was little Bentley. "See, it is me," he said in a small voice.

Kimi emitted a giggle that seemed to be free of nerves.

"What's so funny?"

"You're weeny."

Bentley looked down at himself. "Oh!" He screwed his face, shuddered then expanded again. Now he looked about Kimi's age. "That do?"

"I guess," Kimi said. "So *you* did all the poltergeist stuff?"

Bentley nodded. "I was trying to scare you into using your fear to make me materialize the same way you used to. Only it wasn't as easy as it used to be. Guess you got braver, ay?"

"Braver? I flipping fainted." Kimi rubbed her chin.

"Ah yes. I didn't see that coming."

"*And* you've broken the hall mirror."

"Hmm, impulsive. Sorry."

"Mum'll go mad."

"It's good to see you anyway. How've you been?"

Kimi looked at the regenerated dolly in her hand and then back to Bentley. "I'm eleven tomorrow."

Bentley nodded.

"And, erm, eleven-year-olds don't have imaginary friends. Do they?"

Bentley's face changed from sunshine to thunder. "We have to be going." He jumped to his feet and held out a hand. "Come on. There's no time to waste."

Kimi shook her head. "Thanks for visiting, but Mum and Dad'll be back soon. And when they get here, I'm forgetting all about talking birds, whirlwinds and imaginary friends I haven't seen in years, and I'm taking off for some much needed birthday shopping."

Bentley sat back down with a surprised look.

"You okay?" Kimi asked.

"Just then Kimi, you mentioned talking birds. What did you mean?"

Kimi hesitated, but only slightly. If you can't talk to your imaginary friend then who can you talk to? "Well, I was actually spoken to by a crow."

"Oh." Bentley's eyes widened. He looked to the floor in thought.

"Don't you want to know what it said?"

Bentley stood up and held out a hand once more. "Not right now Kimi. I've a predicament, see. The biggest predicament ever to face anyone's, uhm, imaginary friend. And if I don't get this right, there's gonna be big trouble. So please, Kimbo. Come with me."

It was years since she'd been called that. Years. "But the crow, Bentley. It flew into the doors, then it attacked me, then it said -"

"No, Kimi. Tell me later. We need to skedaddle!"

"Skedaddle to where? And why? This is about the lightning isn't it? Something's happened to Mum or Dad - or both - or something's about to happen to me. You're here because you know, don't you?"

"What could possibly make you think I might know something?" Bentley pulled the rocker to one side and opened the door. He held out a hand again. "Now come on. I'm serious. We have to go, Kimi. Right now!"

Kimi did not budge. "You obviously know something because you were trying to scare me into making you appear. Why would you do that if you didn't know something bad was going to happen?"

Bentley let out a long breath and closed his eyes. He shuddered then bloomed taller into the old and wrinkled Bentley. "You know, you never used to ask so many questions."

His old eyes were round with anxiety, his creased

face pale and sagging. Long seconds of silence passed between them; time for Kimi to think that maybe she should be trusting him. He had always arrived to help when bad things happened. And Kimi had a feeling that the talking crow was only the beginning. Her heart was banging again.

"Listen Kimbo," Bentley said. "This is not a joke. I really must insist -"

"It's okay," Kimi heard the strain in her voice. "Tell me what to do."

"You'll come?" Bentley brightened a little.

Kimi nodded.

He shrank back to young Bentley. This time she took his hand.

***

Kimi surveyed the mess in the dining room. "Mum'll crap a cow when she sees this. Can't you clean it up?"

"I'm not a magician," Bentley said. He pointed a finger to the air and made a spinning motion. Instantly the wind blew up, whipping the debris into a spin.

"Could have fooled me." Kimi stepped back against the wall as the mix swirled into a vortex.

"We're going to my place!" Bentley yelled over the roar. "You'll be safe there!"

Kimi shook her head.

"Come on," he beckoned. "Step into the wind!"

Kimi squashed herself against the wall.

"Step inside the wind, Kimi. Please. You'll be safe. I *promise!*"

"Nooooo," she whimpered.

Bentley dropped his finger. The wind vanished and the rubbish fell back to the carpet. He looked really anxious. "I thought you were going to trust me?"

Kimi shook her head. "I - I'm sorry, but something's not adding up. It's great to see you again. But would you go off through a whirlwind with an imaginary friend at eleven? Would you? Really? I'm not a little kid anymore. I - I feel something. A vibe. And *you* know what that something is. Don't you?"

Bentley leant forward, palms on the dining table. "Well maybe I do, or maybe or I don't. But that's not the issue. The issue is, we really need to get out of here." He shuddered, swelled, and once again old Bentley stood there looking seriously vexed. "All right," he said in a much firmer voice. "It's truth time. Here's some facts, and you need to listen up because there ain't much time. Understand?"

Kimi managed a single nod.

"Firstly, I'm not imaginary. Never have been. I'm your Tulpa, your protector, created from your essence. Secondly, it's not a whirlwind, it's a localised twirly. Thirdly, you ain't eleven 'til tomorrow. And lastly - and this is the important bit - any second now you'll be getting visitors." He nodded up the hall to the front door.

"Yeah, Mum and Dad," Kimi said. "They'll be back, soon."

"My superiors wanted to snatch you. Take you without your consent."

"What superiors?"

"Quiet!" Bentley raised a hand. "I begged them to let me try first. See if I could get you to come of your own will." He glanced at the wall clock. "It's nine minutes past ten, Kimi."

"But -"

"Quiet, please! We're out of time. Any second now those visitors will arrive." He nodded through the hall. "Please, Kimi. Come with your old friend, Bentley, who you can trust with your life."

Then things moved extremely fast.

The sound of a car - very loud - came screaming up the front lane.

"Hurry!" Bentley stirred the air again with one hand and lunged at Kimi with the other. The rubbish spun and the wind roared. Outside, tyres squealed and the arriving car ploughed into the wheelie bins and sent one bouncing off the front door with a tremendous bang. Kimi screamed and leapt in Bentley's direction. They collided and Bentley almost fell into the spinning vortex. It wobbled until he got his finger up and twirling again. Kimi looked back to the front door. The hum of the running engine was right outside.

No other sound.

No one getting out.

No one coming to the door.

She turned back to Bentley. There were tears in his eyes. "Trust me Kimbo," he pleaded.

She glanced back to the front door where the car outside ticked over. "What if it's Mum and Dad?"

Bentley shook his head. He took a step forward. "Kimi - come on!"

The car outside suddenly revved so loudly that the windows buzzed.

Kimi screamed.

"NOW!" yelled Bentley.

She was already flying towards him. Bentley's hand gripped hers and pulled her into the vortex. The roar became a whoosh. She glanced over her shoulder in time to see the front door opening and the beginnings of a shadow coming inside, before the vortex spinning around them increased its speed and the world outside went into a blur.

It was calm inside the vortex.

The wind was not touching them. Kimi's hair was not blowing around her head. In fact, this was the calmest feeling of all. Kimi, still clinging to Bentley, was about to tell him that someone had entered the house when Bentley began to fizzle. Tiny holes appeared on his smiling face. The holes were expanding, joining, cracking, popping. Bentley was vanishing. The noise was horrendous. Kimi pulled away from him. Then she noticed that her hands and the sleeves of her top were also filling with holes; fizzing, bubbling, vanishing. There was no pain, only a feeling of great calm as she watched herself dissolve away to nothing.

Nothing.

Nothing but white.

No Bentley.

No spinning wind.

No pins and needles in Little Hand.

No Kimi. Only a consciousness floating in white. Kimi thought of home and saw Dad's proud smile when she found her first rat skull, saw Mum laughing - which Mum always did a lot of.

Then back to white.

She looked for her hands, her legs, but could not see nor feel them.

Could not feel herself.

Only a feeling of lightness.

Nothing but white.

One death today.

———

4

~ Disassembled and Reassembled ~

She continued to be there. Amongst the white. Neither floating nor standing. Just there. If she had shoulders, she thought, then white feathery wings might sprout from them any second. Something must have gone wrong, or perhaps she was still in her bed and this was all a dream. But those words - *one death* - in that awful screechy voice - would not let go. If this was death, she wished it to end.

Fizzling sounds resumed from somewhere above. A feeling of weight returned to her body and Kimi was aware of her heartbeat once more. The fizzling grew faster into cracks snaps pops, and Bentley was reforming before her eyes. Tiny bubbles appeared in mid-air, spread, joined up, became a faint face, a see-through shirt, a smile. Kimi checked her hands. They were also reforming. A sucking sensation from above and the spinning vortex reappeared, whirring rapidly around them. Kimi felt solid – twice or three times her normal weight. Beyond the wind, washy colours of greens and blues blurred in and out of each other. Kimi swayed, grabbed for Bentley but missed and fell, still fizzling, through the wind. There was a loud pop and she landed on her hands and knees with a thud that bolted up her arms and rampaged through her bruised and throbbing chin.

"You okay?" Bentley's voice.

Kimi's mouth hung open. The sun's rays were hot on the back of her head. The fizzle was subsiding down her legs to her feet. She was staring at a white pebble on dusty ground.

"Kimi?"

A white pebble.

"You need this?" Bentley's voice again. Kimi looked up through tangles of hair. Bentley was no longer blue. He looked normal, apart from the raggedy clothes. He held out a brown paper bag with a blue heart on the front. "You going to be sick?"

Kimi brushed the hair from her eyes and looked behind to the diminishing vortex. Rubbish and leaves, evidently brought with them, pitter-pattered to lush green grass as the wind died. No one was following. She looked back to Bentley.

He folded away the sick bag. "How you feeling?"

"The pins and needles have gone."

"Huh?"

"In my hand." She inspected Little Hand, half expecting it to be like a normal hand. But it was still bent and crooked and smaller than the right. "Had them since I woke up. But they're gone."

"Right. So you're not going to be sick?"

The memory of watching herself dissolve was strong

38

in her mind. Floating in white as only a pair of eyes had been extremely unnerving. Thinking back, it felt like she had been beheaded. She rubbed her neck. "The noise, Bentley, the noise, it was -"

"I know, I know. First time's always the worst." Kimi's toes gave a final fizzle and her ears popped. She shifted around onto her bottom, stuck her fingers in her ears and gave them a good wiggle. Bentley said something. She removed her fingers. "What?"
"I said that you seem to be okay. It'll wear off in a bit."

"You could have warned me, Bentley. That was scary."

"I know. But you're here now, safe in *my* world." Bentley stepped to one side and swung an arm wide.

They were on a rocky outcrop overlooking a patchwork of rainbow-coloured field and forest which seemed to run for miles. The sun was beating down, and a fringe of pale green mountains shimmered on the horizon beneath a cloudless sky the colour of duck-egg blue. All around, the sound of birdsong, insect clicks, and a distinct banana aroma with a mouthwatering hint of summer-fruit pudding. "Whoa," Kimi said. "I'm dreaming, right? That's what this is. A crazy dream."

"Oh blast!" Bentley was glancing all around. "Blast! Blast! Blast!" He stamped a boot in the dust. "Blasted blast!" He went to the edge of the outcrop and peered down.

Kimi crawled to his side and looked down, too. "What's wrong?"

"We're in the wrong place." He sighed mournfully, went back to where Kimi had landed on her knees, and kicked the white pebble.

It rolled past Kimi and went over the edge. Kimi watched it fall. After two bounces it met steps cut from the rock which zigzagged downwards, bounced a few times more where it met the steps again, before landing on the rock-strewn floor below.

They were facing a similar rock face and outcrop, and the gulley between them ran either way as far as Kimi could see. There was no way over. And behind them appeared to be only vast green field and sunshine.

"I clean forgot about this," Bentley said. "Come on." He found the top step a few metres to their right and quickly bobbed from sight.

Kimi got shakily to her feet and followed. "Forgot about what?" The steps were big and not so easy to navigate.

"This place!" Bentley paused by some strange blue weeds growing from the rock. "This is where all newbies arrive. You being a newbie, the twirly automatically brought us here. We're miles from home. I should have altered the mix to take us closer."

"Well I don't like this. I want to go home."

"Don't be soft."

"Soft? What happened, Bentley? You - *we* - dissolved or something. I thought I was -"

"It's simple," Bentley said. "A simple process, which, after two or three goes, becomes as easy as blinking."

"But it went on forever, the noise was -"

"It gets shorter every time you jump. For me, it's like a blink. I don't hear the noise any more. Don't see the white, either."

"Lucky you."

"I remember it though," he said, thoughtfully. "That fizzy, snappy, poppy, buzzy noise. Gave me the willies. Like a swarm of bees eating Rice Krispies."

Kimi managed a small laugh. "I feel weird. Like I'm not here."

"Listen. Every atom which goes to make up Kimi Nichols has just been disassembled and then reassembled in a different dimension. You're bound to be feeling a bit off."

"I've been disassembled?"

"Yes."

"Every atom?"

"Yes...and there's more atoms in Kimi Nichols than all the stars in the universe. Disassembling you and reassembling you in another dimension is no mean feat!"

Bentley offered a hand up. She took it. "What if you haven't put me back together right?"

"Take some breaths and take it easy," he said. "We

41

need to get a move on." He turned and continued down the steps.

Kimi followed. "Aren't you going to tell me where we are? And why you're not blue anymore?"

"There'll be time for questions later." Bentley picked up his pace.

"But I need to know!"

Bentley stopped and sat on a rock. "You're impatient," he said.

Kimi caught him up. "Start with the blue thing. How come you look real?"

He let out an exaggerated sigh. "A Tulpa - that's *me* - is constructed with the essence of its evoker - that's *you* - understand?"

"Erm, no," Kimi said.

"Okay then," he said and stared up into space. "A Tulpa's appearance, is uhm - diluted – yes! - in the evoker's *Earth* world, my appearance is *diluted*, and humans with a mind for noticing such things, might report seeing a *ghost*."

"You're a ghost?"

"No, no, no, well, yes, no - look, didn't you ever see a shadow out the corner of your eye, but when you looked again it was gone?"

"I suppose."

"Didn't you ever feel a presence, like you were being watched?"

Kimi nodded. She'd had that feeling many times.

"You were tuning in, catching a glimpse of a watching Tulpa."

"Watching?"

"Yes, humans can be interesting, especially when they think they're alone."

"That's stalking."

"No it ain't. We don't always watch. We might be on a mission, or retired, or just plain visiting for a laugh."

"A laugh?"

"Why yes, there's one group makes a hobby of it. They dress up as Roman soldiers and march through people's living rooms. Hilarious."

"Right."

"Ever find something missing, only for it to turn up later?"

"I think I get it, Bentley."

"Where do you think all the odd socks go?"

"I get it!"

Bentley stood. "Look, there's lots to learn, and Rome wasn't built in a day." He turned and continued down the steps.

Kimi followed. Hearing this young Bentley speak like an oldie was freakily weird. She'd have to put him right on that. The air cooled as they descended into shade.

"On *this* world, however," Bentley went on. "The

evoker's mojo is more powerful, lending the Tulpa a fuller figure, if you like." He bounded down the last few steps.

Kimi said, "So you're only blue in my world and only visible to some people." She stopped five steps from the bottom, flexed her legs then jumped, landing in the dust by his side. "So what *is* this world? A faint-dream?" She touched her sore chin. "I'm still out cold?"

"Oh no you're not. Fact is, you're probably more awake right now than you've ever been in your life. This, my dear Kimbo, is the extra-dimensional, supernatural world of Heart. Your second home, from this day on."

Kimi remembered home, the screeching car and the wheelie bin bouncing off the door. The door opening. The shadow coming inside. "Heart?"

"That's right."

"What's going off at home, Bentley? Are Mum and Dad - well - are they okay? I've got this awful feeling -"

"I'm afraid I'm silenced on Mousehole matters for the now, and there's nothing I can do to change that. We'll return to things Earthly in due course. Now's the time to enjoy the wonders of Heart. And firstly, we need to cover health and safety."

"You're kidding me?"

"I kid yee not, fair child. Wondrous things are about to explode from a jack-in-the box. If one does not know one's measure, then one is likely to get burnt!"

"You're talking like an oldie. I don't like it."

"Hmm, yes, I'm out of practice." Young Bentley had a confused look.

"Just keep it simple."

"All right then. Health and Safety, uhm, `*module 1, section 1, rule 1 - induction to quantify mojo measure must always come first and foremost - for the safety of the new Balancer.*`"

"Balancer?"

Bentley grimaced, grasped thin air as if he was holding a glass, then made turning motions at the invisible object with finger and thumb.

"What *are* you doing?"

"Opening a can o' worms." He lobbed the pretend can over his shoulder. "A *giant* one at that!" he added.

"What's a new Balancer? And where's this rule book? And why's the sky that *gorgeous* blue? And how the heck can forests be purple? And what about that crow, Bentley? It flew into the patio doors not twenty minutes before *you* flew through them, and you're not even interested in what it said. What's *that* all about?"

Bentley said nothing.

"Tell me."

Bentley snatched up some tufts of fern, made a fist, shook it vigorously and presented it to Kimi. "For you," he said. "Bentley, at your service!" But his face dropped when he saw there was nothing in his palm but a pile of leaves. "Oh!" he said, clearly unsettled as the leaves blew away in the breeze.

He went to pluck more leaves. Kimi grabbed his arm. "The crow talked about death, Bentley." He stared at her with wide eyes. "*One death today*, it said. How's that for madness? Ever heard of talking crows, Bentley? Have you? Have you?"

Bentley pulled his arm free. "That would be an omen, Kimbo. I'm sorry, but you're going to have to trust me. You're safe here and that's what matters."

"But an omen means something bad, doesn't it?" Bentley was visibly trembling but Kimi couldn't hold back. "Don't mess with me, Bentley. I want the truth. I - I'm worried about Mum and Dad - that the lightning might have hit one of them - one death, like the crow said, *and* -"

"Stop!" Bentley threw his hands up. "This is getting us nowhere. There's something important that I must show you. Can we forget about the crow for a few minutes?"

"Nope."

"You're stubborn as well as impatient."

"I know it." She walked away and sat on a rock with her back to him.

"I need you to watch this, Kimi."

"Nope."

"Kimi!"

"I'm watching a weed die. It's more interesting."

There was no response from Bentley but the silence between them didn't last long. There came a harsh sound, loud and piercing like an electronic zipper. Kimi's hands flung to her ears and she turned in time to see streamers of fire erupting from Bentley's outstretched arm. A small bush fifty metres up the gulley went up in a puffball of flame.

Bentley blew on his fingertips. "Your turn."

In two seconds she was by his side. "Magic? You did magic?"

Bentley shook his head. "Not magic, no. It's mojo. And it's your turn." He picked up the white pebble and bowled it up the gulley floor. "Aim for that."

"*Me?*"

"Yes." Bentley was grinning.

"Like how?"

"Simply think `mojo` and imagine, uhm, imagine you're skimming a stone on the sea."

There was a rush of something, adrenaline, Kimi thought. She grasped an imaginary stone in her right hand, twisted low, drew her arm back. No longer weakened from being disassembled and reassembled, her muscles were tightening. Kimi felt big.

Bentley stepped behind. "Imagine you're gripping that stone, Kimi."

"I am, I am."

"Focus on your target, and *think* - mojo, mojo!"

Kimi focused on the pebble. "Mojo, mojo." A ball of heat appeared in her brow. It pulsed, but not painfully. "Mojo, mojo, mojo." Tingles danced down her right arm. She pulled it fully back, took aim.

That's when she noticed the crow on a boulder behind the smouldering bush. Another crow behind that. More on the rock face. She looked up. The opposing outcrops were lined with crows, tightly packed. More crows in the sky, descended, scrabbled for a place. Stones and dirt trickled here and there. Kimi's arm was numb, burning. "Bentley," she whispered.

"I see 'em," he whispered back. She felt his hand at her elbow. "Easy now." He was guiding her slowly backwards. "There's an alley through the rock just a few feet away. Take it nice and easy, Kimi, and tell the mojo it's not required."

"Not required, not required." The rush subsided. Her arm relaxed.

More crows, twenty, fifty, a hundred, two hundred, three, sailed down into the gulley and took up boulder space. Those packing the outcrops barely moved. Kimi imagined they might all speak at once but they were moving out of view as Kimi stepped backwards into the alley. The crows remained silent. Not a sound. Despite the cool shade of the alley, sweat was running down her face.

48

"It's a short dash to the forest," Bentley said.

The alley was about twenty metres long - a tunnel cut through the rock. It opened to lush green field, a reed-edged pond, and the lilac forest beyond that she'd seen from above. Kimi clasped Bentley's arm and they went slowly up the alley. "Can't see no crows," Bentley said, quietly. "When we go out, I've no doubt they'll be watching up above."

"We're going out?"

"It's the only way."

"Maybe we should think about that. I mean, what could they want?"

"Perhaps they're after that can of worms." Bentley gave a little chuckle.

Kimi didn't laugh at his joke. She had already witnessed one crow attack today. If it hadn't been for the glass in the patio doors, she was certain that crow would have ripped her fingers off. Her legs were beginning to wobble. "I - I don't think I can do this, Bentley, I -"

"I've seen you run, Kimi. You're bloody fast. Just run like the wind, okay?"

"That's it!" she said. "The wind! Whisk up a windy thing and get us out of here!"

Bentley shook his head. "Twirling's out of bounds for at least another mile or so."

"Well can't you use your magic flamethrower thing on them?"

"It's mojo, Kimi. And no I can't and neither can you. There's far too many of them. It would be exceptionally dangerous having mojo flying about willy-nilly."

Kimi's legs were like string. "I don't like this. Really, I don't."

"Once we're in the forest we'll be fine. I know a place we can lay low for a while."

"Maybe the crows are just curious. I mean, all they've done is looked at us. Why should we run at all?"

"I can see your point, Kimi. But crows gathering like that's known as a *murder* of crows - and they didn't get such a name for no reason. We have to run like the wind!"

They arrived at the end of the alley where sun-drenched field awaited. The lilac forest beyond appeared vibrant, beautiful and peaceful. No crows, no sounds, other than the insects humming. But Kimi knew they were up there, waiting. "Okay then." She took a deep breath and wished strength to her trembling legs.

"On three," Bentley whispered, and together they poised. "One - Two -"

Kimi grabbed his wrist. "Do you think *my* crow's among them?"

Bentley stared at her for a second, then looked forward again. "Like the wind, Kimi, like the wind!" He took a deep breath...

———

5

~ Death by Wobble ~

"Three!"

Bentley burst from the alley in a blur. Kimi
followed, sprinted hard, focused on the lilac forest, the sun
hot on the back of her head, and soon they were thundering
past the pond. A single caw rang out from behind. Kimi
glanced back. A glistening ribbon of oily crows was lifting
from the outcrop. Hundreds of wing beats ruffled the air. She
missed her footing, stumbled. Bentley grabbed her by the
arm, spun her round and upright and they were running
again. He was pointing to a gap between two low bushes at
the forest's edge. Kimi's feet pounded the ground and she
sprinted like never before. The screeching was loud and
almost upon them as they reached the gap. Kimi ducked,
dived through. Bentley followed. So did the crows, black
darts, wings tucked behind. One jabbed into Kimi's arm and
cartwheeled away. Another caught her shoulder, its claws
digging in before momentum carried it off. Kimi ran blindly,
tripping on roots and smacking into leafy branches. A loud
caw, a swish, and sharp claws raked through her hair and
tore clumps of it away. Bentley tripped, went sprawling to
the forest floor, turned quickly onto his back. Sparks
crackled around his hands. Silvery balls, like marbles, came

streaming from his fingers, blasting crows into swirls of feathers. The forest floor blackened.

"This way!" Bentley sprang to his feet and ran to a place where the prickly thicket looked impenetrable. He prized it apart and Kimi scraped through. On the other side was the open end of a fallen tree wide enough to stand up in. Behind them, crows were wriggling through the thicket, beaks snapping. Bentley pulled Kimi inside the fallen tree.

"What – the -" she panted.

He shushed her and pulled her deeper into the tree. It smelled damp and buggy. "I – I really don't like this place," Kimi said. She stepped on something squishy. "Not one bit."

Bentley wiggled his fingers and a stream of silvery balls gunned a circle around the inside of the rotten trunk. It began to collapse. They backed off, Bentley still firing until enough trunk and attached limbs had fallen to completely block the entrance. It was dark now. Tiny holes remained where thin beams of light angled in. Kimi felt itchy all of a sudden. Outside, claws scratched and clicked on the trunk above their heads. Bits crumbled and fell in Kimi's hair. She swiped them away, took a step back. More bits pattered to the floor.

"At the other end of this trunk," Bentley whispered, "is the entrance to Doyle's Den. The safe place I mentioned."

"How far?"

52

"Twenty metres, tops."

"Take me home."

Bentley's hand found hers and Kimi reluctantly went along, one hand clenching her collar. Daylight occasionally streaked in through small holes in the trunk and that was good to show the way, but not so good for showing up things that wriggled or hung in webs. She could still hear the crows back at the collapsed entrance. At least they weren't getting in.

The trunk grew thick with sticky cobwebs and Kimi grew itchier. She closed her eyes when she saw the first spider that was the size of her head, kept them firmly shut, and did not open them again until Bentley advised that they had arrived, and that she would have to open her eyes to navigate her exit.

Vines as thick as drainpipes had been weaved into the tree's roots and packed together. It was a squeeze to get through. A shove from Bentley helped. Kimi stepped into darkness. The vines snapped back into place behind her. Bentley slipped through as a blue mist then reformed. Orange light swirled and sparked around his hands. He thrust them above his head and the light erupted like a fountain. Three fat pumpkins could now be seen - one on each of three walls - each pumpkin carved with three eyes and an open mouth. The pumpkins sucked in the light and shone brightly, casting the den in an amber glow.

"Nice," Kimi said.

They were in a triangular shaped room. Tightly-packed vines made up the three walls, stretching upwards for a long, long way. A small jigsaw piece of blue sky could be seen in the darkness at the very top. On the dusty floor the remains of an ancient fire sat in the middle of three tree stumps.

"This it?" Kimi said, after dancing and jiggling and shaking herself free of bugs.

"Keep it to a whisper," Bentley said. "Don't want the crows alerted, do we?" He sat on the nearest stump. "We can stay here for the night if needs be."

"No way. I need to get home."

"Agreed," Bentley said. "But home's miles away. Come and rest for a minute."

Kimi chose the widest of the remaining stumps and sat up on it with her legs crossed. "I mean, *my* home, in Mousehole. All we have to do is make it back to the alley, climb the steps to the top, whisk a windy thing and hey presto we're back in Mousehole. And I'm sure you could keep the crows off with those silver ball things."

Bentley shook his head. "Against orders, I'm afraid. The only way is forward, to Middling, where the people who gave those orders await you. That means getting out of the forest and onto the plain before we can travel by twirly."

"What people?"

"Ay?"

"Who gave the orders. You said, *people*."

"Yes, people, who, like you, entered this world and stayed to fight its battles and advance the cause." He paused. "Anyway," he went on. "Before we think of going anywhere we need to get you up to speed on stunner manipulation. You up for some mojo?" His eyes glowed orange in the pumpkin light.

"I - I guess."

Bentley held out a hand and rubbed his thumb and fingers together. After initial sparks, a silver ball the size of a marble appeared at his fingertips. He flicked it at Kimi and it hit her on the chin. It dissipated, leaving behind a numbing feeling which spread up her face and made her eyes water.

"Hey! Was that what you fired at the crows?"

"Of course. They're stunners."

"You mean the crows aren't dead? You didn't kill them?"

"That's correct."

"That's crazy. They were out to kill us, Bentley. Still are."

"Well, I - I don't think murder for the sake of it is the answer, Kimi."

"Unbelievable!"

"What?"

"You! Those crows will have recovered by now and

55

we're no better off." She rubbed her throbbing chin.

"Let me." Bentley touched his fingers to her bruise. Her eyes closed to the warm glow. The tightness in her jaw relaxed and she felt the pain drain into him. Bentley was good at soothing pain away.

"Thanks," Kimi said.

"Don't fret," Bentley said. "Crows won't get the better of us."

A croaking sound made them both jump. A ginormous toad was squeezing through the vine wall behind Bentley. It was the size of a bulldog, had purpley transparent skin which hung in flabby folds, and protruding yellow bloodshot eyes. Kimi stood up on her stump.

"Ugly, I know," Bentley said.

The toad issued a low, rumbling croak.

Kimi snapped her mouth shut.

"Bellamy's Aunt is its given name," Bentley said. He rubbed his thumb and fingers, produced a silvery stunner and flicked it at the toad. On impact, the toad flipped over backwards then emitted a raspberry from its fat lips. Its eyelids closed and it shivered. It appeared to be smiling. "They love it," Bentley said. "You try."

Kimi tried and yelped when sparks flew from her fingertips.

Bentley shushed her. "Think *power,* Kimi. But also think *restraint* in equal measure at the same time."

Kimi thought of power – and restraint – and when the silvery ball appeared resting on her fingertip the feeling of connection to it was extraordinary. This thing, this stunner, had come from her. "I did it." Kimi said. The stunner faded then vanished.

"Again," Bentley said.

This time the silvery ball stayed. Kimi lobbed it at the toad who had been watching eagerly. On impact, the toad flipped over, jiggled and blew another raspberry.

"That is so cool," Kimi said. "Look!" All around the vines were parting and fat toads were squeezing through. Soon they were surrounded by toads and Kimi didn't wait to be asked. Stunners were flying everywhere and the numerous toads flipped and shuddered and blew satisfied raspberries. "Crap a toad!" Kimi laughed.

Bentley gave her a look. "Since when did you become foulmouthed anyway?"

"Everyone says it at school."

"Crap a toad?"

"You exchange the toad for whatever's crapping you out at the time. Anyway, how the heck'd I do that?"

Bentley got to his feet and strode among the toads who all appeared to be smiling and sleeping soundly. "That's nothing," he said. "We have just witnessed the beginning of what I hope will be a most fruitful relationship!"

"With toads?"

"With yourself, silly. You're empowered now. And every new Balancer must master every facet of his mojo in order to succeed."

"Balancer? You said that before."

Bentley ignored her.

"You called me a Balancer."

Bentley was sweating.

"Hello! You said I was a Balancer."

"Please understand that I'm under orders, Kimi. You're on a need to know basis until you're out of – well, until we're home and safe." He sat down and wiped sweat from his face.

"Okay," she said, pulling her sweater off. She wiped her face and tied the top round her waist. "I'll play along until I wake up. How does that sound?"

"Oh lordy," Bentley said. He was staring at her pink tee-shirt with the Superman S on the front.

She checked for stains. "It's clean on."

"It's not that, Kimi." Bentley's eyes were wide as saucers. "It's the colour. Bliss flies go for pink, see. Nobody wears pink on Heart. Nobody!"

"Well, Supergirl will," Kimi said.

"Trust me, you need to cover up - that's a whole lot of pink - you'll be screaming like a baby when the bliss flies sniff you out - like a baby!"

"It's too hot to cover up. And I'm thirsty!"

"You ain't listening, Kimbo. Bliss flies are nothing like the flies in Mousehole."

"Well you're not listening, either! I'm hot, I'm bothered, and I don't care about stupid flies!"

"You ain't seen a bliss. They're *this* big." Bentley rolled his hand into a fist and came at her making hissing sounds, his fist swooping this way and that until it stopped right at Kimi's nose. "This big! And they got probes. Squirmy little probes that don't give up 'til they've crawled inside your clothes and laid under your skin!"

Kimi leant away. "Grossing me out won't work."

Bentley's shoulders dropped. "Don't you think we've enough with the crows without inviting bliss flies along for the ride?"

There was an awkward silence.

Toads purred. Crows cawed far away.

Bentley lunged, grabbed Kimi by the wrists and instantly she was shuddering much the same way the toads had been. Shuddering enough to make her teeth gnash. Bentley was shuddering, too; and worst of all, the pink from her tee-shirt was travelling down her arms and draining into his hands.

"Dob ih!" she cried, vibrating like a gong. "Dob ih!" she cried, as the pink drained and vanished completely. "Dob, dob, dob," she wailed when the draining continued to her jeans and then her trainers.

Bentley eventually let go and Kimi settled to a stop.

"What the heck was that?"

"Pigment control," he said.

Kimi's clothes had all turned white. "Put it back," she said.

"No."

"Put it back, please."

"No. It's for your own good."

She pulled the turquoise cross from around her neck - the one she'd got for Christmas. It was also white.

"You all white?" Bentley chuckled.

Kimi did not laugh. She checked her hair. It was still dark. "I really want to go now, Bentley. I - I'm meant to be going birthday shopping *and* -"

Bentley shook his head. "Look, Kimi. This can be a scary place if you don't know what you're doing, but right now we need to find a way past those crows, and you ain't really helping."

"Well you stunning the horrible things wasn't the brightest idea either, was it?"

"I did what I thought was best."

"Well I'm not happy, Bentley." Kimi sat back down.

"The crow that spoke to you. Remind me what it said."

"'One death today.'"

"You sure?"

"Well, I wasn't at first because of its horrible screechy voice, but it said it again before it flew off."

"Hmm." Bentley paused in thought. "Well," he said, coming round. "I just can't fathom it. Our only option is to stay here and wait for rescue. They'll soon come looking for us." He stared at the floor and went quiet.

"What are you hiding?"

"Nothing."

"You are, I can tell."

"I'm thinking, that's all."

"About what?"

"Crows, Kimi. Crows defy science. There's a myth that says they talk when delivering prophecies. They fight for the right to play messenger via some form of ancient ritual. Once the prophecy is delivered and executed, the messenger will burst into flames and depart to its own personal little afterlife."

"*My* crow didn't burst into flames."

"Which, according to the myth - means the prophecy has yet to conclude. But it is only a myth."

"So Mum and Dad are okay?"

"I do hope so," he said.

"Then you'll take me home?"

"To Mousehole, no. To Middling…yes."

"But I look stupid," Kimi said. "My necklace is ruined, my Nikes look like cheap copies - and I look like a freaking ghost!"

"I'll take you shopping - get you kitted out."

"There's shops?"

"Yeah there's shops - and food - good food."

Kimi's stomach rumbled.

"And the quicker we get there, the sooner you'll be fed and watered." Bentley had a studious look. "We need to get past them crows, Kimi."

"How long until someone comes looking for us?"

He shrugged. "How long's a piece of string?"

"Well maybe the crows have given up and gone home. I can't hear them anymore, can you?"

"No I can't," Bentley said. "But we need to make a plan before we consider moving out. Now that you've learned to manipulate a stunner, I hope you realise that initiating a more powerful blast - like that which you witnessed when I blew up the bush in the gulley - is not a difficult thing to do?"

Kimi nodded.

"And also, that defence by stunner, should always come first. Always."

Kimi nodded again.

"And also, that one must think power and restraint in equal measure to create the stunner?"

"Yes, Bentley. I know what to do."

"Then we will leave the safety of the den. Once

we're through the vines there's a good mile of forest. If we remain stealthy, we'll make it through and can whisk a twirly from there. The boundary is thereabouts."

Toads were waking up. Yawning and smacking lips they began to disperse, squeezing through the vines. Kimi patted one on the head as it wandered by. Its folds of flab shuddered and its lips rasped before it shuffled away. She patted another which did the same. Then she patted a third which didn't. This one wobbled, distorted, then turned inside out with the most awful gurgling sound which ended in a slop of steaming guts on the floor. Kimi jumped on top of the stump she'd been sitting on.

"What on Heart did you do?" Bentley had jumped on his stump, too.

"I - I just patted it."

"Death by wobble," Bentley said. "Most unusual."

"It's disgusting. I've murdered a toad."

"Please, carefully touch another."

"No way!"

"Only a light touch, Kimi. If your mojo's playing up we need to know."

Kimi carefully touched a finger to the nearest toad. The toad shuddered and rasped and squeezed away through the vines.

"Again," Bentley said.

This time she tried with Little Hand. Same thing

happened. The toad tootled off quite merrily.

"Another!"

Just as Kimi's hand came close to *this* toad's head, its flesh distorted, acting much like an opposing magnet. When Kimi's fingertips grew nearer, the flesh would pull away from it. "This one's gonna blow," she said, and withdrew her hand. She reached towards another and the same thing happened. Its flesh retracted from her advance, and she found that if she got the distance just right the flesh would begin to wobble. Before the wobble reached its feet Kimi withdrew her hand.

"That's the strangest thing I ever saw," Bentley said.

"Is my mojo bust?"

Bentley shrugged.

"You mean you don't know?"

"Guess I don't."

"What is this place, Bentley?"

"It's the world of the supernatural, Kimi, and it just gets more super by the minute." He went to the vines and parted a section enough for Kimi to squeeze through. "Let's get out of here. And uhm – be careful what you touch."

———

6

~ Aliens, dodo, and Sue the guy ~

"Perhaps it's a focusing problem," Bentley said as they pushed through vines.

"Or it could be a disease. Or even a new form of mojo."

A vine sprang back and thumped Kimi on the forehead. She threw it to one side, let out a hefty puff - and moved on. When the vines had thinned and progress made easier, Bentley said: "White suits you, you know, Kimbo. You could be an angel."

Kimi prickled. She'd never thought of that, and the truth was, all the signs were there. Maybe she had to win her wings like in that old black and white film, Mum loves. *One death today* - it was her. She was already dead.

"Don't fret. You ain't dead," Bentley said, waiting for her to catch up.

"Uh? How did you? Can you?"

"Sometimes," Bentley said.

"What?"

"Read your mind."

"You never told me that, before."

"Never had chance. Besides, it's only snippets and *not* recommended."

"Why?"

"Because forced telepathy twixt Tulpa and Balancer can have disastrous consequences, see. So never ever try!"

"What's the point in having telepathic ability if you can't use it?"

"Because it's not really an ability, Kimi. It's more a side-effect of the Tulpa to Balancer, uhm, how should I put it - connection. You might accidentally pick up snippets of my thoughts, as I might pick up snippets from your thoughts, and picking up snippets is fine, harmless. But actually forcing your thoughts on your own Tulpa, well, that's like poking yourself in the eye. It bloody hurts. So best to be careful. Okay?" Bentley went on walking and Kimi followed. The vines had thinned out and the forest was lilac again. Insects hummed, birds chirped. There were no crows.

"Tell me about mojo. What else can it do?"

"Well, your mojo sits within your core, waiting to be nurtured and harnessed."

"But what do I do with it? Kill dragons or something?"

Bentley smiled wryly, as if he'd heard that one a million times before. "No, Kimi. There's only one thing you need do…" He stopped beneath a purple tree bulging with red bananas and wiped his eyes which had begun to water. "…one thing - and I know that Kimi Nichols can do this."

"What is it?" Kimi stared at him. The red bananas - if that's what they were - sprayed out behind his head like a tropical hat. It would make a great picture.

"Make me proud!" Bentley said.

"Are *they* bananas?" Kimi's stomach grumbled again.

"I've waited a long time for this day, Kimbo. A long, long time."

"I don't really like bananas, but if they are -"

"You've got tasks ahead that would normally be undertaken by a prepared Balancer – never mind a premature - that in itself would see most cry off."

"A premature?"

"You won't be crying off, will you, Kimi?" Bentley set off walking again.

"Hope not," she said, hurrying after. She disliked being referred to as a premature but didn't want to cut his flow. "What tasks?"

"Specifics later. Let's focus on keeping moving. And they're not bananas, they're bliss fly pupae."

Kimi made a barfing sound.

"Indeed," Bentley said.

"What other beasties live here?"

"Too many to mention."

"Give me one, just one."

"Well, humans will always wonder over the *paranormal* - as they like to call it. But the likes of ghosties, UFO sightings, corn circles, hauntings, big cats, fairies and `magic`" - he did finger-quotes in the air - "the list is endless. Everything, or almost everything which humans pass off as myth or unexplained, is usually a direct effect of Heart's involvement with Earth matters."

"UFOs?"

"Yes. Or to be more precise – the *greylians*. They do great work for the cause - have done for as long as records show."

"*Aliens*?"

"Yes."

"I'm gonna meet real *aliens*?"

"Greylians," Bentley corrected, ducking under some looping brambles. "No doubt there'll be a few of 'em noshing at the Foot when we get back."

"Eh?" Kimi didn't duck low enough and tangled her hair. She tugged it free and ran to catch up.

"The Rabbit's Foot - where we work, live and enjoy roasted dodo."

"Dodo?"

"Tastes like chicken, pork and beef all rolled into one. It's Big Sue's specialty."

"Who's she?"

"Sue's a he. A Tulpa like me. He's Scottish. Likes to clean a lot. You'll love him and he'll adore you."

"Right," Kimi said, growing weary of the forest and catching another scratch from a branch. "Aliens, dodo, and Sue the guy. That it?"

Bentley stopped walking. "Tell me Kimi, do you

believe in fairies?"

She was about to tell him she really wasn't sure what to believe anymore, when she became aware of a rapid clicking sound. Bentley pointed above her head to where a dozen or more spheres of shimmering light the size of large oranges were descending through the leafy trees.

Kimi backed off from the shimmering spheres. One dropped to head height and hovered in the air before Kimi's face. Its clicking became a furious buzz. "Make it go away!" she shouted, but the sphere shot towards her. She threw up her arms, stumbled and fell onto her backside. Her eyes opened to the sphere settling onto her knee. The shimmering stilled and Kimi saw wings, beautiful luminescent wings like swirling rainbows folded around a slender grey body.

"Whoa," she said. She leaned closer to the sphere, thought about touching it, when wings sprang apart revealing a furry little beast with a whiskery snout, buck teeth and fierce red eyes.

Kimi squealed and tried to waggle it off her knee, but the thing flung itself forward and landed on her chin. Its claws were on her lips, stretching her mouth open.

"*uhg - uhg -*" She tried to bat it away but couldn't get near for the whirring wings.

"Not so loud, not so loud..." Bentley was cringing in the background.

"*Eh 'ih 'ogh -*" Its snout poked around inside her

mouth and its whiskers tickled her tongue. Kimi gagged and was on the verge of being sick, but the little thing had great strength, jamming her mouth open. She could barely breathe. Then her mouth snapped shut and the thing shot a few feet away, hovering once more as a shimmering sphere. The snout and beady eyes poked through the shimmer. "Heeee - no baduns!" it said in a tinny voice. The snout vanished and the sphere flew upwards and joined the others bobbing in the air.

Kimi spat repeatedly into the dirt.

"Must you?" Bentley said. "That's not very Balancerlike."

She stuck out her tongue and wiped her arm across it, over and over and once more for good measure, then spat again. "Yuk! It was in my mouth. Oh bloody - yuk!"

"Keep it down, will you."

She spat again.

"Won't poison you," Bentley said. "Famoose eat bad teeth. Gives 'em the shimmery look."

"They *eat* teeth?"

Bentley nodded. "Only bad ones. You should try 'em. Quite tasty. Like walnuts."

"Bentley that's gross. Stop it! What the heck *was* that thing?"

He offered a hand up. "Like I said. It was a famoose. There are no such things as faeries, Kimi - at least not in the

fairytale sense of willowy ladies with shimmering wings -
although the shimmering wings'd be right."

Kimi could still feel the thing's claws pulling her
mouth open and wished she could scrub her teeth. She was
about to spit one last time when the sound of many crows
cawing from up ahead stopped her.

"They must have circled round us," Bentley said.

The caws were growing in number, getting louder.

"They're coming," Kimi said. "Now what?"

Bentley shrank to his younger self. "Run!"

———

~ 7 ~

~ A Flash of Genius ~

They ran back through the forest the way they had come. The first crows were descending, swooping down through the lower branches. Kimi's pace increased. "They're coming," she puffed, but too late as the first crow flew straight into Bentley's back. He stumbled forwards and the crow emerged from his other side just as fast as it had entered.

"Engage!" he cried - he seemed to be okay - and threw the multiple rounds on the way to his feet. Hundreds of silver balls sprayed the oncoming crows. Kimi got hit on the head by a ricochet which made her dizzy for a second, followed by a stiff wing lashing across her cheek. She fell to her knees, and the silvery balls were growing in bunches around Little Hand. The pulse in her brow matched the pulse in her hand, and without even thinking about it she took Bentley's lead and let loose, spraying the oncoming crows with a continuous barrage of ferocious stunners.

Crows spun from the air. Crows lay ruffled and groaning. Crows were retreating. Kimi was about to announce they were near to triumph when a second wave of crows dropped through the trees. "Hurry!" Bentley shouted. They stumbled through bramble and thicket, launching stunballs over their heads without looking. Whether it was panic or fear Kimi had no knowledge, but when this next wave of crows, which seemed so much thicker and blacker than before, was almost upon them, her stunballs morphed into orange fireballs, and, after she'd launched the first volley which exploded at least fifty crows, the fireballs changed into fire streamers and crows were picked off in quick succession and all of them blasted to oblivion. Some of her shots misfired and sizzled through thick old boughs which came thumping to the ground. Some shots went skyward exploding above the forest like fireworks. This was chaos, but it was working. Now the famoose joined in, moving to Kimi's rear and using their furiously clicking wings to bat crows away. There was a satisfying *frapping* noise when crow wing touched famoose wing. The famoose seemed to enjoy it, shrieking "Wa-hey!" after each successful frapping.

Bentley was shouting something as they ran. Kimi didn't know what and didn't care. They were almost at the den and the crows were dispersing. Bentley saw off the remainder with a volley of stunballs and they kept on running until the vines thickened.

"What?" Kimi said to his horrified look once they'd slowed to weave through the vines.

"You know fine well what."

"I didn't do it on a purpose. It kinda just flew out."

"You're fortunate you didn't start a fire, young lady."

"Got rid of the crows, didn't it?"

"Seems to me," Bentley said. "That Kimbo Nichols needs some serious focal training!"

Kimi shrugged. Little Hand was throbbing warm. "Don't I get a wand or something? Surely that'd help with aiming."

"A wand?" Bentley tutted. "Wands are not a requisite of the Balancer, Kimi. Wands are for those, how shall I say - for those perhaps a little disabled in the mojo department."

She hoped he wasn't referring to Little Hand. "You mean like a retard?"

Bentley groaned and shook his head.

"Chill out," Kimi said. "We're safe, aren't we?"

Bentley didn't answer. He had stopped by a gap in the vines and was staring skywards through the tall trees. The small amount of sunlight that had been getting through seemed to be fading. Dark storm cloud was gathering, blotting out the sky by the second. The black cloud began to spiral like a whirlpool. It was spinning directly downwards towards them. Only it wasn't a cloud. Kimi grabbed hold of Bentley's arm. "Are – are they -"

"Crows," Bentley said.

Kimi heard him swallow.

"That's a lot of crows," Kimi said.

"Half a million at least," Bentley said.

Kimi tugged him by the arm and they ran. The noise came first. Half a million crows screeching all at once. Kimi was pushing through the vines after Bentley with the famoose in tow when the crows broke through the leafy canopy and came thrashing through the branches like bricks. Bentley dived under a crooked old log and Kimi scrambled after. The dozen or so famoose took up the rear, batting away the first crows to arrive. Kimi and Bentley pushed on through the vines and did not stop until they were back in Doyle's Den and the vine wall snapped shut behind them.

"Th- thanks for helping," Kimi said to one of the famoose floating near her head. It poked its snout out. "You're welcome," it said, then vanished again.

Bentley was sat on a stump, panting. "That was a close call," he said. "There's no other thing for it. We're staying here until we're rescued." He did not look at all happy.

Kimi sat on the stump opposite. "How can you be out of breath when you're just an essence?"

Bentley looked offended. "You do have a way with words," he said. "It's simple, Kimi. You sweat – I sweat. You cry – I cry. You pant – I pant."

"What about when I need the loo," she said, and Bentley gave her a look before they both laughed.

Outside, the forest full of beating wings sang like a locust swarm. Kimi looked up to where the vine walls tapered to a small hole at the top. She could only just see the piece of blue sky. "It won't take them long to figure out there's another way in," she said.

Bentley followed her gaze. "We need to think of a way to block that hole," he said. "Now think, Kimi. Think!"

The famoose she had thanked came and landed on Kimi's shoulder. Its wings settled behind and it lay itself down.

"Make yourself at home," Kimi said.

"Think Kimi!" the famoose said.

Bentley went into shudder mode and shrank to the tiny Bentley. "I think better like this, before you ask," he said.

"I – I'm sorry for blasting away with the mojo," Kimi said. "I'll be more careful next time."

Little Bentley glared at her. "Do you think I can allow a next time? Do you realise the severity of our situation? Do you realise the trouble you're in for killing defenseless animals? Do you realise the trouble I'm going to be in when the Adepts get my report?" He stood up. "Do you realise, that as a trainee Balancer, you have broken every rule in the book? Do you realise -"

"Oh shut up," Kimi said. "I'd hardly call them defenseless animals."

"The power you hold is enormous, Kimi. Look at the

mess we're in. And look at the state of you, all blood and sweat and muck."

"Hey come on," Kimi said. "I didn't exactly want to be here in the first place. And what do the crows want anyway? Does this happen with every new Balancer? Is it a test or something?"

Bentley sat back down and said nothing. Behind him, two black feathery heads were squeezing through the vines. A single famoose shot forward and frapped them both back out again. "We're trapped." Bentley said. "And we need to block that hole. What are we going to do, Kimi?"

Kimi didn't have a clue. Then the answer came in a flash of genius - even if she did think so herself. She whispered something to the famoose on her shoulder and the famoose giggled before flying to the wall and slipping through.

"What did you say to it?" Bentley asked. The remaining dozen or so famoose that had made it with them to the den were all pressed together in a shimmering scrum, and chattering excitedly.

"Wait and see." Kimi smiled.

"You need to tell me what you're up to, Kimi."

"I've sent it for ice-creams and a can of pop."

"This is no time for jokes. I need to know."

"Wait and see!"

Little Bentley sighed.

Kimi grinned. "Now who's the impatient one?"

———

~ 8 ~

~ Under the Dome ~

Kimi felt filthy, sweaty and hot. She wished she *could* send out for pop or ice-cream. Little Bentley was deep in thought and staring right through her. She rolled a stunball and flicked it. Bentley blinked to life, ducked, and the stunner hit the famoose returning through the vines right on the snout. It dropped to the floor like a swatted fly. Kimi ran and picked it up. "You killed it!" She thrust it at Bentley.

"Me!?"

"You shouldn't have ducked. Give it the kiss of life or something."

Bentley held a hand over the famoose. "It's only stunned," he said.

It twitched in Kimi's palm. Bentley lifted his hand away and the famoose looked up. Its fierce red eyes had faded to pale pink. "Oooh, could get used to that," it said.

Kimi released the famoose like one might release a dove. It hung heavy in the air, its wing clicks not so furious. "How many did you get?" Kimi asked it.

The famoose blinked and made a sort of smile - if that's possible with a snout and buck teeth. "Four-hundred-and-ninety-seven," it replied, wing speed returning to normal.

Kimi smiled. "That should do it."

"How many what?" Bentley asked, looking put out. "You need to tell me what's going on, Kimi. I'm the one responsible for the situation here. You can't just go off making plans willy-nilly."

"Here they come!" Famoose were squeezing through the vine walls. Hundreds of them. Soon, the tapered ceiling of Doyle's Den was stuffed with hovering spheres which turned the walls into a kaleidoscope of rainbows.

"It came to me in a flash," Kimi said.

"Why you clever so and so," Bentley said, staring up at the shimmering display. "You've only gone and blocked the hole." He folded his arms and was nodding his head. Well done, Kimi. Well done."

"Oh," Kimi said, looking up at the blocked hole. "I never really meant to do that."

Bentley looked at her. "Eh?"

"That wasn't the plan."

"Then what was?"

"We're leaving. With four-hundred-and-ninety-seven famoose to help."

"Four-hundred-and-ninety-eight," corrected the famoose back on her shoulder.

"Right." Kimi patted its head.

"We going nowhere," Bentley said. "The hole's

blocked and that'll do us fine 'til help arrives."

"Well it won't be blocked for long," Kimi said. "I'm getting us out of here and the famoose are coming to help."

"Kimi, there's more crows out there than there's ever been crows anywhere."

"I can leave a few behind to block the hole if you want to stay."

"You're mad," Bentley said. "Set one foot outside and those crows will have your eyes out in seconds. How in the Bellamy's do you expect to get us out of here?"

"How far did you say until we can twirly?" Kimi wiped her brow.

Bentley wiped his. He screwed up his face and ballooned into old Bentley. "I object!" he said.

"You are *not* my boss," Kimi said.

"No, but I am your protector. I can't allow a rookie to go off all guns blazing."

"But I'm not going to do that."

"You already did," Bentley said.

"You're worrying over nothing."

"And you're being insolent and disrespectful of your position!"

"How far?"

Bentley sighed. "Like I already said…a mile or so."

"Good. We can do that easily." Kimi lifted the famoose from her shoulder and lobbed it to the air. "Lead the way!"

"Aye aye!" it said, and squeezed through the vine wall and the other four-hundred-and-ninety-seven famoose followed, draining from the tapered ceiling like bubbles down a plughole.

"Kimi, please discuss this."

"It's your turn to trust me." Kimi pulled some vines to one side and followed the famoose. She thought about focus. She focused on the bat-like clatter of the crows now only ten or fifteen metres away; the thuds and the crashes as they hit the outer walls of interwoven vine; the caws and the screeches that sounded like crazed chimpanzees; the incessant pecking and scratch, scratch.

The vines were thinning. Soon they would be able to see her.

She focused on noting that once her plan was complete, and a stunning success, she would find this Doyle and thank him kindly for the use of his refuge. A black head and beak came darting through the vines before her. Kimi broke a grin when it was instantly descended upon and frapped to the floor by three famoose. She flicked a stunball for good measure which sent the crow tumbling down a rabbit hole.

She focused on her mojo – power and restraint in equal measure - and so many stunballs appeared in her hands that it looked like she was carrying two bunches of silvery grapes.

She focused on the little Bentley - now at her side.

"I'm in," he said. "But please tell me what's going

on."

They reached the log they'd previously dived under. Famoose had spread across the gaps beneath and above it like a shimmering web. Many crows screeched on the other side. Kimi knelt at the gap and beckoned Bentley. He knelt by her side. "Here we go," she said, and the wall of famoose pushed as one and Kimi and Bentley crawled under the log and out the other side, keeping pace with the expanding wall of famoose. As they took to their feet, the famoose closed in above and all around and soon they were encased in a dome-shaped net of shimmering spheres.

"Incredible," Bentley said, as they started forward.

Blackness could be seen through the gaps between famoose; a blur of wing, beak, and claw. To Kimi, they looked like scrabbling beetles. Extra famoose had taken up position at the front, acting like a plough to drive them through the mass of crows. The satisfying sound of crows getting a frapping was quite an orchestra, Kimi thought. They were moving - and safe under the dome of famoose.

"Incredible," Bentley repeated. "How did you think of such a thing?"

"School garden. Ange the caretaker, she puts mesh domes over the veg to keep the birds off. You should see her radishes. And when I saw the famoose frapping the crows, I thought of Ange's domes and knew we could have our own dome..."

"Incredible," Bentley said again.

"…with built-in frapping defence," Kimi finished.

"Incredi -" Bentley winced at an extra-loud barrage of frapping and the famoose wall to his left bulged inwards a little. He glanced worriedly at Kimi. They both looked up and all around but couldn't see the trees and sky – only a black swarm picking away at the famoose.

Kimi realised some famoose might get hurt, or worse. But she knew there was no option now but to carry on. "How long 'til we're out of the forest. A mile did you say?"

"You should have checked this plan with me you know."

They were both shouting to be heard over the din.

"Come off it, Bentley. It's working. Relax. Change to that old bloke if it helps you chill. Admit it. This is an *incredible* plan!" They strode forward, bathed in light from the dome of famoose. "In-flipping-credible!"

"But how'd they agree to it?"

"Seeing as they like teeth, I said they could have my biggest alligator skull. It's got loads of teeth."

"Really?"

"It's okay, I've got five."

"Alright, maybe it is a good idea. I'll give you that much." Bentley didn't change to the old Bentley. He stayed just as he was and grinned.

"You mean you approve?"

"It's certainly ingenious."

"Yes!" Kimi gave the air a punch - but forgot all about the bunch of stunballs hanging round her fingers. The hole blown in the dome was only about the size of a toaster, but enough for five crows to enter before the famoose could knit back together. Kimi quickly stunned the five crows - easy enough under a small dome - problem was she took out half the wall as well. Stunned famoose hung from newly-revealed trees to their right. Crows poured in like black liquid. Claws on Kimi's shoulder, tugging her top, tearing at her hair, clinging, pulling. She feels the power throbbing in Little Hand, she twists, turns, advances. The dome is breaking up. Bentley takes a stumble back. He squashes a famoose under his boot but doesn't seem to notice. He's running now, spraying stunballs in all directions like he's turned superhuman all of a sudden, and Kimi thinks - *well he is* - then there's blood in her left eye. Claws rip across her right ear. She does not cry out. She closes her left eye. It's useless for now. And she bounds into step with Bentley and feels the surge. She focuses and grips the *stone*, sets it away like a skimmer on a pond, then another and another and the flames skim through the masses of crows. Flames flash from her hands like lightning bolts, jagged, ripping apart anything that gets in the way. The death cries of crows and famoose grow louder than the zip-crackle of misfiring mojo.

Crows, famoose, on fire, spin through the air.

Orange mojo fireworks explode in the sky.

Famoose desperately knitting the dome back together.

Bentley, on one knee, crouched beneath Kimi's windmilling arms.

A bunch of stunners in his hand.

His stricken face is weighing up the odds.

A second later the stunners are coming right at her.

Like being dropped in a bin head-first, Kimi thought as she passed out.

She returned to smacks on the cheek that felt a bit too hard. Little Bentley stared at her. All around them, the dome had regrouped. Its walls appeared thinner than before.

"I'm sorry."

Bentley didn't say a thing. He helped Kimi to her feet.

"I know what you're thinking," she said.

"You do?"

"Focus?"

Bentley sighed. "I could get hung in a greylian loo for ten years for this."

Kimi apologised once more but Bentley shook his head. "Despite the famoose casualties and the very good fortune, once again, that you didn't start any fires, it looks as if the crows have all but scarpered."

Beyond the dome, one or two crows flitted here and there. Many dead littered the forest floor. "Good," she said, then: "Look! I can see the edge of the forest!"

The dome set off again. Everything seemed peaceful. Five minutes of silence followed. Even the famoose were quiet. Only the whirr of their wings could be heard. The forest's edge beckoned. They'd be stepping in a twirly soon. Then what? Kimi didn't dare think. Little Hand still had that burning throb. She decided that the next time she needed to blast anything she would use only her right hand. Maybe it would be more accurate.

"Nearly there," Bentley said as the undergrowth thinned to grass, red daisies and a smattering of trees ripe with pomegranate. They stepped from shade into sunshine but the dome did not leave them.

"Oh lordy," Bentley said.

The field was an oily black carpet glistening in the sun for as far as the eye could see. The odd caw sounded and flutters rippled the carpet here and there.

Bentley froze.

"Let me out," Kimi said. The famoose, probably not wanting to get Kimi heated, made a hole at the front immediately. Bentley snapped back to life but not in time to prevent Kimi from stepping through.

"We mean you no harm," she said to the field of

crows. "And I'm sorry for shooting your friends."

"Are you ca-razy!" Bentley said, tugging at her sleeve. "They're not rational enough to bargain with you, Kimi. They'll take your eyes and come back for the sockets given half a chance. The crows jostled and hissed. Kimi knelt and offered a hand to the nearest crow. "I won't hurt you," she said.

The crow hopped forward. It stared at Kimi. She smiled. It stretched its neck and tentatively reached its beak close to Kimi's fingertips. "It's okay," she said.

Bentley was backing into the dome. "Leave it, Kimi."

"No," she said. "It's – oh!" The crow's head distorted, retracted into its neck. Its body wobbled, it jumped back, squawked then turned inside out to a pile of scarlet ribcage. Kimi was dragged backwards sharply. The dome closed up before her as the field of crows went into a frenzy. "Oh crap," Kimi said. "Did you see that? It turned inside out just like the toad."

"What in bothery were you thinking?" Bentley said. He shuddered and morphed into the Bentley similar to Kimi's age. "Might need to run," he said.

"Shouldn't you be able to do a twirly thing now?"

"Good thinking," he said. "Step aside."

Kimi shrank against one wall and the dome spread a little to give Bentley space. He twirled a finger but nothing

90

happened. "Hmm. It can't be far. We'll try again every ten metres or so."

As the dome advanced with caution, the jostling crows parted. They seemed to be keeping a foot or so between themselves and the dome. The odd frapping sound could be heard when one strayed too close. Bentley tried again. Nothing. Another ten metres, nothing. And another. Still nothing. "Can't be far," he said. They were well into the field of crows now. In front and behind was a moving oily slick. The sun beat down and inside the dome was like a greenhouse. Kimi was sweating. She ached for home and the kitchen tap.

Again Bentley tried to whisk the air but again there was nothing. "I don't get this," he said.

"Look!" Kimi pointed. In the distance the crows were lifting off. A plume of dust was cutting through them.

"A twirly?" Kimi asked.

"Ah!" Bentley said. "That's no twirly. Such dust can belong to only one thing."

"Huh?"

"It's the fuzz."

"The fuzz?"

"Yes. We're about to get a lift."

"Cool!"

He shuddered and morphed into old the Bentley. "And maybe even arrested."

91

"Oh."

———

~ 9 ~

~ Free Time ~

The dust cloud charged across the field and crows lifted to the sky in great numbers. Sunlight glinted off something among the dust and the sound of an engine could now be heard. Kimi thought this might be the aliens.

The famoose broke from their dome formation. Most settled to the grass. Some stayed bobbing in the air. The old Bentley pulled Kimi to his side. Brakes squealed, and through billows of dust a sparkling chrome quad bike skidded to a stop. This was no ordinary quad bike. This was bigger than Dad's car, had streamlined mudguards, and a bowl-shaped seat at the back that looked deep enough to lie down in. The driver was quite small, wore blue overalls, black boots, black elbow length gloves and a red helmet with darkened visor.

Nice quad, Kimi thought.

"*Squad*, actually," Bentley corrected.

"Is it the fuzz?"

"It's the fuzz, all right. And the crows know it!"

The crows were all but gone. The squad driver turned off the engine, dropped to the ground and pushed his helmet off. He shook his head vigorously and jet black hair flew all over. Kimi thought he badly needed a haircut, but then saw his face. As sure as she could ever be, she was staring at a monkey - a quad-riding, straight-standing, grinning monkey.

"You made it then," the monkey said, eyeing Kimi up and down and pursing his lips as if he was sending kisses. A fly landed on Kimi's tongue and she spat and spluttered. The monkey laughed. It was a deep creepy ghost-train laugh.

"I can't tell you how pleased we are to see you." Bentley said.

"This the premature?" The monkey jerked his head in Kimi's direction . "Wearing pink was it?" Its lips curled back revealing a yellow-toothed grin.

"Yes, this is the premature, and yes, she was wearing pink, but she wasn't to know." Bentley brought an arm around Kimi's shoulder. "Kimi Nichols, meet Rehd, our delightful chief of fuzz."

"Nice to meet you," Kimi said, shakily, not appreciative of being labelled a premature once again - especially by a monkey.

"Pleasure's mine." Rehd bowed and made a sweeping gesture with his helmet. When he straightened up he looked to the sky. "Launching flares was a top idea, Tulpa Bentley. A top idea! Found you quick-sticks!"

"Ah, actually it was Kimi - uhm, yes, Kimi's idea. We're glad you spotted them. Aren't we, Kimi?"

"Yeah. Really glad," Kimi said, feeling her cheeks

burn.

The monkey stepped closer. "Premature had an idea did it? How sweet." He laughed again.

Kimi thought she might send up a flare where the sun don't shine.

"Actually," Bentley went on. "It was also Kimi's idea to create the dome of famoose. I'm sure we'd have been killed if it wasn't for that."

The monkey was studying Kimi, moving closer, staring at the blood congealing down her neck; the blood on her white tee-shirt; the blood spots on her white jeans and white trainers. "My, my, you are in a sorry old state," it said.

The gash on her ear stung from sweat. Her scalp stung where hair had been snatched. She was filthy, yes, a right old state. "I, I'm sorry." Kimi said, with no idea why she was apologising.

The monkey took another step. "What did you do to rattle the crows?"

Kimi felt a pull, twitches on her skin, just like the toads and the crow. She made a cautious step back.

"Can we get going?" Bentley said. The monkey turned to Bentley.

Oh thank you, Kimi thought.

"You're welcome," Bentley said.

"What?" said the monkey.

"Sorry. Thinking out loud. Can we get moving,

please. My Balancer is badly in need of nourishment."

Chief Rehd nodded. "Of course, of course." He began pacing back and forth with his helmet held behind his back. "But before we can return to base there are a few developments you need to know about."

The monkey's pacing brought him close to Kimi once again. This time she felt a pull down her entire right side. A horrible image of imploding monkey came vividly to mind. She took two steps back and yelped when she got frapped in the butt by a nosey famoose.

The monkey grinned. "I don't bite, little lady!"

"Please," Bentley said. "Tell us what it is we need to know. My Balancer needs -"

"Yes, yes, nourishment, I know. It's pandemonium, Tulpa Bentley. Utter pandemonium is what you need to know. In the hour or so since you left on your rescue mission, we have had close to three-hundred reports of ill health. Symptoms always the same: starts with wobbling flesh, alongside disturbing incoherent behaviour that might yet be explained as madness. Add to that a blighted crow that has developed a habit of spouting prophecies to all and sundry, and you end up with extremely concerned Adepts. Have you or the premature experienced any such wobbles or incoherence? Or talking crows?" the monkey added.

Bentley stiffened. "No, not at all. Although the crows *were* getting a little animated and I can't for the life of me think why."

The monkey glanced at Kimi. "So I see. Very well. Once in town, should you experience wobbling flesh, or think you might be going a weensy bit mad, you must report to Adept Blavatsky immediately." Rehd pulled his helmet on, grabbed the squad's handlebar and swung up to the seat. "All aboard!"

"Can't we go by twirly?" Bentley asked.

"Twirlies outside of Middling are grounded until further notice."

"Well that explains why I couldn't find the boundary. Whose idea was it to ground twirlies when they knew we were out here ?"

"The order came from the highest, Tulpa Bentley." Rehd twisted the throttle and the chrome mudguards rattled. "Move it, move it! Sun quick down - not safe!"

"Come on, Bentley," Kimi said. "Least we're getting a lift. I want to get out of here before the crows come back."

"I don't know what this place is coming to," he said, climbing into the bowl-shaped seat behind Rehd. "I really don't."

Kimi thanked the famoose for their help and got in the back next to Bentley who shrank to the teen Bentley to make more room. "Come get your skull anytime!" Kimi shouted to the famoose as Rehd hit the throttle again. The squad bike jerked, spun round and headed back the way it had come. The ride was fast, bumpy and so loud that attempting conversation was pointless. Kimi clung to Bentley. The last thing she wanted was to hit a bump and get flung against the monkey's backside. If she made him wobble, or worse turn inside out, not only would they crash but she'd get found out. Bentley seemed to realise and held her tightly back. Kimi guessed it was a good thing he was here.

Rocky terrain led to potholed fields which in turn met swampy marshland that smelled like sick and seemed to go on forever. Occasionally a famoose flew alongside for a while. Now and then a crow appeared high in the sky but always kept distant. The range of green mountains loomed and they were heading for the tallest of them all. Its peak seemed to punch through the sky. Near its base, a ridge swept outwards to the right, circling around and down and disappearing into the greenery below. A similar ridge swept from the mountain's left side, also circling down to the greenery. Kimi was reminded of a statue in Mum's office of an Indian Goddess with her long arms wrapped around her followers. These curved ridges were the protective arms, and among the greenery within, Kimi could make out patches of grey-slate rooftops and the odd black spire here and there. She guessed it must be the town. It did feel a welcoming place. In the air above the town, three small black objects were slowly descending. They looked like helicopters but without rotors or landing gear. Setting sunlight glittered orange on the noses of the descending craft. Kimi tingled all over. Glancing to Bentley, she uttered something about crapping a UFO. His smile, his eyes, shone with excitement. Once again her heart was thumping.

Where the two sloping ridges met ground and almost touched each other, two tall pillars of stone came into view, one at the end of each ridge. They flanked a dirt road lined either side with lilac forest. Rehd bumped the bike up onto the road and headed towards what Kimi thought must be the entrance. But only yards from it the squad bike slowed, bumped off the road at the other side and dipped through the trees. They both slid down into the seat to avoid low branches. The trees opened to the ridge's sheer grassy hillside. A sloping dirt track followed its curve all the way to its summit. Rehd revved the throttle, wheels spun, the bike hit the track hard and up they went. Kimi and Bentley were thrown back against the bowl as the bike thundered on. The sky was now smouldering purple. In no time they had cleared the summit and were tearing across it, weaving through scores of stone circles. Rehd stopped the bike beside one of these circles where five monkeys as stiff as the stones themselves guarded its perimeter. These also wore overalls. Theirs were green. They all came forward, and saluted Rehd who did not leave his seat.

Bentley helped Kimi out and moved them both well

back from the monkeys.

"They've had crow trouble," Rehd said to the monkeys. "I doubt any will dare come near, but keep eyes wide."

"Yip, yip," the monkeys all said at once.

Rehd turned to Bentley. "Wait here."

"Very good," Bentley said.

"One of the officer monkeys stepped inside the stone circle and whisked the air. Bits of grass spun into a vortex. Rehd started the engine, drove through the stones and vanished.

"I'm Officer Roddy." Another of the monkeys stepped forward. "Make yourselves comfortable. The chief won't be long, I'm sure."

"Thanks," Kimi said. She thought Roddy a strange name for a monkey then realised all the monkeys looked the same. She was considering suggesting they wear name badges when Bentley steered her away.

"Many thanks," he said. "We'll take a seat while we wait."

Officer Roddy saluted and stepped back against a standing stone.

They were heading to one of many ornate benches that lined the ridge. "Some people call this the goddess," Bentley said. "On account these ridges appear like arms holding the town within."

The mount towered into a purple haze. The sun was edging its way behind. Kimi thought it looked like a halo. "You must have read my mind," she said. "That's exactly what I thought when I first saw - oh - you did!"

Bentley chuckled. "You're right, it does look like she's protecting her people."

"Think it will protect a premature?"

"Don't take offence, Kimi. It's just a figure of speech."

"But why premature? I'm not a baby you know."

Bentley stopped walking. He took hold of Kimi's upper arms in much the same way Dad had half a million crows ago, just before he'd delivered his riddle. "Before we see the town," Bentley said. "There's something you must know."

"You're going to tell me it's my crow isn't it, the one spouting prophecies."

"Yes, I had thought of that. I suppose it might be. But that's not what I was going to say."

"Tell me then. Things can't get any freakier can they?"

"It's nothing bad, Kimi." Bentley smiled. "You're expected."

"Expected? By who?"

"Whom!"

"What?"

"No matter. Look, you were expected to arrive here in five years' time via normal process."

"Five years?"

"A Balancer's life normally begins at sixteen, see, when those humans of only the soundest heart are automatically chosen."

"Then why am I here now?"

"You are here early - i.e. *premature* - because you were in danger back in Earth-space. A danger so fraught with – um – danger, that the Adepts decided that here is safer. Though you wouldn't think it looking at the state of you. How you feeling by the way?"

Kimi remembered the so-called danger back home. The wheelie bin bouncing off the front door. The engine screaming. "When do I find out what's going off at home?"

Bentley's hands fell away. "Like I said, you'll have to wait until you speak with my superiors."

"The Adepts?"

"Yes."

"I want to go home."

"But we've only just got here."

"I need to know what's happening at home, Bentley."

Bentley sighed. "Look," he said. "There's no other option. We can't go back just yet. For starters there's crows out there that'll tear us apart given a half a chance. And for

102

seconds, my superiors will not allow a return to Mousehole until they are satisfied you are not at risk. And like the monkey said, twirlies are grounded."

"But Mum and Dad?"

"Wait and speak to my superiors, Kimi. Have patience. It's all you can do."

Kimi wanted to know more about these superiors. Bentley was always using them as an excuse to stay quiet. But now that actually meeting them was close, she wasn't quite so keen. A cooling wind breezed across the ridge and Kimi shuddered. As Kimi shuddered, so did Bentley, as if the shudder had jumped from her to him. "That was weird," she said, shuddering again. Bentley shuddered back.

"That *is* bizarre!" Bentley said, sweat dripping from his chin.

"Bentley you're sweating like a horse. Not got any of those symptoms have you?"

"Erm no. I'm all right, Kimi. Just a bit warm."

"But it's not so hot now. The sun's going down. *And* there's a breeze. And why do you sweat? How can you if you're not real?"

"I am real. I - I do as you do. I'm your essence, remember."

"But I'm not sweating like a turkey on Christmas Eve, am I?"

"I - I suppose it's the surprise of you arriving early.

103

Got my blood pressure up, see."

"Blood pressure. Right." Kimi wished she knew how to do the mind-reading thing.

"Now you shouldn't be wishing for such things," Bentley said, clearly agitated.

"Well *you* shouldn't keep things from me."

"I don't know what you mean," he said, feigning offence.

"You know a whole lot more than you're letting on!" She prodded him in the chest and he stumbled backwards. "And stop listening to my thoughts!"

"Easy Kimbo, I'm only trying to help."

"And quit with the Kimbo," she said, prodding him again.

Now he looked like he might cry.

"*And* the soppy faces!" She went to prod him again but he was shaking, trembling, changing form. An instant later he was the old Bentley again. "And you can quit being old, as well. I don't like it!"

"Well you quit being horrible," Bentley said.

"Me horrible? That's rich."

Bentley started shrinking but didn't stop at the good looking boy stage. He kept on going until he was five again. Kimi thought he looked a bit scared and was about to back off, when, with a sudden rumbling, Bentley expanded rapidly to an oldie.

"What *are* you doing?"

"It's *your* doing," he said. "You've got me all over the place and I just can't…" He shrank and in an instant became five again. "…stop!"

"All right, all right." Kimi held up her hands in surrender. "But try being straight with me, okay?"

Bentley nodded and changed to an old man again.

"Why the oldie?"

He sighed, screwed his face, and shrank back to the boy resembling Kimi's age.

"It's the time I've been here, waiting, Kimi. The natural progression of my essence is moulded by my everyday duties, I suppose. Holding the form of a boy to match your age requires a bit of focus. You being so horrible was getting me vexed, see, so reverting to my natural state kind of just happens and -"

"What the heck are you on about?"

A look of wonderment overcame Bentley's face. "Ah-ha!" he cried, jumping up and down excitedly. "Oh Kimbo, forgive me. I should have told you this when you first arrived, but you know me, there's so much to remember, and if I had only -"

"Just tell me, Bentley."

"All right," he said, rubbing his hands together. He leaned in close with a deranged yet gleeful look. "Time!"

"Huh?"

"Yes!" he did a little jig. "You're going to be mightily impressed! Your Earth world, yes? It exists in the same *place* as Heart, but occupies different *space*, see?"

Kimi raised an eyebrow.

"Em, em, em," said Bentley, rapidly tapping the ends of his fingers together. "It's Earth, see. It's bigger than Heart, and it's got a really deep gravity well - far deeper than Heart's. So when one transfers through a twirly, one also jumps to a different measure of space-time. Back on Earth, time is still running, but sixty times slower than here. See?"

"Um, no."

"It's easy," Bentley said. "The time difference means that one Heart hour is the same as one Earth minute. Therefore, back in Mousehole, barely a minute has passed." He ended with a loud "HA!" and continued jigging.

"Really? So that means -"

Bentley nodded eagerly. "Like I said. Back in Mousehole, barely a minute has gone by. Which is why I appear older in my natural state than the boy you thought I might have been - what with all the hopping back and forward. If that makes sense?"

"So if what you say is right, then it's only about ten-past-ten at home? And if I aim to return for say, eleven, that means I can stay here for -" Kimi ran through the numbers on her fingers. "Two and a bit days? No way. Is this for real?"

"Two-point-five days, actually," Bentley said, looking deliriously pleased.

"You serious?"

"I might have a poor memory, Kimbo, but I *can* do the math."

"I meant serious about the time difference."

"I'm very serious. I should have mentioned it earlier, but it didn't cross my mind. If you return to Mousehole after two-point-five days on Heart, it will only be 11 AM this morning."

"Then I won't be missed."

"Exactly!"

"So this is like free time?"

"That's one truly excellent way of looking at it, yes."

"You're not pulling my leg? Trying to trick me into not missing home?"

"Kimbo, how could you think such a thing. A Tulpa can't lie to his Balancer. It's not in the science."

Maybe not, Kimi thought. But there's nothing stopping you from withholding info. "Sorry, Bentley, but it is a bit much to believe."

"As much as talking monkeys and fire from your fingertips?"

"Good point," Kimi said.

"Now, perhaps you'll stop worrying about home and

107

enjoy your *free time*."

Kimi stared into his hopeful eyes. "You promise about the time diff?"

"You have my word."

"You sure?"

"Time can't be tricked, Kimbo. It is what it is."

"Say you'll crap a cow if you're lying."

"Do what?"

"Say - *if I'm lying, I'll gladly crap a cow*."

"Really, is this necessary?"

"Say it!"

Bentley sighed. "If I'm lying - I'll gladly *blab a bow*." He rubbed his nose at the same time so his words came out muffled.

"Couldn't hear you." Kimi folded her arms.

Bentley glanced at the monkeys then back to Kimi. "Kimi, if I'm lying to you, then I promise to crap a whole herd of cows. Now please, believe me." His cheeks were glowing.

Kimi burst out laughing.

He offered a hand and Kimi took it. "Come on, let's show you the town."

———

~ Middling ~

They reached the edge of the ridge and sat on the nearest bench. Kimi didn't speak immediately. Dusk had begun to settle over the scene below, but detail appeared the longer you looked. The centre of town was a huge dark circle glimmering with tiny lights of all colours. Each light illuminated crackled patterns of leafy branches around it. It was spectacular - like an entire wood of Christmas trees. All around the wood's circumference, street after street of spires and angled rooftops ran off in straight lines. Some streets were longer than others and all were lit up with coloured lights, just like the wood, and tiny figures were going about their business.

"Triple wow!" said Kimi, at last.

"That's Pommy Wood in the middle," Bentley said. "The lights are pomegranate lanterns."

"Don't you have electricity? Telly? Computers?"

"Oh, we have better than that."

"Like what?"

"We're in the beta stages of *BUG*. Computers are brain-link only. As for your telly; over five million Earth broadcasts are at your disposal." He grinned.

"Neat."

"If you look close," he went on, "around the outside

of Pommy Wood you can see the giant standing stones. Forty two of them surround the wood in total."

Kimi *could* see them. Each stone as big as a house and taller than the trees within. There were famoose, too, zigzagging round the tops of the stones like fireflies. Then movement beyond the farthest street lights, two pulsating amber lights were rising from the darkness. Slowly they came higher, side by side and soundless. When the lights cleared the far ridge and were hovering, silhouetted against the purple sky, they appeared not like helicopters as Kimi had previously thought, but smoother and sleeker like teardrops turned on their sides. Their dark surfaces glittered with the light from the town. They vibrated in unison before shooting into the inky distance in a blink. Kimi giggled and half-closed her eyes. The town went out of focus, diffusing to a dreamy blur and she felt lifted by it, or held by it, or maybe both. Enchanted, she decided. That was the word she was looking for. She gazed up at the mountain, fading into darkness, its sun halo now a smudge of pale yellow. "Tell me what the aliens are like?"

"Oh…a bit slippy and slidey, which is weird at first, but I suppose they're decent enough chaps. They certainly work hard and play hard. I remember the -"

"I meant what they look like."

"You're asking the wrong one there, Kimi. I'm rubbish at descriptions."

"Try."

Bentley smiled. "You'll probably get to meet Granp first. He's General Cohn's right hand man. He dines in the Foot most nights. You'll like him. He's a particularly good friend of mine."

Alien friends? Kimi threw her head back and laughed so hard it echoed back to her. She kept on laughing until Bentley shook her still.

"What's so funny? Keep it down or you'll have the officers over."

Bentley was a blur. "I know I might be mad." She wiped her eyes and breathed. "Or even that this is all a crazy dream, which it probably is, I mean, talking crows, famoose - I even got a few killed, don't you know. *And* I blasted crap-loads of crows from the sky - oh, Mummy will be proud. I even took a ride with a stranger - that'll be Daddy proud, too - even if it was with a cheeky talking monkey. And don't forget *you*, good old *you*, my trusted Tulpa made by me from me who talks back to me - would you believe? And to top it all, I'm gonna meet aliens. I'm cracking up - *Wawawawawawa* -" she stuck her thumbs in her ears and waggled her fingers and felt way too hyper.

Bentley said: "It's the town, Kimi. Power from the forty-two giant stones has this effect. You need to get acclimatised. Take some deep breaths."

She took some.

"And anyway, what do mean by `I talk back to you`?"

Kimi shrugged.

"A Tulpa is a precious thing to have, I'll have you know."

"Sorry. I didn't *mean* anything. How'd I end up with you anyway?"

Bentley sat back down. "It's simple really. Most humans meet their Tulpas when they're little."

"Like I was five."

"Right. To come into existence, a Tulpa has to be invoked. Usually it's the result of a fright or a great worry on the part of the evoker. In your case, you happened on a black cat and your fear made me materialise - I'm really a product of your inner strength, see. Pure fear made you do that."

"But you're a boy - or you were. How can you be from me?"

"A boy in a story book your mother used to read to you. He bravely saves a drowning puppy. That was your favourite bit. His name was Bentley. The boy not the puppy. A hero character you subconsciously called upon in your time of need."

"I remember that book," Kimi said, drying her eyes. "So I made you into a boy? Sorry about that."

Bentley grunted. "Don't be saying sorry. It's not surprising how many Tulpas materialise as characters from

112

books. Believe me when I say I got off lightly. You'll meet some weird Tulpas in Middling. Big Sue for starters - *he*'s unusual."

"Oh yeah, the Sue guy."

Bentley nodded.

"So how come I haven't seen you for years?"

"Well, as kids get older they tend to get wiser, often learning to deal with fears and worries by themselves - so the Tulpa is no longer required and gets left behind."

"Here? On Heart?"

"Exactly. Waiting, hoping, that one day, their creator might show up. I always knew you would make it of course. Never bargained on getting you so early though."

"So me and you, Bentley. We're stuck with each other?"

"That's right. Until you, uhm, you know -"

"Die?"

A whooshing sound from behind.

"This'll be us," Bentley said, getting to his feet.

"Bentley."

"Yes?"

"Are we going to fizzle again? The white?"

"Yes. But we're not crossing dimensions so it is a lot quicker."

"How much quicker?"

"Kimi, come on, it's nothing, really."

"What if I make people wobble? You heard what the monkey said about people wobbling. I already turned a crow and a toad inside out. If I do that to a *person* -"

"Don't worry. I already thought about that. Stick close to me and I'll explain when we get down there."

Wind swirled among the stones. As Kimi and Bentley arrived, Rehd stepped from the vortex which then instantly vanished. "The Adepts are still in discussion," he said. "You're to go straight to the Rabbit's Foot, nourish the premature, and wait."

"Wait for what?" Bentley asked, steering Kimi to his other side away from Rehd.

Rehd's eyes were on Kimi, even though he was talking to Bentley. "As with all new Balancers, Tulpa Bentley, the premature will be scanned, logged, and tested. Nourish your premature and I will return for her when the Adepts are ready."

"What about the illnesses you mentioned?"

"No new cases. Wobbling flesh, along with the incoherence, comes and goes. Those affected are allowed to go about their normal duties. Apart from driving and operating machinery."

"And the crow?" asked Bentley. "The one spouting prophecies?"

"Locked up tight." Rehd gave a little shriek and swept a long arm toward the stones. "To the Foot," he said.

114

Bentley looked reasonably happy with this, but Kimi had serious jitters. Bentley saluted the monkey, stepped into the stone circle and whisked the air. The monkey pursed his lips, clicked his heels and returned the salute.

"Come along, Kimbo. I can already taste that dodo." She took his hand and was pulled into the wind.

———

- The Sweet Lump of Gorge -

Inside the vortex seemed faster than before. Kimi had that terrible nervous feeling you get when starting a new school, only a zillion times worse. She gripped Bentley's arm.

The vortex slowed groaned and vanished. Sudden change from grass to damp cobbles made Kimi slide a little. They were on one of the streets. Bentley dragged her backwards into the shadows. He pulled a key from around his neck and opened the door they stood next to. Kimi glimpsed a luminous green monkey painted on the door before she was shoved inside. Bentley followed her in. "Wait here, don't move, and don't put the lights on. I'll be back in a tick!"

"Wait!"

But he was gone. The door closed. The lock locked.

Two steps through the darkness and Kimi reached the one small window. She lifted one of the blind slats and peered through. Across the lane, Bentley was growing into his old self. He brushed his hair back and disappeared through a doorway. The large frosted window next to it was lit up bright green from the inside. Above it, a sign in squirly letters said, *The Rabbit's Foot.* And there was music, like a harp playing, and the faint sounds of chatter and laughter.

Thin shadows moved behind the frosted glass - thin shadows with big ovular heads. Kimi's pulse was so rapid, she realised she had been holding her breath and gasped for air. She needed to sit. She turned away from the window and sunk to the floor. Her eyes were becoming accustomed to the darkness. In the grey-black, the wall opposite, behind a hulking black sofa shape, appeared to be all bookshelves. She could make out two chairs and two small tables with lamps on. A hint of lavender caught her nose and reminded her of the fabric conditioner Mum used. Kimi closed her eyes and breathed.

"All set!" Bentley said, flinging the door open. Kimi jumped and yelped for the six-millionth time today...before sinking back to the wall. Being on Heart was like taking a walk with a pet defibrillator who liked surprising you every five minutes.

"I said - we're all set." Bentley's hand waved in front of her face.

Kimi clasped it and got to her feet. "There's something we need to discuss," she said. Bentley appeared to give a little fuzzy shake and let go of her hand. Then he froze, staring right through her. He was calculating, hiding something. Deffo.

"And what might that be?" he asked.

Kimi hesitated. She had so many questions.

Bentley turned, locked the door, turned back,

dropped the key in his shirt. "I'm sorry, Kimbo. You know the situation. Only the Adepts can provide the answers. They always do. And we need to get you fed and watered before they send for you."

Kimi sighed. "Please don't leave me again."

"I was only gone a minute, Kimi. And you were quite safe in here. Belongs to good friends of mine. Look, we couldn't risk walking straight in the Foot. General Cohn's in his favourite pew by the window with Granp - *and* the place is jumping. You give anyone the wobbles - particularly a greylian General - and we're done for."

Kimi was trembling. "Oh Bentley."

"Your roasted dodo is waiting."

"I'm not hungry anymore."

"No buts!"

"I didn't say *but* - I said I'm not hungry."

"We will travel directly to the kitchen!" Bentley twirled a finger and the resultant wind made Kimi close her eyes. She was tugged forward into it and, after a momentary fizzle, her eyes opened to brightness and a steaming plate of dark meat, oozing with juice. It looked like a ginormous turkey leg. Juices trickled to a bed of crisp lettuce. Pots of coloured sauces were arranged to one side. The smell was divine. Saliva squirted into her mouth. Her stomach expanded and opened its hungry mouth.

"Hallo deary," came a sweet voice from above. Kimi

looked up. The feast was in the hands of a giant. Well, a tall skinny bloke who almost reached the ceiling. He was dressed in chefs' whites, had a chequered tea towel over each shoulder, and a blue tartan chef's hat with straggly grey hair poking from under it. His face was creased and tanned like the old Bentley's. He had a kind smile, and a blue plastic bag tied round his beard.

Kimi had to swallow before she could reply. "Hi."

"What a gargantuan relief," the big man said. "I don't appear to be wobbling, do I? Welcome, Kimi. Take a seat won't you, and tuck right on in. You look like you've been in the wars, poor thing." He placed the plate on a small table by the back door. Kimi liked him instantly. She thanked him and sat, drooling. Bentley joined her. He passed her a knife and fork rolled in a green napkin with a rabbit foot printed on it. "Enjoy!"

"I'm Big Sue," the towering giant said. "You can call me Sue." He swiped a tea towel from his shoulder. It flicked out with lightning speed, whipping a crumb from the table.

Kimi startled again.

"I'll fetch wee Stella." The giant headed for the door at the other side of the kitchen. This was a big kitchen. Digital readouts blinked from five big blazing ovens. Saucepans, pots and bigger things like cauldrons boiled and bubbled. Colourful salads made tall piles on two islands,

120

herbs and onions hung from the walls along with plucked birds the size of pigs - all ready for the pot.

"Who's Stella?" Kimi asked Bentley, once certain the giant had left.

"She's Sue's Balancer, also your roomy, and your um - mentor."

"Mentor? That means teacher, right?"

"Come on – eat up!"

"How old is she?"

"Seventeen. And she's nice. Stop fretting and eat."

Kimi gave him a look. Her stomach creaked and groaned. "Change to the younger Bentley, please."

Bentley gave the look right back. "Why?"

"Because. If I'm going to be stared at while eating, then I'd prefer to be stared at by someone my own age."

Bentley looked puzzled.

"Just do it. Please."

Bentley shrugged, did a quick vibrate, then -

"No! Wait!"

Bentley stopped.

"Not my age. Two years older."

He looked puzzled again.

"Do it will you. My belly thinks my gob's healed up."

Bentley's head shook fast from side to side, and while it was shaking, his features smoothed and shrank away, flecked hair became dark, and the resulting smile was extra shiny.

"Thank you." Kimi lapped the drool from her lips, jabbed the fork in the meat and cut a mouth-sized slice. The taste was as Bentley had promised. An initial smack of roast chicken was soon rolled over by a wave of juicy pork. Then came the succulent flavour of tongue-melting roast beef. Juice was dripping from Kimi's chin. She dipped a finger in a pot of plum coloured sauce. It tasted like strawberries and beetroot. "Very nice," she said, going in for another dip.

"Told you," Bentley said.

Kimi was about to cut another slice when the whole dodo leg was suddenly wrapped in a swirling green mist. It lifted into the air before her, dripping juice and bits of lettuce back to the plate.

"Ach, take the bull by the horns, I always say!"

The giant stood in the doorway, his palms resting on the shoulders of a very short but very pretty girl. Her white-blond hair was tied in pigtails. She had a big mouth, and lots of teeth with a gap at the front. The green mist was coming from her outstretched right arm in undulating waves, holding the dodo leg before Kimi's nose. "Go on!" the girl urged. Her eyes were bright and full of mischief.

Kimi smiled, shrugged, and grabbed the dodo leg at each end. The green mist whipped away back into smiley-girl's hand. Kimi took a big bite.

"I'm Stella," smiley-girl announced. "And you're Kimi. It's good to meet you."

Kimi quickly swallowed the mouthful of meat. "Yeah. Pleased to meet you."

"Ohh, trust you," Big Sue said. "Now you've got her hands all greasy. As if she isn't in a bad enough state."

"Quit your whining," Stella said. She broke away from under Sue's hands, took three steps forward, then froze when one of Big Sue's tea towels whip-cracked at her ear. Stella rolled her eyes and continued towards the table. She wore an amazing black leather jacket covered in straps and buckles. She sat opposite Kimi.

"Can't feel anything," she said, then made a fist and held her knuckles towards Kimi.

Kimi put the dodo leg down, wiped her hands on the napkin, made a fist, and slowly, and very, very carefully, moved her knuckles towards Stella's.

There seemed to be no pulling sensation.

Knuckles touched to knuckles.

Not a hint of a wobble.

Kimi breathed again.

"Excellent!" Bentley said.

"Ohh, indeed it is," said Sue, polishing a fridge.

Stella looked pleased. "Kinda knew it," she said, sitting back in her chair.

Kimi felt a bit embarrassed, like she had the plague

or something. She cut another slice of meat, dipped into a yellow sauce, and shoved it in her mouth. Bananarey lemons was the taste.

"So far so good," Bentley said. "But we need to do another test."

Kimi stopped eating.

"Come in, Perry!" Bentley said, loudly.

The door through which Stella had arrived opened a crack. Harp music and the sounds of chatter and clinking glasses became instantly louder.

"Come on, lad, don't be shy," Bentley said.

The head that popped around the door was wide-eyed, white-toothed and had deliciously dark skin and a shocking hairstyle not too dissimilar to monkey Rehd's.

Kimi sighed inside. She realised she must look horrendous and tried not to show her squirm. "Hi!" she said, tucking her hair behind her ears and giving a little wave, which she instantly thought must have looked pathetic.

"Hello there," the sweet lump of gorge said, stepping inside. His open-neck white shirt and washed out jeans brought more internal sighing. "I'm Perry," he said.

Kimi smiled and nodded. She kicked Bentley under the table then thought,

Make yourself five again.

Bentley raised an eyebrow.

Ten then.

"What?"

Okay an oldie then. I prefer you as oldie. Change to an oldie.

Bentley huffed, stuck his tongue out, shook his head and swelled into the old Bentley - complete with creases and flecks.

Kimi smiled at him, but he didn't smile back.

"This is our pot lad, a fine Balancer-in-training, the lovely Perry Sunder," Big Sue said, indicating to the gorgeous one. "But the awful thing is," Sue went on. "Poor Perry is one of those that has shown the symptoms."

"That's right, Kimi," Perry said, still smiling. He took a few steps forward. "It's a horrible and weird feeling - like your flesh is floating. Makes you feel sick. Then there's a feeling of being completely crazy, like you don't know who you are, like you might just go and paint a giraffe or poke your -"

"Okay Perry. That's enough," Sue said.

Stella stood. "So we need to do the old the knuckle test, sister." She took Kimi's hand, pulled her to her feet, marched her across the room, and halted three feet from Perry. Kimi swallowed hard. Her mouth had stuck. Her heart was currently somewhere near her left big toe on the rebound from the top of her skull.

Bentley came and stood between them and off to the side. "You first, Perry."

Perry looked nervous. He took a breath, lifted his arm slowly towards Kimi, fist clenched. He was shaking.

Kimi didn't have to raise her arm. She could feel it already. A low hum all over, a magnet ready to grab. She took a step back. "No!"

Perry dropped his arm.

"I didn't see anything," Stella said. The others confirmed the same.

"I could feel it," Kimi said.

"Me too," Perry agreed.

"We need to actually see the effect," Bentley said. "Please, try again - very carefully. I'll keep hold of you just in case."

Big Sue was staring, slowly polishing his watch at the same time.

Bentley came behind and placed both hands on Kimi's shoulders.

Kimi steadied herself. "Okay."

Perry took up position. "I'm ready, I think." He looked worried.

Kimi's skin tingled all over. Bentley's grip tightened. She knew he could feel it too. She watched her knuckles rising in the air before her. Ten centimetres away from Perry's knuckles and his skin began to wobble. Kimi paused.

"I see it," Bentley said, and gently moved Kimi back

a step.

Perry also stepped back. "What does it mean?"

"It's a puzzle," Bentley said. "And for the time being, we need to keep this to ourselves and ensure Kimi has no contact with anyone who has shown the symptoms. Now Perry, I want you to return to your duties, keep your mouth shut and your ears open for any developments. Yes?"

"Of course Mr B. See you, Kimi," he said. "I'm sure we'll get this figured out."

Kimi smiled and did the pathetic wave again. His worried white smile went swishing out the door.

"Here you are deary." Sue was offering a glass of something green. "Pommy juice. To buck you up a bit."

Kimi took a long, long drink and emptied the glass. A minty explosion watered her eyes and nearly blew her toes off. "Cra -"

"Ah-ah!" Bentley stopped her.

Kimi swooned, returned to her seat, grabbed up the dodo leg, took a big bite, then declared. "I wuv dish plashe."

Big Sue arrived with a glass of water. "You're meant to sip it," he said.

Kimi drank the water down in one. Then burped.

"What's the plan, then Mr B?" Stella asked.

"Here's what I think," Bentley said, sitting back at the table.

Big Sue drew a chair and sat down. He folded his

arms and Kimi realised his hands were in perfect position to grasp at either of the tea towels hanging over his shoulders. She checked around for crumbs then wondered what book he came from.

"As you know," Bentley began, "Kimi's been assigned to Stella despite her being a prem -"

Kimi kicked his foot.

"- despite her being here early. And although I'm not entirely happy with that, because of all the wobbling and Kimi attracting crows like flies to a cowpat -"

"Thanks," Kimi said, wolfing more dodo.

" - we do know that Kimi is in danger. The Adepts have made that known plain enough and that's why she's here. Why Kimi would make Perry wobble and not Stella is beyond me. Though we do know that Stella has not yet shown any wobbling symptoms. I think there must be a connection, somehow, but I'm certain that that's what the Adepts are working on. So for now, Kimi, you must stay away from others, upstairs in your room. Get cleaned up. And Stella, will stay with you at all times. All we can do, is keep you out of harms' way until Rehd returns for you."

"But then what?" Kimi asked.

"All newbies go through the same procedure, Kimi. After tasting the dodo, they get summoned to the library for scanning and logging."

"But I'm obviously a freak, aren't I? I'm something

to do with all the sickly people and - and - and the scanning is bound to show something up."

"Then maybe that will be a good thing," Stella offered. "I think B's right. Let's get you freshened up and keep you out the way 'til chief Rehd comes for you."

"It does sound like the right thing to do," Sue said. He reached a big hand over and patted Kimi's shoulder.

"I guess," Kimi said. She took a small bit of lettuce and dipped into a pot of blue sauce. Sprout and onion, she thought.

Bentley reached over and picked off a piece of meat that had fallen onto the lettuce. "That's settled then," he said, threw the piece of meat in the air and caught it in his mouth. *You eat?* Kimi thought.

"Right, let's get moving before the chief arrives." Bentley looked at Stella. "Remember what comes first?"

Stella's eyes lit up. "Aye - *The Balancer On Board.*"

"That's right! Kimi - you're meant to get a welcome pack to fill you in on all the do's and don'ts, but of course your early arrival put paid to that. Maybe Stella can dig hers out and run through a few things once you've had a shower. Things like why you shouldn't attempt telepathy with your Tulpa unless in dire need."

Kimi felt her cheeks warm.

"Okay, sounds like a plan," Stella said.

Kimi wiped her mouth. She was really quite stuffed,

but didn't want to stop eating dodo. "Can I, um, take this with me?"

"Of course you may," Sue said. "Just be sure and leave no mess or I'll have you on scrubbing duty!"

Stella slid from her seat with a twinkle in her eye. Kimi carefully picked up the heavy plate and followed Stella to the door.

"Oh - one last thing," Bentley said. "Do you have any fillings?"

"Um - yeah, two I think. Why?"

"They need to come out. Get that sorted will you?" he said to Stella.

"Ach - it'll be a pleasure," Stella said, opening the door.

Kimi looked worriedly at Bentley, but he was waving her away.

———

~ 12 ~

~ Is that a plan? ~

The kitchen door led to a small hallway. Straight ahead, double doors shared a small circular window which emitted the same green light Kimi had seen from the front of the building. She saw Perry carrying a tray of drinks, glimpsed a golden harp and the long platinum hair of its player, saw thin shadows swaying behind the frosted glass of the cubicles.

"This way," Stella said, starting up stairs to the right of the double doors.

A shaded wooden staircase spiralled up three floors where wall-mounted pomegranate lanterns cast a faint yellow glow around each landing. The large oval plate was heavy, and Kimi went carefully up each step, staring at the trembling dodo leg.

"Hurry up," shouted Stella, already on the top landing.

"Okay, okay." Sweat was running down Kimi's face when she finally reached the top. She took her eyes off the plate and went a bit woozy.

Stella was leant at the frame of a small wooden door. A painted sign pinned to it said:

*** NO UNAUTHORISED TULPAS ***

Stella pushed the door open and snapped her fingers. Yellow lights came on. Kimi swayed inside, wondering vaguely what else Stella might be able to do.

"Ach, sorry about the mess," Stella said. "I've been using your half for storage."

This bedroom was six times the size of Kimi's, back in Mousehole. Its ceiling went up to a high point beyond a criss-cross of rafters. Kimi guessed they must be inside one of the spires. On the right stood a chunky four-poster bed with blood-red drapes that looked old and worn. A tall Welsh dresser stood at its side, brimming with clutter. Kimi spotted a pair of familiar bug eyes on the dresser. They were peering through a glass dome. "Is that real?" she said.

Stella made a squealy giggle. "You like it?" She pulled the glass dome forward, her face twinkling. Within the dome sat a Bellamy's Aunt. It was obviously dead. Its skin pallid and corpselike, and its bloodshot eyes bulging enough that they might fall out. A fat white fly clung to the side of its face, its coiled probe penetrating the toad's tongue which was pink, plump and glistening and hanging right out.

"Bloody hell," Kimi groaned. "Is that what I think it is?"

"Bliss fly meets Bellamy's Aunt," Stella said. "This piece is called, Bellamy's Bliss."

Bentley was right about bliss flies. It *was* the size of a fist, and its probe, all greasy and slimy. Eurgh! She knew it was only varnish. But still. Kimi's cheeks seemed to be scooping themselves up.

"Shot and stuffed them both myself!" Stella said, proudly.

Kimi turned away, pretending to check out the rest of the room. A bulky wardrobe faced the bottom of the bed and a wicker ottoman. A chunky orange teddy bear sitting on the ottoman had a shock of spiky black hair which reminded Kimi of *what's-his-face* - the pot lad - Barry, or something. "Are you allowed to do that here? Shoot things and stuff them, I mean."

"Well, not really. I told Sue and Mr B, that they were dead when I found them. Don't sprag, will you?"

"Course not," Kimi said. "But would you mind covering it up?" Stella looked wounded. "No, no," Kimi said. "I meant, I, well, it's a good display and everything, I just feel a bit sick and -"

"Aye okay." Stella picked a jumper from the floor and covered the display. "Sue doesn't like it either. And, Mr B says I need my head examined - and all because I want to do a big cased display with branches covered in famoose. It's not like anyone's going to miss a few famoose. And hey, it's nature isn't it?"

"Yeah," Kimi said, absently. She was staring at *her* bed. Her side of the room was in complete disarray. Shelves of small boxes, bigger boxes on the floor, all filled with books, old clothes and rolled up pictures. A single, much dimmer lantern hung over this side, and a tattered fold-out camp bed stood in the pale circle beneath it.

"We'll soon get sorted," Stella said, taking the plate of dodo from Kimi and placing it on the dresser. She patted the four-poster's chunky covers. "Have a seat."

Kimi was glad of a seat. She flopped onto the four-poster. It was soft and bouncy.

"B' said you killed loads of crows and famoose." Stella hitched up on the bed.

Kimi swayed with the mattress. "I feel awful about the famoose," she said. "They were so willing to help me. I wish -"

"I wanted to go and collect the dead ones," Stella said. "Would have been perfect for my display. But B' said it was too dangerous. That the crows were pretty nasty. Were they nasty, Kimi? Though I guess they must have been, looking at the blood on you."

"Oh yes. They were nasty alright."

"Tell you what. Let's get the official stuff out the way, then you can get cleaned up and tell me all about what happened." Stella slid off the bed, went to the dresser and pulled open a drawer. "Ready for this?"

"What official stuff?"

Stella removed a green bundle from the drawer. It was a roll of felt, tied with an old leather belt. "Used to belong to my Great Granddad," she said, undoing the buckle. The felt unrolled with clinks and clanks and Kimi's heart stopped when she saw all the tools. There was a scalpel, pliers, a mirror on a stick, and all manner of spiked things.

"Wa - was he a torturer?" A film of sweat oozed through Kimi's brow and she felt the urgent need to pee.

"Ach, these are high quality dental tools, I'll have you know. Now, like Mr B' said, those fillings have to go. It won't hurt much." Stella selected pliers and a rusty scalpel and held them up to Kimi.

"Wh - wh - why do fillings have to go?" Some distant voice was telling Kimi to make a run for it, but the command was not connecting with her legs.

"Earth fillings interfere with mojo. Oh - and metal hips. You haven't got a metal hip have you?"

Kimi shook her head, glaring at the old tools. "I - I don't want to do this. Isn't there a dentist in Middling?"

"Aye - me!" Stella frowned, her eyes went small and black and her mouth contorted. She snapped the pliers and made a twisting motion with the scalpel.

"Du, du, du, du, don't I get gas or something?" Kimi *really* had to pee.

"Nonsense," Stella said. "Lie down!" She kneed up onto the bed and pushed Kimi onto her back. Kimi's head landed square on the pillow, but still she couldn't move; Stella had straddled her.

"Pommy juice numbs the pain a bit," Stella said. "So you should be okay - ish!" She brandished the scalpel. "I'm going to make a few small incisions in your gums. Might sting a wee bit. Open wide!" She leant in close, twisting the scalpel around and around in her fingers.

"I - I need to pee - desperately!" Kimi sank further into the pillow, sweating profusely. That distant voice urged her to throw Stella off the bed, but Kimi was numb. She went to speak, to beg, to plead, to shout, "I - I -," but could barely catch her breath.

"Open up!" ordered Stella, eyes bulging. "I pwomise you I'm weally good at this," she said in a scary, little-girl voice. "There'll hardly be any bwood!"

Sweat trickled into Kimi's ears amplifying her pounding heart. Stella moved in and the scalpel trembled right by Kimi's nose. Kimi panted desperately - she had to do something - and quickly.

"*Logos, Thymos, Eros*," whispered Stella. "*Make this work first time!*"

"What do you mean, first time?" Kimi blurted.

Stella smiled, snapped the pliers and made for Kimi's mouth.

The scream came from nowhere. She was screaming like a baby.

At that moment the old Bentley appeared at the side of the bed in misty blue form.

Stella vaulted sideways off the bed and proceeded to put the tools away.

"You've still got it then," Bentley said once the screaming died.

Kimi sat up deflated and breathless - the need to pee no longer apparent. "Wh - what's going on?"

"Sorry," Bentley said, slapping Stella a high-five. "Scary but necessary. Page one of the welcome pack, see. All newbies must undergo the evocation test. That fear you first used as a little one - when you came across a Shuck and summoned me up - has to be tested for working order. Only *real* fear does that - and beneath *real* fear lies your mojo - can you see that, Kimbo?"

"But I already made you appear, back home, in my rocking chair."

"Ah yes," Bentley said. "But only because I prompted you with the corn dolly. When I tried to scare you into making me appear in your dining room, you went and fainted. So it had to be tested again here on Heart, see?"

"Think so," she said, still breathing heavily. She could partly see some sense of reason in what Bentley was saying, but thinking was a bit swishy after the minty explosion from the pommy juice and the bucketful of adrenaline Stella had released. Kimi wiped her damp face on her sleeves.

"Grand job," Bentley said, slapping Stella's hand

again. "Oh - and well done, Kimbo. You did good!" Bentley smiled, twirled a finger and vanished in an instant.

"Sorry about that," Stella said. "But like B' said - it had to be done." She sat on the bed next to Kimi. The wide-eyed mad girl had gone and Stella looked sweet and doll-like again. "You okay, Kimi?" Her big mouth grinned.

Kimi nodded, relieved her heartbeat was slowing. "I really thought you were serious. You had me terrified."

"I've had lessons," Stella said. "Uncle Sean from Ireland is a Balancer and so's Grandma Joyce in Glasgow. What about you, any Balancers in the family?"

Kimi hadn't thought about that possibility and immediately pictured Aunt Lizzie. Maybe that would explain her craziness. "Um - no idea," she said. "I suppose it's possible - but this is all new to me. Though I think I'd know about it if there were."

"Not really. You're underage remember."

"Premature. Right. What were those funny words you said before - Logos something? It sounded like you were doing a spell."

"Didn't B' give you the focusing words?"

"Well, no," Kimi said. "At least I don't think so. It kinda got a bit hectic with all the crows and stuff."

Stella nodded. "You'll learn them soon enough. Why are you here early, anyway? I can't get that out of Bentley or Sue no matter how much I grovel. Go on, tell me

- what's the big secret?" Stella leant close.

"I've no idea myself. Honest."

"You must have some idea. You don't get brought here early for nothing. Did anything strange happen before Bentley turned up?"

Kimi tried to think back. The details were clouded but the talking crow stood out. "Yeah," she said. "I guess a talking crow is strange."

"Really? You had a harbinger from Heart? How cool! What did it say?"

Kimi heard its screechy voice in the depths of her mind and goosebumps tickled up her arms. "One death - one death today!" She shuddered.

"Oh -" Stella leant away as if Kimi had B.O.

"So what's that all about?" asked Kimi.

"That's all it said?"

"Yes, but what does it mean? I think - I think my Dad's been killed."

"Killed? You mean - murdered?" whispered Stella, leaning back in again.

"No - no, I think, well, there was this great blast of lightning right where Mum and Dad were meant to be meeting someone - and Dad had said, well, oh I don't know - it's all so mixed up and -"

"But what about Mr B' - how'd he come into it?"

"Bentley just suddenly turned up. Even though I

139

haven't seen him for years. He said there was trouble coming to the door - and then a car crashed into the bins - then the engine revved up really loudly, and someone came in the front door, and seconds later I was falling out of a twirly."

Stella looked captivated.

"But *who* crashed into the bins?" Kimi went on. "Bentley obviously knows - he knew they were coming and he was pretty desperate to get me out of there."

"Ach, secrets ay? Did he say anything? Any clues?"

Kimi thought for a moment, considered mentioning Dad's secret riddle, but then thought better of it - for now at least. She felt strangely merry and buoyant. The rafters started to revolve. She closed her eyes and grabbed the covers to still herself.

"Invigorating stuff, pommy juice," Stella said. "A good blast in the shower is what you need."

After a good blast in the shower, Kimi felt a hundred times better now the caked on blood had been washed away. She really wanted to curl up in Bentley's bath robe and have a good nap, but Stella was insistent that she should be ready because chief Rehd could return at any time. She'd even somehow cleaned and dried Kimi's clothes. She turned her back while Kimi got dressed.

"I've an idea," Stella said, talking to the door.

Kimi fastened her jeans. "I'm done," she said.

Stella turned round. "I think there's skulduggery afoot, Kimi. Something that me and you are obviously not wanted in on. Typical Tulpas - think they know best - bless them. Now I'm not saying old B' and Biggie aren't capable of whatever it is they're up to, but I can't see any harm in doing a wee bit of investigating of our own - can you?"

Kimi sat on the bed and yawned.

"Aren't you interested?"

Kimi struggled to keep her eyes open. "Yeah, go on."

"Well, when you go for scanning, I'll tag along. You can say you're scared to go alone or something."

"Won't Bentley be with me?"

"Can't. When you're in the scanning machine, your Tulpa automatically disengages. He'll be lying down in his room for the duration."

"Oh. Why do I have to be scanned? I'm a bit, well, frightened."

"Don't be. You'll be seen by Patina. She's sweet."

"Is she one of Bentley's superiors?"

"Patina is the most superior of superiors. And while she's attending to your scanning, I'll try and sneak a look at logs and records. See if I can find out why you're here. All *you* have to do is keep old Patina occupied. Is that a plan, or is that a plan?" Kimi nodded. Eyelids fell.

———

13

~ The Library ~

Then a hooter went off.

Kimi bolted upright. Her temples throbbed and her mouth felt like it was coated in famoose fur. "What the?"

"Just one of the ovens going off," Bentley said. He was standing by the bed. "The chief's here for you."

Kimi remembered about scanning at the library - and there was something about a plan. "How long was I asleep?"

"Five minutes," Stella said. "Put this on." She was holding out a jacket similar to the one she wore. This one was red, scuffed and torn, and the arms were missing. Kimi got to her feet and tried it on.

"It's my original field jacket. You can borrow 'til you get yours. Sorry about the arms, though. Kind of got ravaged by dodgy mojo. Beginners eh?" Stella's eyes twinkled.

"I'll get one of these?" Kimi asked.

"Aye - standard issue, Balancer's field jacket. We'll get you fixed up later, but right now the chief's waiting."

"Are you feeling okay Kimi?" Bentley asked. "Nervous or anything?"

"A bit," Kimi replied. "But I'm okay." She thought of the first thing that she could so Bentley wouldn't read her mind. She thought of geraniums. Orange geraniums.

Bentley raised an eyebrow.

She made quickly for the door.

***

Big Sue was at the bottom of the stairs. He ushered her through to the kitchen where Rehd was sat at the small table. He was staring into what looked like a video-phone. "I know babes," he was saying to the phone. "I won't be too late. Yes, yes." His lips pursed. "Me too, babes." He pressed a button, stood up and collected his helmet from the table. "Let's get this done," he said to the room.

"Good luck, Kimbo," Bentley said. "I'm afraid I can't come with -"

"I know. Stella told me. You enjoy your nap."

Bentley hugged her. "Right then. Be good. And watch your back."

"Take note!" Rehd said. "The crows are thick tonight. And the Adepts have not yet made the answer. Until they make it, I will be the premature's escort." He moved two steps closer to Kimi. Not close enough to wobble. Kimi held her ground.

Stella went quickly to Rehd's side, moved him back to the table. "Chief Rehd," she said. "I'd like to volunteer to come along and help with the premature."

Rehd laughed.

"I'm serious. She's a wee scaredy, and I'd hate for

144

her to, I dunno, freak out or something."

"I can handle a premature, Balancer O'Brien. Thanks for the offer."

Stella said quietly, "She might even wet herself. Make a mess in your bike."

Rehd gave Kimi a `you-cannot-be-serious` look. A smile was pulling at Kimi's face. But she held it down. Stella was good. "Oh yes," Kimi said. "Proper babies, us prematures."

Rehd flapped a gloved hand and grunted. "Very well. There's some rules." He read from his video thingy, "The premature must immediately desist from mojo applications and all corvine interaction of any nature until Adept Blavatsky says otherwise."

Kimi didn't have a clue what he just said.

Bentley's hand came on her shoulder. "He means -"

Stella cut in, "He means no shooting stuff, sister - especially crows."

"Right," Rehd said. "Let's get going. My lady's getting cold." He flicked his visor down and headed out the back door.

Stella clapped her hands silently, whispered "Yay!" and dragged Kimi into the back yard. The night was pitch, the sky sprinkled with stars, and Rehd's gleaming squad bike was waiting at the gate. Stella climbed in. Kimi joined her.

The engine roared and they were pressed back in the

seat. The back lane was empty apart from many bins and a few small cats prowling menacingly to and fro; their attention held by the yard walls which were lined with crows. Kimi noticed the rooftops were dotted with crows too. She clung to Stella, crows lifting as they sped past. At the end of the street they passed a tall statue of a man in a chair, a black figure in the night. Kimi glimpsed `CARROLL` on the nameplate as the squad weaved around it.

Now they were into trees and scrub, the squad's lights on full beam. Weeping willows loomed and passed, loomed and passed. Black crow figures darted across their path. They reached the base of the left hand ridge, the throttle screamed and up they went, the twinkling town rapidly shrinking beneath them. The summit arrived with a blast of cold and they tore towards the mountain. Blackness enwrapped them as the bike sped on and the mountain grew broader and taller. A pinprick of white light blinked into existence directly ahead and the bike sped towards it, headlights cutting through the dark. Soon the tyres were leaving grass and hitting concrete, or probably flat rock, and in a few more seconds, Rehd was braking and the bike spun to a stop beside the white light. He killed the engine and the silence echoed.

The white light was a pomegranate lantern above a small door in the mountainside.

"I'll be right here," Rehd said.

Stella jumped out and dragged Kimi to the door. "Cheers," she said to Rehd.

Rehd sat on the handlebars, put his feet up on the seat. His video-thingy was beeping. He waved them away.

There were no crows about, Kimi noticed.

Blue paint flaked from the twisted door. Ivy crawled the frame and dripped with cobwebs. Kimi shuddered.

An engraved sign on the door said,

HEART LIBRARY

Est. 1926 - A Christie.

"The library's inside the mountain?" Kimi said.

"Yep." Stella pushed the door and pulled Kimi inside.

Rehd's voice, "Yes babes, I know babes," before the door shut behind them.

They were in total darkness along with a smell like dusty curtains.

"Good morning!" yelled Stella in a sing-song voice.

There was a loud `phut` and what looked like a pumpkin, illuminated on the very high ceiling, casting them in an amber shroud.

"*Remember the plan?*" Stella whispered.

Kimi nodded. "*I think so.*"

147

"You keep old Patina busy, and I'll sneak a look on the computer. Okay?"

"Okay."

Stella looked to the ceiling and shouted to the pumpkin, "O'Brien with the premature!"

There was a small pause, then another `phut` and another pumpkin lit up, then more and more went `phut - phutting` a great long way to a back wall and a tiny little door. Double rows of towering bookshelves ran the length of this room, all of them angled inwards. Kimi and Stella walked between them towards the door at the back.

Kimi sneezed and the sneeze echoed. "Big isn't it?" she whispered, staying close to Stella. There appeared to be no one about.

"Ach, this is only the lobby," Stella said. They arrived at the door in the back wall and Stella reached for the handle. "Ready?" she threw open the door and brilliant white light burst from within. Kimi shielded her eyes, squinting. The silhouette of Stella's head and shoulders vanished into the glare. Kimi made a grab for Stella's jacket and followed.

"Blink and you'll get used to it," Stella was saying from within the light. Kimi did blink and the scene forming before her was so huge, so vast, so silvery shiny, it took a few moments to settle. Polished marble chequered the floor in white and green and there was the zingy smell of lemons. Pairs of chrome columns stood either side of this vast room, a great many of them supported the ceiling above and ran a long way back to a small point in the distance. Kimi had the feeling of being completely surrounded by thousands of tons of mountain as if she was in the belly of a giant whale. Through a large oval-shaped hole in the ceiling, the same arrangement of columns repeated for many floors after that. Between all the columns were shelf after shelf with what Kimi thought must add up to millions of books. Many desks filled the ground floor with young women sat working at them. The women all appeared identical with straight blonde hair and bright yellow jumpers. They all had their heads down, working feverishly.

"Ahem!" Stella coughed. The women all looked up at once. Each had a gleaming white smile and the same black glasses. More appeared on the floors above, peering down with glinting teeth.

"Crap a clone," Kimi said.

"Secretaries," Stella informed.

A dozen or so of these secretaries left their desks. Instead of legs, wispy trails of light swirled from their waists. They floated over, swaying and giggling and gleaming smiles. "It's the early one!" exclaimed the secretary nearest.

Makes a change, Kimi thought.

Stella jerked her head at Kimi. "She's here for scanning. Can we go up?"

"Yessss," the secretaries hissed in unison. They began fading and fusing together in a sea of blonde hair, yellow jumpers, spectacles and bright white teeth. Kimi moved behind Stella. The secretaries converged before them into one bright beam of giggling light that began stretching upwards through the many floors.

"Ready?" asked Stella. "Just step inside."

"I've heard that before," Kimi replied. They stepped into the shaft of light and took off with a fast swishing sound. Through the see-through wall of fused yellow sweaters and smiles, row after row of bookcases whizzed downwards. Kimi's cheeks pulled and flapped. She had to shut her eyes and hold on to Stella. All she could hear was swishing and giggling.

"We're here," Stella said, calmly, as the shaft of light curled into a high alcove and set them gently down. Then it sucked away giggling back down to the ground floor.

"Awesome," Kimi said, feeling a little sick.

"Just wait 'til the ride down," laughed Stella.

Kimi took in the surroundings. There appeared to be a series of windowed labs. Through large windows, she could see desks and computers and machines that might be heart monitors and stuff like that. Movement in one of the labs, a shadowy figure gliding by a window. Kimi expected an alien to emerge.

The door opened and a tall woman came sweeping

through. She wasn't as tall as Big Sue, but almost. Her golden hair was styled in enormous waves that swept along with her. She wore a lilac dress all flowers and lace that reached to the floor. It wasn't clear if she had legs or not, but her movements were smooth and gliding, so Kimi guessed not.

The woman arrived and smiled down at Kimi, her blue eyes swirling dreamily. "You must be Kimi," she said in a voice so soft.

Kimi nodded.

The woman turned to Stella. "Thank you, Stella. You may wait here. We shan't take long. This way, Kimi." She swished around and Kimi followed into the lab from which she'd come, relived that she felt no wobble from this woman.

She handed Kimi a spotted hospital gown and indicated a changing screen. "If you could pop into that, sweetheart. And remove any jewellery."

Kimi changed nervously behind the screen. She had hated hospitals ever since she'd had her tonsils out. At least this place didn't smell all antiseptic and stuff. She tied up the gown and stepped out, shaking a little.

"I am the fortunate keeper of this fine place," the woman said, floating over. "From this day on and for ever more, you, Kimi Nichols, are under my careful eyes - and I must offer you a little warning; they are demanding eyes,

151

preferring nothing less than *purpose*, *pride* and *perseverance*! What is it that I prefer nothing less of, sweetheart?"

Kimi stared into swirling hazel eyes. "Uh-huh -"

"All the P's. The P's, remember the P's!"

"Erm," Kimi couldn't think at all.

"Purpose! Pride! Perseverance! You can learn that, yes?"

A nod was all Kimi could manage. This lady was a weirdo and Kimi felt dizzy every time she came close. Not the wobbly thing. Just dizzy.

"My name," the weirdo went on, "begins with a P, ends with an A and is exceptionally long. You may use the abridged version. It's Patina *just* Patina."

"Yes, Patina," Kimi said, realising she'd been holding her breath. She took a great gulp of air.

"Good, good. Now - if you could step into the scanner."

The scanner was chrome and bell-shaped with a hole in top and looked like a sit-in sauna. Kimi stepped inside and the doors closed around her neck. Patina clapped her hands and the scanner began to hum. Kimi felt warmth, in her toes first, then it spread slowly up her legs. She must have looked quite terrified, because Patina floated right over and leant on the scanner, her purple eyes swirling; "It's all right, my love. Keep still and enjoy the warmth. We're just recording every atom. Doesn't hurt at all and only takes a minute."

Out the corner of her eye, past crazy lady's waves of hair and through the lab window, Kimi saw Stella slipping into the room beyond and duck down behind a monitor. But she wasn't ducked far enough. A small amount of blond hair was showing over the top of the monitor.

Kimi stared straight back into Patina's eyes, which wasn't easy as there were no pupils - only deep blue eyes turning like whirlpools. Patina was smiling. Kimi smiled back. The band of warmth rising up her body was at her ribs now and would soon be finished. She had to somehow keep crazy lady from turning round and spotting Stella. Then came the second flash of genius of the day.

"P!" she said.

Crazy lady frowned. "You need?"

"No. I thought of another P - surely there should be a fourth: Perfection!"

"Aw, bless you," crazy lady said with a sweet smile. "Purpose, the first P, is required, because without purpose there is no drive - and drive one must! Pride is important because pride, if used correctly, provides fuel for the drive. And Perseverance is forever ahead of you, pulling you forward. Never let perseverance fall behind…"

Kimi was warm all over now. She saw Stella's head move and wished her out of there.

"…but *perfection* is never a requirement for it is

only a *perception*. Can you see that, sweetheart?"

Kimi shook her head. Stella was moving, slipping back out the door. Kimi breathed. "I - I'm not sure what you mean."

"You can think about it for a while."

The scanner's doors swung open.

"Hand please, my darling," Patina said, holding out a chrome contraption that looked ominously like a heavy-duty stapler. Kimi had held off trembling, but now her legs felt like spaghetti. "A teensy prick is all you will feel. A pinprick of your precious blood is all I require." She took Kimi's hand and jabbed her wrist with the stapler.

"OW!" Kimi said, purposely loud, noticing Stella creeping back to the landing.

"And a miniscule scrape of your glorious DNA. Open wide please." Patina waved a cotton bud.

Kimi opened wide and gagged when the bud rubbed the inside of her cheek.

"And a hair!" Patina's hand moved super-fast, plucking out what felt more like a handful.

"OW, OW, OW!" Kimi felt she might just go and pluck a few back, but Patina was staring again, orange eyes, swirling.

"Get dressed," she said, swishing around and gliding to a work surface. Kimi dashed behind the screen and changed quickly. She shrugged Stella's old jacket on, hung

154

the gown over the screen, then almost fell over when she stepped out. Her trainers were on the wrong feet.

"This way!" Patina was holding the door open.

Kimi quickly swapped feet.

"Please wait with Stella while I update your file. There is only the oath left to do. I shall be with you in a heartbeat!"

Kimi smiled and hurried past the weirdo. Stella had taken a seat back out on the landing. She was leafing through a book from a table piled high with them.

"That was way weird," whispered Kimi.

"Ach, you know," Stella waved the book at her. "I've read a lot of books. When I was little, Narnia was my favourite. Still is I suppose. Do you read?"

"Never mind that. Did you find anything?"

"Not here," Stella said quietly. "The big lady's got big ears."

"Erm yes, Harry Potter," Kimi said, loudly, hearing the door opening behind.

"Prefer Stephen King, myself." Stella threw the book back on the table.

"This way girls," Patina swept past. "Stella, sweetheart, you can be witness." She went gliding up the landing, her lace hem brushing the floor.

They followed the landing to its end where it curved and met the opposite landing. A narrow but tall passageway led off from here - long and brilliant white. At the end of the passageway, Patina hovered in silhouette. Her tall slender body and massive hair made her look like a tree. Stella entered and Kimi followed. Halfway through, Kimi realised the brightness was sunlight. She could make out bits of greenery behind the weirdo lady but that was impossible because it was the middle of the night when they had arrived. When they reached the hovering Patina, she was smiling into the air and her eyes were closed. Kimi wondered what colour they'd be when she opened them. She guessed green and Little Hand tingled for the first time in a while.

The passageway opened to a white-railed balcony in the shape of a semi-circle.

"Take a good long look," Patina said, gliding to the railings.

Kimi and Stella joined her. Breeze flicked at their hair and the sunshine warmed their faces. The sunburst of Middling was stunning, even in daylight. Kimi turned and looked up, thinking they must be near the top of the mountain. But there was still a way to go, at least until you hit the clouds, then who knew how much farther. She turned back to the panoramic beauty of it all and let out a long sigh.

"It has that effect on most." Patina said.

"It's - *it's -*"

"Awesome!" Stella finished.

"Yeah -"

"Kimi, sweetheart, believe me when I say, that it is an enormous privilege to be here." Patina opened her eyes. They were emerald green. Kimi startled, then tried to hide her surprise with a coughing fit which ended when Stella whacked her on the back a few times.

"Take it all in," Patina said, sweeping her hair back. "This is Heart - a home for heroes and heroines with hunger…" Kimi gazed into the swirling green eyes. "…hunger for knowledge, a greater existence, and for hope and pride. Can *you* be that heroine, Balancer Kimi Nichols? Can you?"

Kimi felt so light that her feet were leaving the ground. Her breathing quickened and a smile broke across her face. She knew immediately what the answer was, but could not speak nor take her eyes from Patina's.

"Right answer," Patina said.

Kimi returned to the ground as if a big puff of air had blown right out of her. The balcony began to shake and Kimi grabbed for the railings. Rumbles sounded in the distance where darker mountains shimmered on the horizon. It lasted a good few seconds.

Then quiet.

Patina tutted in the direction of the dark mountains, then swished around and floated close to Stella. "Balancer O'Brien. You have proved to be a very worthy Balancer to date - and I must applaud you, despite the occasional impish

157

iniquity. However, you must realise that you are now *more* than a Balancer. You are a very privileged witness and mentor to a newbie - a responsibility so enormous because the future of a potential heroine is at stake, and *that* must *never* be shirked. *You*, Balancer O'Brien, will never shirk - will you, sweetheart?"

Stella was pressed against the railings, staring up at Patina with a dopey grin and big round eyes. Patina turned her gaze to Kimi and Stella slumped, panting.

"Good, good," she said, clicked her fingers and the sun went out. Instant black. Kimi was speechless.

"Now, pay attention, Balancer Nichols. I have arranged an induction for you. Adept Blavatsky has kindly offered to put you through it. And of course I expect you will give your all. Yes?"

Kimi nodded.

"Do you have any questions?"

Kimi hesitated. "Lots," she said.

"Hmm," said Patina. "I understand this must all seem so strange, my love, but you will learn, you will grow, you will understand. And I think that's the best way. Adept Blavatsky is the best in the business at getting to the bottom of matters, and so we shall see what unfolds. Take heart." She clasped Kimi's hands in hers and squeezed them gently. They were warm, soothing hands.

"And Stella, I expect you to accompany and give

help where needed."

"No worries," Stella said.

"Then we are done." Patina let go of Kimi's hands and went gliding into the passageway. "Report straight to the Shed for induction. Tell Rehd to say hi to Ruthie for me."

As they neared the end of the passage, the sound of the giggling secretaries came from below and the column of pulsating light arrived once more and curved across to the landing. Patina swept right through it and the light quivered. "And don't forget your P's!" she shouted back.

Kimi took Stella's hand, closed her eyes tightly, and they stepped inside the shaft of light, whooshing away instantly. Kimi's stomach shot upwards and lodged in her throat. She made a funny "*Nghhhhhhhh -*" noise all the way down until their feet slapped to the marble floor. The light dispersed, forming back into a crowd of smiling secretaries who quickly returned to their desks.

"Byeeeee -" they all said, grinning like toothpaste adverts.

Kimi and Stella ran for the little door and on through the long lobby.

"She is freaky," Kimi said. "Did you see her eyes? And how the heck did she switch night to day?"

"Come on. We need to hurry!" Stella jogged ahead.

"Did you find anything?" Kimi ran after.

"What?"

"On the computers, about me?"

"No, nothing. Come on we need to get a move on."

"To where?"

"To the Shed. You heard the lady - induction."

They were running now, back through the rows of bookcases, pumpkin lights turning off as they went.

"But you were checking the records for long enough. Didn't you find anything at all?"

They reached the outer door. Rehd's voice could be heard. He was still talking to *babes* who Kimi reckoned must be Ruthie.

"Aye I did," Stella said. "I got lucky. Your file was already up on screen. Thing is, it said the file was updating and wouldn't let me click on anything else."

"Oh," Kimi said, frowning. "And that was all?"

"Yeah."

"I wonder what the update is?"

"Who knows," Stella said, heading outside.

——

14

~ The Shed ~

Conversation was impossible with the squad's engine crackling into the night; and as they hurtled down the sloping ridge, Stella was looking everywhere but at Kimi. She knew Stella was hiding something. Call it another vibe or call it intuition or maybe the two are the same? Whatever. This place was weirder than dreams. Crows were following, circling in the black sky. When the squad hit bottom and headed into the trees the crows swooped down and followed, launching from one weeping willow to the next as they passed through. Rehd slowed the squad and they were entering the same street they had left by. Crows cluttered the statue and jumped and jostled on every wall, gutter and roof. Cawing horribly, scurrying and squabbling in forward waves as the squad bike trundled up the cobbles. The Rabbit's Foot's luminous green windows came and passed, and ahead the twinkling lights of Pommy Wood beckoned. Kimi clung to Stella.

Rehd brought the bike to a stop at the end of the street, which was unbelievably stupid because the place was dark and deserted. An empty dirt road lay between them and the giant stones and the glowing wood beyond. Somewhere behind them a dog howled, then another somewhere else.

Kimi's spine ran cold. She shivered. The bike jerked forward. Rehd took the bike between two of the enormous stones. They followed a pathway dappled with light from pomegranate lanterns nestling in branches like glowing gems. Kimi checked over her shoulder for crows. Some had crossed the road to the wood. Five of them stood in silhouette in the gap between the stones. Something was stopping them from coming further. She loosened her grip on Stella who was smiling at the passing trees. Kimi realised she would have to wait until they were alone before interrogating Stella further. As Stella swept her gaze and their eyes met, Kimi smiled. Stella smiled back but quickly looked away. The quantity of lanterns in the trees tripled, brightening their way considerably. Warm fruity aromas filled the air. Famoose played in the branches and a dozen or more flew alongside for a while. If Santa was real, then they could be in his grotto right now. Kimi felt lifted by it all, and thought that this *shed* might actually be something to look forward to. She held on to that thought.

The magical brightness suddenly halted and the black night sky opened wide. Stars glimmered around a pale blue crescent moon. They had entered a grassy clearing. A small ramshackle shed stood in the middle. It was twisted and wonky and looked like it would easily collapse if leant on. Wooden tubs brimming with pomegranates were piled high out front and a three-legged stool stood by the door.

Rehd killed the engine and dismounted. Kimi got out quickly before he could offer a hand. She helped Stella from the bowl seat.

A faded sign on the door:

THE

Scholarium for Harmonious

Extrasensory Development

sitvis vobiscum

"It's just a garden shed," Kimi said. Stella shushed her.

Rehd hung his helmet on the handlebar. He looked to Kimi. "Pick a pommy," he said, then added, "Any pommy. Show it to the folks at home but not to me!" He smacked his lips and laughed his ghost train laugh.

Kimi looked to Stella for help.

"He's trying to be funny," Stella said. "But you do need to pick one."

"I don't really like pomegranate, to be honest," Kimi said. "Thanks anyway."

"Not for eats," Rehd said. "You pick, I eat, you keep."

Kimi again looked to Stella.

"Just pick one. You'll see." Stella pointed to a tub well away from Rehd. "There's some nice ones there!"

Kimi went over, picked one. It was perfectly round. She put it back, spotted one with a dent on the side and

163

picked it up. "I like this one," she said, and lobbed the fruit to the monkey.

Rehd snatched it from the air, gave it the once-over, then stabbed a fingernail into the fruit and it spun in his hand and he carved it with quick jagged movements. Blue sparks flew from the fruit, along with a high-pitched whine like a dentist's drill. When he'd finished, the pomegranate sat in Rehd's palm oozing red flesh through the newly carved holes. He stuck his lips to it and slurped out the insides before gazing at his creation, juice dripping from his chin, his head cocking this way and that way. He wiped the dribbles on his overall sleeve and lobbed the pomegranate back to Kimi. "Voila!" he said.

Kimi caught it one handed. It was sticky and warm and had perfectly carved birds running around the outside. She guessed they were crows. Stella was nudging her arm.

"Erm, thanks." Kimi stuffed the pomegranate in her jacket pocket.

"You're welcome," Rehd said. He reached for the shed door. "I'll be right here," he said for the second time tonight.

The old battered door creaked open revealing a film of pale blue light which filled up the doorframe like coloured clingwrap. At first, Kimi thought it was another door, until Stella said thank you to the monkey and then walked right through it.

"Hurry up will you," Stella's voice echoed from within. "It's weird in here with the light on."

Rehd pursed his lips, retrieved his phone-thingy from his overall pocket, and said, "Are all prematures this slow?"

Kimi stepped up, touched a finger to the film of light, but her finger went straight through and touched something soft. She yanked her finger back out.

"Oi! Mind where you're poking!" Stella's hand came shooting out from the blue light, grabbed Kimi by the collar and dragged her inside. There was that familiar fizzling feeling, but only briefly.

"Can I look yet?" Kimi said, as the floor began to shake and rumble. She opened her eyes to coal black darkness and held on to Stella to steady herself. "We're moving," she whispered. "I can't see a thing. What's happening?"

"Going down!" A pair of red glittery eyes appeared in the corner.

Kimi yelped.

Stella giggled.

"Such insolence!" bellowed the voice, and a garlic breeze washed over Kimi's face.

"Sorry, Your Adeptness," Stella said.

The red eyes shot to Kimi.

"Erm, sorry," Kimi said, trying to exhale the garlic

air she'd swallowed. The shed continued to groan and rumble. The red eyes vanished leaving them in total darkness. Kimi guessed this must be some kind of antiquated lift. "How much further?" she whispered.

"Any second," Stella said.

Kimi's heart had begun to race and she knew why. Answers were coming soon, answers she needed but might not like to hear. Vague thoughts of home wavered dreamily in her mind; Dad's intense eyes, his riddle of secrets - followed by a resounding bang - not the bang from the lightning, but the wheelie bin as it bounced off the front door. Then came Bentley's kind face and she wished he was here. Maybe if she got too scared he would materialise and whisk her away. But to where?

The floor stilled and Kimi's stomach pinched. The doorway of pale blue light reappeared before them.

"This is us," Stella said.

Kimi clung to Stella and allowed herself to be pulled through the light into moonlit darkness. Wooden boards creaked beneath their feet. A white wooden rail encircled them, its posts supported a pointed, cobwebbed ceiling above. Stella went and leant at the rail. The blue light they'd stepped through had vanished and it appeared they were standing in an old-fashioned bandstand. Kimi went through a gap in the rail, down five wooden steps onto grass and looked back. This was no longer the old shed or the lift or whatever it was; this was absolutely a bandstand. Just like the one in Mousehole park.

A single crow sat on the point of the roof, preening itself under an almost full moon in an inky sky. Kimi froze, expecting the crow to spout doom.

"You okay?" Stella asked, her blonde hair had an eerie shine from the moonlight.

The crow continued preening.

"Discombobulated," muttered Kimi. She wandered off around the bandstand. Fallen leaves lay still on the grass. Nearby, crows like silent statues peppered the branches of two extremely tall, gnarly trees. *These* crows seemed to be showing no interest in Kimi.

"What do you think?" Stella jumped from the rail to the grass with a thud which echoed all around. About two hundred metres away, moonlit grass met a red-bricked wall with many arches. The wall itself was so tall, it was hard to see where it ended and the night sky begun. It appeared to run in a huge circle around them, putting the bandstand in its centre. Kimi went twice around the bandstand, trying to take it all in. Pathways worn through the grass led from the bandstand to all of the arches.

"How can this be?" Kimi said. "I mean, where's the shed gone? And how come we're back outside?"

"Ach, we're all a bit freaked the first time," Stella said, starting towards the arched wall. "Come on."

Stella's words echoed just as her thudding feet had. This place felt more like inside than outside. Kimi looked up to the sky. A distant crow passed over the base of the moon and one or two stars could be seen if you focused hard enough.

She hurried after Stella, sensing something powerful, some hidden force among the stillness of it all.

"Did you see the sign on the door on the way in?" Stella asked.

"Yeah -" Kimi had, but couldn't remember what it said.

"The Scholarium for Harmonious, Extrasensory Development," Stella reminded. "And this is it - the SHED hasn't gone anywhere - you're in it!"

"Well I don't get it. And if this is a school, where's all the pupils?"

"It's Saturday, you nit."

"Oh right." Kimi sighed. "God, I really want to get this over with."

"See the arches," Stella said. "Forty two of them run in a circle the exact same size as Pommy Wood up above." She pointed to the sky.

"And I guess they line up with the standing stones?"

"That's right." They arrived at the arches. A turquoise glow illuminated a cobbled corridor and more arched doorways sat in the wall behind.

"Where we going?" Kimi asked.

"Room seven. Blavatsky." Stella pointed to the arched doorway nearest. It held a darkened passageway and carved into a dimly lit turquoise lantern at the top of the arch was the number 7. "How you feeling?" Stella asked.

Breathing was not easy. And fizzy cotton wool had filled Kimi's head. "Like I've had five coffees," she said, then jumped as a flurry of crows lifted from the trees by the bandstand.

Stella stepped into the gloom and Kimi followed. Up ahead, a small, rounded figure stood in the darkness of another arched doorway. "Ah brilliant! Come in girls, come in," a woman's raspy voice came. The figure turned and disappeared and Kimi and Stella followed. They stepped into an unexpectedly big, pyramid-shaped room with many lab benches like those back in Mousehole Primary. The walls were made of glittering stone; the twinkling surfaces reminded Kimi of the UFOs she'd seen.

In each corner, and intermittingly down the walls, globes of pearlescent light shimmered on ornate metal columns. Kimi did a double-take at the globe nearest and realised that the light was made up of at least a dozen famoose. They were gnawing happily on a pile of what looked like rotten teeth. Kimi remembered walnuts and stifled a gag.

"Welcome girls." This woman looked ancient. Her

green wool suit stretched at the buttons. Grey hairs curled from two enormous rubbery chins. Her lips were big, like false ones stuck on, and little piggy eyes sat in bags like hammocks. Her hair consisted of a few grey wisps, and Kimi saw veins running like tree roots over a flaky scalp. "Miss Nichols," the woman said. "It's exciting to have you here. Premature Balancers are such a rarity." Her oversized lips smiled and pushed her cheeks up so much that her eyes disappeared. "And, Miss O'Brien," she said, turning to Stella. "I see you being a fine mentor!"

"Thank you, Helena," Stella said, bowing her head a little.

They were ushered to the front of the room where a single seat sat before a blank screen mounted on a stand. Kimi sat in the padded chair while Stella stood by her side. Blavatsky blinked at the screen and it flickered to life. The words that Kimi had heard earlier appeared: *Logos, Thymos, Eros. Invoking your mojo...*

"Now, Miss Nichols," Blavatsky said. "Let us see what you are made of. Hold out your hand."

Kimi imagined this woman going into a furious wobble and turning inside out. The mess would be pretty yucky. She noticed Stella take a step to the side and guessed she must be thinking the same.

"There's a problem, Miss Nichols?"

Even the famoose lamps had gone still. All eyes were on

170

Kimi.

"Miss Nichols?"

"Yes there is," Kimi said. "I – I have a problem." The old woman appeared affronted, but Kimi couldn't stop herself, "I would like some answers," she blurted, then added, "Um, please -"

"Answers?" The woman's eyes appeared to emerge on stalks from their tiny sockets. "You must realise, Miss Nichols, that I am Key Adept, Helena Blavatsky, inductor extraordinaire, tester of the testy. It is *I* who receives answers, Miss Nichols. Now - let us get down to proper business."

Kimi stood up. "I - I know you're hiding something!" she said in a voice that came out shaky.

Stella gasped.

The old woman looked shocked. "Hiding something? Me?"

"Everyone," Kimi said. "You, the fuzz, Bentley, Big Sue, the weird woman in the library. There's something you're not telling. And I think it's to do with - with my parents."

Stella's hand came on her shoulder. "Sit down Kimi."

"Poo-poo and piffle!" the old woman spluttered. "There's no place for paranoia in the Shed, Miss Nichols. We will continue with no further interruptions. Sit!"

171

Kimi sat, trembling.

"The first and most vital lesson," Blavatsky went on, "is to realise the power within. I'm sure your Tulpa has already given sufficient warning, however, you must be aware that the granite walls, deep in the heart of our wonderful Shed resonate on a frequency which accentuates mojo to higher levels. Gives it more *oomph,* one might say. The crystalline powers of the granite, coupled with the pyramidal design of each lesson room, enables a much tighter focus than can be deployed elsewhere. Therefore, Miss Nichols, using mojo within the Shed must go hand in hand with extreme caution at all times. Is that clear?"

Kimi nodded.

"That's why you feel like you've had five cups of coffee," Stella said, squeezing Kimi's shoulder.

"Exactly," said Blavatsky. "As this is your first time in the Shed, you should indeed be feeling quite invigorated. Now - I need to see your lantern."

Kimi felt more than invigorated. She felt like she could sprint a marathon or balance a car on her head. Or even sprint a marathon *with* a car on her head. Then she remembered the squeal of tyres, the bin banging off the door and -

"Your lantern?" Blavatsky was standing right in front of Kimi, her podgy hand held out. Kimi's heart leapt and she almost left her seat but came straight back down again.

Blavatsky startled but she was not wobbling. Kimi closed her eyes and exhaled loudly.

"Miss O'Brien…some water please. It seems the premature may be too immature in her years to partake in induction."

Stella ran some water from the nearest lab bench and returned with a beaker. "Come on, Kimi. Drink up. You'll be fine."

Kimi drank.

"Good. We'll try again." Blavatsky held out a hand. "Your lantern?"

Kimi looked at her, puzzled.

"Chief Rehd, he carved you a lantern did he not?"

"Oh that." Kimi took the sticky pomegranate from her pocket and dropped it into Blavatsky's palm.

Blavatsky turned it in her hand, examined it closely. "Hmm, seven little crows."

"Pretty isn't it," Stella said.

"Seven for a secret," said Blavatsky. She handed the lantern back.

"Isn't that magpies?" Stella asked.

"No my dear, they are crows in disguise," Blavatsky said. She returned to the screen and rested a podgy hand upon it. "You are a Balancer, Miss Nichols. Or at least I hope you are. Do you know what a Balancer is?"

Kimi shook her head.

"In the simplest of terms, Balancer Nichols, you

keep the peace."

"Like the police?"

"No, not like the police…I mean the harmony, the equilibrium, the *balance*. Think of it as aiming for *good* at all times, being a good person and -"

"Helping old ladies cross roads and picking up litter?"

Stella tittered.

"No, yours is a much bigger job than that. Much bigger! Consider this if you will. Heart is Earth's control centre. And the bottom line, Miss Nichols, is that Balancers and their Tulpas alike are responsible for the continued protection and evolution of *all* species, striving *always* to retain the balance of life." She clasped her hands behind her back and plodded back and forth. "A Balancer, you see, will encounter difficult situations. From the simplest, single-celled amoeba requiring atomic manipulation, to the cultivation of new life-forms, and to the complexities of humans, with desires to rob, cheat and kill one another. You may nurture your mojo towards a scholarship in genetics, or you may become a brain surgeon, an astronaut, or even a secret agent, out in the field. Whatever it is you become, Miss Nichols, you must always remember that every living thing has internal scales. There are no exceptions. A Balancer's ethos is to balance those scales." She stopped plodding and faced Kimi, still with her hands behind her back. She raised her nose as if she were looking down spectacles at her. "A Balancer's job is *all*-encompassing - do you see that?"

Kimi nodded.

"And each Balancer will find their own dedicated path. It is today, Miss Nichols that we uncover the beginnings of such a path for Balancer Nichols to stride forth upon." She finished with a satisfied smile. Her piggy eyes sank into her face like currants in dough.

"So, erm, do we do the magic stuff?" Kimi asked tentatively.

"Miss Nichols!" Kimi winced. "I remind you that I am a Key Adept. I am also nearly two hundred years-old. You are here to be inducted by me. Nothing more or less. To that end, I shall assess your mojo, conclude its worth, and hopefully set you on the path which you may be destined for. I do understand, that as an immature premature, you may be eager to get to work on your mojo, but you must first learn patience and -"

"I really just want to go home," Kimi said, taking every ounce of effort to swallow the lump in her throat. "I - I'm worried about -"

"Listen to me child," Blavatsky said. "If you have questions about home, then I suggest you go back to the library and enquire there. And the quicker we complete induction, the quicker you can go and ask your questions. Agreed?"

"Come on, Kimi -" Stella winked. "- we can ask questions later."

"Okay. Sorry," Kimi said.

"Then we shall continue. Realise, Miss Nichols, that there is much to learn and master. There's always a way where there's a will, always a glitch to mould, a sight to see, a trickster to uncover. Do you get that, Miss Nichols?"

"Yes," Kimi said, but not taking in a word.

The old woman smiled and gave a little chuckle and her suit buttons braced. "Helena is pleased," she said. "A lesson has been learned."

"So I can go now?"

"No, no, no - not yet, Miss Nichols. Two things must be ascertained before you may go anywhere." The old woman leaned forward and spoke very slowly; "Can you Shift and Separate?"

"Sounds like a bra," Stella said, hissing. Blavatsky threw her a look.

"I erm, haven't a clue what you're on about," Kimi said.

Blavatsky stood up straight once more. Let me show you by example," she said. "Firstly the Shift - discovery of self at core level." She gripped her head in her hands. "Do not attempt this on your own. Only the years of an Adept or a helping greylian hand can invoke the shift. Now watch." She closed her eyes and went still, her hands seemed to be

176

applying pressure to the sides of her head.

Stella nudged Kimi. "This is amazing."

Blavatsky gave a little moan. Her face was changing, the podgy flesh shrinking. Her skin smoothed out to a clear complexion. Her wisps of hair filled out, spilling from her scalp in shiny brown waves. Her cheekbones rose and blushed, her lips reduced to those of a model. She took her hands away from her head and smiled at Kimi. She looked really strange. A fat woman with a supermodel's head.

"Shifting is still one of life's mysteries," Blavatsky said in no longer a raspy voice but one as smooth as silk. "With greylian help, it seems that we can assert our flesh towards its ancestry and reveal our pedigree. The core of our being can be exposed. Why do you think my shift state might be such a beautiful woman, Miss Nichols?" The beautiful woman's head cocked on the fat woman's body, and smiled.

Kimi thought for a second. "Erm, you had a pretty mum?"

Blavatsky nodded. "Something like that," she said. The woman came forward, put her fat hands on Kimi's arms. "Do you have any idea what your shift state might be?"

Kimi shook her head.

"We'll find out soon." She returned to the screen where the words of mojo incantation still awaited explanation. Blavatsky pressed her hands to her head and the features filled out, the shiny brown hair shrank away, and the podgy Blavatsky returned. There was loud a gurgling sound which appeared to come from Blavatsky's stomach. She let out a burp which echoed the room. She smacked her lips. "Shifting always makes me hungry," she said. The raspy voice had returned. She adjusted her wisps of hair and Kimi wondered why she didn't just stay in the shift state.

"Any questions?"

Kimi shook her head.

"Good, good. Now the Separation. Watch!"

Blavatsky's head was rising from her shoulders, her neck stretching and thinning, up and up until it was thin as a pencil and Blavatsky's head seemed to be in the very point of the pyramid roof. "I can see youuuuuuuuuuuuuuuu!" she called in a small voice.

"Awesome," Stella said.

Kimi was speechless.

With a super-quick swoosh Blavatsky's head came whipping down on its super-thin neck and sat bobbing in the air before Kimi. It smiled.

Kimi swallowed.

Another rush of air and Blavatsky's neck was shrinking, whipping back up to the ceiling and down to the fat body in a green wool suit. The old woman appeared normal again. Without warning, she flicked her wrists and her arms shot out like tentacles and wrapped Kimi to her chair. "Got you!" she said then chuckled before letting go and returning to her normal state. "You see, Miss Nichols, to experienced users, one's mojo can be used to great effect. Are you ready for your test?"

Kimi could only stare at her.

"Just say yes," Stella said.

"Erm, yes."

"Very good. Follow me," Blavatsky said.

"I'm gonna do that?" Kimi asked Stella as they followed Blavatsky out of the lab and back down the passageway.

Stella's arm reassuringly linked Kimi's. "Like the lady said - Shift and Separate - I'm sure you'll be good at it."

They went through the arches and across the grass, around the bandstand, and to an archway on the other side. This one was numbered `14`

"This way." Blavatsky walked into the gloom.

This passageway opened to vast darkness and a chair sat under a spotlight. It looked like a dentist's chair, had straps across the arms and legs, and before Kimi knew it, she was sat down and strapped in. There seemed to be something in the darkness around her; whispering perhaps, and maybe small movements. Kimi had the impression she was being watched by many eyes.

"Miss O'Brien," Blavatsky said. "Take a seat." She snapped her fingers and the darkness vanished, replaced by a bright glow of yellow provided by a ring of lanterns around the wall. They were in some kind of circular auditorium, and the whispers Kimi had heard now became chatter. Kimi's heart took off once more. As far as she could tell, at least half of the audience – *and there must be hundreds* – appeared to be aliens. Big grey heads with black staring eyes and really thin bodies. Some were clapping, some standing. The remainder of the audience were people, young, old, and extremely old. Kimi guessed they were Balancers and Adepts. Stella went up a few steps and took an end seat next to an alien she obviously knew because they slapped a high five with each other.

Blavatsky raised a hand. The applauding and the chatter died. The audience sat. Apart from one. This was a tall slender being, its skin grey, its head bulbous, its big oval eyes as black as oil. As it came down the steps it appeared to slither and slide, its movements snakelike and sleek. It was carrying a blue cool-box and seemed to be entirely naked – apart from a band around its right upper arm which held what could have been pens – or maybe they were probes. The alien came to the chair and stopped at Kimi's side. Its huge eyes were sheened with an outer layer which blinked, but beyond that Kimi could see no depth. It had two nostrils but no nose to speak of, and a slit for a mouth which turned up into a pleasant smile. Kimi gave a trembling smile back.

"Our greylian friends provide enormous help in the field of human genetics, Balancer Nichols," Blavatsky said.

180

"This is Leilani, my long-serving and most brilliant assistant."

The greylian blinked and gave a single but small nod of its huge head.

Kimi swallowed. "Hi."

"Our greylian friends are also extremely gifted," Blavatsky went on. "Leilani here will perform the cortell and we will discover what you are made of. When she asks you to Shift, and also when she asks you to Separate, you must aid her by focusing. Is that clear?"

"I – I don't – I -" Kimi shook her head.

"Just go with the flow!" Stella shouted from the seats.

"Yes, thank you, Miss O'Brien." Blavatsky nodded to Kimi. "I suppose she's right. Just go with it. Alright?"

Kimi nodded.

The greylian took Kimi's right hand in *its* hands, its long thing fingers wrapped twice around Kimi's. They felt neither warm nor cold, as if they weren't living. The greylian blinked rapidly, then let go. She examined Little Hand, blinked rapidly again, then made a slight purring sound. "Thisssss," the greylian said. There was silence from the audience as the greylian went to its knees and wrapped a single hand around Kimi's left wrist. The greylian lifted its head and stared at Kimi. "Shhhhhhift!" it said.

Kimi felt her heart miss a beat. A warm glow

appeared in her forehead. The warmth reached out like veins crawling down her eyes, her cheeks, her neck – no, not crawling…draining. That was it. The heat travelled down her left arm and into Little Hand. The indentations running diagonally over her thumb and forefinger and again down the little finger did something they had never done before. They went black like horrible dead snaking veins. Kimi started to shake.

"Shhhhhhift," the greylian repeated.

"Do as Leilani asks, Miss Nichols. Focus!" Blavatsky said from behind.

The audience were whispering again, straining their heads. Hundreds of black oval eyes blinked in Kimi's direction. She didn't have a clue what she was meant to do. She closed her eyes and saw Bentley. "Make me proud," he was saying. Then Dad: "You'll get through this." Then Mum, smiling – but not the weird smile, the nice one, the one that sang with pride. "Be yourself," she said. "Follow your heart!"

"Miss Nichols!" said Blavatsky again.

"I know," Kimi said. "Go with the flow…" She relaxed into the chair, and instead of feeling the warmth drain from her brow and down her arm, she imagined that she was pushing it, feeding the warmth into Little Hand. The blackened grooves tingled.

The greylian raised its head and smiled. "Yesssss," it

182

said, and the audience hissed. Kimi almost yelped when the flesh on Little Hand began to shrink and pale. Blavatsky came closer, watching as the skin shrank to the bones and the bones shrank too, elongating, twisting. Kimi's head was floating. She thought she might faint, but then came a sudden jolt from her wrist and a crackle of bones and her fingernails stretched from their roots. Gasps came from the audience. Stella was on her feet. The greylian released the straps and pulled Kimi to her feet. It held her arm up high. Kimi stared in disbelief at the black claw jutting from her wrist. The audience went into raptures. Blavatsky's mouth was agape.

Stella came running over. "Slap me silly with a deep-fried Mars bar," she said. "You're a crow!"

The applause died and the greylian released her grip and slid to one side.

"Thank you, Leilani," Blavatsky said, never taking her eyes from Kimi's blackened claw. Slowly at first, the claw began to change. The nails shrank back into their roots, bones crackled, flesh filled out and pinked once more, and for a few seconds, Little Hand was like a normal hand. Kimi flexed her fingers just in time before they bent and the indentations returned. She slumped back into the chair.

"Interesting," Blavatsky said. "Never had a corvine before. Bring the box!" She indicated to Leilani. The greylian slithered silently over with the box in its arms. Blavatsky removed the lid and lifted a cage from within. In it was a crow. When it saw Kimi it thrashed its wings and hissed. Feathers flew through the cage bars.

"You know this crow?" Blavatsky said.

Kimi nodded.

"It's been asking for you, Miss Nichols. It seems it wants you to hurry things along. Do you know what that might mean?"

Kimi swallowed. "I – I think – I think I'm going to die."

"Oh don't be silly, Miss Nichols. You couldn't be any safer here."

"The crow," Kimi said. "It told me there'd be one death today."

"But that doesn't mean it would be you, Kimi." Kimi noticed Blavatsky had used her first name, and that made her uneasy. "Then if it isn't me, I think it must be one of my parents. I had a – a feeling that something bad was going to happen. Then I saw the lightning strike -"

"Miss Nichols, I do think the Shed's powerful constitution is taking its toll on your young soul. Perhaps we should take a break and continue tomorrow."

"No," Kimi said. "I'm sorry, it's that crow – I think it knows the answer and-"

Blavatsky screamed and the cage went looping through the air. A thin fountain of blood spurted from her fat hand and spattered her face. "It bit me," she said. The cage hit the floor and broke into bits and the crow took off. It flew twice around the auditorium before screeching away through the passageway entrance.

"After it!" Blavatsky bellowed, and Kimi was first to her feet. Feeling fully invigorated with springs in her heels, she sprinted down the passage and out onto the grass. There were crows everywhere. On the grass, the bandstand, in the trees. Kimi scanned them, searching for a clue. Then she heard the familiar screechy voice: "*One death*," it said, "*and hurry up about it.*" It came from the highest of the two gnarly trees. She ran towards it, eyeing every shadow and every cluster of leaves, searching for movement.

"*You won't get me up here*," the crow said.

The warmth returned to Kimi's brow. Blavatsky's huffing and puffing was coming from behind along with many hundreds of pattering feet. Kimi knew the auditorium had emptied and that she was the star of the show. She reached up with Little Hand and fed the warmth through her arm and into the marrow of her bones.

Her arm began to stretch upwards through the branches of the old tree, weaving round limbs, flicking crows out of the way.

"Kimi!" Stella's voice.

Kimi spotted the crow, a few branches up, but her arm was slowing down. It appeared she was at full stretch. She relaxed and her arm began to shrink back to her.

185

"No!" Stella's hands were at her waist. "Try it from here, Kimi. This is Separation – the second part of your test. Use your abdomen – the thicker the part of the body you use, the further you can get."

Without thinking, Kimi felt her waist tighten and her arm resumed its stretch followed quickly by her torso. She was moving up through the branches and leaving her legs firmly on the ground, pulling her way through with freakily long outstretched arms.

"Come down, Miss Nichols," Blavatsky shouted. "This instant do you hear?"

Kimi looked down. Blavatsky was looking up with hands on hips. Stella was punching the air and the hundreds of greylians looked like eggs. Kimi looked back to her target. The crow had moved again, now on the uppermost branch. "I'm coming," she said through gritted teeth and weaved around another branch. "And nobody's gonna stop me!"

The crow took off, hovered ten feet above the tree.

"Oh," Kimi said.

The crow was squawking but it sounded to Kimi like laughter.

"Miss Nichols!" yelled Blavatsky. "You have three seconds to disengage Separation then I will open fire!"

Kimi kept on going.

"One!"

If she could reach the top branch, pull her legs up

186

from there, then maybe she could get to the crow.

"Two!"

Her hands reached the top branch. But that's as far as she got.

"Three!"

There came a fast rattling sound first, then a barrage of stunballs aimed mainly at her back. The crow flew skywards and disappeared into the ink as Kimi shrank back to earth quickly and furiously with an intense feeling of being sucked down a plughole. She slapped through the branches on the way back down and jolted in her trainers before falling onto her backside. Stray stunballs bounced around her.

Greylians were snickering, Adepts and Balancers were clapping. Stella arrived, clapping too. "Way to go, sister!"

Blavatsky wheezed and stuck her chins out. At that point, the middle button on her suit eventually gave and popped off. It spun through the air and landed at Kimi's feet. A crow darted to it, grabbed it up in its beak, flew over to Blavatsky and dropped it in her hand. She looked cross and was breathing quite heavily.

"Was that um - okay?" Kimi asked as the applause died. She had a feeling she was in trouble.

"If you had awaited your test instructions, you would have learned that six feet was your Separation target," snapped Blavatsky.

"I - I'm sorry. It just kind of happened. I -"

"Fifty feet you went. Fifty feet or more!" she bellowed. Crows leapt out of the way as she stomped back and forwards on the grass. "You, Kimi Nichols, are more than what I hoped," she said, stopping in front of Kimi. "Much more!" She turned to Stella. "O'Brien. As I'm sure you will know from your studies, vertical Separation to anything more than twenty feet is considered quite exceptional."

"Aye, I do," Stella said.

Blavatsky had a smug yet hungry look on her bloodied face. "I have a proposition," the old woman said, shuffling closer. "Never before have I witnessed such power in a newbie, never mind a premature."

"Good isn't she," Stella said.

"Yes," agreed Blavatsky. "For a premature, you are exhibiting the skills of at least a fifth year - no offence, Miss O'Brien."

"None taken," Stella said.

"And to that end, I would like to escalate your training module and personally oversee it. Would you be all right with that, dear Kimi?"

Stella was grinning and silent clapping, so it must be okay. "Suppose," said Kimi, not entirely convinced by Blavatsky's change of tone, but she didn't care. She was out

188

of here anyway and going after that crow.

"Then for now," the Adept went on, "It's important that you keep this to yourself until we have chance to study you properly. As Kimi's mentor -" she turned to Stella. "- I am holding you fully responsible for her wellbeing."

Stella shrugged. "No probbies."

"But what's the big deal?" Kimi asked. "I'm sure I could have gone a lot higher."

"The big deal, child," Blavatsky's lips slapped. "Is that you could have killed yourself. Separate too far and you Separate for good!"

"Oh!"

"Oh indeed. Now, ladies. You are dismissed for today. See to it, O'Brien, that Miss Nichols does not attempt further Separations. Keep her safely indoors. I shall be taking urgent consultations and may call you back at any time. Understood?"

"Okey dokey," Stella said.

Kimi nodded.

Blavatsky padded off toward the arches muttering something about new Heart records, and the greylians followed, apart from Leilani. She smiled at Kimi and gave a little bow before following the others.

"Come on." Stella pulled Kimi to the bandstand and up the steps. Once in the middle everything went dark and the floor rumbled.

"I don't like her," Kimi said, gripping Stella's arm. "If she thinks I'm coming back here, she can crap a crow - feet first!"

"Ouch!" Stella laughed.

In seconds, which seemed a whole lot quicker than coming down, the rumbling ceased and the floor stilled. Bright blue light appeared all around and a moment later they landed in the clearing on their backsides.

The Shed door slammed shut.

"Afternoon!" the monkey, Rehd said from his stool with a rake in his hands.

"This is a crazy place," Kimi said, surveying the now bare pomegranate trees, the many bulging tubs of fruit, and the great heaps of leaves all around.

"Crazy but cool," Stella said, getting to her feet. "How about we go shopping and get that new jacket?" She held out a hand to Kimi.

Kimi took it and pulled herself up. "No. I want to go back to the library and see what those updates were."

"But Blavatsky said to keep you indoors and-"

"Yeah? Well she also said I could get answers at the library. Come on I'll race you!" And off she went, running through the leaves.

Stella was shouting something, but Kimi couldn't stop. With an amazing burst of energy, she sprinted through the wood, running faster than she'd ever done in her life.

190

Answers awaited at the library - and she wouldn't stop running until she got there.

———

~ 15 ~
~ The Secret Room ~

Kimi burst from Pommy Wood and tore blindly across the road. Chrome flashed, brakes squealed and dust went up in a wave. "Sorry!" she shouted, leaping clear of the squad bike. The monkey driving it yelled something but Kimi didn't stop to listen. She sprinted down the first street she came to, weaving around people and obstacles with the silky deftness of a gazelle; the power in her heels kept coming and coming.

She could no longer hear Stella, nor did she look back to see where she was. Kimi's heart felt huge in her chest as she hurtled past the weeping willows and raced up the steps around the ridge, leaping ferns with gravity-defying ease. She reached the top landing in no time at all, ending her run with a hard sprint to the library door.

Only now did Kimi stop for breath, becoming instantly aware that she wasn't out of breath at all. She raised a hand to the door and pushed. It creaked open and Kimi stepped into the darkness.

"Lights!" she yelled to the ceiling, and the first pumpkin lantern came on with a `phut` - "Keep it coming!" she shouted, striding forward. The lanterns lit up, one after the other `phut`, `phut` - she broke into a trot, `phut`, `phut`, `phut` - her pace picked up to match the speed of the igniting pumpkins, and once again she was sprinting, eyes fixed on the small door in the back wall - and with great leaping strides - she was there and grasping the handle.

It wouldn't budge.

She looked down. No keyhole.

She put her ear to the door - silence - not a secretary to be heard.

A distant cough came from behind and Kimi spun round. Back in the entrance stood a small, wiry silhouette. Kimi suddenly lost her breath and a stitch appeared. She bent at the cramp and clasped her hands to her side.

"It's closed." Stella stepped into the amber light.

"It's what?"

"Closed. Shut. Not open."

"You could have told me."

"Ach, didn't you see the notice on the door?"

Kimi shook her head and started towards Stella, but barely had the strength to stay upright. She was clutching her side and dragging her feet.

Stella sprinted down the long foyer and grabbed hold of Kimi a second before her legs gave up. She hooked Kimi's arm around her shoulder and took her weight. "You're as heavy as a pregnant coo!" Stella puffed.

Kimi didn't respond.

Stella paused in the doorway and lifted Kimi's chin up. A small note pinned to the door said,

`Closed until further notice.
By order of Adept Blavatsky.
Appointments only.`

Kimi groaned and her chest made lurching motions.

"Nooo!" Stella cried, and seemingly finding new strength, scuttled towards the landing wall with Kimi's feet trailing the ground. Kimi grabbed for the wall and threw her face over just in time. She vomited in one huge splurge and watched it rain down into the darkness.

"You overdid it, you numpty," Stella said. "Remember what Blavatsky said about the energy being accelerated. You have to drain it slowly, not sprint like a big cat."

"Okay," Kimi said, and below, the colourful sunburst of Middling began spinning. She closed her watery eyes and groaned.

"Take some deep breaths. You'll be okay in a bit."

Kimi sucked in deeply and slowly breathed out.

"Again!"

Kimi did, and finally some feeling returning to her legs. "I need an appointment," she said, between breaths.

"Right -" Stella bit her lip and looked hesitant to say anything further.

"What?"

"Ach, you're not gonna like this. But only Tulpas can make appointments."

195

Kimi slumped to the wall and leant over it, thinking she might be sick again. "So I have to ask, Bentley?"

"I guess," replied Stella.

Kimi looked her in the eye but she turned away. "You know something, don't you?" Kimi said, certain that Stella was holding back. "Are you gonna *tell* -"

"Shush!" Stella was pointing in the direction of the black mountains to a pinprick of white light in the sky. The light was moving and bringing with it a high-pitched whistle. Stella put her fingers in her ears so Kimi did the same. Even with her ears plugged, Kimi heard the piercing sound as the light grew rapidly bigger. It travelled towards them faster than any jet and left a trail like a shooting star before stopping directly above the weeping willows. Stella removed her finger plugs and nodded to Kimi to do the same. A low hum had replaced the whistling.

Kimi sidled behind Stella and peered over her shoulder. The light, about the size of a bus, was descending slowly to the grass.

"What is it?" she whispered in Stella's ear.

"The Starburst," Stella replied as the light faded, revealing a slender blue craft with a bulbous front. The clear cockpit slid forward and two greylian figures moved quickly, slithering over the side of the craft and dropping to the grass before skating off in that snakelike way. The one in front had a bigger head and appeared to stoop as he went.

"What's going on?" asked Kimi, still whispering.

"It's Granp and General Cohn. They visit every Saturday."

"They're scary. Wouldn't want to meet them," Kimi said.

"Ach, you'll meet them alright..." Stella gave one of her gap-toothed grins. "...tonight in the meadery. The General does the rounds, usually with Granp in tow. He walks the streets, says his hellos' - sometimes pops into the Shed for a chat with the Adepts to talk the talk and stuff. Then they end up in the Foot. So be sure to bow when you meet him."

Kimi groaned, still feeling queasy. "Do I have to bow?"

"Dunno," Stella said. "Can't think no-one's ever not done the bowing thing. You could try it and see what happens." Stella's eyes suddenly sparkled. "Oh!"

"What?"

"Dodo brains!"

"Huh?"

"The brains are a delicacy."

"Yeah," Kimi said. "Somehow, I don't believe you."

"Ach it's right," Stella said. "Greylians love them. Big Sue serves up the same thing every time. After Cohn's done meeting and greeting, they finish up in the Foot like I said - usually for a feast. Starter is always bliss maggot and -

"

"That's sick." Kimi's stomach rolled.

"No kidding. Sue fattens the maggots on dodo guts 'til they're this big!" She held her hands apart like a tale-telling fisherman might. "Greylians suck the juice right out of them. Then the main course is dodo brains, served still inside the head, although they're not quite raw, they're liquefied *and* -"

Kimi's jowls quivered. She clamped a hand to her mouth and shook her head.

Stella continued, "The brains are mushy and still inside the skull when they -"

"You!" Kimi cut in. "Are bloody evil!"

"Ach, I was only -"

"Well I don't find it funny," Kimi said. "And another thing - I think you know more than you're letting on."

Stella looked surprised. "Away with you! Why would you say that? I've been nothing but good to you since you got here."

"Well…" Kimi started, but hot scratches appeared in her throat. She tried to gulp them away but the tears were unstoppable. Her head dropped, her shoulders fell and she sobbed into her hands. Stella's arms came around her.

"Sorry, Kimi. I know you're missing home, but you shouldn't worry. It'll sort itself out. What say we go into town, show you a few sights, go to BoZone and get you kitted out with your new jacket. Come on, what do you say?"

Kimi really wanted to scream. If she hadn't felt so weakened she would have. She calmed the sobs, wiped her eyes and drew away from Stella. "Whu - whenever I - ask questions," she said in broken voice. "Whenever I ask what's going on - I get fobbed off - even you do it, Stella. Even you."

"No way," Stella said. "Why *would* -"

"Look, I need to go see Bentley and see if I can get in there," she pointed to the library, "I need an appointment! And all you can think about is getting me a new bloody jacket. Don't you get it? Don't you understand what's happened to me? Don't you get that my Mum and Dad might be in danger - or worse! Don't you? I'm not bothered about a new jacket. I want answers and I want to go home!"

"Okay, okay," Stella backed off. "Calm down. Most girlies would jump at the chance. And Mr Purse - wait 'til you meet Mr Purse. Mr Purse is a *scream* -"

"Shut up!" Kimi yelled. "I'm going to see Bentley." And with that, she trudged toward the steps, wishing she knew how to whisk up a twirly.

***

Kimi made the descent slowly with a chill wind in her face. Behind, Stella's footsteps kept their distance. Kimi wished her friend Julie was here; a familiar face from home. She looked down to where the blue craft hovered inches above the grass and imagined Julie standing by it with her happy smile. She was in her pink cardigan of course. And that's another thing; how can anyone even think of banning pink - wouldn't you think they'd have the sense to ban the bloody bliss flies first? She reached the bottom step thinking once again that she might really be going mad, when the footsteps behind grew nearer and Stella's arm slid through hers. Not one word was spoken as they strolled over the grass toward the humming craft, not a word as they passed dodos in pens, not a single word until they entered Carroll Lane.

Stella stopped and looked at Kimi. "I'm sorry," she said. "I - I just - well -"

"It's okay," Kimi said. "My bad. I didn't mean to tell you to shut up," and she took Stella's arm and no more was said.

* * *

"He's out back beheading dodos," Big Sue said when Stella asked where Bentley was. Sue snatched some paper towels from a dispenser on the wall, ran them under the tap, then came for Kimi with his mouth in a big O. "Dear, dear, dear, dear, dear," he said, dabbing Kimi's face. Kimi startled at the cold water but couldn't move very far with Sue's hand clamped on her shoulder.

"Have you been scaring the lassie?" Sue threw a sharp look to Stella.

200

"I'm fine thanks," Kimi spluttered.

Sue's mouth twitched beneath his beard. "We all like to keep ourselves clean and presentable when under my, erm, *your* roof. Just remember that. And why are you still wearing that mangy old jacket?"

Stella must have sensed Kimi was on the verge of bursting into tears again. "She's had a hard morning," she said, taking Kimi by the arm and guiding her away from Big Sue. Kimi heard a *tut*, followed by the sound of tea towels flicking at tables.

They stepped into a cobbled backyard enclosed by high stone walls. In the middle of the yard was a blood-stained tree stump with two large nails sticking from it in a V. The old Bentley, next to it, straightened up, an axe in one hand and a wriggling dodo clasped by the feet in his other, dangled to the floor. "Ah!" he said with a welcoming smile. "How'd you get on?"

"We didn't, really," Kimi said. "I need to see the librarian again, but the sign says appointments only - and Stella here, tells me you're my P.A."

"Ah," Bentley said again, but this time not so welcoming. "Then Stella would be right I suppose. What is it you want of the library? - I have to have a reason, see."

"She wants to know where she stands," Stella said.

Bentley swung the dodo up onto the old stump and its neck slid swiftly into the V of nails. Kimi winced when it wriggled and made weet-weet sounds.

"Just let me finish this one," Bentley said, raising the axe.

"No you won't!" Kimi started forward with a hand raised. "I don't want to see that, thank you very much."

Bentley gave a look of displeasure. "You have to start at some point you know," he said, offering her the axe.

"Yeah well maybe I will one day," Kimi replied. "But right now I've more important things on my mind. Can you please make me an appointment?"

"Alright then," Bentley said, straightening up and removing the dodo from the V in the process. It flopped back by his side, twitching and making the weet-weet sound. The axe hung from his other hand. He closed his eyes and began to vibrate, fading to the familiar see-through blue. Behind him, more dodos in a small run became excited adding more weet-weets to the air. Bins trembled, as did the cobbles under Kimi's feet. Garden tools propped against the back wall tumbled over as Bentley's eyes darted beneath their lids. His mouth opened and closed but made no sound. Gradually the vibrating slowed and Bentley became whole again. He opened his eyes.

"Week on Monday, five pm," he said, swinging the dodo back into the V as if his announcement was matter of fact.

"Wait!" Kimi took another step forward. "I can't

wait a week. Haven't you done the math, Bentley?"

He put the axe down and released the dodo. It waddled to the back of the yard and clicked beaks with those in the run; all of them bursting into weet-weets.

"Of course I've done the math," Bentley said. "It's really not that bad, you know."

Kimi felt herself shaking. "Not that bad? Time is multiplied sixty times, Bentley. If I wait a week, that means sixty weeks will have passed back home. Sixty weeks! That's more than a year. Don't you think Mum and Dad would report me missing? Hmm? I'd be a missing kid, Bentley. A missing kid!"

"No - no," Bentley shook his head and made towards Kimi with his arms outstretched.

Kimi took a step back. "You promised me answers when I got here, and I'm not getting any!"

"No, Kimbo. You did the math wrong," Bentley laughed. "It's sixty times the other way. A week here is barely three hours back on Earth. So no, I doubt you will be missed." After a moment he added; "Actually, it's 2.8 hours to be precise."

Sweat had formed on Kimi's brow and the ball of heat sat throbbing behind. She squinted against it, eyes narrowing on Bentley.

"Stop it now, Kimi," he said, holding up a hand and stepping to one side. "Let off one of your Roman Candles and you'll fry everything in this yard!"

Stella's hand came to her shoulder. Kimi shrugged it off, turned and stormed back inside.

"Feet!" Big Sue said, pointing to the doormat. Kimi gave a half-hearted shuffle on the bristly mat before bursting into tears. She ran inside and up the stairs, not stopping until the bedroom door was slamming behind her. She tore Stella's jacket off, threw it on the four-poster, then sank solemnly and breathless onto the camp bed and sobbed into the pillow. Thoughts of home were stronger than ever. Julie's bright smile. Mum's fingers running soothing circles on her shoulders. `Fancy one of my special pastas?` Dad was donning the apron with the six-pack man on the front.

Kimi had a fancy for that pasta. Much more than the fancy for the pink Limo. She'd give that up anytime for Dad's pasta. Anytime. And when they go birthday shopping, she's going to ask for a set of pink bowls to eat it from. And a new pink Superman tee-shirt. And pink trainers.

A flicker of orange light brought her eyes open. On the floor stood a glass of water and two tablets alongside her pomegranate lantern that Rehd had carved. It glowed burnt orange.

"Brought you some headache tablets," came a tired voice from the four-poster. Stella sat up, yawning. "Guessed you'd have a beauty!"

"Thanks," Kimi said, wondering how long she'd

204

been dozing. Her head was thumping at the temples. "How'd you know I had a headache?" She took the tablets and washed them down gratefully.

"Figures," Stella said. "Abuse the mojo and that's what you get."

Kimi rubbed her eyes. "How long have I been -"

"Five hours."

Kimi stared at Stella. It didn't seem five seconds, never mind five hours.

"You drained yourself with all the mad dashing around, that's all," Stella said. "Your lantern looks good though, doesn't it?"

"Suppose," Kimi said, gazing round the room. Seven shimmering crows projected from the lantern and hung gracefully on the walls.

"Watch this!" Stella flicked a hand at the lantern and misty strands shot from her fingers. When they reached the lantern, Stella whipped her hand and the strands in turn whipped the lantern like a top. The illuminated crows outstretched their wings and spun rapidly round the walls. As the spinning slowed, so did Kimi's breathing. Suddenly she was feeling more relaxed and the headache was receding. Stella smiled at her. Kimi smiled back.

"That's your mood lantern," Stella said. "Better than a massage."

I doubt that, Kimi thought, but Stella was obviously

making an effort. "Well thanks," Kimi said.

"No worries." Stella whipped the misty strands again and again. The crows went faster, stretching into one solid ring of orange light, spinning the walls like a giant hula hoop. "Watch!" Stella said as the spinning slowed and the ring shrank back to seven crows. Only now they weren't the cut-out shapes that Rehd had carved; they had form - real fiery crows swooping and gliding. Kimi watched in amazement. Draught from their wing beats felt real on her face. The sound of the beating was also so real. Stella slid from the bed, dropped to her knees, and placed a hand on the spinning lantern. The crows stilled and faded back to hanging shadows.

"Wow, that was pretty cool," Kimi said. "And my headache's gone too!"

"Your mood lantern's made specially. The monkey doesn't think of what to carve you see. He carves what you are."

"I'm a crow, aren't I?"

"Dunno," Stella shrugged.

"The claw thing proved that, didn't it?"

"Yeah, that claw thing was pretty icky, Kimi. It does seem you're connected somehow." Stella picked up the lantern and handed it to Kimi. "I found this on the floor by the door. Must have fell out my jacket when you threw it. I suggest you look after it from now on - it's a useful tool, your mood lantern."

"Right, sorry," Kimi said, finding her head a little swimmy. "I've really been out for five hours?"

Stella started to say something about how awesome Kimi's Separation abilities were, but was drowned out by the great blast of a hooter from below which seemed to lift the floorboards. Kimi jumped, "What the heck?"

"Big Sue's warning horn," Stella said. "He's firing up." Stella's eyes lit up. "Wanna see something really scary?" She didn't give Kimi a chance to reply. "LIGHTS!" she said, and the main lights came on. "Follow me - no time to spare," she said, dashing to the door. "Bring your lantern and be quick or we'll miss it."

"Miss what?" Kimi asked when she caught her up on the next floor down. Stella paused, glanced all around, stared over the banister to the next flight, then put a finger to her lips. "Quiet as you can - I'm gonna show you my secret room." She clicked open a door labelled; STORE, slipped inside and dragged Kimi with her.

"*Moodirecto!*" she said in the darkness and a beam of green light shot across the room. Stella held up her lantern. Its carved surface showed knives, swords and hammers. Kimi decided not to ask.

"Now you," Stella whispered. "*Moodirecto!*"

"*Moodirecto!*" Kimi said, touching her lantern. Only one of the crows lit up, projecting an orange beam. Heavy shelving filled the room, holding catering-sized tins and large drums. Stella dropped to her knees, pulled out three drums labelled; `*OIL OF BULL BOIL*` and crawled beneath the bottom shelf. "Come on!"

Kimi crouched and crawled under.

Stella unhooked a panel from the wall. "Air vent," she said, disappearing inside. Kimi followed, pushing her lantern in front as she went and soon catching aromas of roast meats and gentle harp music. Stella stopped at a small gap in the venting wall and slid her lantern inside.

"It doesn't look wide enough to get through," Kimi whispered as Stella pulled herself in.

"It's a squeeze," Stella said, "but only for ten feet or so."

Kimi waited for Stella's feet to disappear then pushed her lantern inside and watched Stella's backside getting smaller until she vanished through a flap at the end. Then the flap lifted and Stella's face appeared. "Come on yer numpty!"

Kimi squeezed her way through, a tight fit to either side. As she neared the end, Stella's hands were there to pull her out.

The secret room was not much bigger than the average toilet. It had bare floorboards and wood-panelling to the walls. A single pomegranate lantern, shrunken and wrinkled, hung from the low ceiling. Stella snapped her fingers and the lantern sputtered, gave up a pallid yellow glow, and three spiders ran out. She tapped her lantern and its beam vanished. Kimi did the same.

"Neat huh?" Stella said.

"Erm, suppose." Kimi looked around to see if she could find anything to justify `neat`. Two wooden stools that might have once been used under a cow stood against one wall, and propped in the corner was an old walking stick with a long curved handle that looked like it might be the skull and beak of a dodo.

Kimi thought she'd better show some interest. "Erm, so how did you find this place?"

"Big Sue found it when he was cleaning. Well, he found the entrance hole leading from the first duct and I offered to investigate. I told him it was probably an old store cupboard that had been sealed off at some point - and that all there was in here were two old stools and a walking stick."

Kimi gazed around again. "So if Sue knows, then it's not really a secret room is it?" It smelled dusty and the dim glow along with distant harp music tinkling up from the bar made it positively spooky.

"Ach - I didn't tell Sue the whole truth. Take a seat and push yourself back against the wall."

Kimi pushed one of the old stools firmly behind her and sat. Stella sat at the opposite wall and their knees almost touched. Stella reached for the walking stick. "See the knot," she said, swinging the point of the beak over their knees and down to the floor, coming to a stop in the centre, next to a dark circular knot in the wood. She pressed the knot with the end of the beak and it sank slightly into the floorboard, gave a double click and then released. Kimi detected the smallest vibration through the legs of the stool and dust rose on the floor in a circle about the size of a manhole cover.

"Keep back and let it rise," Stella said.

Kimi pressed her back to the wall and spread her feet as the circle of flooring kept rising between their legs. It was some kind of black metal cylinder, making double clicks every few inches it rose, eventually stopping at just above head height. Around its circumference ran a series of hooded eyepieces. Headphones dangled from each side. Stella hunched her stool forward and popped her head around.

"Didn't expect that, did you?"

"What the heck is it?"

"A periscope of sorts," Stella said. "There's six viewports, each feeding into a different part of the bar. Obviously a spy once lived here." She peered into a viewport. "No -" swung the cylinder round to the next one and looked in. "No -" then the third viewport, "Yes!" and swung it around to Kimi. "Take a look!"

"At what?" Kimi asked.

"Remember the hooter when Sue fired up the liquefier?"

"Erm, yeah."

"That means, Cohn and Granp will be served dodo brains any minute."

"Right."

"Well this neat little rig will take your pretty eyes right inside Cohn's cosy cubicle. And trust me, seeing is believing. Get the headphones on!"

"I'll puke," Kimi insisted.

Stella handed her a handkerchief. "Get your eye to the scope!"

Kimi put on the headphones and did as Stella said. The image was circular and a little distorted; the harp music much clearer through the headphones. She was looking from the side and slightly above at a table. A bald, grey figure sat either side. The General, she knew had the bigger head. His skin was not as smooth as the other greylian. Red mottles ran up his arms, his chest and over his large forehead. His one eye that Kimi could see was very creepy - evil creepy - changing from a slit to a wide black oval and back again in a blink - and when it was wide with glossy blackness, it made Kimi hold her breath. Plates on the table held what appeared to be wrinkly old banana skins - then Kimi remembered the first course.

"Bliss maggots," she muttered, trying not to retch. She spun the scope and looked in the next eyepiece. Her heart gave a sickly flutter. It was Perry, his hair all spiky and he was carrying a tower of glasses. He was watching the golden-haired harpist who Kimi could only see the back of. Heat spread through Kimi's cheeks.

"Oi," Stella said, and Perry zoomed away as the scope returned to its previous notch. "Eyes!" she nodded to the viewport in front of Kimi.

Kimi leant into the eyepiece quickly, more to hide her blush than anything.

Tartan, dressing-gowned arms removed the plates and wiped the table. Moments later, Big Sue's bearded face dropped into view as he bowed to the General before sliding a bowl of steaming dodo heads onto the table. The greylians were talking in whispery voices. Kimi pushed the headphones tight to her ears and caught the end of a sentence.

"- how sssssoon do we take the girl?" Granp's slender arm and long spindly fingers reached out and picked a dodo head from the top of the pile, grasping it by its beak.

"Not until -" replied the General, then came a screech of microphone feedback and Big Sue's voice announcing `thank you - we'll have a wee break for the harpist -`

"Damn," Kimi muttered before stifling a gasp with the hanky as something began to emerge from Granp's mouth. It was like a see-through straw, growing longer and longer, drooping downwards until it came to rest against the dodo's eye. With one sudden movement, the straw-like protrusion jabbed and the dodo's eye disappeared into its skull. The greylian's cheeks sucked in and a reddish-brown fluid began travelling up the straw, vanishing into the slit-thin mouth. Kimi pressed the handkerchief close.

Granp jerked his head and the protrusion jumped clear from the eye socket, spotting the table with liquid brains. He threw the dodo head over his shoulder and nodded to the General who took one for himself. Kimi saw the General's protrusion begin to emerge. It wasn't as see-through as Granp's, but slightly reddish like his chest. The sight of both greylians sucking up brains was too much. Kimi sat back, keeping the handkerchief to her mouth.

Stella was grinning. "Nasty ay?"

Kimi nodded and made a gagging motion.

A double click and the scope began to descend. Stella's face appeared over the top. "Don't you think that's cool? You get to see some pretty outrageous things sometimes. I once saw Sue scatter some crumbs then come back and clean them up."

Kimi shrugged. "Yeah, I suppose."

"And you're the only one who knows about it. Apart from me of course. And you can come and use it whenever you want. Anytime!"

Kimi gave a weak smile. "Thanks. Sorry if I'm not doing cartwheels. I know this is probably all really cool, and thanks for sharing, it's just -" and she let out a great sigh.

"Ach, you're peeved because you have to stay a whole week aren't you?"

"Something like that," Kimi said as the scope clicked and dropped further.

"Next Sunday is the Festival of Cohn - bonus if you're still here. You'll love it - promise. Listen, all you have to do is chill out and accept that you're stuck here for a week. Let your hair down and enjoy. This place can be really great if you let it."

"Okay," Kimi said. "I suppose I can believe that. But how does that explain what I just heard?"

"Ohhh." Stella rubbed her hands. "What'd you hear?"

"It's what the alien things were saying. I only caught the end of it, but one of them said something like `when do we take the girl` and the other one went to say something but Sue's announcement cut in and, well, what girl?"

Stella was shaking her head. "That's what the greylians do, Kimi. Abduct people - from Earth, that is -"

Kimi stared at Stella with thoughts of home and Dad with his boxed sets of the X-Files. She wondered if Mulder and Scully were Balancers. Then there was Dad's favourite film - Close Encounters. They'd watched that like a zillion times.

"They do genetic work and stuff for the Adepts,"

Stella went on. "Vital stuff. Good stuff."

"So all those reports of people saying they've been abducted. They're all true?"

"Ach no, not all," Stella said. "Only some."

"What about the others?"

"Nutcases."

"Oh, so they could have been talking about any girl - I just thought, well -"

"I know what you thought, Kimi. They abduct millions, well not millions but you know what I mean - lots, all the time. It's their job. Look, it's no wonder you're feeling a bit paranoid. You're in a strange place, that's all. I remember walking around in a daze when I first got here. Trust me. This is a good place. You've just got to try chilling a bit."

Stella was probably right, but how could she relax with all the worry. "I feel trapped here, Stella. It's like I've got no choice in anything. And I'm sure that people are hiding the truth. And I'm worried about Mum and Dad. Not to mention myself. That crow - `One death today` it said - and I really do think that's gonna be me - and well, nobody seems to be too bothered."

"Can't be you," Stella said brightly. "The crow said someone would die `today` right?"

Kimi nodded.

"Well that was yesterday."

Kimi shook her head. "Not in Earth time."

"Ach, right. All the more reason to stay here then."

Silence between them. Only the return of the tinkling harp below. This was all so confusing. Death, greylians, dodo brains and secret scopes. Kimi had many questions yet no answers at all. She had promises of answers to come from people she wanted to trust, but wasn't sure how to. And now she had to wait a week, yet it felt as if those answers were there but just out of reach. Kimi saw her Mum and Dad's smiling faces. Dad was good at figuring out answers and getting to the bottom of things. What would he do? He'd start talking all logical and doing breakdowns - that's how you get answers. Kimi felt a great urge to reach out and throw her arms around her Mum and Dad and hug them and squeeze them for at least a full day without letting go. She caught the faint scent of Mum's perfume - sweet lavender - just for a second, then it was gone like a memory lost. Swallowing back tears, she stared at the floor as the scope settled into its hole with a final click and a puff of dust.

Then it came to her from nowhere. Kimi sat up straight with a spreading smile.

"You okay?" Stella asked, nervously.

"I've got an idea and I need your help. - *Moodirecto*!" Kimi tapped her lantern and the orange beam shone out. She pushed her stool to one side, dropped to the

216

floor, lifted the flap and squeezed inside the vent.

———

~ Wrong Answer ~

"Lock the door," Kimi said quietly. "And talk in whispers."

Stella locked the door and joined Kimi on the four-poster bed, legs crossed and eyes eager.

"The files at the library," Kimi began. "They were updating, right?"

"Aye." Stella nodded.

"And now, I've been mysteriously locked out and told to wait a week, right?"

"Aye again," Stella nodded.

"Well I'm not waiting a week. I'm going in tonight."

"Tonight? How? You can't…"

"I can and we leave right now. You gonna help me or not?"

Stella looked worried. "But how?"

"Your scope gave me the idea," Kimi said. "That balcony we stood on with what's-her-face -"

"Patina -"

"Yeah, potty Patty. Anyway, there was no door was there? Only a narrow passage connecting the lab floor with the balcony, and there was no door on either end. That's how we get in!"

"But there's no way up there," Stella said. "It's way too high."

"Haven't you figured it out yet?"

Stella shrugged and threw her arms up. "I - I give in."

Kimi leant forward, put her cupped hand to Stella's ear, and said in the lowest whisper: "Separation!"

Stella looked at her as if she'd gone mad. "You'll kill yourself!"

"Not if we do it together and keep an eye on each other."

Stella seemed to shrink away.

"What?"

"I - I can't - ach - I can't do the bloody thing -"

"The separating thing?"

"Aye."

"At all?"

"Well - only a little."

"How high can you go?"

Stella slumped from the four-poster and stood in the circle of light by the old camp bed. Her eyes closed and her stomach began to expand. It looked like she was heavily pregnant. Then it shrank and Stella was Stella again. "That's it," she said, looking embarrassed.

"Oh," Kimi said. "Sorry - erm - then I'll go up there on my own."

"It's too far, Kimi. You could kill yourself. And you know it." Stella returned to the bed. "You heard what

220

Blavatsky said."

"Stuff Blavatsky! Down there in the Shed, when I Separated, it was easy, no pain, no bad after-effects, nothing. I'm sure I could have kept on going to the moon!"

Stella looked at her worriedly. "You're serious aren't you?"

"I need to see those files. You in or not?"

"If you get caught, you'll be in such deep crap."

"If *I* get caught? So I'm on my own then?"

"Listen," Stella said. "I've got another secret. And I'm sorry for keeping it from you, but it was forced on me, and well, I think I need to tell you before you go and get yourself killed."

Stella had gone pale and Kimi knew a truth was coming. She felt the urge to reach out and clamp a hand over Stella's mouth. Instead her hands began to shake. She drew them to her stomach and stared at Stella. "Go on."

"Ach - I saw more on those files than I told you." Stella paused as if waiting for a reaction. "What are your parents called?"

Kimi swallowed. "Jack - and Val."

Stella nodded. "Your file wasn't the only one updating. Two Balancers - they live across the street from here - Balvalerie, nice woman, early-forties, mousy hair, always smiling…"

The warm ball of pressure reappeared behind Kimi's

eyes. She threw a hand up and rubbed her brow hard.

"…and her hubby," Stella went on. "Pajackok, handsome guy, slicked back hair - that's Pa-*jack*-ok and Bal-*val*-erie - sound familiar?"

"Oh my God. You're saying that my parents are Balancers?"

"Well, their weird names are typical of those Balancers with, how would you say it…ancient connections. Do you see? On Earth, such a Balancer will often change his name to something less conspicuous."

"I - I - surely I'd - I mean, my parents, Balancers?"

"I can't swear to that," Stella said. "That's why I asked if you had any Balancers in the family. You see, *your* file said it was updating, but seeing as you were still in the scanner, I had time to do a search - so I typed in, Nichols and a list came back - the two at the top of the list were also updating."

"And those were the two Balancers from across the street?"

"Yes," Stella said. "Only -"

"Only?"

"Well - next to each of the names - well - it said…"

A long silence followed. Kimi felt herself tense up. She wasn't breathing, just staring at Stella, waiting for the hit.

"…*said*…"

"What?" blurted Kimi. "Said bloody what?"

"Erm, `missing in action` - or something like that."

Kimi shook her head. "Just tell me the truth, Stella."

Stella placed a hand on Kimi's. "It said - presumed dead," she said, softly.

"Wrong answer!" shouted Kimi, sharply pulling her hands from Stella's. Her heart made a different sound. It was the bang of the bin hitting the front door over and again, bang, bang, bang, bang, bang.

"I'm sorry, Kimi."

"Well they can't be my parents then can they," Kimi snapped. Tears filled her eyes. She wiped them away. "Can't be!"

"Okay," Stella said. "You're probably right." She stared at the floor.

Kimi shrank back up the bed. "If they *were* my parents, then surely, with you living across the street, you would have known that, wouldn't you?"

Stella moved closer. "Kids aren't always kept in the loop around here, Kimi. Some Balancers work the top secret stuff, and they often lie low. All I know is that Pajackok and Balvalerie live over the street. They have lived there for a long time. They keep themselves to themselves. I don't even know what they do. But I do know that their names are weird, and that your Jack and Val could well be shortened versions."

"Then why haven't I got a weird name?" Kimi said.

"Ach, who else do you know called, Kimi?"

"Good point."

"I also know," Stella went on, "that I haven't seen either of them since the day before you arrived, and when I asked Sue where they'd got to, I got done for having mucky shoes."

"I guess it's all adding up," Kimi said, as thoughts whizzed and the hot ball, pulsed in her brow. She knew what she had to do. "You said the files were updating, right?"

"Erm, aye."

"Then I'm still going in. I have to." Kimi jumped from the bed.

"Ach, have you no been listening?"

Kimi made for the door. "I'm going - with or without you. If you'd rather stay here and not risk getting caught, then that's fine by me. Thank you for sharing your secrets!"

"Wait up," Stella said, thudding her feet to the floor. She grabbed her old jacket from the bed and threw it to Kimi. "Best get that on. It'll be chilly up there!"

***

On Stella's suggestion that Kimi should conserve energy, guided only by moonlight, they climbed the first run of steps at a creeping pace, but it wasn't long before Stella was pulling Kimi back.

"You're speeding up - cool it will you! You need to go slow," Stella insisted, linking into Kimi and holding the pace. "You're about to attempt the craziest Separation in history and you need to be focussed."

Kimi tutted.

"Do this my way or I'll scream for the fuzz."

"You wouldn't!"

"Watch me. Last thing I want is to be slung in the slammer for aiding your death!"

"There's a slammer?"

"Shush - and focus!"

"Why'd they call it Separation anyway when it's really like stretching?"

"Ach, you separate alright, Kimi. It might feel like you're stretching, it might even look like you're stretching, but really you're taking your mojo to its extreme, altering yourself at atomic level, separating bone and tissue from its solid state, altering it to a fluid state. That's not a stretch, Kimi. That's real separation. Like Blavatsky said, you go too far and you're out of here. You sure it's worth the risk?"

"It's worth the risk," Kimi said without a second thought.

Eventually, at the library door, Stella took out her lantern. "*Moodirecto!*" She stepped inside. Kimi followed. The lantern's green beam shone all the way to the door in the back wall.

All was quiet.

"We're clear." Stella tapped the lantern off. They shuffled back outside and looked up. The sheer mountain disappeared into the night.

"That's some way up," Stella said. "Are you sure about this?"

"Not a hundred percent," Kimi said. "It might be an idea if you sit on the floor and hold my legs steady just in case. We need a thingy though -"

"Thingy?"

"Yeah, what's the word? A code - that's it! I know - I'll tap my left foot if I hit trouble, and my right foot when I reach the railings so you know to let go. How does that sound?" Kimi positioned herself.

"Okay." Stella dropped to the floor behind Kimi, shoved her legs through Kimi's and gripped her arms around them. "It's the middle one you want!"

"What?"

"Computer - there's three of them - logs and records is the one in the middle."

"Right," Kimi said, drawing a deep breath. "Ready?"

"Ready!"

"Remember," Kimi said, "left foot means trouble - right foot means I'm there and you can let go - okay?"

"Got it," Stella said. "Left's for trouble and right's to let go. Good luck, and erm, no squeezing cheese!"

"Trust me," Kimi said. "I'm clenching too hard for that!"

Stella snorted.

"Here goes." Kimi steadied herself. She closed her eyes. Focus, Kimi, focus and make it a good one - nice and smooth - like pouring water.

"Whoa!" she heard Stella say. Kimi was stretching from the waist. It's working, Kimi thought, her eyes on the rock face passing by. Small creatures scurried under tufts of grass. A line of small birds on a ledge all raised their heads as they went by. After a while, the pace seemed to slow and Kimi began to waver. She tried to speak, but couldn't. Come on, come on, come on. Don't give up. Give it more. I can do this - I - can - do - this. Kimi's torso tightened like a rubber band. She stared up into the darkness, praying for the balcony to come into view. Surely it couldn't be much further. Her vision went blurry, her head heavy. Her stomach gave a sickly judder. It felt so tight, she realised she might be sick any time soon and fleetingly imagined vomit raining down on Stella. But that comical thought was quickly swept away by a series of hard tugs that seemed to come from deep inside and she thought that was it. Death would come any second with Blavatsky's fat lips shouting her warning. She was barely rising and breathing wasn't easy. She gulped for air and saw her arms start to fade. She had to stop this. She closed her eyes and focused on returning to the ground.

Nothing happened. This wasn't looking good.

Which foot to tap? Right? Left?

Right for trouble. No. Left - left for trouble. She tried to wiggle her toes but there was no connection. No feeling in her legs. She continued to inch upwards, but she had no control and the feeling of tightness was beginning to burn. Would she snap? Or just pass out and die?

She was about to close her eyes when the familiar white railings emerged from the darkness. Something leaped in Kimi's chest and the stretch quickened. Ten more feet. That's all. She concentrated on the railings, reaching, straining, tightening, shaking, and then the railings were there, damp and cold in her hands.

She grinned to herself, and in that instant, some small feeling had returned to her legs and a long, long way below - her right foot was tapping. The ensuing rush was like being pinged from a catapult.

A little yelp escaped from Kimi as she was propelled up and over the railings. She landed on the balcony floor with a too-loud thud that made her wince. She took a moment to check that nothing was amiss, shaking her arms, then her legs. Apart from a pain in the gut which felt like she'd been punched, everything seemed in working order. She looked back over the rail but couldn't see Stella - only mist. She wanted to shout that she was safe but knew she'd made enough noise already. With thoughts of getting in and out of there as quickly as possible, Kimi crept into the darkened passageway and was soon emerging onto the dimly lit landing.

Loud purring came from below. In fact, it was a great deal of purring, as if a hundred cats were sleeping at once. Kimi looked over but it was dark down there. She guessed it must be the secretaries sleeping, so slinked away from the rail and continued carefully up the landing. The lab rooms were in semi darkness with only monitors giving out flickering light. She went straight through the first door and into the room where Stella had been, carefully peering around at the shadows, her heart thumping madly at the thought of potty Patina suddenly appearing. She took the carved pomegranate from her pocket and tapped it.

"Moodirecto!" She aimed the orange light to the floor, and crept to the computer in the middle.

LOGS AND RECORDS the screen informed. She typed `Kimi Jo Nichols` in the search box and pressed return.

Truth time, she thought as the screen whizzed through names too fast to make any out. And suddenly there it was, all blocked together on the same entry:

Nichols, Kimi Jo - Balancer Status: Premature. Case study: H Blavatsky.

Father: Nichols, Pajackok Joseph - DNA confirmed -

DECEASED

Mother: Nichols, Balvalerie - DNA confirmed -
DECEASED

Kimi stared at the screen. The shadows around her seemed to draw in close for a look. The only sound was Kimi's heart knocking in her ears.

DECEASED

DECEASED

She stared at those words forever.

DECEASED

DECEASED

A single tear ran into Kimi's mouth and Dad's words came to her - his pained face - `You can do this`!` - and she remembered Mum's vibe, dismissed with a smile which didn't match up with her eyes. Tears spilled over and Kimi slumped to the desk and sobbed into her arms.

A crackling sound and the lab lit up. Out on the landing; more lights blinked on. The secretaries weren't purring any longer. Through the lab window, Kimi saw the beam of yellow light curl up onto the landing. Patina emerged in a long flowery dressing gown and curlers in her big hair. She looked angry and swept up the landing dragging Stella by the collar.

The lab door flew in and Patina's eyes blazed red.

"I know the truth," Kimi said, choking back sobs. "Do whatever you want with me, but don't blame Stella.

She's done nothing wrong."

Patina released her grip and Stella dropped to the floor. She scrambled away as Patina glided forward, stopping when Kimi held up a hand. "Don't come near me!"

Patina sighed. "Sweetheart, I know how upset you must be, but -"

Kimi's mouth opened and terrible screams came out. Awful screams that tried to pull her guts out with them. Arms came round her shoulders. A head against hers.

Stella.

"I wan - I want, Ben - Bentley," sobbed Kimi.

"Your wish," Patina said, clicking her fingers. Bentley appeared by Patina's side in an instant. The tray of glasses in his hands wobbled while he caught his balance.

"Good job they were empty," he said, glaring at Patina. Then he saw Kimi. "Oh," he said, and the glasses crashed to the floor.

"Your Balancer," Patina began. "Broke into the library and discovered the news, from which we have tried so hard to protect her."

"I didn't break in!" Kimi snapped. "And you," she said to Bentley. "How could you?"

"Wha- what?" Bentley whimpered, wringing his hands.

"You knew all along that my - that my - that they - that they were - and you kept it from me. You're meant to

231

look after me, not trick me. What do you think I am? A soft baby? Is that what you think? Is it? Is it?"

Bentley dropped to the floor, his clasped hands never parting as his knees crunched onto glass. His face sagged. Tears rolled down his cheeks. "I - I'm sorry, Kimbo. Forgive me, please. I was forced to keep the secret - or they were going to put you in the deep freeze and…"

Kimi shook her head in disbelief. "What kind of place is this?"

Patina's eyes went yellow and wide. "A place of good heart!" she affirmed with a nod and her arms folded across her chest.

"Could have fooled me," Kimi said. She went to Bentley, her trainers crunching glass, and helped him to his feet. "You've cut yourself," she said, picking shards from his bloodied knees. He was shaking. She led him to a swivel chair and sat him down.

"I'm sorry," he sobbed.

"I want to go home!" Kimi squared up to Patina, whose eyes were now pastel blue and spinning. "Now!"

"I'm afraid I can't allow it," Patina said, producing a disc from her dressing gown pocket. "I need you to see this." She went to the middle computer and slipped the disc in. "Please sit," she said, ushering Kimi into the chair. Bentley and Stella came to the side.

"These are stills from cctv footage of the golfing

course," Patina said. The screen flickered and a black and white image of the course appeared.

Bentley gasped and so did Stella. Kimi trembled and stared at the screen. Stella's hand came to her shoulder. Kimi reached up and held it.

"Try not to be alarmed," Patina said. "These are selected stills - nothing too horrendous, I promise you." She reached a finger to the screen and the image changed. In the top left corner stood two small shadowy figures.

Kimi's hand went to her mouth.

"Those are your parents," Patina said. "Notice, beyond them, if you look closely, you might make out the flaggy thing."

"The flagpole at the hole," Stella said.

"There's a crow on it," Bentley said.

"Correct." Patina tapped the screen and the image altered once more. "Note two things at this point - one; our beloved Pajackok, your dear father; is throwing his golfing stick to the ground. Note also that the crow has alighted at the same moment."

"Dad knew something was about to happen," Kimi said.

"Indeed!" Patina tapped the screen again and this time the two figures had started to run. The departing crow was almost off the screen. "Watch," Patina said. She ran her finger in a circle on the screen and the image magnified, revealing some bushes that previously were barely noticeable. "Tell me what you see."

"Bushes," Kimi said.

"I see shuck," Bentley said. "Well I'll be!"

Patina outlined the triangular shape among the bushes with a long fingernail. "Correct, Tulpa Bentley, that would appear to be the head of a shuck," she said and then magnified the scene further. "Now what do you see?"

"Three of the buggers!" Bentley said.

"Yes, hanging around like feline vultures. Odd don't you think? But that's not all. The next still is the actual lightning strike," she said. "Brace yourself, Kimi, sweetheart."

Kimi squeezed Stella's hand. Stella squeezed back.

Patina tapped the screen, but there wasn't much to see. In fact the screen had gone white. "Now look at this." Patina circled a finger in the middle of the screen. The image magnified, revealing a black jagged line running from top left to the centre. "Any idea what that might be?"

"The lightning strike?" Kimi offered, swallowing hard.

"Noooooo," Bentley said. "Can't be - surely not?"

"Can't be what?" Stella asked.

"A centre core!" Bentley said. "Always comes last, see."

Patina nodded. "My girls have scoured the archives

234

and I can assure you that not one lightning photograph marries this image - not one. On the other hand, magnified images of mojo show the centre core as a thin black line. Just like this one!" she tapped a long nail on the screen.

Kimi stared at the image, shivering. Stella's arm closed around her shoulders.

"So you're saying they were murdered?" Bentley's words didn't seem real.

"I'm saying nothing of the sort," Patina said. "I'm merely looking at facts which investigation has thrown up thus far - and in this case we appear to have some out of place shuck sniffing where they shouldn't and a killer blow which surely looks like mojo!"

"But how?" Bentley said. "That's a mighty blast to be mojo - and where would he shoot from? He'd have to be up a tree or…"

"I *have* explored the possibilities, Tulpa Bentley," Patina cut in, casting a hand in his direction and silencing him immediately. She floated gently to Kimi, cupped a hand under Kimi's chin and lifted her head. "You will be all right, dear," Patina said. "I hope you now understand why you can't yet go home. And also, that you have good, caring friends here."

Kimi dropped her head and rubbed her eyes. She could feel Bentley staring, but could not look at him. Thoughts ran fast. Important thoughts. But she could not grasp them for the image filling her mind of Mum and Dad burnt black in their coffins, side by side. That's all. Just that one image.

"One death -" came from Kimi's lips. She looked to Bentley who quivered. "One death - the crow said. I - I don't understand."

"Crows have been wrong before," said Patina.

"So question the crow," Kimi snapped, struggling to hold down the tears.

Patina shook her head. "Crows answer to nobody but penguins."

"What?" Kimi looked at her, puzzled. Bentley opened his mouth to say something but was silenced by another flick of Patina's wrist. "Listen Kimi," she went on. "The crow was obviously wrong - the cctv footage in its entirety shows quite clearly that two deaths most certainly occurred -"

Stella's grip gave a squeeze.

"- and DNA evidence collected at the scene confirms without any doubt whatsoever, the identities as being your parents -"

Stella began stroking Kimi's hair. Kimi thought she was trying to cover her ears.

"- we even found a finger - and the prints, although a little *singed* -"

Kimi burst.

At least that's how it felt. Her vision blurred through juddering tears. She tried to speak but her teeth would only gnash, gnash, gnash. Stella was stroking and Bentley was saying something. Tears raked up through Kimi's chest and she wailed into Stella's armpit.

"Whisk us!" she heard Stella shout. "Can't you see she's too upset - whisk us!"

"To where?" Patina shouted over the wailing.

"My room!"

"Agreed!" Patina said, and everything went silent.

Kimi's head sank into the soft feather pillows, the red drapes hung warmly around her. Stella pulled the covers around Kimi's chin and kissed her brow.

The door opened then closed.

Kimi pulled the covers higher and cried.

————

~ 17 ~

~ Too Many Secrets ~

Skittering and scratching brought Kimi awake. It was as if the room was full of rats. She raised her head from the damp pillow, trying to see through sticky eyes. The noise was coming from the pointed ceiling. Birds on the tiles outside, that was it. This bedroom may be bigger than hers back in Mousehole, but lack of windows made the place depressing. It could have been any time of day, but Kimi guessed from the birds on the roof that it must be daybreak. The only light came from the dim yellow lantern hanging over the camp bed which had clearly been slept in; thrown back blankets, squashed pillow, and Stella's mood lantern on the floor by its side. Kimi sat up. Her ribs ached from the constant sobbing. She rubbed some clarity into her eyes and peeled matted hair from her face. She imagined looking out the window at the harbour like she would every morning; the red boats in a line on the sand; the water smooth as a mirror. But this image wasn't there for long. Two words slid across it - big and bold and engraved in gleaming metal on a heart-shaped plaque - NO PARENTS - those words were here to stay. Kimi stared at them, wishing for a window.

Small footsteps sounded on the stairs and the birds were skittering and scratching again. Kimi took a deep breath. The door swung open.

"Hi!" Stella stepped in carrying a tray. She heeled the door shut and ordered the main lights on. "I've brought you some brekky." When she put the tray on the bed, a large bump was revealed in her fastened up jacket. "Coffee and toast!" She sounded chirpy, but Kimi could hear her nerves. "Bentley said you often had it - and I know you might not, erm, you know, fancy anything much, and so I, erm -"

"It's okay," Kimi cut in. "*I'm* okay." She didn't feel like smiling but tried for Stella. When she did her swollen eyes closed up completely.

"You look awfully puffy," Stella said.
Kimi took a sip of coffee and caught another glance of the engraved plaque. It now sat artistically on lush grass and was surrounded by wilting red roses.

"So then," Stella said, sitting on the bed.

Kimi noticed Stella's eyes were bloodshot. "You look worse than I feel."

"Ach, no, I'm fine - just tired. Been up most of the night."

Stella looked as if she was itching to say something. "You're gonna burst if you don't tell me." Kimi pointed to the lump in Stella's jacket. "You either got pregnant overnight or you Separated and got stuck."

Stella giggled and pulled a plastic Tesco bag from her jacket. Kimi almost dropped her mug. "Where the heck did you get a Tesco bag?" She reached out and took it with a

240

shaking hand. It was like having home arrive. Or at least a part of it.

Stella snatched the bag away and swung it from side to side. "You know how Potty Patty said you couldn't go home just yet?"

"Yeah," Kimi said, eyes fixed on the swinging bag.

"Well, she didn't say nothing about me not going - so I did!"

"You went home for the night? Oh you lucky sod."

"Not for the night. It was only an eight minute jump, but it took all night - with the time difference, aye?"

"Right." Kimi continued watching the bag.

"And it's *your* home I've been to - not mine."

The bag stopped swinging and Kimi felt like she'd just been dropped in an icy bath. Only one trickle of tear escaped. Kimi managed to hold back the rest. "Was anyone there?" she asked, wiping away the tear.

"Sorry Kimi, but the place was erm - empty -" she paused for the smallest moment, "- but look what I brought." She fished into the plastic bag.

"Surely there was somebody there?"

Stella pulled a jar of Marmite from the bag. "To go with your toast."

Kimi took the jar.

"I didn't really see much to be honest." Stella picked up the knife from her tray. "Go on. You should try and eat something."

Kimi wasn't really hungry, but she undid the jar, held it to her nose. The meaty aroma smelled like home.

"Ach - nasty stuff," Stella twisted her face. "Smells like cat's fart."

"Tell me what you saw," Kimi said, spreading Marmite on a triangle of toast.

"Not much, really. The patio doors were open and there was obvious twirly disruption in the dining room - erm, I found a smashed mirror on the floor by the stairs."

"That was Bentley," Kimi said, biting into the toast.

"I had a look round upstairs - the only sign of disturbance was in your room - which is really wee by the way."

"And there was no one there?"

"No one," Stella said, holding out the still bulging bag to Kimi.

"But there must have been," Kimi insisted. "Who crashed into the bins and revved the engine so loudly? Did you check outside?"

"Shit!" Stella smacked her forehead. "I - I only went to get you some stuff," she said, miserably. "Nobody sent me - I just thought I could cheer you up a bit and took my chance before someone saw fit to ban me as well."

"But what about the car outside, you dumbo?"

Stella shrugged. "I'm sorry. I didn't think. I just

242

grabbed you some stuff, shoved it in a bag, and got back here quick as I could before I got caught."

"Right," Kimi said, knowing an opportunity had been wasted. "Look, don't worry about it. And I'm sorry for getting arsey, it's just -"

"You don't have to apologise for anything, Kimi. You're right though. I was too busy trying to surprise you, when really I should have talked to you first - ach, Kimi, I'm just a blonde butthead!"

Kimi shook her head. "No you're not at all. And you need to ignore me. I guess I'm not really thinking straight. Thanks for this." She dipped into the Tesco bag and pulled out her thick cream jumper and her black jeans. She brought them to her face and inhaled the lavender fabric conditioner. Sometimes that smell would get too much, but today it was heavenly.

"Autumn's on us right now," Stella said. "I thought you'd like a cosy jumper and a change from them white jeans."

Kimi had no intention of hanging around for Autumn or anybody. She had to go back home, of that she was certain. Anyway, it wasn't Stella's fault. "You're a star," she told her. "I appreciate it, really."

"I'll jump again tonight if there's anything else you'd like."

Kimi imagined herself in her own bed tonight. If

Stella could go back without anyone finding out, then surely she could too. "Maybe," she said. "Thanks - I'll have a think about it."

"Ach, listen, I have to go - Bentley's waiting for you downstairs and he's crapping himself because he let you down. He wants to see you as soon as poss - so eat up and I'll see you in the bar." Stella went to the camp bed and picked up her mood lantern.

"Did you sleep there?" Kimi asked.

"Ach - you were, erm, snoring a bit. Besides, I was away most of the night - no worries!" She made for the door.

Kimi suspected her crying had kept Stella awake. "Stell!"

"Aye?" Stella stopped in the doorway.

"Thanks for last night - helping with the Separation - and, well, after that."

"Ach, no worries – that Separation was awesome by the way. Right, I'll see you in a bit." She turned to leave.

"One more thing."

"Aye?"

"What do you say we get a window or two fitted in here?"

Stella grinned. "Aye, nice one - see you downstairs!" And she was gone.

Kimi kicked off her white jeans which she'd slept in and now looked more grubby grey than white, and pulled on

244

her clean black jeans, deciding to stick with her Superman tee and not bother with the jumper just yet. She shrugged on Stella's old field jacket, checked the pocket for her grass dolly and mood lantern, and made her way downstairs, trying not to think of what Bentley might have to say and trying not to look at the NO PARENTS plaque which practically filled the whole of her head and now had vines curling around it and a crow perched on top.

***

Big Sue was stood at the bottom of the stairs in his tartan dressing gown. He had a tea towel clutched to his mouth and looked as if he'd been crying. He smiled from behind the tea towel.

"Hi," Kimi said, attempting a smile.

"How are you, dear?" he said, ushering Kimi towards the front door where the old Bentley was talking to Stella.

"I'm okay," Kimi replied as Sue's tea towel dusted her shoulders.

As Kimi approached, the old Bentley slid into the cubicle by the door. Stella gave Kimi the thumbs up and took a seat in the cubicle opposite, disappearing behind the frosted partition.

Sunlight diffused by the frosted windows produced a pinkish haze. Bentley sat among it looking ill and older than normal. Kimi could tell that he'd been crying too. He smiled and gestured her to sit. Kimi didn't even try a smile this time.

"Hello," Bentley said, looking as if he could blubber any second.

"Hi," she said, which came out like a squeak.

"I'm very sorry," Bentley said, pushing his face through his hands. "I let you down, Kimi. I shudder to think what you must think of me - and, and well, I'm deserving of whatever punishment you see fit."

"Punishment?"

"Oh yes," Bentley said, resignedly. "The first decree of the forty-fourth amendment to the Balancer's manual, section five; *Punishments for Unbalanced Tulpas* - I could be hung in Pommy Wood, or sent to the deep freeze for a year, or turned into a light bulb. Bulb duty is terrible. They tend to hang you in toilets and -"

From the corner of her eye, Kimi saw Big Sue join Stella in the other cubicle while Bentley babbled on among the pink haze. "*These windows,*" Sue was saying. "*Do you think I should clean them mid-afternoon as well as morning and night -*"

"*Shut up, Sue,*" Stella said.

"- and if you ask me," Bentley went on, "I deserve nothing less than the worst -"

"Stop it!" Kimi said. "It's okay. You did what you had to do."

246

She reached a hand across the table, and Bentley took it. "You're not mad at me?"

Kimi shook her head. "How could I be? I would have done the same thing."

"You would?" Bentley was smiling now.

"Deffo," Kimi said, noticing that Sue and Stella had gone quiet.

"Well I am really, really sorry," Bentley said. "It wasn't pleasant keeping things from you and -"

"Bentley - I said it was okay." Kimi patted his hand.

"So you forgive me?"

"On one condition," Kimi said.

"Of course - anything."

"That you ask no questions about where I got these jeans from." She stood up to show him.

"Oh. Alright - as long as you don't go mad when you hear what I have to say."

Kimi thought that things couldn't get much worse and really wanted to broach the subject of getting back home soon. "Yeah, what's that?"

"It's just, well," Bentley started. "There's erm, well, there's something else I've been keeping from you."

Stella and Sue's heads popped up from behind the glass partition.

Kimi looked at them then back to Bentley and her stomach gave a little roll.

"It's this." He reached down the front of his shirt and pulled out a large silver key on a string. "The key to your parents' place."

It felt as if a famoose had suddenly awakened in Kimi's chest. Bentley looped the string over his head and pressed the key into Kimi's hand. "Your father gave me this key the day before he -"

"-*died*," Kimi finished.

"- left on a mission," Bentley went on. "He was quite cryptic about it. Of course it all adds up now."

"What did he say?"

"He said, well, he said that bad news was arriving, and that so was his daughter, and that as soon as you knew the truth of the situation, I was to hand you the key and ensure that all three of us accompanied you over there - no exceptions. He was firm about that. Made me repeat it. No exceptions!"

Kimi gazed straight through Bentley. She had completely forgotten what Stella had said about Mum and Dad having a place here - the crow perched on the NO PARENTS plaque repeated, `*one death*` over and over - and now she had the key. What if the crow was right. One death. Only one. What if...

"Kimi! Kimi!" Stella was knocking on the partition. "You okay?"

"Huh?"

"- of course I was dumbfounded -" Bentley was still talking.

"Where is this place?" Kimi rolled the heavy key in her hand. Stella stepped up onto a chair. "Right there -" she pointed through the top of the window where the frosting gave way to clear glass. Kimi climbed on her chair. The house across the lane was in shadow but she recognised it. The glass-balancing monkey on the door's Pommy Juice advert grinned at her. Up the side of the house, painted on the brickwork, was a man in a black suit and hat. He was shooting flames which curled around and down to the front door.

"The painting is your great-grandfather," Bentley said. "Holds the all-time Heart record for fireball hurling. Could shoot more than half a mile - accurate to within a foot. Incredible. No one's come near, since."

"Right," Kimi said, not really listening. The feeling that there might have been only one death was very strong. As strong as an undeniable truth. A fact so plain as day, that when she went over there and opened the front door, either Mum or Dad would be waiting. One of them - deffo - waiting. She almost voiced this, but couldn't, or wouldn't - she still wasn't really thinking straight, she knew that much, but something had awakened inside. Something bright. Hope! "Right," she said again, trying to contain her nervousness. "Let's go and take a look."

They stepped into sunshine and an empty lane. Fifty yards to the right stood a row of red cones along with a couple of yellow plastic signs like the ones you get in McDonalds when the floor's wet. Kimi looked to her left and saw a similar row of cones and the same yellow signs some fifty yards down the street the other way. Beyond the signs, people went about their business.

"Cleaning in progress!" Big Sue winked at her. "I thought a little privacy wouldn't go amiss." He held an arm out and Kimi took it.

"Thanks," she said, wishing her heart to slow down as they approached the door with the grinning monkey. The key was a perfect fit. It felt as if the lock had sucked it from Kimi's grip. The door opened silently to darkness. "Lights," Bentley said as they stepped inside and two table lamps blinked on.

Kimi eyes darted around, looking for movement - anything. The door led straight into a small living room containing only a black leather sofa with a small reading table and lamp to either side; the shapes in the dark she'd seen when she first arrived. Book cases full of books ran the back wall behind the sofa, and off to the side, narrow stairs spiralled upwards. She ran up the stairs and found an empty, slept in bed. NO PARENTS. A few tears escaped. She allowed them to pass, wiped her face and went back downstairs.

"What do you think?" Bentley handed the key back to Kimi.

"It's tiny," was all she could think of.

Bentley went to one of the reading tables and picked up a small brown book. "Not so tiny," he said, handing the book to Kimi.

`Dylan Thomas - The Code of Night` said the tattered cover.

"It's a key," Bentley said, pointing to a gap in the bookshelf. Kimi went behind the sofa and slid the book into the empty space. There was a click and a whirr and the whole bookshelf slid upwards into the ceiling. Kimi imagined it popping up in the bedroom she'd just left.

"The workshop," Bentley said.

Kimi stepped inside. This was big. Banks of monitors ran along the long wall to the right with at least ten computers lined up beneath, blinking lights in all colours. A lone jukebox looked lost on the wide back wall. It must have been connected to the door opening because it flickered to life and the classical tunes that Kimi had heard and detested so often began to sing softly. A single tear escaped. Kimi quickly wiped it away.

Two large leather chairs sat before a desk on the left holding two more computers. More bookshelves sat behind. Bins full of rolled up papers dotted the floor. Rubbish overflowed from wire baskets. Cork boards filled every free bit of wall space, blazing with stick pins and notes written in Mum or Dad's scrawl. Kimi went and sat in one of the big leather chairs. On the desk in front stood a framed photograph of her and Mum taken one wet and windy day at the Minnack theatre, and another showed Dad leaning against a standing stone and a very young Kimi sat grinning on top.

NO PARENTS - the engraved plaque slid back over her memories. It was new and shiny again - no grass - no wilting roses - no crow - NO PARENTS

Kimi could hold it in no longer. Terrible cries came wailing from her in huge unstoppable retches. Three hands came at once to her shoulders and she cried until the classical music had stopped.

It was Stella who spoke first. "Cool place isn't it," she said.

Kimi stood up and wiped her eyes. "I've got no parents," she said.

"You've got us," Stella said.

"Yes," Bentley and Sue agreed.

"And we've got you!" Stella added.

They all looked so worried, so kind. These were good people. New friends. Friends for life, Kimi thought. A life that had to go on. "You're right," she said, wanting to change the subject. "Let's have a look around. Make yourselves erm, at home!"

"Hang on," Stella said, picking a notebook from a pile on the desk. "Aren't we forgetting something?" They all stared at her. "Kimi's dad gave you a message?" she said to Bentley.

Bentley looked uncomfortable. "Yes - to give Kimi the key."

"And?" Stella tapped the notebook on her chin, her stare fixed on Bentley.

"And um - to come over here with Kimi and make sure she got the brown book on the table with which to open the bookcase door – yes." Bentley affirmed.

"No," Stella said. "You forgot something. Didn't he say that you were to ensure all three of us came over with Kimi - no exceptions!"

"Yee-gads!" Bentley said. "Yes. But why?"

"For support obviously," Big Sue said.

"Ach, I don't think so," Stella said. "He wants us to look for something. The more eyes the better. I reckon there's been a clue left somewhere - and I think we should all get looking!"

"Oh dear," Big Sue said, fiddling with a tea towel. "Let's have some more music!" He went to the jukebox, pushed a couple of buttons, then began polishing it before the classical tunes started up again.

"Okay," Kimi said to Stella, happily buying into the distraction. "Let's get looking!"

253

And so they did; Bentley and Kimi rummaging through boxes of notebooks, of which there were at least a thousand, all filled with mysterious calculations and strange symbols; Stella scanning through files on the computers though not really knowing what to look for; and the conclusion Kimi came to was absolute: "My parents were geeks!"

She was having second thoughts. Perhaps Dad's insistence on them all coming over together, was in fact to keep her company and nothing else. If she'd come on her own she would have probably just sat and cried for hours. She was also having second thoughts about the need to go home. This house, this workshop, felt a bit like home. It was warm, somehow, as if hands were there to hold her - or to show her the way. Then she spotted something unusual. Something out of place. Something pink.

A small triangle, poked from a book on the shelves behind the big desk. It looked like a bookmark, but it was vivid pink. Kimi stared at it with an overwhelming feeling surging through her that made her gasp for breath. It felt like she'd connected with something - and in her brow the prickles danced.

Bentley muttered something and threw another notebook on the pile. Stella remained staring at the computer screen. Big Sue continued polishing the juke box while humming along to the classical music. Kimi stood up. "I think - I think I might have found something."

The others stopped what they were doing. She went around the desk to the bookshelves. All eyes were on her as she slid the thin book from its place. It was yet another notebook. She turned the cover. Blank. And the next few pages - also blank. There was nothing in this book, only the pink triangle poking from the top.

Kimi didn't grasp it straight away. A loud voice shouted NO, put it back, hide it, burn it, this could be confirmation of something most terrible. Another, equally loud, yelled, TAKE IT, this could be hope, you don't give up on hope! Her brow grew hot and tingles rushed down her arms and burned through her hands. The notebook was suddenly bathed in yellow light. The pink triangle glowed hot. There was no longer a choice to make. Her finger and thumb were about to clasp it, and when they did, Kimi's forehead throbbed powerfully. She winced as the card slid out and drew a huge breath when she saw what it was.

"Crap a bliss fly!" she heard Stella say.

Kimi stared at the shiny pink card. A gleaming pink Limo sat under the *Ride a Limo Co,* logo, and neat handwriting along the bottom of the card said;

`booking confirmed - Sunday 9^{th} Oct - 2 pm pick up at Penzance Plaza.`

Kimi stared at the writing with tears brimming. She wiped them away and sniffed them back. "Nice one, Dad," she whispered. "Nice one."

Stella's nose arrived at Kimi's shoulder. Kimi handed her the card.

"Neat," Stella said. "But what's this on the back?"

Kimi took the card and read the reverse; `back in a jiffy - 271` Goosebumps ran up her arms. "Back in a jiffy!" she said, "Dad's last words."

"What last words?" Stella said as Bentley nosed in for a look. Big Sue remained over by the jukebox and was now dusting the wall.

"Dad was acting real weird," Kimi said. "Just before they left for the golf course - he must have mentioned about being back in a wiffy at least six million times - and even though I corrected him and told him he meant jiffy he still kept saying wiffy – he even changed his mobile voicemail message and said it in that. He wanted me to remember."

"Then this is one big clue," Stella said, eyes twinkling.
"So what does it mean?" Bentley said, taking the card for a look. "What's the number, 271?"

"Might be a page number?" Kimi offered.

Bentley gazed around at the many bookshelves. "Must be least a thousand books here - so which book?"

"I've no idea," Kimi said. "But we have to start somewhere, and I'm not stopping until I find out what this means. Dad's done this for a reason. Dad always has a reason!" Bentley and Stella were both smiling at her and Kimi knew why. Her voice. It had new energy and it felt good. She smiled firmly back.

"Okay, books it is," Stella said. "Look for one with Jiffy or Wiffy in the title." Then added, "And check page 271 in every single book."

Bentley clapped his hands. "Let's get moving."

Suddenly Kimi wasn't so sure. "There is a lot of books," she said, gazing around and hoping for a quicker solution. "Dad would make it easier than that, surely."

"Come on," Stella said. "If we do it methodically, and we all help, it won't take us that long - unless anyone's got a better idea?"

Kimi was on the verge of agreeing that Stella's suggestion made sense when her eye caught something golden in one of the wire rubbish baskets. In fact there were many things golden and they dawned over her like a warm sunrise. They were the envelopes Mum used for sending out the software. Big fat padded *Jiffy* envelopes. The rubbish baskets were stuffed with them.

"Jiffy envelopes!" she pointed at the bin nearest. Stella picked it up and tipped the contents onto the floor. Kimi dropped to her knees and grabbed at the envelopes - "Empty - empty - empty" throwing them to one side. Bentley tipped up a next bin and then a third and Kimi and Stella worked through the Jiffy Bags finding nothing but air, nothing that is until the very last bag caught in mesh (or trapped there purposely) at the bottom of the bin. Kimi freed it up. It was heavier than the others. "There's something in it," she said and Stella and Bentley closed in. Big Sue, seemed disinterested, now back to polishing the jukebox and singing along to Ava Maria - badly.

Kimi peered inside the Jiffy Bag and pulled out a further notebook. This one was full from front to back with Dad's scrawl. Calculations, symbols, long scientific names and words Kimi had never heard of. One thing did stand out though.

`*Calculus key to the Jiffy.*` was repeated on many pages.

"This is it," Kimi said, flicking through page after page of calculation. "This is what Dad wanted us to find."

"What on earth for?" Bentley said.

"You're not on Earth," Kimi said with a grin that came easily. "Don't you see? Dad's laid down the clues well enough you must admit. All we have to do is figure out what this `Jiffy` is."

"How?" Bentley said.

"Page 271 - I hope," Kimi said, sinking into one of the leather chairs.

Bentley and Stella moved in as Kimi flicked through the page numbers. Big Sue remained by the jukebox and was chewing his tea towel.

"Here it is." Kimi held the notebook open -

Page 271

The Jiffy - the calculation for reverse time travel (in brief)

First stage ingredients for non-Jiffy, vacant time jump:

1) two opposing twirlies (see diameter limits)

2) an essential angle entry of 42 degrees

3) high speed

~}~

Final stage and essential ingredient to upgrade to non-vacant travel - the final ingredient which completes the Jiffy - find it within, and we'll be back in a Jiffy!

~}~

"We're gonna do time travel," Stella said in a dreamy voice. "Time travel."

Bentley held out a hand for the notebook. "Let me look."

"Wait!" Stella said. "Read the last line again."

Kimi read out the line: "*Find it within, and we'll be back in a Jiffy!*"

"Yes!" Stella said. "What's within yourself?"

"Mojo?" Bentley offered.

"Ach no," Stella said. "What comes from within?"

259

"Ahhh," Kimi said, sure that she'd somehow just grabbed the answer right from Stella's forehead. She rose from her chair. "Why the heck didn't we ask this question before now?"

Stella shrugged, "Never thought. Well, I never really saw much of them anyway. Kids aren't kept in the loop round here you know." She looked to Bentley who went around behind the desk and folded his arms across his chest. "Would you care to let me in on whatever it is you have discovered?"

"Tulpas," Kimi said. "Where are Mum and Dad's Tulpas?"

Bentley's eyes went wide as saucers. "Yee gads!"

"Retired to Mercurial Waters, that's where they'll be," Stella said. "We have to find them - find out what they know. Jack - your Dad – he's probably left a message with them - or another clue."

"But you can only twirly part way there," Bentley said. "After that it's at least a week's trek!"

"A week?" Kimi said.

"Oh yes, a trek that would take us through at least a fifty villages and settlements, whose interest in us would draw more attention than we -"

A high-pitched shriek from Big Sue made them all start.

"Ohhhhh," he was saying, stepping slowly back

from the film of blue light which had appeared on the wall beside the jukebox. It reminded Kimi of the blue light filling the frame of the Shed's door, only this was much bigger.

"It's a door," Stella said, going for a closer look.

"Bloody big door," Kimi said, as the shimmering light spread up to the ceiling and stretched to at least ten feet wide before finally settling.

Stella reached out and touched the shimmering blue. Her fingers did not go through it as Kimi expected. Instead there was a BEEP and a previously unnoticed panel on the wall by the jukebox lit up red. "A touch pad," Stella said, then touched it with a finger. Another BEEP sounded and the panel remained bright red.

"Where in the creation could this lead to?" Bentley said, moving closer to inspect.
Stella was staring closely at the touch pad. "It's covered in prints. It's a fingerprint reader," she said, and the room filled with silence.

The heat behind Kimi's eyes returned with such force that she cried out loud and held her head in her hands. "That bloody hurt," she said, feeling something very strong and powerful coming from the shimmering blue wall. She took a few steps back and the heat in her brow receded.

"We need to get in there," Stella said. "And I don't really want to be the one saying this, but there's fingerprints all over that pad. And, well, remember what Patina said -

you know - what they found at the scene."

"Oh God," Kimi said, suddenly recalling her last seconds with Patina. She looked to Stella. "She said they'd found a - a finger. A burnt finger. Then you got us whisked." Both of them turned to Bentley.

"No way," Bentley was shaking his head.

"Way!" Stella said, firmly. "I know it's awful, but if we want to get any further, then we need that finger."

Kimi's mind raced. She didn't much like this idea either, but it seemed the only way and although the thought of being in the same room as a burnt black finger that might prove to be the only thing left of either her Mum or her Dad, made her feel like crying again, she knew there was the possibility that Dad had left that finger behind, somehow - maybe for the very reason of opening that door. She told herself it was just a finger and no longer any use apart from being a key. She would do it. Had to. They would somehow get that finger from Patina. All they needed was a plan.

Kimi's thoughts were interrupted by great thuds coming from the living room. She spun round. Big Sue was through there, shoving the bolts in the front door. He came hurriedly back through the bookshelf door and entered the workshop looking nervous. Red patches formed on his cheeks as he fished something from his pocket. "I - erm - I'm afraid I have a secret," he said, unfolding a piece of paper. "Ahem -"

"More bloody secrets?" Kimi muttered, shooting Stella a glance. Stella blushed as Sue read from the sheet of paper.

"To my trusted friend, Tulpa Big Sue – This is extremely Top Secret! - In a short time from now you will hear of-" he paused: *"Two deaths -"*

Stella's gasp was loud enough to drown Kimi's. Kimi sat down.

"I ask you do not worry," Sue continued. *"- and do not confide in anyone. In due course, once Kimi learns the truth, Tulpa Bentley will lead Kimi to my house - watch out for this and ensure that you reveal the entrance to the IPC -"* Sue pointed to the shimmering blue wall. *"-once my daughter has realised what she must do, you must ensure that the front door is bolted, and despite any objections, personal or otherwise, you must summon the Chief of fuzz, post haste! - yours, Pajackok."*

Sue stuck the note back in his dressing gown pocket, grabbed a tea towel from his shoulder and began twirling it in front of him.

"Wait!" Kimi yelled, darting forward. "We should discuss this first -"

It was too late, tiny though it was, the twirly was in full swirl beneath Sue's tea towel and before any further objection could be voiced, the twirly slowed, groaned, and monkey Rehd stepped out.

"'Bout time," he said to Big Sue, straightening his waistcoat and flattening down his hair which looked like he'd been electrocuted. "I have note," Rehd announced, flicking open a piece of paper.

"Bloody hell," Kimi said. "Was everyone in on this but me?"

Stella's arm came to Kimi's shoulder. "Let him speak," she said. "I've a feeling this is about to get interesting."

Rehd pursed his lips, shook his head furiously, then began to read; "*To my dear friend, Chief of fuzz, Rehd – this is top secret - once summoned by Tulpa Big Sue, you will find my daughter and her companions planning to travel - I ask that you help with passage through Bridgetown -*"

Bentley nodded, "Where the trolls live."

"But that's east of Mercurial Waters - that can't be right -" Stella said.

Bentley raised a finger to hush her. "Let him finish!"

Rehd cleared his throat and continued, "*- give Kimi the key to the IPC and ensure that all five of you step through at the same time - no exceptions - a challenging time awaits - I wish you good luck, Balancer Pajackok.*"

"What's an IPC?" Kimi asked.

Rehd pointed to the shimmering wall. "*Internal Passage Chamber - Balancer Jack invented.*" From his waistcoat he pulled a white plastic bag which unfurled from an outstretched furry fist. `**EVIDENCE**` it said across the front in big red letters.

Kimi glared at the bag.

"Good grief man," Bentley said.

"Oh -" Stella said, reaching for the bag. Rehd snatched it back and dug his hand inside. Kimi turned away, swayed a little and held onto a desk.

"Here, Kimi Nichols," Rehd said.

Kimi felt her heart drop into her stomach. She didn't want to look but knew she had to. It's just a finger, just a finger, she told herself as she turned.

It was hair Rehd was holding not a finger but a lock of dark hair.

"From Jack's head," Rehd said. "For DNA lock -" he jerked his head towards the shimmering blue wall. "Swipe root on pad."

A whole lot of air escaped from Kimi's lungs at this point. Stella, Bentley and Big Sue all seemed to follow, breaking into chatter and making a grab for the lock of hair. Kimi sat down with her head in her hands and went looking for the plaque. She closed her eyes against the babble and the first word she saw was MUM in big capital letters. DAD slid in alongside a second later. There was no plaque to be seen. She opened her eyes to a hand on her shoulder.

"Yours -" Rehd said. Bentley, Sue and Stella loomed behind him with eager eyes.

Kimi took the lock of hair and closed it in her hand.

"When do we leave?" Stella said, breathlessly.

"When do we not!" Bentley said, looking worried. "It could be dangerous!"

Big Sue, towering over them all, was stuttering nervously. "May - maybe I should stay here and - and keep things in order -" Then he ran to a bookshelf, whipped the tea towel from each shoulder and began flicking rapidly at the rows of books. Bentley, Stella and Rehd all started talking at once.

"QUIET!" Kimi shouted. The room came back to silence and she stood up, straightened Stella's old jacket, and popped the lock of hair into a small front pocket and zipped it. "Secrets!" she said. "All of you had secrets. Too many secrets!"

"But not one of us knew that," Bentley said. "Well, we knew we had our own but not that *others* -"

"I know that," Kimi said. "I'm not stupid." She slipped the notebook into her inside pocket and started forward. Bentley, Stella and Rehd parted to let her pass. "Come on," Kimi said, and led them to the back wall. She arrived at the touch pad which still glowed red and turned to the group, now stood in a line. Kimi, despite her inner turmoil, couldn't help the breaking smile.

"What's so funny?" Stella said.

The line was size ordered. Big Sue first, less than a

foot from the ceiling, then Bentley, then the smaller Stella, and lastly the smallest; monkey Rehd, his arms trailing the floor. "Nothing," Kimi said. "Secrets," she continued. "All of you had something to hide. Well I don't like it."

"You're only jealous," Stella said jokingly, obviously trying to lighten the mood.

"My point is," Kimi said. "If you'd let me finish. I was going to ask if anyone has any more secrets?"

The line shook its heads all at once. "Well if you do, then now's the time." All heads shook once more. "Good - then erm, then erm-" All eyes were on Kimi. "- then we best erm,"

"Make a plan?" Stella offered.

"If I may," Bentley said, looking to Rehd on the end. "But what's behind this TLC chamber thing?" Bentley pointed to the shimmering wall.

"IPC," Rehd corrected. "Internal Passage Chamber - Balancer Jack says it will take us somewhere deep – real deep."

"Can we set off now?" Stella said, eagerly.

"What else did Dad say?" Kimi asked Rehd.

"That's all," Rehd shrugged.

"Can anyone see any reason not to go straight away?" Kimi asked, fishing the lock of hair from her pocket.

"Yes," Rehd waved a hairy finger. "Before coming here. I heard Adept Blavatsky say you would be summoned soon – they want to do tests. Reckon your mojo's a tad wonky."

"Ach, that'll be right. Typical," Stella said.

"I'm not going," Kimi said.

"But Kimbo," Bentley began.

"End of, Bentley. This is way more important. Old Mrs Potato Head will have to wait!"

"I'm in," Stella said.

"Oh dear!" Bentley said as the line shuffled forward.

"Link arms everyone," Stella said. "Don't want to lose anybody."

Kimi joined Big Sue on the end and took hold of his dressing gown sleeve. She reached carefully to the touch pad, hand trembling a little. "Everyone ready?"

No one answered so she took that as a yes, closed her eyes and swiped the lock of hair across the pad. Nothing seemed to be happening.

"The root - the root!" Rehd shouted from the other end of the line.

"Oh right," Kimi examined the lock of hair, found a good bunch of roots, and once again reached for the touch pad. She took a deep breath. "Ready?"

Unsettled murmurs came back.

"Just do it," said Stella, and so, Kimi closed her eyes and did just that.

———

~ 18 ~

~ KIMI'S SECRET ~

BEEEEEEEEEEEEEEP

Kimi opened her eyes. The touch pad had turned green and the blue light on the wall no longer shimmered. It was crackling into a spiky surface and growing out from the wall. The line shuffled backwards.

"Be still!" Rehd ordered.

The shuffling stopped, replaced by five sharp intakes of breath. Kimi instinctively turned her head as the blue light passed through her, the crackling fading in her ears. A feeling of lightness buoyed her, followed by the unpleasant sensation of being sucked into a hole with a rush of icy coldness. She was floating in shadows, her breath misting the air.

"Wa-hey!" Stella's voice broke the silence. Kimi's hand was sliding up Big Sue's arm. She grabbed it tightly. All five of them were bobbing in a line, five or six feet in the air, and the temperature in here, wherever here was, must have dropped at least twenty degrees from where they'd stood a second ago. Everyone was breathing fog. Kimi's teeth began to chatter. As her eyes became accustomed to the darkness, this room was appearing as vast as the inside of a cathedral.

Far above through a domed glass roof, two crescent moons hung in a star-pricked sky. Something fluttered in the rafters. Crows, Kimi thought, although she couldn't see them for the darkness. Across the immense room in a far corner, a pale yellow light blinked on, illuminating a raised platform holding a bank of computers arranged in a semi-circle. Before them sat a black, bulky figure, which looked pretty much to Kimi like a fat man in a suit.

"Lights!" came the gruff voice of the fat man.

The place did not light up as brightly as Kimi expected. Many rows of tables holding glass cases appeared, spread over the huge floor area, each case lit up inside by a single blue light. The case in front of Kimi contained a stuffed crow on a branch. The taxidermy wasn't so good. The stitches down its breast were crooked and lumpy. Gaps between the tables created a long, meandering pathway to the fat man at the computers. The cases on these tables also appeared to hold stuffed crows.

"Ahem – hello there - don't think you could get us down from here, could you?" Bentley's voice repeated over the vast space.

"I get sick with heights," moaned Stella.

Kimi was about to voice a similar plea when the empty grey wall above the fat man caught her eye. Small, childlike figures appeared to be growing out from it. Kimi counted five emerge. They sucked from the wall and swam in the air above the fat man. She couldn't see much detail from here, but they seemed to be morphing into little clowns with painted faces and white gloves. They tumbled weightlessly in the air before the fat man spoke again.

"Bring the visitors," the gruff voice said, and the clowns all swung to the ground, each effortlessly swiping up a chair, before rejoining the air again. The five clowns drifted over the cases of crows, balancing chairs on heads, shoulders and fingers whilst paddling the air.

"What the heck are they?" Stella said.

No one answered. All eyes were on the floating clowns. They arrived chuckling and swept around behind the bobbing line. Without warning, Kimi's knees bent as the chair slid in and small gloved hands were pushing on her shoulders. She dropped quickly to the ground, the chair legs clattering. Thankfully the seat was padded. More commotion followed as Big Sue's chair crashed down beside Kimi and he gave a whooping shriek. Bentley came next, screaming as he almost fell off. The clown behind him threw himself over the chair and pulled Bentley back on by his ears. Then came Stella's exaggerated yell, which Kimi suspected was done to hear the resulting echoes. And lastly, monkey Rehd's chair came down hard, making him bounce and squeal.

The clowns whizzed around in front and hovered in a line before them, their golden slippers inches from the floor. They all looked identical. Young boys, with faces

271

painted pastel blue and one darker, star-shaped eye, red button noses and cherry red lips turned up into a smile; although Kimi could clearly see that these boys weren't smiling beneath their face paint. Their suits were grubby beige with faded flowers. Each wore a white frilly collar and white gloves. The rip on the pocket of the clown hovering in front of Kimi was repeated on every other clown. They were identical right down to rips and grubby patches.

"Please have a seat!" the clowns all said at once in little boy voices, each gesturing with a sweeping arm. No foggy breath came from the clowns. Kimi guessed they must not be living.

"They're already sitting you buffoons!" came the gruff voice. "The grips! The grips!" The fat man was no longer visible from this new position on the floor, but his voice carried well enough that the birds in the rafters got rattled every time he spoke.

"Please hold the grips!" the clowns all said at once as dust and feathers floated down from above.

Bolts of metal with indented finger grips rose vertically from the chair arms, but nobody made an attempt to hold them. Everyone stared at the clowns. Kimi's heart was beating hard.

"They're gravity chairs," the fat man said. "Take hold of the grips or sit in the rafters with the crows - your choice!" He sounded irritated.

The clowns cocked their heads in unison.

"Do it!" Rehd said, grabbing awkwardly at the grips on his chair.

"Do it!" the clowns repeated, cocking heads the other way.

Stella took hold of the bolts on her chair and the others followed suit. Kimi had somehow expected an electric shock and was mightily relieved to feel only cold metal.

"Seatbelts!" the clowns declared, all of them snapping their fingers.

Metal straps sprang from the arms of every chair and clamped themselves over unsuspecting wrists. The whole line shrieked, startling the clowns who shot to the air in a vertical whoosh. The unseen fat man laughed a thunderous laugh and the birds in the rafters scattered, sending more dust and feathers wafting down. The clowns bent their knees all at once and swiftly somersaulted through the air, landing behind the chairs and turning them quickly so they all faced forwards. Kimi was at the rear, staring at the back of a clown. The line began to move, each chair gliding silently inches from the floor, pushed along by a floating clown.

The line turned into the pathway of lighted cases and Kimi began to count the crows in the cases as they passed by her left and right, but she stopped at nineteen, when up ahead, Stella made gagging sounds and a gasp came from Bentley. She soon found out why. A long wooden table passed slowly by holding a huge glass tank. Its sides were grimy, but she could clearly see what was piled up inside. Human brains. Lots of them, plump and glistening, each connected to a cable, each cable twisting out of the tank and away into the shadows. More gasps came from up front when ornate cages on stands came into view. Half a dozen passed by with skinny grey rodents scratching about inside. Kimi's eyes widened as a little snout twitched through the bars, pale red eyes blinked at her. She noticed little stumps on its shoulders. These weren't rats, they were famoose with their wings cut off. The famoose gave a quiet sniff and the line continued past more cases of badly-stitched crows until eventually arriving below the raised platform and the fat man at the computers.

"Welcome to Paradise," he said, and the clowns in front of Kimi moved their chairs to one side, settling them into a neat line. Bentley was placed nearest the fat man, then Big Sue, then Stella, and lastly, Rehd - they all stared up at the fat man. They looked terrified, especially Big Sue whose fingers twitched madly. The clowns remained motionless behind each chair. Kimi was sat on her own, away from the line and facing the fat man, and was trying desperately to hide her trembling.

"Big cat got your tongues?" the fat man said. His black suit appeared ancient and worn. Thin legs and grimy shoes dangled from an incredibly large belly which seemed to be sitting snugly within a metal ring. The metal ring sat within a circular rail, thereby holding his shoes just off the floor. Behind the man, was a semi-circle of computers. Kimi guessed the rail was a quick way for the fat man to get from one computer to the next. He had no neck that Kimi could see, and a face so wrinkled and mottled with brown spots made him appear more turtle than human. His fat head lifted towards Kimi, though he didn't seem to be looking at her because his eyes stared in opposite directions. And jammed into the sagging skin around one eye was a monocle, which made that particular straying eye so much bigger. "I said - welcome to Paradise!"

"Th-thanks," Kimi said, her teeth still chattering. The others murmured thanks and greetings and all of the clowns gave a lengthy sigh.

"I am Key Adept Charles Babbage," he said. Gloopy strings of saliva slopped from his mouth to an already greasy jacket. "But you can call me, Charlie." His magnified eye stared at Kimi.

"Where are we?" Kimi asked. The clowns shifted their gaze to her.

"You can let us go now," Stella said, straining at the straps around her wrists. The clown behind her placed his hands on her shoulders and Stella went still.

"The straps are necessary," the fat man said. "As I already said, you'll join the crows in the rafters if the straps are removed." He grunted and a dollop of snot dropped from his nose and swung from side to side. The fat man didn't seem to notice. Or care. The clowns gave a throaty snigger which made Kimi shudder. Bentley shuddered back and gave a weak smile.

"You have an awful lot of stuffed crows," Stella said.

The fat man nodded and the snot dropped an inch. "Make a point of stuffing at least twelve a year," he said, sucking the gloop back up his nose. The sound turned Kimi's stomach.

"Shows them who the boss is," Babbage added.

"So you're the boss?" Stella asked in a tone that Kimi would never have dared. She expected the clown to clamp Stella's mouth.

"Shush now, dear," Big Sue whimpered.

The fat man raised a hand. "Your attention please." A greasy wad of saliva spilled over his lip, swung from his jowls, and slapped to the ground beneath his dangling feet. Kimi noticed there was a grate in floor. She imagined a whole river of Babbage's gloop running beneath them. He pulled what looked like a small microphone from his breast pocket, and with his free hand, swung himself along the rail. His gangly legs trailed behind as if they were dead, or not real legs at all. He arrived at the first computer and pressed a few buttons on the keyboard. Above him, the grey wall with the flaking plaster from where the clowns had emerged, lit up. He swung back along the rails and faced Kimi once more, his stick-thin legs swinging. The microphone turned out to be a clicker. He pressed it with a fat thumb and the word; JIFFY appeared on the wall behind him in tall, golden letters.

"I'm going to show you some slides," he said, "but first, headphones!"

From behind their backs each clown pulled a set of golden headphones. Sticking from each earpiece was what looked like a really big drawing pin. The clowns placed headphones on her friends heads in unison. Kimi cringed as hers slid over her ears, but nothing bad happened, at least not until the fat man raised his hand and spoke again.

"Engage!" he said, indicating to the clown behind Bentley. The clown raised a gloved finger and pressed the headband of Bentley's headphones. There was a squeaking sound and the giant drawing pins began to slide into the earpieces. Bentley's eyes went horribly wide and moaning sounds came from his throat as the pins went deeper. As they came to rest flush to the earpieces, Bentley's eyes rolled up into whites, his tongue fell out, and he gave a shudder.

Kimi shuddered back but didn't get a return. Bentley looked deathly still.

Big Sue was whimpering. His fingers twitched so fast. Kimi realised he wanted his tea towels. The clown behind Big Sue had to rise a foot or so in the air to reach a finger to his headphones, but when he did, and the drawing pins began to squeak, Big Sue sobbed and the tears glistened in his beard like dewdrops.

Kimi jumped when the fat man raised a hand and the clown behind Big Sue clapped the drawing pins in quickly. Sue shut up immediately, his eyes rolling up into his head and his tongue hanging out, just as Bentley's had.

The clown behind Stella placed his hands on her shoulders. "Shit!" Stella said, with worried eyes. "Shit!" the clown behind her said, and pressed the band of Stella's headphones. The drawing pins squeaked in and Stella's face went milky white.

Kimi's adrenaline was steaming through her. She wanted to rip free from her cuffs and smack each clown on its cute little nose; wanted to tear into fat bloke too and ask him what he was playing at; wanted to scream out loud and fire mojo from her eyes - but something wasn't right. Her brow, that pulsating throb - was missing.

No mojo.

But still.

"Stop it!" Kimi screamed, first to the clown and then to the fat man. "You're hurting my friends. Stop it now!"

"Has to be done." The fat man nodded and rubbery strings of slobber swung up and stuck to his chin.

Stella moaned and tears pushed from her eyes as the

278

drawing pins slid right in. Her eyes rolled into whites and a small triangle of pink tongue poked through the gap in her teeth.

"Stop this!" Kimi said, now crying. The clown behind Rehd, pressed a finger to his headphones.

"Uh-oh," Rehd said, and the drawing pins sucked in with an effortless rush. Rehd shrieked so loudly that the echo sounded a dozen times, scattering the birds up on high. Rehd slumped forward, only the wrist cuffs preventing him from rolling off the chair.

Kimi swore and screamed, shuffling her chair, fighting against the straps on her wrists. Her fingers flicked rapidly as she tried to fire mojo, to do something, anything, but there was no prickle, no mojo. Clown hands arrived and pressed firmly on her shoulders. Kimi stopped fighting. Sweat trickled down her face. "STOP THIS MADNESS!" she yelled, trying frantically to shake the headphones from her head. The fat man's big eye glared through his monocle. He raised a chubby hand. Kimi screwed up her face, waiting for the pins to squeak - and her heart almost exploded when the clown's hands left her shoulders.

She held her breath, waiting - and then came a sensation of release, as if the headphones had been lifted away. Kimi opened her eyes and shook her head. They were off. The clown's gloved hand came into view, the headphones hooked over an outstretched finger. Kimi panted fog plumes. "Wha - wha - wha -"

"You really need to calm down and pay attention," the fat man said. "Now, where we - ah, yes-" He clicked the clicker and the golden JIFFY on the wall was replaced by an image of a misty swamp. "Merculial Wa-ers," he mumbled, pausing to wipe away a particularly thick blob of slobber, which had grown so heavy it was pulling his lip and impeding his speech. Now it glistened on his sleeve like a giant slug. Kimi gagged.

"Mercurial Waters," he confirmed. He clicked the clicker and the misty swamp was zoomed into. Many pearlescent forms huddled together. They had only the faintest features, but did appear to be mostly happy, some smiling, some in obvious conversation, some sleeping - apart from two. Fat man clicked and the picture zoomed in closer.

"Meet, comedy duo and the bane of my life; Stefan and Ronnie," he slobbered. "Your folks' Tulpas."

Kimi stared at them, partly with fear but mostly with curiosity. She wished they weren't misty like ghosts so she could see what Tulpas Mum and Dad had invoked. These two had their mouths stitched up and didn't look happy but that was about it as far as detail was concerned. "So you silenced them," Kimi said. "Just like you've silenced my friends."

Fat man shook his head and the gloop swung. "Your folks did the silencing, not me. Though I've enjoyed the peace and quiet I must say. Should have done it myself years ago. And believe me, silencing the Tulpas was merely the beginning. Tell me, Kimi Jo Nichols, why do you think you are here?"

"Wu - we followed my dad's clues," Kimi said, in the strongest voice she could muster. "My parents have been killed, and we think we have to make a Jiffy work, then we can go back in time and save them - and we think, well we think that Dad might have left more information with their Tulpas, or another clue - and Dad *said* -"

"No, no, no," the fat man said. "Listen - and pay good heed because what I have to convey is of vital importance – vital! Do you hear?"

Kimi looked at her friends, still and silent in their chairs, and to the motionless clowns behind them, staring at her. She looked back to the fat man. "I'm listening."

"Your quest, Kimi, is not, not, not, to head for Mercurial Waters. Your clever father calculated that you would come to this conclusion, but of course, for reasons of security both his and your mother's Tulpas had to be silenced."

Kimi suddenly realised what *two* retired Tulpas meant, and the fat man must have seen the horror in her face.

"Spit it out," he said. "We haven't got all day."

"It's - it's just, well - if two Tulpas have retired, then that - that means there definitely was two deaths."

"What?" The fat man looked puzzled.

"The crow, it said `one death` when this all started - when it flew into the patio doors. *One death today,* it said, but if there's two Tulpas then -"

"Never mind bloody crows," Babbage said. He clicked the clicker with a sharp jab and an old black and white photograph of her father filled the wall. He wore a cricket jumper, a white smile, and had a big wave of hair.

"Some twenty-three years ago," the fat man began, "a handsome young Balancer came tugging my coattails, expressing a desire to learn more of my famous calculations. For that has been my life, you see - *calculating.*"

`Click` and the picture changed. A younger, slimmer, Babbage, posed beside a strange looking machine the size of a shed. It seemed to be made up of pistons, levers and buttons.

"This, is the Difference Machine - entirely mechanical," Babbage said. "My prototype for Earth's first calculator."

"Big calculator," Kimi said.

"Yes it is. It's over there, somewhere, covered in dust," he nodded towards the mass of cased birds. "Anyway, I did a foolish thing and turned this young Balancer away. Thought his interfering would bring zero to my already superior brain. That he'd only be a drain and a hindrance. He objected of course. Gabbled on about time travel and how

282

his mojo and my calculus could be a perfect marriage; the key to time and space itself he said. But I brushed him aside - sent the rascal packing."

"You did?"

Babbage grunted. More snot joined the pile on the floor and rolled down the grate.

"Many years later," he went on, pausing to add another slug to his sleeve. "On the 13th April, 1993, to be precise, a Bellamy's Aunt appeared from thin air and dropped onto my breakfast plate - are you familiar with the Bellamy's Aunt?"

"Yeah," Kimi nodded.

`Click` and on the wall appeared an old photograph of a giant toad on a plate with egg and beans splatted out from beneath it. "The toad was pale, shivering and barely alive. I found a scroll of paper tied round its neck and removed it seconds before the creature turned inside out." `Click` and the picture on the wall showed a plate full of bones and crimson innards. Blood ran into the eggs and beans.

Kimi gagged again.

"At first, of course, I assumed some dark and dangerous mojo was at work. Either that or someone was trying to make a fool of me. Because I have always had my objectors as any genius does. But then I found the note on the scroll and immediately I knew -"

`Click`

Attempt 403

Intended for the table of ACB

DOS 13th April 1994

If successful, contact Balancer Nichols at the Rabbit's Foot.

"Wow," Kimi said, her pulse racing.

"Yes wow," Babbage said. "Your father's note had to be slightly cryptic of course, but it didn't take long to work out that *DOS* meant *Date-Of-Sending*. Somehow, he had figured out how to send this toad back in time by exactly one year, and that, my dear was the beginning of a long and rewarding relationship. I consider your father, and your wonderful mother, my greatest friends."

"I see," Kimi said.

"And so did I," Babbage said. "For many years we calculated. Calculate, calculate, calculate. This man's genius brought me great hope. My studies took off on fresh, exciting tangents, buffeted along by your father's infectious enthusiasm. Now, tell me what you see-"

`Click`

Kimi examined the new picture on the wall. "Erm, a pea, a paperclip, a marble and a ladybird."

"And what do they have in common?"

"They're all little?"

"Yes, but not only that, Kimi - they all travelled

284

back in time to within one inch and one second of their target. After many years of calculating and achieving little but misplaced objects and inside-out amphibians, we eventually succeeded in discovering the final ingredient." He leaned forward and gloop spilled over his lip and rolled into his shirt pocket. "Can you guess what that ingredient might be, Kimi?"

Kimi shook her head.

"DNA is the answer, Kimi. But not just any DNA, no, these marvellous little items succeeded in flying through time without fault or hindrance because of *your* DNA, Kimi Jo Nichols."

"My DNA?"

Babbage nodded and dropped more slobber. "Every time we sent an item with a single root of your hair attached, the bounder succeeded, whereas those without your DNA attached, would not."

`Click` and this picture showed a squashed pea, a bent paperclip, a cracked marble and a lump of yellow mush with spotted wings that Kimi guessed might be an inside-out ladybird.

"Oh," she said, and the clowns sniggered.

`Click` A head and shoulders image of Kimi's mum filled the wall. She was bright and smiling. Kimi had to bite her lip.

"Three days ago," Babbage said. "Right here in this

room, your mother and father were enjoying a slow dance to Ravel's Bolero; it is the most wonderful rising crescendo, Kimi. One of our favourites. The finale was near, every instrument joining the beat. Your mother and father, aided by the low gravity and Separation techniques, were almost in the rafters. Then something terrible happened. Your poor mother had a skeppy. Now a skeppy, Kimi, is the most real of visions. Skeppies are rare for even the most prolific of seers. When you have a skeppy, you don't just see glimpses of what might be, you live the scene as if you were in it. Your poor mother dropped to the floor with an awful cry, and after a few worrying moments of deathly stillness, as if she had taken leave of her body and left a statue in its place, she returned to the living, sobbing hysterically."

"She did?" Kimi was absorbed in his words and almost not seeing the snot swinging from his chin.

"Your father was in a state. He eventually calmed your mother and she recalled the skeppy. She was on a golf course. Your father was also there, reading a note. There was a crow on the flagpole. The air turned and the next second they were running before being blown apart by a thunderbolt!"

Kimi gasped. "Was that it? Was that all she said?"

"No. Before everything went dark and the skeppy was over, your mother was insistent that she'd seen at least three shuck peering from the bushes."

"Big cats - yes," Kimi said. "I've seen them on the disc at the library - they were caught on the cctv."

"Really?" Two small bubbles blew from Babbage's right nostril and drifted to the floor. "My intelligence is yet to report. That's good then," he said, nodding more snot to his jacket. "You see, Kimi, we knew that if shuck were present, then so would be a thimblerigger."

"A thimble-whaty?"

"A charlatan, a flimflam man, a trickster. Such beasts are like magnets to the shuck. Your father always feared this; always spoke of safeguarding the treasures of our work. Because that's what they are Kimi - treasures - especially valuable to those who would choose the wrong path."

"But who?"

"I don't know that," Babbage said. "But what I do know, is that an hour after your mother's unfortunate skeppy, your father received a note, delivered by a crow."

`Click`

BALANCER PAJACKOK - BE AT THE FIRST HOLE AT GALA GOLF AT PRECISELY 10:00 AM ON SATURDAY - BE PRESENT WITH WIFE AND DAUGHTER - FAILURE TO COMPLY WILL RESULT IN RANDOM DEATHS - ONE FAMILY WILL BE ELIMINATED FOR EVERY FIVE MINUTES YOU ARE LATE - DON'T BRING THE FUZZ!

"That's not the note, Dad had -"

"Of course not. He wrote a different note to show you. We knew two things, Kimi. Time was an important commodity, but it was also against us. We had to move quickly and tough decisions had to be made. Your father was certain that we could pull this off - your mother not so - she feared for you, of course."

Kimi's heart fluttered.

"Balvalerie, bless her, knew we were right, that they would need to turn up to their deaths."

"But why? And why not me? Why did they have to be killed?"

"Your distraught mother agreed to be hypnotised. Your father took control. He made up a false note and made sure you would stay at home. We placed the clues and engaged those we could trust -" he indicated to her motionless friends and the clowns behind them did a little tap dance and made jazz hands. "- and now you are here, preparing for the task ahead."

"So you sent Bentley to get me?"

"Not me," Babbage said. "But it was in your father's calculations. He knew that, allowing for the time difference between Heart space and Earth space, you would be rescued within a few Earth minutes. He also knew that his and your mother's deaths would bring death cries from their Tulpas.

When a Tulpa dies the whole of Heart hears the death cry, and so the Adepts would be instantly investigating. They would learn that you were home alone and they would despatch a greylian craft to abduct you. Abduction by greylian is a little painful though, so your father bargained on your loyal Tulpa to intervene." Babbage paused while his mouth emptied with a glug and sheened his suit. "And intervene he did, begging the Adepts to let him try and coax you here by your own free will."

Kimi looked to the motionless Bentley. "I didn't make it easy for him did I?"

"No matter," Babbage said. "You're here now, just as your father knew you would be, preparing for the task ahead."

"Which is?"

"You have the ingredients for time travel, do you not?"

Kimi nodded to her jacket. "Well, I've got the notebook."

"Opposing twirlies to the correct volume and velocity pertaining to the size of object to travel?"

Kimi nodded. "Well, yeah, I suppose, it's all in the notebook."

"Not forgetting of course, the vitally precise forty-six degree, angle of entry?"

"Erm, no -" Kimi remembered. "Forty-two - yes, it's

forty-two degrees."

Babbage smiled. "Just checking!"

She smiled back.

"Then you know what you must do," Babbage went on. "We need to get you back through time to the precise location just before the lightning...*or the mojo*...strikes, so that you can prevent it from happening in the first place. However, the speed and accuracy required to take you through the opposing twirlies can only be achieved by a greylian craft."

"Okay."

"Listen, Kimi. General Cohn is due back in Middling next weekend for his festival, but that is too long to wait. You must visit Cohn, and persuade him to loan you a pilot and a ship. His craft have the speed and computer power to ensure success. We plug you in and presto! You arrive back in time above the golf course, the pilot drops ship and whisks your folks to safety with its abductor beam - situation saved - and also the murderer – if there is one - will no doubt reveal himself at this point."

"You're kidding," Kimi said, glancing at the others slumped in their chairs.

"Don't worry about your friends, Kimi," Babbage said, sniffing up snot. "Do you think you can achieve such a feat?"

"Can't we just phone the General?"

Babbage laughed. "Greylians don't do phones - or visits come to that."

"But what if I go back in time and turn inside out like the toad?"

Babbage shook his head. "Turning inside out only happens to those things not pure - so that is not a concern. Though what is a concern, is the Doppelganger Paradox - to the very best of calculation that your father and I could fathom, arriving back at the correct place and time depends solely on your thinking - your thought process is the driver - you think of the golf course and the time you wish to arrive and that is undoubtedly where you will jump to - you must not think of your other self during this process or the Doppelganger Paradox will initiate - you will find further explanation within the notebook. I suggest you study it!"

"But what about the toad and the crow I turned inside out? Is that something to do with the paradox thing?"

"You did what?"

"When Bentley brought me here – to Heart I mean – we were chased by crows. We hid in Doyle's Den. Bentley was teaching me to do stunners and these big toads came. They seemed to enjoy it. Afterwards, I patted some of them, but one wobbled horribly and turned inside out. I killed it. Then I did the same thing to a crow."

Babbage was nodding.

"Then when Rehd arrived, he came close and I felt a

pull like a magnet, and I knew I had to step back."

"Astounding," Babbage said. "And what about the others, does anyone else suggest a magnetic pull?"

"Yes, Perry. He works at the-"

"Yes, Kimi, I know the boy."

"And chief Rehd said hundreds were sick – experiencing wobbling."

"That's true. Your father and I figured for such a thing. Time is a great mystery, Kimi. Your father suggested that if the mission ahead is successful, and we change the past to create a new future, then there will be some disruption apparent before the event takes place. It seems, Kimi, that the Jiffy does go ahead. Those people experiencing the wobbles were accounted for in our calculations. Though why any creature might wobble so badly that they turn inside out when touched by you, the one who changes time, is beyond me."

"So you don't know?"

"No."

"But what if I kill someone?"

"That's a risk we'll have to take. There's too much at stake here, Kimi. Let us be grateful that this wobbling evidence is apparent. At least we know that the Jiffy worked. Or will work."

"It - it all sounds scary," Kimi said.

"Yes it does, but we don't have a choice. Simply

ensure that you don't go bumping into yourself and you'll be fine."

"If I do meet myself, I guess I wobble and turn inside out?"

"We tested that on a Bellamy's Aunt." Babbage said. "Sent it back to meet itself. Both toads' eyes exploded then the things began to shrivel. Nothing left but two lumps of skin. But you'll be fine. If you see yourself, be sure to run the other way."

"I'm not sure I can do this." Kimi wished she was really back in time - like five years ago.

Babbage nodded and dropped more snot. "I understand your trepidation," he said. "But you must understand that *you* are the only one who can pull this off." He reached for the rail at his bulging waistline and unclipped what Kimi had thought were braces. The top half of his body began to rise leaving the legs behind. Those legs were false after all. He kept on rising until he had floated completely out of his trousers. All of the clowns turned away. Kimi stared in disbelief. The bottom half of this man was rounded like a spacehopper. There was no evidence of any legs, only lumps, spidery hairs and the odd boil, oozing with puss. Babbage grabbed the chrome rail and his rounded base came down to rest, squashing over its sides. He reached up, removed his monocle and shook his head. Kimi yelped as Babbage's eyes fell from their sockets and swung on his cheeks by their optic nerves. Then came a crack as his jaw dislocated and a waterfall of gloop gushed down his front. This horrible monstrosity sat there gurgling for a few seconds with its eyeballs swinging before another splurge of saliva spilled from its twisted mouth. Kimi was nearly sick.

Babbage dragged himself off the rail and dropped back into the trousers. He fastened the clips, shook his jaw back into place, threw his head back to get the eyes back into their sockets, helped them in with his thumbs, and re-fixed his monocle.

"*That* is the unfortunate result of too much time travel without enough purity," he said. "I cannot risk another jump. I must remain here, bound by my disgusting disfigurations. But you, Balancer Nichols, *can* do this. Of that much I am sure - and so was your father. Would you agree?"

"I – I hope so, sir," Kimi said.

"One last thing. There's a secret. Can you guess what that secret might be?"

Kimi shook her head.

"Why do you think your friends are skewered so?" Babbage asked.

She looked at her statuesque friends with the drawing pins still firmly embedded in their brains, their eyes white and their tongues poking out. "I - I don't know."

"Selective hearing!" he said. "They will come out of

294

this remembering only what we need them to." He pressed the clicker again and an ancient map appeared on the wall. On it were drawings like cave paintings showing headdresses and totem poles and arrow heads and weird looking names like *Pennacook*, *Cheyenne*, *Kickapoo*, *Micmac*, *Sac* and *Fox*.

"Your heritage," Babbage said. "You come from the ancient natives of America, Kimi. The peoples of the Algonquin - the earliest Balancers!"

`Click` and the screen zoomed in on one tribal name:

KICKAPOO

"Your father is a pure from a pure from a long line of pures. Your mother also. Therefore you, Balancer Nichols of the Kickapoo tribe, could not get any purer."

"Kickapoo?" Kimi said, a little disgruntled. "I'm a bloody Kickapoo?"

"You derive from that tribe, yes. Your name, *Kimi*, means `secret` and my, what a delicious thing fate is to bring you such a name. We realised you see, your father and I, that purity of thought is the final thing - the thing existing at the very end - the very last calculation!"

"Erm -"

"Your friends are skewered for reasons of secrecy and security. Once released from the headsets - your father's invention by the way - they will remember everything about our conversation apart from one single fact - and that is?"

"The purity?"

"That's correct," Babbage said. "You must never reveal that *you* are the secret ingredient. It is imperative that you persuade your friends, and General Cohn, that you must be the one to travel with the pilot, but you must not divulge the reason why. After all, nobody likes a bragger do they?"

Kimi shook her head.

"Your father and I reached the conclusion that such disclosure would dilute the power of your purity. Does that make sense?"

"I suppose it does," Kimi said.

"Not a word then," Babbage said. He raised his hand once more and the clowns pressed fingers to the tops of headsets, drawing pins squeaked back out and the headsets were whipped away.

"Interesting!" Big Sue said, as his eyes rolled back into view and his fingers twitched for his tea towels once more.

"Yes, very," Bentley said, shaking his head which brought squelching sounds.

Stella's head raised from her chest. She yawned and blinked her eyes before focusing on Kimi. "Well, well," she said. "Kickapoo? Couldn't you just crap a clown!"

A small hiccough escaped from Kimi's mouth. When she realised it was actually a laugh, she laughed again. It seemed to be infectious. Stella hee-hee'd, Bentley chuckled, Big Sue's shoulders jigged as he whooped, Rehd made ooh-ooh sounds and his head shook vigorously, and the clowns behind joined hands and started body popping. This made Kimi laugh harder. Even Babbage's grotesque features had broken into a grin. Tears soaked Kimi's cheeks and her ribs ached - she'd become accustomed to that of late, but never accompanied by such a warm feeling. She smiled at her friends, bizarre though they looked, strapped into chairs with a dancing clown for company, every one of them had happy faces. There was no longer coldness in this vast room.

"So," Stella began as the laughter subsided. "It's greylians we're after - how the hell do we get there?"

"Easy," Rehd said. "Now I know why Balancer Jack needed Rehd." He grinned at the others. "I can get us a short cut through Bridgetown."

Kimi thought he already knew that. The headphones must have done something to their memories. She'd have to remember to tell Dad.

"Got it in one," Babbage said, dribbling more gloop. "Now, here in a nutshell are your individual mission tasks - read and memorise lest we might fail!" The fat Adept turned in his trousers to look at the wall. He read aloud from the instructions;

`Click`

1) Big Sue:

Feed the troops for the journey.

Stay at home and keep lookout.

Anything out of the ordinary - report to Charlie.

"Good idea," Big Sue said. "I'll get some sandwiches made up."

`Click`

2) Bentley:

Guard the troop with your whole being.

Ensure by any means that Kimi gets into the mission craft.

Oversee twirly operations.

Good man!

Kimi was pleased to see old Bentley nodding with a determined look on his face.

`Click`

3) Rehd:

Gain passage through Bridgetown.

Safeguard the aim of the mission.

And get Kimi into that craft!

"Figures," nodded Rehd.

`Click`

4) Stella:

IF YOU CAN'T BE GOOD, BE CAREFUL

"Ach - away wi' yer," Stella laughed, and so did Kimi. Okay it wasn't much of a joke, but it was humour - Dad's humour. She could see him grinning as he wrote it.

"One last one," Babbage said. They all stared at the wall.

`Click`

5) Kimi:

Do what you have to do and we'll see you in a Jiffy! Love you lots, Mum and Dad xx

Kimi managed to read it three times before the click came again and the wall went blank. Then she let her breath out. "Okay then," she said, blinking her eyes clear. "When do we go?"

"I need one hour," Rehd said. "To explain absence and secure a decent bribe for our troll friends."

"What would everyone like in their sandwiches?" Big Sue asked.

"How exciting is this," Stella said. "A real mission!"

"Hang fire," Bentley said. "Hasn't everybody forgotten something?" All eyes were now on Bentley. "How, for the love of bafflecakes, do you think we can safely travel half way round Heart with every crow and its mother after Kimi's eyeballs?"

"Good point," Rehd said.

The others chorused agreement. But not Babbage. Babbage was snorting snot. When the gloop had cleared from his nostrils, he looked up and said: "I thought you'd never ask." He nodded to the clown hovering behind Big Sue. The clown summersaulted backwards into the shadows and came springing back seconds later holding what looked like a bread basket. Sitting in a nest of crumpled green napkins was a crow. There was blood on its head, though it appeared to be asleep.

"That's my crow," Kimi said.

"Of course it is," Babbage slobbered. "It came to me for help."

"And you're going to stuff it, right?" Kimi said. Babbage sighed. "Now that's a nice thought, Kimi, but it's never going to happen. You see, Audrey here-"

"It's got a name?" Kimi said.

"Of course it has name, Kimi. As I was about to tell you, poor Audrey cannot die. She is exhausted, at death's door you might say. But death's door cannot open until it is meant to."

"The prophecy crow," Bentley said. "It's been niggling me all along."

"Yes," Babbage said. "Audrey prophesised one

death, and despite the evidence pointing towards two deaths, I suspect that time is waiting for your presence, Kimi. Only then can the prophecy conclude."

"My death?" Kimi said. "It's going to be me, isn't it?"

Bentley looked worried. In fact, Big Sue, Stella, even Rehd, they all looked glum.

Babbage breathed heavily. His wayward eyes gazed around the vastness before he spoke again. "I have brains in tanks, Kimi. And famoose with clipped wings." He smiled and spilled some spit. "Do you trust me, Kimi?"

Kimi hesitated. "I – I think so."

Babbage said: "The brains in that tank were donated by Balancers gone. Long gone. But they're still alive, Kimi. Kept alive, by me, until advances can be made to restore their bodies. The wingless famoose are here to be cured. Wing disease has caused theirs to fall. My miraculous potions, aided by my lair's low gravity, will give them back their wings. Know that you can trust me, Kimi, and that what I am about to tell you is the truth, the whole truth. I do not know who the one death relates to. Prophecies can be fickle things, you know. It could be something as simple as Audrey's own death; the circle of time demanding its completion before the old bird can burst into flames and enjoy her passing. It may not be simple at all. You may only manage to save one of your parents. If this alleged lightning

301

strike turns out to be mojo, and your killer is up a tree, then it may be the killer who gets his comeuppance." A gurgle then a gush of fresh saliva spilled down Babbage's front. He sighed. "Talking too much," he said.

"So what do I do?" Kimi said.

"You take Audrey with you."

Bentley coughed. "I have no problem trusting you, Adept Babbage, but this crow set whole armies on us. How can it be trusted?"

The others murmured agreement.

Babbage licked his lips. "We've made a deal," he said. "Audrey has called off the crows on condition that when Kimi secures a greylian craft and the Jiffy is executed, then she must travel too."

Bentley was nodding. "No crows sure makes things a lot easier."

Babbage looked to Kimi. "Can you see any problem, Balancer Nichols?"

Kimi shrugged. "S'pose not."

"Good." He nodded to the clown holding the crow and the clown did a double flip, landed before Kimi, and handed her the basket. The crow was breathing but remained asleep – or unconscious, Kimi wasn't sure.

"One last thing Balancer Nichols," Babbage said. He clicked the clicker and the image of a rifle appeared on the wall. "Tell me what you see."

"A rifle," Kimi said.

"Correct." He clicked again and the image turned to face Kimi so that she was looking down its barrel. "Now what do you see."

"Erm, I can see down the barrel."

"And what is inside the barrel?" Babbage coughed. A snot bubble grew from his nose and burst leaving a sticky film on his monocle. His tongue came right out and licked it clean. Stella made a gagging sound. Kimi kept a straight face.

"Damned bogies," Babbage said. "Sorry about that. Now, tell me what you can see, Kimi."

Inside the barrel was a series of scored lines or grooves which appeared to run in spirals. "I can see funny, whirly line things," Kimi said.

Babbage nodded and Kimi was sure she heard him fart. "Helical grooves cut into the barrel, Kimi. Do you know why?"

"I know," Rehd said, after seeing Kimi shake her head. "Improves accuracy. Keeps the bullet in a straight line."

"Those whirly lines," Babbage said, "impart a spin to the bullet. The spinning bullet holds itself true – more focused, you might say, than a bullet flung out with no focus. Now Kimi, hold out your left hand."

The strap around Kimi's wrist clicked open and sank

303

back into the arm of the chair. Kimi held out Little Hand.

"The grooves on your hand, Kimi. Do you know what they are?"

"I – I know they happened before I was born."

"That's right. Your hand was constricted within your mother's womb, leaving grooves or indentations where tissue had been pressed against them. Your father calculated something else, Kimi. And I must say it is pure genius. I want you to ready yourself." He clicked the clicker and the image on the wall above his head changed to a small dartboard. "A Balancer, will, on most occasions, use the index finger to direct his mojo."

"Ahhhhh," Bentley was saying. "Genius!" He was nodding his head.

"On the count of three," Babbage went on. "I want you to project the most powerful blast you can, Kimi. And I want you to hit the bull's-eye."

The red bull's-eye on the dart board was a very small target. Little Hand pulsed and Kimi's heart seemed to jump into gear along with it. "I – I don't think I should," she said.

Babbage smiled. "A little bird told me that your mojo tends to fly off in all directions, Kimi. Now, look at your hand, clasp your fingers and thumb together as tightly as you can and force them to a point."

Kimi did as he asked. With her fingers and thumb

pressed as tightly together as she could get them, the grooves lined up, forming an almost continuous curve from her wrist and around her hand to her fingertips. "It looks a little like inside the rifle."

"Absolutely, Kimi. Your father believes that firing from the wrist will force your mojo to go spiralling around your inbuilt grooves, and that you, Balancer Nichols, will become the hottest shot on Heart."

"Genius," Rehd said.

"That's what I said," Bentley said.

"Wow!" Stella said. "Just wow!"

Big Sue looked worried.

"Go on then," Babbage said. "Take out the bull's-eye." He made an `O` with the thumb and forefinger of his right hand and held it above his head. "I want you to shoot it through here."

Kimi looked to Bentley, unsure whether his look was one of approval or concern.

"Your father will be right," Babbage said. "Focus from the wrist, imagine a pencil-thin stream of mojo flowing around your wrist and direct it straight through my thumb and finger and into the dartboard - the bull's-eye. You can do this!"

Little Hand was buzzing. Kimi glanced at the indentations. "There might be a problem," she said. Babbage brought his hand down.

"When I was with Adept Blavatsky," Kimi went on. "The alien made my hand change, and the grooves went black and -"

"Yes, the cortell," Babbage said. "That same little bird reported that you might have corvine connections. What of it?"

"Well, the grooves in my hand went black, and when my hand changed, it felt like-" Kimi swallowed, "-it felt like that's where the claw came from – from the grooves, as if – oh, I don't really know how to explain it."

Babbage smiled and added more gloop to his right shoe. "Legend says, Kimi, that corvine warriors are the greatest of all warriors. If you've crow in you, then that is something to be celebrated."

"Oh," Kimi said.

Babbage remade the `O` and held his hand above his head. "Now, Balancer Nichols, focus on producing the thinnest beam of mojo, use those grooves, and take out the bull's-eye."

Kimi pointed Little Hand towards Babbage's hand. She closed her eyes, clasped her fingers and thumb as tightly as she could, imagined a pencil-thin stream of perfect mojo, thought of its course and the target, and opened her eyes. There was a zipping sound as the brightest stream of purple mojo spiralled round the grooves and shot from her fingertips, through Babbage's `O` and burnt a hole through the bulls'-eye.

Big Sue yelped. The others cheered. The clowns applauded.

Babbage smiled. "You have an exceptional addition to your Balancing armoury, Kimi. Use it well."

"I will, sir," Kimi said, her heart beating soundly. "I will."

"Now remember, all of you, be very discreet," Babbage said. "If any Adepts find out about this mission, they'll put a stop to it immediately. Good luck!" He raised a hand. At that, the clowns formed the chairs into a line once more and off they went, Kimi in front this time, meandering through the cases of crows and the cages with wingless famoose and the glass tank stuffed with brains.

They arrived back at the wall and the clowns turned the chairs to face it. "Goodbye!" the clowns all said together and the chairs were tipped forward into a momentary blink of crackling blue and the workshop's floorboards came up fast to the sounds of knees cracking off them - apart from Rehd, who had screwed into a ball and rolled comfortably up the room.

"Ach, I'll have to remember that move," Stella said, rubbing her knees.

Kimi was on *her* knees holding the basket with the sleepy crow still installed.

Bentley was helping up Big Sue, who seemed to have taken the hardest knock.

"I'm fine, I'm fine," he said. "Oh, what a rush!"

"So what now?" Bentley asked.

"Hem," Rehd coughed. He was stood on one of the desks. "Like I said, I need an hour to explain my absence and secure the bribe."

"Good," Big Sue said. "I'll go prepare some food. You need your energy up before you go."

"So what can me and Kimi do?" Stella asked.

Rehd shrugged. "Be ready to leave in one hour."

Stella rushed over to Kimi, rubbing her hands. "We've a whole hour to kill!"

Kimi guessed what was coming. "New jacket?"

Stella's eyes lit up. "Aye! And you can't argue. We're going in the field and you can't do that without your field jacket."

"It's alright," Bentley said. "I'll stay here and look after the crow."

"Audrey, you mean," Kimi said.

"Right. Audrey." Bentley took the basket from Kimi.

Kimi couldn't help but smile. She had hope. No, *more* than that; Dad was behind all this. And if it wasn't for Mum's vision, Kimi realised she wouldn't be here at all. She also realised that the plaque had vanished. Her parents were with her now.

———

~ 19 ~

~ Mr Purse ~

"The new version's got double buckles on all the straps," Stella said. They had arrived at the ring road to a warm blaze of setting sunshine and not a crow in sight.

"Looks like Babbage was right, the crows have gone," Kimi said, scanning the trees and almost getting run over by an old woman in some a chrome buggy.

"Watch your toes, youngin!" the woman shouted, sunlight glinting off the mudguards as she trundled by. Kimi gazed after the woman, wondering if what Babbage said about the purity was true. Surely there were other Balancers with the purity thing who could do this mission a million times better than she could. Maybe even relatives could be a match.

"You okay?" Stella was tugging at her arm.

"Yeah, yeah," Kimi said, continuing across the ring road, smiling at those who smiled at her. "There's some freaky Tulpas round here," she whispered as a six foot cat in a top hat sauntered by on his hind legs. He tipped his hat and winked.

"Aye there is," Stella said, quickly adding; "watch it, sister!" as she dragged Kimi out of the way of a trio of squad bikes zipping by. "Your first mission hasn't even started and you're going to get yourself killed!"

"Sorry," Kimi said, allowing Stella to pull her to the safety of a standing stone on the edge of Pommy Wood. The wood was a quilt of purple and yellow leaves, its trees bare but for the many lanterns. "What if Blavatsky's looking for me?"

"Don't worry about her," Stella laughed. "She's not left the Shed since I've been here. Worst she'd do is send a monkey looking, but I'm sure Rehd'd get you out of that one. Come on, let's twirly across the wood. It's quicker, and saves being spotted."

"Teach me how." Kimi took a step forward to show willing.

Stella paused for a moment, eyeing the people going about their business on the ring road. "Nah," she said. "We don't want to attract attention."

"Like who's gonna care," Kimi protested. "Look, we go a little further into the wood, hide behind some trees, twirly from there, and we can be at the other side in, erm – a jiffy."

"There's no time to teach you. It takes a lot of practice. Do it wrong, like most newbies, and you either end up puking or twirling your clothes right off. I will after the mission though." Stella pulled Kimi behind a thick bramble patch. She glanced around before whisking the air. Purple and yellow leaves swirled into a neat vortex, just big enough for them both to fit. Stella took Kimi's hand and pulled her inside. The groaning sound came and immediately went, there was barely a fizzle, only a blink of white, then the leaves dropped to the ground and they'd reached the other side of the wood.

"This way," Stella said, starting through the trees for the ring road.

Kimi ran after her. "About the mission," she said. "I - well, I think -"

"Stop your worrying," Stella said. "Just think of it as any old mission."

"But that's just the point," Kimi said. "I've never done a mission, so how the heck can I think of it as any old one."

Stella put an arm around her shoulder as they came to the wood's edge. "Listen," she said, pulling Kimi behind one of the huge stones. "You have to go and meet the trolls - if Rehd's bribe isn't right, they might torture you; if you smell sweet enough, they might eat you; if, by some miracle, the trolls let us pass, then the trip through the black hole at the end of their canal might kill you."

"Black hole?"

"Aye."

"A real black-holey type thing?"

"Aye - and if you're still alive after that, you have to persuade the greylians to lend you a spaceship, which they might if they're in a good mood, but then again, the brains of an underage Balancer just might be more appealing. And *if*, just *if*, the greylians are favourable, and *if* the Jiffy thing works, and *if*-"

"All right, all right, enough," Kimi said. "You're not really helping."

"Don't be scared," Stella said. "You've got a good team behind you. When we succeed," Stella said this with fierce determination in her eyes, "and all this gets out - remember that statue at the end of the lane? There's a statue of a famous Balancer at the end of almost every street in Middling, more up the ridges, and a dozen more dotted about the wood here. Where would you like your statue, Kimi? You'll be a hero, Kimi - a hero!"

Kimi could imagine such a statue, only it was a joint one of her and Stella, and Bentley was there, posing all brave; and Sue, waving a tea towel; and Rehd, probably on a stool; and Mum and Dad, and maybe even weirdo Babbage and his clowns. "It's still a heck of a mission though," Kimi said. "Have you ever done anything like this before?"

"Ach, we save old missions for campfires. Can you just go with the flow?"

"Okay, I'll try."

They stepped onto the ring road in shadow. The sun was setting fast. A young man in a smart suit danced by, singing merrily but badly out of tune.

"Is he drunk?" Kimi asked.

"Wounded in action," Stella said. "Sings and dances from the minute he gets up until his head hits the pillow. Must go round the ring road fifty times a day. Can't remember his name. He's happy here, I guess, but he'll never work again."

Two old men, side by side in chrome buggies, trundled by, chatting and laughing with each other. Kimi noticed the walking sticks propped against their knees. And the scars on their faces. And the fact they each only had one arm. *And* that one wore an eye patch. It seemed to Kimi, that being a Balancer meant getting hurt.

"Ach!" Stella was pulling her by the arm. "Quit thinking about it. Look - we're here."

`Karnaby Street.` proclaimed a colourful banner strung across the narrow street. Multi-coloured bunting zigzagged all the way down. People and Tulpas wandered from shop to shop and the air had a pleasant smell to it - like leather and chocolate. Steps took them from the ring road down to street level, where stood one of those colourful seaside organs with chrome pipes poking from its top. Gilded green panels with painted balloons decorated the front. It looked antique, and as they drew closer, so did the old man at its side; white-haired, a grey wrinkled face and dressed only in a sack. Kimi's eyes didn't stay on him for long. She stopped dead and grabbed hold of Stella when she noticed the creature hunched on a shelf by the side of the organ.

"What the heck is that?" she whispered without moving her lips. The creature must have heard because it's head twitched. A long hooked nose curved down over a wide mouth and a pointed ear flopped out from under a purple beret. The creature stood up and bowed, its lean arms and legs had the look of silvery blue rubber and it was naked, apart from a red ribbon around the waist which was tied at the front in a bow.

"It's a piskie," Stella said.

The creature raised its head and stared at Kimi with protuberant white eyes.

"He's blind," Stella added.

"A piskie?" Kimi stared, transfixed by this thing. "Cornish piskies are real?"

"Nope - they're French. Any spotted in Cornwall, came over on the ferry. Come and see." She dragged Kimi to the organ.

"Spare an old man some mojo?" the man in the sack said. He took some sort of long glass sabre from a hole in the organ and held it out to Stella.

"Ach, why not." Stella took a thumb and forefinger and pinged the glass. The sabre glowed electric blue.

"Merci!" the piskie said, and began turning the handle rapidly. The old man poked the glass sabre back into

314

the hole in the organ's side and the pipes on top began to tremble.

Phut - phut - phut - oily blue flares shot from the pipes, forming a ghostly display of a horse on its hind legs, and there was Stella on its back and waving a sword to the sound of bagpipes, while men in the background with bloodied faces held shields to the air in victory. "Wahey!" Stella cheered and clapped. The piskie slowed and the image misted and vanished back into the pipes.

"You're so kind," the old man said, admiring the sabre which now carried a faint blue glow.

"Bonjour," the piskie said in a deep, smooth voice. He stood up to his full height and bowed to Kimi. "Will Madame be doing zee pinging?"

"Zee what?" Kimi said.

"This is Barry," Stella said, indicating the old man. "He's lost his mojo. Ping the glass and you donate. Old Marcel, here," she pointed to the smiling piskie, "he grinds his magic handle and part of your donation creates a display from the pipes - and the rest, Barry gets to keep for himself."

Kimi couldn't think what use donated mojo might be, but couldn't resist a ping. Marcel had sat back down and was filing his long nails into points.

"Okay, what do I do?" Kimi said, wondering what her image would be. "Do I focus on something or?"

"Nothing," Stella said. "Just clear your mind and

315

ping the glass."

The old man swung the sabre toward Kimi. Marcel put the nail file down and assumed position at the handle. Kimi tried to think of nothing, brought her thumb and finger together and pinged the glass.

Fierce orange light filled the sabre and it glowed hotly. The old man's face lit up. He quickly poked the sabre into the organ's hole and Marcel began turning the handle. Once more the pipes on top trembled - then they rumbled.

BANG - BANG - BANG - orange crows shot like rockets into the air, spreading their wings into a fiery display. Then BANG - BANG - BANG - as more and more crows erupted from the pipes, accompanied by the thumping tune of the Ting Tings singing `that's not my name`.

By now, quite a large space in the air above Karnaby Street was alight with a spectacular display of fiery crows, and Stella was dancing along to the music. Marcel's pointed ears had pressed themselves flat and his hands went faster and faster on the handle, so fast that Kimi thought his arms might snap any second. The old man was holding his hands to the air and laughing out loud. A crowd was gathering, ooh-ing and ah-ing at the display, and some of them were dancing too. Stella was shouting something, but Kimi couldn't hear for the noise. Next thing Kimi knew, Stella was shaking a fist and hurling a string of small stunballs at Marcel (who by now was a blur) which knocked him clean off the shelf. His backside slapped to the cobbles and the fiery din vanished as the crows sucked back into the pipes at incredible speed. The organ shook and rattled before settling with smoke curling from the pipes.

"Zut alor!" Marcel exclaimed, recovering his beret and scrambling wearily back onto the shelf. "Merci, merci," he said, bowing to Stella. "I zought my arms might snep erf!"

"You're welcome," Stella said.

"Erm, bloody hell," Kimi said, her cheeks burning.

"Oooh thank you!" The old man staggered towards her with open arms and Kimi received the biggest hug followed by two kisses on each cheek. The crowd clapped and cheered.

"Erm, right, okay then," she said, when she was released.

"Yeah, we best be going." Stella pulled Kimi away.

"Y'all come back soon now!" Barry shouted.

"Au revoir and good *reedance,*" Marcel muttered, stroking his rump.

"That's probably the biggest donation he's had since Elton paid a visit," Stella said.

"*Who?*"

"Never mind." They hurried on down the street. "Good though wasn't it?"

"The Ting Tings were brilliant," Kimi said. "Might

317

have known it would be bloody crows, though."

"Aye," Stella said. "They'll be getting you to do the fireworks for Cohn's festival. Think you could keep that up for an hour or two?"

"Doubt it. I feel a bit drained," Kimi said. "Don't you get tea and a biscuit after donating? You know like when you give blood?"

Stella laughed. "Maybe you can suggest that to Barry on the way back."

"So what else does this Mr Purse, sell?" Kimi asked.

"Nothing," Stella said. "We don't have money here."

"Okay, so what else does Mr Purse give away?"

"You can ask him yourself," Stella said.

The curved shop front had many windows. Golden paintwork flaked here and there. The silver sign above said;

BO : ONE

In the doorway stood a tall man in a baggy cream suit. He wore a red shirt, a grey bow tie, and sandy coloured shoes. In his hands was a large silver **Z**

"Such a commotion!" he said, holding up the **Z** as they approached. "Rattled right off!"

"Sorry," Stella said. "Kimi here was giving it big."

"Oh." The man smiled at Kimi.

Kimi liked him already. He had a kind face. Or was it a funny face? His broad nose was twisted as if it had once been badly broken. He wore rounded spectacles, most of

318

which were hidden by a large quiff of greying hair.

"And this is Kimi, you say?"

"Aye, Kimi from Kickapoo," Stella said to a dig in the ribs from Kimi.

"Kimi Nichols." Kimi held out a hand. "Pleased to meet you."

"Ahhhhh, at larst, at larst - I'm Mr Purse, and I'm so jolly glad to meet you also." He shook her hand with vigour. "Do come along in - I've never fitted a premature before." He shoved the door and a bell tinkled.

They passed through a small waiting area with comfortable chairs and paintings of landscapes on the wall and into a small, circular room. There were no clothes or jackets in here, only a silver pole in the room's centre, running from the red carpet up into a domed ceiling which carried a stunning painting of two hands with lightning crackling between pointed fingers. Balancers, obviously, Kimi thought.

"Now, where do we begin," Mr Purse said, clasping his hands together. "As I said, I've never fitted a premature. So this is really quite an interesting challenge."

"It is?" Kimi said, wishing people would quit with the premature.

"Oh yesssss," Mr Purse said. He snapped his fingers at the silver pole. Many slots appeared and metal arms sprung out all around it with empty coat hangers dangling from them. "Nightdresses, for example. I've done thorough research!" He reached and grabbed one of the metal arms and spun the whole thing. The hangers whizzed around for a few seconds before slowing to reveal many different nightdresses in gaudy patterns. Some had teddy bears on them. Some had kittens. One had cupcakes with cherries.

"Eurgh," Kimi said. "No thanks."

"*Okayyyyy*," Mr Purse said, looking a little put out. "Undergarments then!" He spun the hangers once more which settled to a drab array of brown and grubby grey vests and stupidly long pants, the material of which looked elasticated and not at all comfortable.

Stella was tittering. Kimi shook her head.

"Are you certain?" said Mr Purse. He stuck his hand up a pant leg and stretched it with his fingers. "These aren't just any old pants you know. Oh no, they're pull-in pants, especially designed as the perfect deterrent against tickants!"

"Tickants?" asked Kimi.

"Oh yes. Essential wear for field work," Mr Purse said. "Why, it was only yesterday that Balancer Oddie was granted permission to renew his pants thrice a year instead of two."

"She only needs a jacket," Stella said. "And we haven't much time. Could you?"

"Oh very well," Mr Purse said. He spun the hangers once more and they settled to an amazing ruckus of rattling buckles and the heavy aroma of new leather.

"There are three colours to choose from." Mr Purse lifted a black jacket from the rack nearest and held it against Kimi. "Standard black, which suits you I might say - or -" he turned the hangers and removed a khaki version, "-standard khaki," he said, holding this one under Kimi's chin. "Hmm, not sure -"

"I like the season's special," Stella cut in. "Can we see that one?"

Mr Purse swung the hangers and the pole turned, revealing rows of the season's special. "Much admired and sought after," he said, removing one carefully from a hanger and handing it to Kimi. "Periwinkle blue - or some call it periwinkle purple. But I do much prefer, simply *periwinkle*, don't you? It reminds me of the shells on the beach."

"It's beautiful," Stella said, stroking her fingers down an arm.

"I love it," Kimi said. "It's gorgeous. Why don't we both get one?"

"Ah," Mr Purse raised a finger to Stella. "Miss O'Brien has had her allocation, I'm afraid. The only things due to Stella are two year's supply of pull-in pants - at which she has already turned up her nose!"

"Ach - I can wait," Stella said as Kimi shrugged on the jacket for size.

"It fits perfectly," she said. "How much do I - oh,

erm -"

"Nothing my love," Mr Purse rubbed his hands together. "All you owe is good service to the cause. Now, what else can we do you for?" he said, smiling. "Persian cat leg-warmers? Famoose wing umbrella? A deliciously cosy yeti hat?"

"Just this, thanks," Kimi said, handing him the jacket and putting Stella's old one back on. Mr Purse dropped it into a brown paper bag which he seemed to snatch from the air behind his back.

"Well, you're easily pleased," he said, handing the bag over. "Are you absolutely certain about the pants?" He gave a concerned look. "Winter drawers on, as they say - and the pull-in range of undergarments protects from the elements as well as the bugs!"

"Erm, maybe next time," Kimi said. "We're in a bit of a hurry."

"Until next time then," he said, gesturing to the door. "Do look after your new jacket - keep it polished!"
"I will - thanks," Kimi said, thinking Big Sue would probably take care of that. They were ushered through the waiting area. Mr Purse swung the front door open and the bell tinkled.

"Be safe!" he said with a nod, his quiff bouncing off his nose.

They walked quickly up an almost empty street. It

322

seemed most had gathered at the end by the organ where the old man was proudly showing off his glowing sabre. "I'm telling you - filled it right up in a single ping!" he was saying to the crowd.

"Eet 'az never bin so *fool*!" Marcel pointed out.

"Made a right old roar - almost blew me sack off," the old man said.

"Zee mojo - eet wuz *power-fool*!" Marcel stood with hands on his hips. "Eet took all of my courage to bring eet under control!"

Kimi and Stella hurried past unnoticed, Stella, holding back the giggles until they were back in the wood and safely behind a bramble patch. "That was a hoot!" she said, twirling a finger. Leaves lifted from the floor.

"Hang on," Kimi said. "On second thoughts, I kinda like the sound of a yeti hat - wait here and I'll be back in a -"

"Jiffy!" Stella finished. "Okay, but run, we need to be getting back."

Minutes later, Kimi returned tightly clutching her BoZone bag. "Right - twirl away!" she panted.

"Show me your hat first," Stella said.

"I erm, no, let's get twirled first."

Stella whisked up the leaves into a vortex and they stepped inside, immediately reappearing at the other side of the wood. "Come on," she said. They hurried over the ring road and down Carroll Lane.

"You go in," Kimi said as they reached the house with her great-grandfather painted up the side. "I'm gonna nip up to our room and get my jumper. Might turn chilly out in the field."

"Righto, be quick!" Stella said, and Kimi ran into the Rabbit's Foot.

***

Kimi was last to return. In the small living room, the old Bentley and Big Sue were on the sofa drinking tea and eating nibbles.

"Dodo sandwich?" Sue pointed to the piled high plates one of the side tables.

"Nibbles?" Bentley pointed to the other table. "Limpet cakes are good!"

"Thanks," Kimi said, taking a dodo sandwich and going around the sofa and into the spacious workshop. Rehd, dressed in camouflage gear, was sat at a computer with one arm resting on a large upturned crate by his side. Stella was munching a sandwich and looking at the songs on the jukebox.

"Here you go," Kimi said, handing Stella the BoZone bag.

Stella looked inside. "There's no hat. Only your jacket."

"*Your* jacket!" Kimi said.

Stella pulled the periwinkle jacket from the bag.

"It's my size!" she said, grinning back at Kimi. "What did you do that for? You didn't have to."

"Because you loved it. And you've done loads for me."

"Ach -" Stella said, her pale cheeks reddening slightly. "How did you persuade Mr Purse?"

"Well I had to give mine up of course. Mr P said he could only let one leave the shop otherwise the balance would be upset. So he agreed to swap for your size."

"Right. But even so, you must have fluttered your eyelashes to pull that off."

"Not really." Kimi stuck a thumb into the waist of her jeans and hooked out the brown elastic. "Had to agree to these," she said and Stella burst out laughing.

"Ach, this is braw!" Stella said, trying on the jacket.

"Suits you better than me," Kimi said as Stella hugged her.

"Now we're all here can I have your attention," Rehd said, waving a hairy hand.

They all brought their sandwiches and gathered behind Rehd at the computer. Kimi stood behind Stella so as not to wobble the monkey.

"Here's our twirly target," Rehd said, clicking the mouse. On screen, a small stone circle on a grassy slope appeared. At the bottom of the slope ran a grey canal, spanned by a tall redbrick bridge. Wrought iron gates sat in its arch with `BRIDGETOWN` in ornate letters across the top.

"How far is it?" Stella asked.

"Five hundred miles, according to Google Heart," Rehd said. "We bribe the trolls here!" He tapped the gates with a fingernail.

He clicked the mouse again. "Plan view," he said. On screen, a thin blue line began in the bottom left, running straight up the screen before curving into an ever-decreasing spiral and ending at the centre of the screen where a small white circle was labelled `black hole.`

"We ride the canal, pass through one thousand bridges -" Rehd followed the spiral with his finger and ended at the white circle in the middle. He tapped the screen. "-then jump in black hole!"

"Is it really a black hole?" Kimi asked, swallowing the last of her sandwich. "You know, like the ones in space?"

"Similar," Bentley said. "Bridgetown was the first ever greylian project, see. Their olive branch, if you like. Trolls were once a dying breed, but the greylians removed them from Earth, thousands of years ago. Something to do with their loutish behaviour. Humans were forever ganging up and killing them. The bridges, the canal, all built from scratch by the greylians. They transported every last troll to their new home and made sure that passage to their settlement was easy enough, by placing a little black hole at the end of the canal. I suppose it's their version of a twirly."

"Right," Kimi said. "That explains that then."

"What about where the greylians live?" Stella asked. "Can you Google that?"

Rehd shook his head. "Not mapped. Okay, it's time we go!" and he clambered down from the chair, grabbed the ropes hanging from the crate and tugged it to the centre of the workshop.

"What about the alien settlement?" Kimi asked, keeping well out the way. "What do we do when we get there?"

Rehd shrugged. "Found no pictures or info, so we play it by ear. Come and hold the ropes – this is a long jump!"

Big Sue lifted a bulging backpack onto Bentley's shoulders, gave it a little pat and winked at Kimi. "A little something for later," he said.

Bentley stood with his boots touching the crate and clasped the ropes. "Shouldn't we do a checklist?"

"Right," Rehd said. "Umm," he pulled his lip with a long finger and stared at the ceiling. "Checklist - troll bribe," he said, patting the crate. "Check!"

"Dad's notebook," Kimi said, patting Stella's old jacket. "Check!"

"Where'd you get the jumper from?" Bentley asked.

"It's not from Mr Purse's stock, I know that much."

"Same place as my jeans, which you promised not to ask about," Kimi replied.

"Oh," Bentley said with a puzzled look.

"All ready?" Rehd asked, lifting a finger to the air.

"As I'll ever be," Bentley said, getting a firm grip on the ropes.

"Good to go," Stella said, stepping up to the crate and grasping the ropes.

They all looked at Kimi. "I guess," she said in a quiet voice, stepping up to the crate at the other side from Rehd. When she took hold of the ropes it felt as if a cold boulder had appeared in her stomach.

"This is it!" Rehd said, twirling his finger and immediately Kimi's hair began whipping around her head.

"Be careful, won't you!" Big Sue shouted from over by the jukebox. He was holding the basket with Audrey in it. A few loose papers from around the room sucked into the vortex and the walls of the workshop began to waver. Sue waved his tea towel and was saying something, but the only sound was the groan of the twirly as the room and Big Sue vanished.

———

20

~ Smell the Coffee ~

After a few long seconds of fizzling flesh followed by a brisk wiz through whiteness, Kimi jolted and so did Bentley, Rehd, and Stella as the crate found new level. In the darkness around them, a whirring grey ring of stones slowed to a stop. Kimi's hands were tight on the rope handles, her hair a tangled nest.

"Everyone okay?" Bentley was first to speak.

"Okay, I think -" Kimi prised her fingers from the ropes, stepped away from the monkey and cleared the hair from her eyes. The stones encircling them looked like headstones, shrouded in the darkness. The air was still and smelled like pond water. Kimi guessed it was the canal she could smell. She already didn't care much for this place.

"Twirlies are murder for split ends," Stella said. She tapped her lantern and shone its beam onto her hand. It was full of scrunchies. "Emergency supplies. What do you think all those pockets are for?"

"Thanks." Kimi chose a red one to match her jacket.

"Come on," Rehd said. He tipped the crate towards himself and took its weight. Bentley grabbed a rope handle and they set off down the grassy slope to the canal.

Kimi tied her hair back and linked into Stella's arm.

"Have we really travelled five hundred miles?"

"Aye," Stella said. "Beats the train, doesn't it?"

"What about back home on Earth? I mean, if I was coming up to Scotland say, to visit you. Are we allowed to use twirlies?"

"Aye. But only via stations, and only at night - excepting emergencies of course."

"Stone circles are stations, right?"

"Aye. Back home I use a scooter to get around. Good idea for you to get one once you're old enough."

"Why would you need a scooter when you can twirly?"

"Like I said, excepting emergencies, you can only twirly using stations, and the nearest station to me is a mile away in Moira Pollock's field. So if I was visiting a friend in say, Mousehole, I would drive up to the field in darkness, take the scooter through the twirly, and exit seconds later from the Merry Maidens - which I think is the nearest station to you."

Kimi knew the Maiden stones. She'd been with Dad many times and watched him sketch. "Yeah, I know them," Kimi said. "There on the outskirts of Mousehole."

"Aye. So if I didn't bring my scooter, I'd have a long walk to yours wouldn't I."

"Right," Kimi said. "Best oil my bike, then."

When they arrived at the deserted pavement by the

canal, previously unnoticed lampposts ignited in a blaze of white, illuminating the gates and the pathway either side. The bridge looked bigger than it had in the picture. Through the gates, the black water ran in a straight line. In the darkness, Kimi could only make out another two bridges, but it was just as Kimi had imagined from the image on the computer. On the other side of the gates a little way up, a large wooden hut jutted out over the water and at its doorway beneath the light of a lamppost, lay what looked like an overfed cow, still and awkward on its side. Kimi thought it might be dead.

"Careful of the pooch," Rehd said quietly as he and Bentley approached the gates.

"Tell me that's not a dog," Kimi said, taking a seat on the crate.

"It's not a dog," Stella said, joining her on the crate. "Hunch up!"

Rehd slid an arm through the railings and stared up at the underside of the bridge. He was shaking a fist. Kimi looked up to where Rehd was looking and in the shadows, spotted what appeared to be a cluster of bells hanging from the brickwork. An oversized stunner shot from Rehd's hand and scored a direct hit. The clanging echoed and the cow-shaped dog thing jumped to its feet with a thunderous roar.

Rehd backed off from the gate as it came bounding down the path, its flabby sides wobbling, slobber flying from its face as it bellowed, its brow contorted with rage.

Kimi squeezed into Stella as it slammed into the gates.

The bells settled into silence, the dog thing quietened, gave a whimper, padded back to the hut and flopped to its stomach. It stared at the gates with piercing green eyes.

"Well," Bentley said. "They should at least know we're here."

"The monkeys have mojo, too?" Kimi asked.

"Of a kind," Stella said. "Though nothing as great as human mojo."

"Oh." Kimi spotted a gap between the top of the gates and the underside of the bridge. It was only about twenty feet up. If there was a key or a mechanism on the other side to open the gates, she could easily Separate up there, drop to the other side, and have the gates open in seconds. But the big dog thing was now panting clouds and she thought better of it. "Are there really trolls here? You know, like that, Shrek dude - or was that an ogre?"

Bentley went to answer but Stella got there first. "Aye, they're real - grotesque, with green skin and horns!"

"Right -"

"I'm serious. They're drunk most of the time. Big Sue calls them stinky buggers. Won't let them in the Foot what with the smell and the puking."

"No wonder they keep them locked up."

"I'll try again," Rehd said. He edged back to the railings and slipped an arm through. The dog thing got to its feet and snarled. It was probably nerves on Rehd's part, or the speed at which the dog thing began to charge - so many stunners flew from Rehd's hand in quick succession that a permanent silvery streak was formed, sending the bells into a frenzy that even drowned out the dog's roar. Rehd scuttled backwards as the dog thing slammed into the gates once more. The bells settled and the disgruntled looking dog thing, turned sideways and raised its leg. A fountain of pee squirted through the railings, narrowly missing Rehd who leapt out of the way with a squeal.

"The little scamp!" Bentley said, stepping away from the approaching puddle.

"Maybe there's nobody home," Kimi said. "Maybe we should come back in the day time."

"They're home alright," Rehd said. "They just lazy!"

This time the dog thing didn't lie down. It stood watching, tensed ready to charge. A light breeze rippled the canal, the bells tinkled gently and the dark outline of trees on the other side swayed a little. Leaves drifted along the pavement. The sky was as black as the water, the smell in the air predominantly swampy. They were five hundred miles from Middling, and it felt like they were in a different country. Kimi made to tighten her scrunchie and Little Hand tingled.

"Something's coming," she said. As they all turned to look at her, the ground began to rumble - so much so that the crate Kimi and Stella were sat on began to jump and judder.

Stella shrieked and they both leapt up and ran to the grass. It wasn't the earth moving - it was the metal grate the crate had been laid on. It lifted and slid to one side taking the crate with it.

"All right, all right, who's the raving clever clogs?" a hoarse voice said as a bulky figure clambered from the hole. He struggled to his feet, grunting. "You!" he said, pointing at Kimi who happened to be nearest. "You been waking up, Buster! I hope you got good reason!"

Kimi was at a loss to do anything but stare. This was no troll. He could only be an inch taller than she was. His shabby grey coat was padded out and tied with string. His trousers and boots were holed and grubby. A mass of fuzzy black hair crawled from beneath a pork pie hat and bristled onto his shoulders. He had a similarly fuzzy beard, matted with bits of food, and a plump, purple nose which looked horribly like a real heart, as if someone had wrenched his from his chest and stuck it there. His right eye winked non-stop; and this was disturbing enough until Kimi noticed the smell. He stunk like a bus shelter on a Saturday morning. Kimi took a step back.

"Gooch!" Rehd said, scampering over with an extended hand.

"Gahhhhhhh!" the tramp bellowed, stuck out his chest then thumped it before offering a hand to Rehd. "Rehdo! My favourite chiefy weefy!" His dirty great hand engulfed Rehd's, shaking it so enthusiastically that Rehd did some unexpected body-popping. Stella tittered but Kimi dug her in the ribs. The big dog thing had decided to come closer. It padded up the path, steam rising from its head.

"Good to see you," Rehd said, flexing his squashed fingers.

"And you, little man," the tramp said, one eye on the crate. "So what's so important you're busting my bells without proper notice?"

"We need quick passage," Rehd said, gesturing to the others. "Everybody - meet Mr Gooch."

"All four of you, eh?" Gooch said, not waiting for pleasantries. "You can afford the fare I take it?"

Rehd nodded to the crate. Gooch knelt at it, pulled a tool from his pocket, flicked out a forked lever, and began breaking in. "Gahhh," he said, grinning beneath the beard as the top splintered and flew off. "Hope this is what I think it is!" He rummaged among the straw packing and pulled out a clear glass bottle, sealed with a spring-corked top.

"Molar," Rehd said. "Twenty-three bottles!"

"Twenty-three?" said Gooch, in a surprised tone. He

snapped open the spring-loaded top and took a sniff.

Kimi wondered how he would smell anything on top of the overpowering eau-de-bus shelter, then her mouth gaped when he held the bottle up to examine it. Curled inside was a dead famoose, its pickled wings shimmered in the lamplight. "God, those guys get a bad deal," she said. Gooch raised an eyebrow and winked at her rapidly.

"Yes, twenty-three bottles," Rehd said. "But you must keep this visit secret."

Another tramp appeared on the other side of the gates. A tubby woman smoking a cigarette. An enormous bosom bulged beneath a shabby raincoat, and a bright ginger afro sat on her head like a blow-dried tabby. It was obviously a cheap wig. She had the same purple, heart-shaped nose like Gooch.

"Who is it, hun?" she said in a croaky voice.

"Passengers!" Gooch replied. He took a swig of molar and smacked his lips. "Open the gates!"

The woman took a last drag and flicked her cigarette. It landed with a hiss in the puddle of pee. She blew a cloud of smoke then stomped a few yards back up the path and began hauling a chain which hung from the other side of the bridge. The gates slowly opened outwards to the sounds of cogs and pulleys. Kimi got behind Bentley as the big dog thing came out sniffing.

"Buster won't bite," Gooch said, picking up one end

of the crate by a rope handle and dragging it through Buster's puddle. "Providing you don't fart, sneeze, cough, hiccup or speak without warning," he added.

"That's no troll," Kimi whispered to Stella. "So much for green skin and horns. He's just a smelly tramp with an alcohol problem and we've just added to that *prob* -"

Gooch stopped, laid the case to the pavement and returned, winking at Kimi.

Silence prevailed and wind rippled the water again. Nothing moved apart from Buster, returning to his space by the hut. Kimi cringed. Surely he couldn't have heard?

Gooch arrived with his stink and a stern face. "And you be?"

"Erm, Kimi Nichols, sir," she said quietly while trying not to breathe.

"It's a pleasure, Kimi Nichols," Gooch said, removing his hat and bowing deeply.

Kimi gasped when she saw the top of his head. His hairline stopped where the pork pie hat had been and two stubby green horns protruded from the top of a lime green scalp. Under the lamplight, Kimi thought he looked radioactive.

"I'm Gooch," he said, straightening up. "Fraser Gooch. Do you know how to identify a troll, Kimi Nichols?"

Kimi shook her head.

"Exceptional hearing," he said, pointing to the

337

stubby horns, before replacing his hat. "Now, let's get you
out of here. You're making me nervous." He went back
under the bridge, passed the crate over to the woman with
the afro, and carried on to the wooden hut. Everyone
followed and Kimi made sure she went last, taking a wide
berth and saying nothing as she passed the woman, knowing
that horny ear things would be lurking within her afro.
Buster sniffed every one of them as they entered the hut
which turned out to be a mooring place. Under a single
pomegranate lantern which glowed a similar green to
Gooch's scalp, what looked like fifty pogo sticks bobbed in
the dark water.

"There's plenty waddlers here," Gooch said,
stepping onto the jetty. He whisked a drumstick from his
pocket, flicked it, and four strands of red mist shot from its
end and into the crowd of waddlers. Gooch tugged on the
drumstick and the strands tightened, drawing four of the
strange machines to the side of the jetty. The red mist
vanished and Gooch quickly stowed the drumstick inside his
coat. Kimi remembered Bentley saying those not proficient
with mojo might need a stick to aid them. "Help yourself,"
said Gooch, winking profusely. "As far as I'm concerned,
the gates were left open, someone slipped Buster a few
steaks and borrowed some transport for a while."

"Deal," Rehd said, not offering a hand this time.

"Um, yes, very good of you," old Bentley said,

staring at the things bobbing in the water and scratching his head. He shrank to teen Bentley, obviously thinking the smaller he was the more balance he might have.

"Alrighty!" Gooch said, turning for the door and muttering; "*Tramp indeed* -" as he left. Buster lay back down, its spread backside filled the doorway.

"What the heck are these?" Stella said, once Gooch's footsteps had disappeared.

"Waddlers - like Gooch said." Rehd stepped onto the wooden jetty, took hold of the stem of the nearest waddler and lifted it clear of the water. It *was* just like a pogo stick, only it had a long fin underneath instead of a spring. He held the waddler over the wooden jetty and the fin retracted. Rehd let go and the waddler hovered an inch off the wood. "Goes on land, too," he said.

"Very versatile," Bentley said, looking awkward.

Rehd held the waddler back over the water until the fin came back out. He settled the waddler back into the water and stepped on. It seemed to find its balance in a second. Rehd grinned.

Bentley and Stella seemed more assured by this and wasted no time in choosing a waddler each and following Rehd's example. "You can swim, can't you?" Stella asked Kimi, who was hanging back.

"Course she can swim," Bentley said. "Come on, Kimbo - hop on."

"Hurry," Rehd said. "Before Gooch changes his mind and doubles the fare."

Kimi reached for the handlebars of the last waddler. "How do I make it go?"

"Greylian technology," Rehd said. "Hold handle and think where to go. Waddler does rest."

"Okay," Kimi said, taking Stella's hand and stepping on carefully.

"Mojo gives power," Rehd said. "Waddler detects how drunk rider is and adjusts speed accordingly. Mostly, trolls are drunk, so they go slow, waddle from party to party."

"But none of us are drunk," Kimi pointed out. "Does that mean -"

"Whoa," Rehd exclaimed, as his waddler jerked forward.

Stella did whoop-whoop shouts as her waddler gave a little shake and followed.   Bentley's waddler began to move and he muttered something, maybe a prayer, Kimi wasn't sure. She gripped the handlebars with both hands and felt a tug as her waddler joined the line leaving the mooring hut. When they entered the canal, the waddlers seemed to have minds of their own as they settled, side by side into a row.

"What now?" asked Stella, looking excited.

Kimi grinned through gritted teeth, staring ahead at

the straight line of water.

"Don't we simply think of where we want to go?" Bentley asked.

"That right," Rehd said, removing his cap and stuffing it in his pocket. "Everybody think - black hole!" His waddler gave a jerk and started forward with a little splash of water. Kimi gripped tightly, thought `black hole` and hers did the same.

"Black hole!" Stella yelled, shooting off in a rush of spray, the lamps either side of the canal blinking on ahead of her.

Kimi turned back to Bentley who looked a bit scared and had barely moved. "Come on, Bentley," she shouted. "Think, black hole!" and at those words, Kimi's arms almost popped from their sockets as her waddler wrenched forward and tore off at incredible speed. Rehd and Stella were already way ahead, Stella's blonde pigtails flying out behind her. Now Kimi knew why Rehd had taken his cap off. His thick monkey hair flew back in spikes, reminding Kimi of Perry. Suddenly, the hunk of gorge is there by her side, tears streaming from his windswept face as they tear through the water. He smiles, lets one hand go from the handlebars, reaches to Kimi. She does the same.   Their fingers meet -

"Black hole!" yelled Bentley from behind and seconds later he was coming up alongside, his grin replacing Perry's silky smile.

"Black hole!" he shouted again, tearing ahead with one arm raised to the air.

"Black hole!" shouted Kimi and her waddler shot forwards, cutting through Bentley's wake. This was pretty cool. Balance seemed effortless too. When the first bridge passed overhead, Kimi and Bentley had almost caught up to Rehd and Stella. Another giant dog thing like Buster went bounding up the side of the canal, its roar fading as they left it behind. No sound came from the waddlers at all which made the ride even more surreal than it already was. A second bridge whizzed by where two Buster type things beneath it were fighting - or playing. A third bridge and then a fourth, where a pair of trampy looking trolls stood gossiping. Under the next bridge, there were so many trolls and music blaring that it looked like a party was going on.

"Look out!" Bentley cried, as they zipped past at least a dozen drunken trolls waddling on waddlers. Kimi heard a couple of splashes followed by shouting and swearing but she didn't look back, she wanted more speed. `Black hole, black hole, black hole,` she thought and bridges went by in a blur. The others must have cottoned on and thought similar thoughts because soon they were caught up and riding in a line again, ripping through the water. Tears streamed from Kimi's eyes. She ducked down to the handlebars to try and go faster, grinned like an idiot and imagined taking a few waddlers back to Mousehole and zipping round the harbour with her mates.

"Got ya!" Stella shouted, swerving close, sending up spray and drenching Kimi down one side. Kimi was about to dart sideways and drench her back when Rehd shouted above the breaking water; "We're going into the curve!" and all four waddlers went into a lean. Kimi remembered the plan view she'd seen on the computer. They were heading into the spiral now.

"No time for games, you two!" Bentley yelled, his shirt billowing in the wind.

As the waddlers tore on, Kimi leant into the curve and tightened her grip. Bridge after bridge whizzed by, the lampposts igniting in rapid succession, illuminating the path and the trees and party after party. Kimi glanced to her left and nearly fell off laughing when she saw Stella. She had her mouth wide open and her cheeks wobbled furiously. Her usually small head looked enormous. Kimi did the same and the rushing wind sent her face into contortions. The pair of them grinned at each other. Trolls waved from the canal side and big dog things roared as the curve of the canal grew tighter and tighter.

Beyond the trees on Kimi's right, the night sky had become noticeably brighter. What looked like a vertical searchlight was lighting up the clouds. She guessed it must be coming from the black hole. And that's when all the fun went out of the waddler. Thoughts of actually going into a black hole seemed more daunting than they had before. The waddler tore on regardless and Kimi was at a constant lean, the curve of the canal growing tighter and tighter. She thought briefly of home and had a momentary wish to step through those patio doors and smell the coffee. The waddler gave a sideways jerk and slowed a little. Kimi wobbled, almost lost her grip.

"Any second now!" shouted Rehd.

The last bridge zipped overhead and the water opened to a silver lake. Kimi's waddler surged forward. Orange barrel-shaped buoys sat in a ring in the centre of the lake where a beam of white light projected skywards from its middle, illuminating the fir trees around the lake as if it were daylight.

Kimi glanced along the line of speeding waddlers with her heart beating fast. No one was speaking up and saying what to do. Stella had shut her mouth now and was glaring ahead and looking terrified. In fact, they were all glaring ahead as if they were about to go over Niagara Falls.

"What do we do?" Kimi shouted, but the question remained unanswered as the waddlers separated and formed themselves into a line with Kimi's waddler falling to the rear.

The orange buoys were seconds away, the white light within, blinding.

Kimi braced herself, expecting they'd be thrown

344

over the handlebars into the light, but up front, Rehd's waddler lifted gracefully from the water and he went sailing through the air towards the light. A second later and Bentley lifted clear, water trailing from his waddler. Kimi saw the fin retract. Stella looked back to Kimi, but she too was lifting from the water and the three of them were silhouetted against the light.

Kimi had the urge to jump into the lake, but the urge never got a chance to be acted on. Her waddler lifted to the air. Kimi gripped the handlebars, her eyes squinting at the brightness. It was pulling her in like a magnet. The silhouettes of her friends sucked into the light and vanished. Kimi closed her eyes as she was swallowed too. She expected a splash but there wasn't one, only whiteness all around and a dreamy, drifting sensation as if she had gained a parachute. She couldn't see the others - only herself on the waddler floating down into whiteness. She called out for Stella but no reply came.

The faintest suggestion came to mind that she hadn't made it. Maybe this was heaven. Maybe when she stopped falling she'd find Mum and Dad waiting for her. But again that's as far as her thoughts got. A scratching sound all around which sounded like an army of scuttling spiders was quickly accompanied by blue sparks and streaks of jagged lightning. The scratching grew into a frenzy. Kimi wanted to cover her ears but couldn't let go of the waddler.

Just as she thought her eardrums might burst, the noise suddenly ceased and Kimi stopped dead still. She hovered in the whiteness, only the odd spark of blue, the odd blink of lightning.

Then she dropped.

Fast.

Swirling and curling at super speed. Bangs, cracks and lightning flashes seemed to add to her speed as well as her heart rate. Her cheeks wobbled and her hair flew wildly above her. She could barely breathe and found her knees bending, expecting somehow, a very hard landing.

Then she slowed to a drift as if the parachute had engaged once more. The bangs and cracks faded, the whiteness returned and Kimi looked down past her feet balanced on the waddler.

Blue.

Icy blue.

Coming up to meet her.

"Hurry Kimi -" Bentley's voice.

"Nnnghhh," she said as the waddler crunched into something like snow.

Someone grabbed her hand and pulled hard, so hard she stumbled from the waddler and left it behind. "Run!" came Bentley's urgent command, dragging her through the icy blue. They were in a huge cave with walls and ceiling of glistening blue crystals. Powdery frost crunched underfoot as she gambolled into greyness as if charging from the mouth of some giant ice monster.

Bentley swung her by the arm and flung her from the cave so hard she went sprawling sideways into dust - or maybe it was sand.

"Nnnghhh -"

"Get down! Get down!" she heard Rehd shouting, and looked out to the vast greyness of a long road pointing to the distance. There was a high-pitched whistle, and the air trembled as a black greylian craft only feet above the road's surface hurtled towards the cave. It shot overhead almost sucking Kimi up with it as it flew into the icy blue and vanished with a tinkle of crystals. Then came another black craft followed by two more. Kimi flattened herself to the floor as they zipped overhead and into the cave.

"How cool was that?" Stella said when the last one vanished.

Kimi took Stella's hand and got to her feet. "Cool?" she said, glad to hear sound coming from her lips. "Bloody hell. I thought I was dead in there."

"Yeah, crap a cave or what?"

"We would have been dead if we'd arrived a few seconds later," Bentley said in a heated tone. "Maybe next time we should ring up and get tickets first."

Rehd shrugged and put his cap back on. "We safe. Stop moaning!"

Kimi examined the cave more closely. It stood in a sheer wall of rock which stretched far to the right and to the left before vanishing into fog. The icy blue portal they'd emerged from was like a huge mouth in the rock's surface, its blue crystal interior sparkling like thousands of teeth. Kimi gazed into it, mesmerised. She wondered if her waddler got smashed.

"Let's get a move on," Bentley said, hunching up his backpack and setting off. "It's getting dark in case no one's noticed."

"Agreed - move out!" Rehd said, fixing his cap back on. "And stick to the side of the runway!"

Kimi shook her eyes away from the alluring crystals and set off walking with Stella. The runway cut through barren, dusty land, leading into a great canyon where stood enormous grey structures that looked like anthills. On the horizon beyond, bigger than ever before, stood the dark mountain silhouetted against an amber sky. Great winged creatures swooped and dived around it. Kimi gaped for many seconds at this, unable to put into words what she was seeing. "No way!" she eventually managed. "Dragons? Real dragons?"

Stella laughed.

Rehd said nothing - his eyes fixed ahead.

"No," Bentley said. "But they're probably where the myth originated. They're pterosaurs. One of my favourites of

348

the old beasts!"

"Like dinosaurs? Real live dinosaurs?"

"Not strictly. Flying reptiles to be precise. The last of them were removed from earth at the time of the -"

"No time for lessons!" Rehd said. "Follow me and keep to the side."

"Aye," Stella said. "Let's get there before it gets totally dark. I don't fancy hanging around out here. Feels like we're being watched."

They fell into a line and continued down the runway, Kimi not taking her eyes off the flying reptiles in the distance. She could tell the mountain was still some way off, so that would mean those things must be some size close up. She was about to ask if they were meat-eaters when Bentley spoke up.

"Looks like we got their attention," he said, nodding down the runway. Another craft was approaching, though not as fast nor as low to the ground as those that had zipped through the portal. "Stay still," Bentley said. The craft grew closer before stopping and hovering in silence some twenty metres away.

"What's it doing?" Kimi whispered.

"Dunno," Stella said. "I hope it's Granp."

A low humming sound filled the air and the craft descended, coming to a stop inches from the runway. There was a hissing sound and a cockpit appeared, lifted to one side and unfurled, creating steps down the side of the craft. A large oval head with big black eyes peered out.

"Yoo-hoo!" Stella cried, waving frantically.

Kimi guessed it *must* be Granp, but couldn't understand how anyone might tell the difference from one greylian to the next. The greylian climbed out with what looked like a rocket launcher hung over his shoulder. Its legs swung down onto the first step and it dropped to the runway, pausing briefly before skating over.

Kimi's heart thumped as the greylian arrived, eyes black and shiny.

"Sssssstella," it said in a hissing voice, it's thin mouth turning up into a smile.

"Hey Granp," Stella said. "Neat place you got here!"

"Aye," the greylian said, blinking its shiny black eyes. This brought a giggle from Stella. "You almossst got yoursssself killed!" Granp said. "You have an appointment?"

"Well, no," Stella said. "But we do need to see the General to ask him a favour."

"Yes, a favour," Rehd confirmed.

Granp looked from one to the other before skating gracefully back to the craft and climbing inside. The cockpit closed back up and the craft remained hovering inches from the runway.

"What's happening?" Kimi asked, beginning to feel the cold.

"I guess he's talking to base," Bentley said. "Just hold tight, everybody."

After another minute, the cockpit unfurled once more and Granp slithered to the ground and skated over. "Permission granted," he said. "But only for one."

Rehd took a step forward. "Me. The General will trust in the chief of fuzz!"

"No, my friend," Bentley said, planting a hand on Rehd's shoulder. "I must safeguard the mission with my entire being. I'm certain I can persuade the good General to help us. I'll be the one to go."

"Rehd does have a point you know," Stella said. "He's chief of fuzz. If anyone can pull this off he can."

The greylian seemed never to keep still. Watching its floaty movements, Kimi was beginning to sway herself. She knew she had to speak up. She was the one, after all. Granp fixed his stare on Kimi and moved slowly towards her as if he'd been reading her thoughts. From the corner of her eye, Bentley, Rehd and Stella had all turned to look at her but she couldn't take her eyes off the greylian's shiny black stare. "I'm the one," she said as Granp arrived before her. "I insist. It has to be me."

Granp's slit mouth smiled, the tip of his straw-like tongue flicked out.

"Yesssss," he said.

"But that's outrageous," Bentley said. "Kimi has no

351

experience in such matters, and it's plain to see that I would -"

Granp raised a hand and Bentley shut up. "The General will sssee only one. The ressst of you go ssstraight back!" His long slender finger pointed back up the runway to the blue cave, its crystal teeth glittering.

"I *can* do this," Kimi said, in a tone that came out too deep and made her cough. "You lot get back to the workshop and wait for me there." She wanted to add something like `come looking for me if I'm not back in an hour` but Granp was staring right at her.

"Kimi is right," Rehd said. "It is her mission after all."

"Well I suppose you'll need *this*," Bentley said, in a resigned tone and handed over the backpack. "Best not open it here, though."

"What is it?" Kimi asked, pulling the backpack on.

Bentley whispered in her ear; "A dozen liquefied dodo heads sealed in a stayhot bag. Might just tip the scales in your favour. You be careful now!"

"And this." Rehd sheepishly pulled a bottle of molar from his jacket. "Thought it might, er, come in useful - extra leverage."

"Thanks," Kimi stuffed the bottle in her jacket. "Okay then, wish me luck."

"One more thing," Stella said. She took a disc from

her pocket and handed it to Kimi. "It's the stills of the cctv footage. I swiped it just before Patina whisked us away. Had a feeling we might need it at some point."

"Clever," Kimi said, taking the disc and shoving it in her jeans pocket.

"Good luck," Stella said. "And you've got your dad's notebook don't forget. Now you go in there and charm the General."

"Easier said than done," Kimi said, thinking back to watching the greylians through the spy scope. It was Granp who had talked about taking a girl. What if any old girl would do? What if this was it? What if Stella was wrong? What if -

"Go, pleassse!" Granp said to the others, indicating towards the blue cave.

Bentley gave Kimi a hug and stuttered a good bye and good luck. He turned and started walking up the runway. Kimi heard him sniff.

"Bye!" Kimi said after him in a choked voice.

"See you soon," Rehd said, scampering after Bentley.

Stella slapped Kimi on the back. "Be strong, sister. You can handle the General. Just be honest with him - and be nice - and if all else fails, flash him your pull-in pants and he'll laugh into submission!"

"Yeah right," Kimi said, managing a grin.

"See ya, Granp!"

Granp waved as Stella ran after the others. Kimi watched as they entered the blue cave and vanished in a flourish of tinkles.

"You know you musssst bow to the General?" Granp said.

Kimi spun round. She'd forgotten all about that. "Erm, yeah," she said.

Granp smiled before skating back towards the craft. "Ssstand in the middle of the runway and I'll lift you in the beam," he said, climbing back inside.

"Can't I ride with you?"

"Not allowed," Granp replied, shaking his head as the ladder curled back into a cockpit and sealed itself once more.

Well that's a great start, Kimi thought, moving to the middle of the runway. The craft lifted a good thirty feet and swept directly above her.

There was a humming sound like when you walk under a pylon in the rain and a blue light snapped on, engulfing Kimi. She was about to comment when her feet left the ground and suddenly she was ten feet in the air and sweeping down the runway. It felt as if she'd been picked up by a powerful magnet. This was cooler than the waddlers. She'd seen UFO's sucking people up on the telly and had a strange feeling of having great power, or knowledge, or something, she wasn't sure quite what it was as the light swept her along, legs dangling.

At the end of the runway, the craft swung between two of the enormous anthill structures and the dark mount vanished from view. Kimi's feet touched down into dust and the beam of light vanished. The craft swept to one side and sank to the ground, joining rows of more gleaming black ships.

At the base of one of the anthill structures, what looked like one of those rectangular metal detectors that you walk through at airports lit up in a blue light and a greylian stepped out, followed by four more. All of them carried those rocket launcher things. Kimi noticed a difference with these greylians as they skated towards her. They had yellow stripes across the top of each arm which looked like they'd been swiped on with a paint brush. She guessed they must be guards of some sort. The greylians came to a stop and the one nearest pointed his weapon directly at Kimi.

"In-ssssside," it said, jerking its gun toward the metal detector.

Little Hand gave an unexpected tingle. This was it, there was no turning back now. She must have looked frightened because Granp slid over and patted her on the shoulder. She managed a smile which she hoped didn't look too forced. "Okay," she said, starting shakily towards the metal detector. `I can do this - easy peasy.`

The greylian who had pointed the weapon, skated in front, pointing it again at the metal frame.

"Thank you," Kimi said in a squeaky voice coming to a stop in front of it. She could see straight through it and into the entrance of the clay like structure behind. There was no blue film across it like the entrance to the Shed or the IPC chamber.

"In!" the greylian with the weapon said, tapping her elbow with its bulbous end.

"Okay, okay," Kimi said. "Let me get my breath, won't you."

She took a deep breath and could have sworn she caught a whiff of freshly brewed coffee. She blew it out slowly and decided not to close her eyes this time. She hunched the backpack tight to her shoulder, huddled her arms into her chest so as not to touch the metal framework and stepped through - *straight* into her dining room.

———

21

~ A Greylian Tradition ~

The sudden change knocked Kimi off balance and she fell back against the patio doors. She was home. Wonderful, wonderful home. Something bright and golden surged through Kimi from her toes to her nose. It lifted her. Literally. She was floating, she was home, and the coffee smell was ultra-devinearundo! Kimi laughed.

"Sssit!"

Kimi's feet hit the carpet, fast. The General had appeared at the dining table. Kimi instantly recognised the red hue on his bony chest and arms and his forehead. He sank effortlessly to the chair and began tapping slender grey fingers on the table with a rhythm that seemed to resound in Kimi's ears like a little bass drum. Cohn's ovular head was bigger than the other greylians; the features sharp and shadowed. Wide-set, glossy black eyes swept sideways over high cheekbones and his slit mouth was turned up in an absurdly cute smile.

Kimi swayed. The coffee smell was really strong. If Cohn had put the coffee on then Kimi thought he must have used the whole bag. She leant to the patio doors. It was dark outside. Night time. Then she realised there were no lights over the bay. No lights at all. The panes of glass in the doors

357

were pure black. Kimi let go of the handle.

"Ssscared?" the General hissed. "Pleassse, sssit and ssstill your pulssse." He accentuated every hiss and Kimi's heart was up and running. His fingers ceased tapping and pointed to the chair she would normally take. The chair slid out from the table.

Kimi suddenly remembered to bow, but didn't take her eyes from the General when she did. "Wh - where am I?" she said, creeping shakily to her seat. She put the backpack on the table and sat down. The General didn't reply straight away. He just stared with those deep black eyes, while retaining the childlike smile. Kimi thought he might be probing her. Although there was no physical discomfort, no voice in the head, but it felt like she'd lost something - lost connection to the outside world - to Bentley.

The General sighed and the hue on his chest bloomed like a rash. Kimi's brow tightened and the beginnings of a headache set in. "Where am I?" she asked again, attempting to break whatever connected them.

The General sat up and drew a great breath. The blotches on his chest diffused and his smile dropped to a slit. "You are where it pleassses you to be," he said. "I can change it if you wishhhh." He swept out an arm and instantly, Kimi was sitting on her bed.

"Thisss?" the General said from the rocking chair.

Kimi turned quickly to the window and was met

again by pure blackness.

"Or thisss?"

Now she was on Stella's four-poster and the General was sat cross-legged on the camp bed. Thoughts of Stella's secret room came to mind and Kimi urgently shook them away. She had to think of something - fast!

Now she was in a cubicle at the Rabbit's Foot, embraced in Perry's arms. His silk complexion, crazy hair, white smile, his lips moved in -

"Noooooo!" Kimi screeched, her face aflame.

Now she was on the stool in the secret room, staring into Cohn's black eyes. He was on the stool opposite, his knobbled knees touching Kimi's. Her headache morphed into a thumper. "Ssstrange place," Cohn said, gazing up to the wrinkled pomegranate on the ceiling. A hundred spiders scuttled out.

"No!" snapped Kimi. "The dining room at home - that's where I want to be - that's where I *need* to be!"

And in a blink she was back at the dining table, panting at the smiling greylian.

Kimi looked away, wincing at her banging temple and trying desperately to think of anything but the secret scope. She got the feeling he knew about it. And not just that, she also had the feeling he knew every single thing she'd ever said or done (and wished for – apparently). Her hands were trembling. She touched them to the table, with the strong urge to call for Bentley. She imagined him appearing in a misty blue fog and slapping Cohn on the nose. Realisation occurred that that might just happen if she tried any harder, and the last thing they needed was Bentley in trouble for assaulting an alien. Cohn's eyes were still on her. Kimi could feel his stare but did not look at him. She stared at the cup ring on the table instead. The cup ring she'd got in hot water about when the table was only a day old. She gazed around the dining room and up into the hall. It all looked so real, but she knew it wasn't. The clock on the wall was the old one, not the one mum had bought last week. The mirror in the hall was intact. And on the side, behind Cohn, was the jar of Marmite, which of course was really on Stella's dresser. Yes, this was all projected from her mind, somehow, and Cohn was making her feel like a specimen in a jar. She had to get a grip. Take the lead.

"Thanks," she said, finally looking at Cohn. "This is nice - thank you."

Cohn leaned back in his chair and folded his arms behind his head. It was at this point she realised that greylians didn't have nipples or a bellybutton.

"Ssssso, what brings you halfway across your planet, that could not wait until my next visssit?"

Kimi hadn't thought of Heart as a planet before. "It - it -" She didn't know where to start, so went to open the backpack, but her hands froze on the straps. With a gush of

360

air, the walls wavered and five greylians stepped through, all pointing rocket launchers at Kimi's head.

"Shhhow me," the General said.

Kimi unbuckled the straps and carefully pulled out a bulky silver foil bag with `STAYHOT` printed across it. "Erm, dodo heads - freshly erm, liqui-thingied - for you." She pushed the bag across the table with the tips of her fingers. "From Big Sue."

The five greylians relaxed their rocket launchers and made approving whispers. The General gestured with a hand and the guards disappeared through the walls. He pointed at the foil bag and it slid back up the table to Kimi. "Open!"

She found a tear-strip running across the top and slowly peeled it open. Steam curled into the air along with the damp smell of boiled feathers. Cohn's little nostrils flared and a rapid ticking sound came from his mouth. He beckoned with a long curled finger and the bag slid back to him.

"Ssscintillating," he said, removing a dodo head and dropping it to the table. His long fingers rested over the beak to keep it still, and his straw-like tongue emerged.

Cohn's attention was with the steaming dodo and Kimi was grateful for that. When those black eyes bore into her, she felt he was inside her head. As the greylian's straw-like tongue grew closer to the dodo's eye, Kimi tried to look away, but somehow, she couldn't not watch. Its rounded tip touched gently to the wrinkled film and scraped it away. Then it settled perfectly over the eyeball.

Kimi jumped when the tongue jabbed and the eyeball disappeared inside the head. Liquefied brains rose up the straw. Cohn's cheeks were sucked right in and the brains were gone in seconds. His tongue popped from the dodo's eye socket and retracted quickly into his slit mouth. Cohn shivered and reassumed his absurd smile. He selected another head. "You are Sue's messenger?" His tongue slipped out once more and dropped to the awaiting eyeball.

Kimi watched, revolted, as the wrinkly film was scraped away. It reminded her of picking the scabs off winkles. "Erm, no. I'm Kimi. Kimi Nichols, sir. I've come to ask a favour, please."

Cohn's tongue rammed into the skull and Kimi jumped again. Ruddy-grey mush oozed from the dodo's nostrils. Cohn sucked up the brains much slower this time, closing his eyes as they entered his mouth. When the last of the brains had vanished, his tongue withdrew from the dodo's head and small meaty bits dripped to the table. Cohn sighed before the tongue slipped back into his mouth. "Nicholsssss," he said, selecting another dodo head and flopping it on the table. "Sssssounds familiar. You are human, yesssss?"

"Yes, sir," Kimi bowed again. "Oh - and I brought you this." She took the bottle from her jacket and placed it on the table, not looking at the famoose curled up inside.

"It's molar - from Rehd - the monkey, erm chief Rehd."

The General's eyes grew impossibly bigger. His mouth formed a perfect crescent grin and he made snakey hisses under his breath. Kimi thought it must be an alien laugh.

"Molarrr," he said. "Famoossse in its rightful place!" He beckoned with a curled finger and the bottle tipped over and rolled up the table with the famoose slopping around inside. He swiped up the bottle and flicked off the spring-cork top with a knobbly thumb. His tongue dropped lazily inside and half the contents were sucked up in no time.

"Woah," Kimi said as Cohn's tongue pulled out and a couple of bubbles escaped from the end.

"Favour?" he asked, before holding the dodo head flat to the table and positioning his tongue over the eyeball.

As gross and surreal as this was, it seemed to be going down well with Cohn. Now was the time. She had to get this right. "Yes, sir. I do need a very big favour – please." The tongue jabbed and the eyeball popped.

Kimi winced.

Cohn sucked up the brains.

"Well, erm, I need to borrow a craft, sir - and - and a pilot, please, if I can. It won't be for long. If that's all right?"

Cohn stared at her for what seemed like forever.

Kimi thought of Bentley again, but didn't even get a twinge in her brow.

"For what purpossse?" Cohn said, dragging another head from the stayhot bag.

"Well sir -" Kimi jumped again when the eyeball popped.

Cohn slurped vigorously, his head shuddering.

Kimi went on to explain about the murder of her parents, while Cohn continued with the dodo heads. She showed him the notebook with the time travel calculations, and told of the workshop and the computers and how her thought direction and the speed of the greylian ship could take them back to the exact moment to swoop down and save her parents.

Cohn looked up. "And what -" The black stare fixed on Kimi. "- makesss you think they were murdered?"

"Oh," Kimi pulled the disc from her pocket. "These are cctv stills from the golf club. Patina, back at the library, magnified the images and you can see three shuck - and the lightning strike's got a core. Patina says it's like a Balancer's mojo."

Cohn's eyes bore into her. "And Patina – she'sss aware you ask such favourssss?"

"No sir, I wanted to do this myself."

"No Adeptsss know of thisss?"

The image of a slobbering Babbage arrived swiftly

In Kimi's mind and her heart came booming at her breast. She desperately thought of anything - Perry - then sprouts - why sprouts? Then Bentley. Smiling Bentley. "I - I - n, n, no sir. I thought it better to involve as few people as possible, and -" She was going to go on and plead that Dad's discovery - if they could pull it off - would be the greatest discovery in the history of mankind, but apparently no pleading was necessary.

"Yesss - okay then -"

"S - sorry?"

"Yesss," Cohn repeated, then his tongue slipped back in the molar bottle.

Kimi was momentarily speechless. That was a whole lot easier than she'd imagined. "Great! Thank you. That's just great! Absolutely great!"

Cohn leaned forward, his bony fingers splayed on the table. "I will need to sssee these computers."

Kimi nodded, not quite believing she'd pulled this off.

"I will also need to inssssspect the dissssc, *and* your father'sss calculationsss -"

"Makes sense," Kimi agreed.

"Good," Cohn said. "The starburst will be suited to this mission - it's the fastessst of my fleet - more advancccced."

Kimi liked the sound of that.

"And *I* will be your pilot."

Kimi didn't like the sound of that. She wasn't getting a good vibe from Cohn. The hue on his chest and head, she'd just realised, had turned purple as if blood was pooling beneath his grey skin. "Erm, I don't want to put you out or anything, sir - but couldn't erm, Granp do the flying?"

Cohn fell back in the chair, stared up to the ceiling and made the breathless hissing sounds again. Kimi wanted to ask him what was so funny but didn't dare.

The hissing stopped and Cohn sat up with teary eyes. "Lassst time Granp flew the starburssssst, he entered Earth spacccccce at the wrong coordinatessss and collided with a wind turbine. No, Kimi Nicholsss - *I* am your pilot!"

"Oh, right."

"Yesssss, all Earth operationsss must be handled mossst delicately."

"Right, thank you. So erm, when do we set off?"

Cohn picked up the stayhot bag and tipped it. One last dodo head dropped out. He pointed a finger and the damp head slid up the table leaving streaky marks. Kimi's stomach gave a squirm of objection.

"Greylian tradition," Cohn said. "Imperative to a mission's successss."

"I - I can't eat brains," she said. "I - I'll be sick, and -"

"Then we have no mission!"

"I - I can't," Kimi protested. She thought of Bentley, but got no vibe. "I - I haven't got a tongue thing!"

Cohn raised his hand and something chinked in the kitchen behind. An old knickerbocker glory glass with bits and bobs in, rose from the windowsill and came floating over Cohn's shoulder towards Kimi. Among the things in the glass were the two curly straws her and Julie had bought at the school fair. Cold sweat pushed through Kimi's brow as the glass landed gently on the table before her.

"Now you have the meansssss." Cohn smiled.

No way could she do this. She'd puke for deffo. But then again the brains did look a bit like Marmite. Maybe you either loved them or hated them. A trickle of sweat salted her lips. What was she even thinking of? Her jowls were tugging from the very thought of mushy brains sliding down her throat. "I really, really will be sick," she said, trying to put some authority in her voice.

"Good," Cohn said. "Human vomit has its meritsssss." His tongue fell out an inch. He flicked a finger at the knickerbocker glory glass and one of the curly straws lifted to the air and floated into Kimi's hand. "Sssuck and the mission can commenccce!"

The dodo head smelled rank - like mum's floor rags when she puts them in to soak. Its wrinkled eye stared back at Kimi. She nipped the beak between thumb and forefinger and brought the head carefully in front of her. Cohn was leaning forward again, his tongue hanging limp. Kimi held the straw and touched the end to the dodo's eye. The wrinkled film covering it moved and she gagged.

Cohn gasped. His expression one of expectant delight.

Kimi took a breath and gripped the straw with both hands to keep it steady. But the straw slipped and the wrinkled film slipped to one side revealing a sleek brown orb. She yelped and covered it quickly with the end of the curly straw. Unfortunately it was a perfect fit.

"Go ahead!" Cohn nodded.

As if invisible hands had grabbed hers, the straw was pushed down hard. The eye went in with a pop and a bubble of rusty mush grew from the dodo's nostril.

"Go on, go on!" Cohn ordered, bobbing in his seat. He might have been funny if not for the upcoming meal. Kimi reluctantly put her lips to the straw, the smell from the damp feathers much stronger now. "Sssuck!" Cohn said, tapping the table impatiently.

Pretend its Marmite, Kimi thought. She gave a little suck and the liquid brains rose an inch up the straw.

"Yesss!" Cohn stood up.

The straw had three curls in it. When the brains reached the first curl, Kimi stopped sucking and placed a finger over the end, exaggerating her gasps for air. Cohn leaned across the table. "Want to ssshare?" he said, swiping up the other straw from the glass and then falling, hissing into his chair.

So much for greylian humour, Kimi thought, quickly releasing her finger for a second while Cohn wasn't looking. The brains dropped an inch. That's all.

"Get on with it," Cohn said, righting himself. "Turnsss to jelly if you wait too long. Give them a ssstir!"''

Sweat was cold on Kimi's face. Cohn was enjoying this. She had to do it quickly and get it over with. Maybe she could swallow it without letting it touch her tongue, like when she had to eat sprouts. What was it with sprouts? She released her finger and let the brains sink back into the dodo's head, then, with the biggest effort not to be sick on the table, she gave the straw a little stir. Cohn nodded his approval.

"Right," Kimi said. "Here goes." She took a deep breath, blew it out nice and slowly, nipped her nose, placed her lips back to the straw and sucked as hard as she could. The brains shot up the straw, zipped around the three curls and -

The greylian guards surged through the walls, rocket launchers lunging towards Kimi. She screamed and went over backwards to the floor while the curly straw went spinning into the air, spraying mush in every direction. Kimi closed her eyes and mouth just as brains spattered a trail across her face.

Cohn objected to this intrusion furiously. Kimi stayed on the floor until he'd stopped shouting.

"Apologiesss, General," one of the greylians was saying. "It's thisss one's Tulpa. He's outside, convulssssing and insisssssting his Balancer is dead - we cannot have any deathsssss here, General."

Kimi grabbed the table and pulled herself up. "Bentley? Bentley's here?"

Cohn waved a hand and the metal frame reappeared in place of the patio doors. Through it, Kimi could see old Bentley writhing in the dust, two greylians stood over him, weapons aimed.

"Go to him!" shouted Cohn. He looked worried.

Kimi took no persuasion. She grabbed the backpack and the notebook, and leapt through the frame. As soon as she was on the outside, Bentley stopped writhing and the greylians backed off. His face was grubbier than Gooch's. "Oh - you're alive," he said, looking more embarrassed than relieved as he got to his feet. "I thought, well, that I'd lost you. I couldn't feel you at all and -"

"So you came back here doing the squirmy dance? Thanks," Kimi said. "I was just about to puke. Remind me never to go on a greylian picnic. Where are the others?"

"It's erm, only me I'm afraid," Bentley said, straightening his shirt. "I really thought you were a goner, and I expected to do the death cry any second - sent me into convulsions it did. The others tried to stop me, but I had to find you - see if you were alright."

"I know what you mean," Kimi said. "In there with the General felt weird - like we'd lost contact." Kimi smiled at him.

"Hope I didn't blow anything," he said as the General stepped through the metal frame.

"Far from it." Kimi wiped brains from her face.

As the General arrived, his craft descended from the sky and Kimi's heart leaped again.

The starburst shimmered a beautiful blue that was not unlike the ice cave. It hovered inches from the ground. Its bulbous, streamlined front looked similar to the rocket launchers the guards carried. The clear cockpit slid forward and a greylian slithered out and dropped to the dust. He bowed to Cohn then stepped aside.

Cohn turned to Kimi and Bentley. "Climb aboard!"

22

~ The Ring of Truth ~

Inside the cockpit was egg-shaped, narrowing at the rear where Kimi and Bentley were squeezed together on a padded box-seat. Cohn sat up front in a chair which looked similar to the jaws of a venus flycatcher. It tightened and gripped at his sides when he sat down. Kimi noticed there were no seatbelts and pulled even closer to Bentley who had readily agreed to her request to be teen-sized for the journey.

As the cockpit closed, Cohn whispered to himself, tapping at various buttons in front, and with a low hum the craft began to rise before slipping easily through the forest of anthills. Cohn wasn't even watching where he was going most of the time and the ghostly structures came within scraping distance on more than one occasion. It was totally dark on the ground now and the night sky held a pinkish tinge along the horizon. The red lights of the runway came into view, dotting into the distance, where the ice cave twinkled like a jewelled eye.

"Thanks for coming back for me," Kimi whispered to Bentley, squeezing his arm as the starburst began making a whining sound.

"Only doing my duty," Bentley said, staring anxiously over Cohn's shoulder. Kimi felt a bit queasy and wasn't keen on going back through the portal. She hoped she wouldn't get airsick.

Cohn pressed a small panel on the wall to his right and it flipped open. A metallic cable snaked out as if it was alive, its tip was long and pointed and it searched the air like a snake sniffing for prey. Cohn leant his head towards it and the cable moved to a small hole in the side of his head. He held still as the slender point slipped inside. There was a click and the cable detached and retracted snakelike into the panel and the lid flipped shut. Slowly, the craft turned away from the runway, pointing instead towards the dark mountain; the flying reptiles' silhouettes barely visible in the night sky.

Cohn hissed, and the starburst raced forward. Kimi clung to Bentley, expecting to be forced backwards, but soon realised that even though they were zipping along at some speed, there was no feeling of movement inside the starburst.

"Oh lordy," Bentley said, as the craft rose higher and the mountain shot towards them. The starburst veered to the right and the first flying reptile swerved past the cockpit, its vast leathery wings spread to the size of a small field.

Kimi screamed. Cohn turned his head. His mouth was formed into that toy-like smile, his black eyes, unblinking. The starburst continued around the mountain, dipping, rising, diving, narrowly missing the snapping jaws of the flying reptiles before tearing upwards through thickening cloud.

One of the huge creatures appeared from nowhere.

They were going to collide head on.

Kimi screamed again and Bentley shouted something but his shout was drowned out as the starburst veered sharply left. A spiked wingtip came scratching up the glass of the cockpit accompanied by the reptile's piercing shriek.

"K - keep your eyes on th - the road," Bentley said, but Cohn only continued to smile as the craft lurched and continued upwards into the cloud, emerging into darkness seconds later. They hovered in silence with the stars. Kimi was breathless.

Cohn hissed and the starburst tipped forward into a dive, rushing back through the clouds. The mountain flashed past and the canyon and greylian settlement loomed into view. Cohn leaned back in his seat and brought his hands behind his head. His slender fingers interlocked as the starburst skimmed the tops of the giant anthills.

The runway lights approached and the craft dropped lower and headed straight for the blue cave. In seconds it was upon them and Kimi threw her head into Bentley's arm. Then came the familiar crystalline tinkle. She opened her eyes just in time to see the icy blue all around them - soon replaced by whiteness.

The spidery scratches came quickly, accompanied

by blue sparks and lightning cracks. Now the starburst was rising at a terrific rate, its framework shaking. Cohn juddered in his seat. Bentley made a low moan and Kimi knew her fingernails were embedded in his arm but could not let go.

The cracks and bangs slowed and the starburst emerged from the white. They cleared the ring of barrel-shaped buoys and lifted into bright sunshine.

The starburst swept above the spiralling canal, quickly clearing Bridgetown, and the countryside went into a blur. Moments later, the craft slowed over thick forest and began to descend through a ring of tall fir trees.

"This isn't home," Bentley said.

"No," Cohn said, as the craft lowered into a wide, grassy clearing. He pressed the panel by his side and it flipped open. The cable snaked out and went straight to Cohn's ear. There was a click and the slender point was pulled out and the cable recoiled into the panel. The cockpit slid forward and Cohn climbed out. Kimi followed with shaking legs, jumping awkwardly to the grass.

"Is there ssspace in the workshop for the starburssst?" Cohn asked.

Bentley's boots thumped down and he staggered. "I - I guess there'd be room if we shifted a few desks out the way," he said, staring around at the tall trees. "Where is this place?"

"The Ring of Truth," Cohn said.

"Oh," Bentley said. "An old gobblean haunt."

Kimi didn't want to ask.

"Arriving in Middling, unannounced," Cohn went on. "Will cause a ssstir with the Adeptsssss." He leaned against the hovering starburst and folded his arms. His grey skin looked dolphin-like in the sunlight.

"Good thinking," Kimi said. "So what now?"

"Your sssslave," Cohn pointed at Bentley, "will create a wind traveller and go make us some ssspaccce."

Cohn obviously disliked Bentley, or disliked Tulpas. "Right, erm, so, we're gonna go through a twirly in your spaceship?"

"Yesss - directly into the workshop - away from prying eyesss. I mussst also link the ship with your father's computer and ensure its capabilitiessss are sufficient for the tassssk."

"Yes, good idea," Bentley said. "And you're right, of course. This must be kept quiet. If Patina gets wind of what we're doing, she'll throw me in the freezer without a second thought."

"Now would be good!" Cohn gave Bentley his sickly smile.

"Oh. Right. Of course." Bentley got to his feet and had a vortex swirling in an instant. He bloomed into the old Bentley and jumped inside looking flustered without even saying goodbye.

Cohn looked on edge as he watched the twirly

vanish. He shuddered then climbed back into the starburst. Before Kimi had a chance to ask what he was doing, the craft began to rise with the cockpit still open. From some twenty feet up, sunlight glinting off it, Cohn's bulbous head came over the side.

"You have good mojo, Kimi Nicholsss?"

A strong breeze swept through the clearing and the surrounding fir trees rustled. The hairs on Kimi's neck bristled and Little Hand tingled so fiercely it made her yelp. "I - I'm just a learner."

Cohn smiled. "Shhhhow me."

Kimi heard rustling among the trees. The thick skirt of a tree bulged and waved along to the next as if something large was moving behind. This was no *old* haunt of a gobby-thing, or whatever Bentley had called them. They were here, waiting, and probably under Cohn's command. Kimi imagined terrible little men jumping from the trees in pointy hats with green teeth and long floppy ears.

The tree where she'd last seen movement, moved again, and its lower branches pushed outwards. A large black head came through. The big cat stared at Kimi for a second before slinking out onto the grass, its eyes glowing amber. The sunshine glossed its coat just like it had in the cornfield all those years ago.

Adrenalin kicked in immediately. Kimi felt it surging through her.

Sprouts.

She remembered the smell of the cat's breath, the hot sun glinting behind its head, the saliva dripping to her ladybird dress. Her brow pulsed and Little Hand tensed and relaxed, tensed and relaxed. To her left, low branches parted and a second big cat stepped through. Up above, Cohn was hissing, but Kimi didn't look up. Little Hand went firmly to her chest and her tingling grooves felt magically energised. She recalled the invoking words and focused.

Logos, Thymos, Eros...

Which cat to take out first? She turned slightly, getting both cats in her sights. This was not a good position to be in, Kimi thought, her heart thumping soundly. She started thinking about how stupid Bentley was leaving her in the middle of nowhere with an alien who couldn't care less whether she got mauled or not, but the cat to her front bared its teeth and gave a low growl.

Concentrate, concentrate.

Logos, Thymos -

Then an idea struck. She brought both hands to her chest. Both barrels. She would take the two cats at once. All she had to do was get the aim right first time. That's all.

Logos, Thymos -

Cohn's hissing stopped.

"EROS!" Kimi bellowed and the resulting mojo really did come like magic.

As if control was not hers, Kimi watched her hands shoot out before her and swing into beautiful motion, performing opposing figure-of-eights. Orange flames shot from one cat to the other in quick succession. The cats lifted twisting and screaming into the air before exploding in fireballs. The blast knocked Kimi backwards onto the grass and the flames went floating up through from clearing like Chinese lanterns. Cohn ducked inside the starburst as they went by.

Something rustled from behind. Kimi threw a quick glance.

Branches moved everywhere. She sprang to her feet. That feeling of raw power was rebuilding itself in her arms and across her chest. She felt so strong - so ready.

"Too easssy," she heard Cohn say, and the skirts of all the trees lifted at once. Black heads emerged from every one. Kimi guessed fourteen - maybe sixteen big cats. They padded the grass, sniffing towards her.

With no further thought, Kimi's mouth opened and a great bellowing "NO!" thundered around the clearing and she went into a spin, arms outstretched and firing jagged forks of orange fire. All of the cats exploded at once filling the air with a ring of orange tatters which floated skyward as the others had done.

Kimi stood there panting, her throat was on fire, her heart still loud but sound, yes so very sound. She allowed

380

herself a small smile. Every muscle in her body now seemed to breathe in time like a weapon primed, a warrior ready to spring the next parry.

This was a Balancer.

The sound of clapping. It was Cohn. This was merely a test and she'd passed it. That was all. She looked up, expecting the starburst to be on its way down. Cohn was still peering over the side of the cockpit. He wasn't smiling and he wasn't coming down.

"Try again," he said. "Anyone can blasssst a pussssy." He put two fingers to his mouth and whistled. An ominous silence settled in the clearing. Then the trees rustled once more. Kimi's breathing remained heavy, like bellows carefully pumping power to her focus. This was all new but there was no time to dwell. Movement in the branches, but not the big movements made by the cats, these were made by something smaller.

They came through the trees quickly. These had to be the gobby-things Bentley had mentioned. Like little men with clothes made of leaves. Ears and noses dropped down past their chins. Disfigured eyes and mouths gave their faces the appearance of melted plastic. Kimi was surrounded. Each creature had a wand pointed at Kimi – at least it looked like a wand. Blue sparks fizzed at the ends. They were closing in.

The idea that she could fire from her foot as well as both hands and maybe take out half them at once seemed a good one, but then there was a lot of them. Maybe a twenty or thirty; teeth bared, sneering.

Kimi's legs were turning to water.

Cohn had gone quiet. Only the low hum of the starburst and its shadow on the grass told her it was still there. She might be able to take out half of them but then she would surely be pounced on by the other half. She wanted to look up, plead with Cohn, but couldn't tear her eyes from the ring of prowling monsters. She was at a loss. Was this to be her end, after all she'd been through? They were closing in. This was her only chance. She would do a one foot spin, just like she did at the ice rink, and take out as many as she could using the more focused thinner beam that Babbage had showed her. She drew a deep breath and tensed her stomach muscles in readiness for the spin. This had to be perfection.

Logos, Thymos -

The ugly little creatures were lowering themselves into attack positions. Every single one, growled in unison, saliva dripping from snarling jaws.

Logos, Thymos, focus, focus, focus, but the focus would not come.

Her heart was no longer sound, it faltered as if missing beats.

Kimi swayed and the trees swayed with her. With the thought that she was about to faint - and then surely be ripped apart - she found herself rising into the air. She was

Separating, but not slowly as she'd done before. She sped towards the hovering starburst, grabbed onto the rim of the cockpit, and her legs shot up to meet her body. Cohn hissed and shrank back looking more surprised than Kimi was. She clung on tight and smiled at him, hoping he didn't think about closing the cockpit.

"Nice mojo," Cohn said, eyes wider than usual.

Kimi was about to ask if he would kindly get them out of there when below, wind roared and the little men scattered back into the forest. The grass in the clearing swirled and the old Bentley reappeared.

"Don't ask," Kimi said, as Cohn brought the starburst down.

"But -"

"I said don't ask." Kimi jumped the last few feet to the grass. "We were practising mojo while you were gone - that's all."

"Yesssss," Cohn said. "Practicccccce."

"Oh," Bentley said, with a jealous look.

"Ssssspace?" Cohn said, peering from the cockpit. "Have you made ssssspace?"

"Of course," Bentley said. "Shall I?" He stuck a finger into the air and spun up a vortex once more. Cohn made his sickly smile and extended a hand to Kimi. She didn't like that stupid smile at all and thought she could happily punch him. She took his cold hand and climbed in while Bentley kept the twirly going.

Cohn closed the cockpit and stared at the spinning vortex, but the starburst wasn't moving.

"Come on," Kimi said. "Just drive into it. Bentley knows what he's doing."

"I dissslike," Cohn said. "They make chaossss with my innardsss."

"Come on," she said, reluctantly reaching a hand to his bony shoulder. He felt like a dead fish. "You'll be fine - I promise!"

Cohn placed a cold hand on hers, closed his eyes and the starburst nudged forward into the vortex. The walls of the ship began to waver and Cohn's eyes opened with an expression of sheer terror. As the familiar groaning sound came and papers slapped and fluttered outside the cockpit, tiny beads of sweat covered Cohn's face, his red hue paled to the faintest pink.

The groaning stopped and the workshop walls appeared. Kimi looked around for the others, finding the three heads of Stella, Rehd and Big Sue sticking up behind the sofa in the living room. Stella waved and Kimi waved back, then turned quickly at the awful sound of vomiting.

Cohn was gone. She scrambled past his seat and lifted herself up on the rim of the cockpit. He was crouched on the workshop floor adding more sick to a steaming pile, his once grey face now pearly white.

"Eeww," Stella said, striding into the workshop. "If you think I'm clearing that up!"

"No need," groaned Cohn, remaining bent over the sick pile. His tongue dropped out and sucked it all up like a hoover.

"That is not good," Kimi said, as Cohn crawled to a chair and slumped into it.

"Hate those thingsssss," he hissed, rubbing his stomach

***

Big Sue chose some classical music on the juke box then scurried into the workshop with his tea towels flapping, fussing over General Cohn as if he was royalty; while Rehd took the notebook of calculations and the disc with the cctv footage and sat with Cohn at the main computer. Bentley arrived moments later, his twirly appearing between the nose of the starburst and the chair where Cohn was sat, which caused the General to groan again. Kimi remained on the sofa in the living room, eating one of the crackers that Sue had fetched over. The cheese tasted strangely like creamy carrots.

"So what's it like, flying in a real alien ship?" Stella asked, taking a seat.

"Okay, I suppose," Kimi said, still a little shaken from the confrontation with the gobby-things.

"Just okay? Ach, you're a jammy cow. I've asked

385

Granp for a lift loads of times but he never will - did you come back through the black hole thing?"

"Oh yeah, yeah we did."

Stella's eyes twinkled. "Ach, I so wish I could have a go."

Kimi glanced into the workshop to check that Cohn was out of earshot. He was at the far end, engrossed in the computer with Rehd. Audrey the crow was standing up in its napkin nest and showing some interest. "What bothers me," Kimi whispered. "If he hates twirlies so much, how the heck is he gonna fly the starburst through two at once *and* go back in time?" Then added as an afterthought; "Maybe we should take some sick bags. If he pukes in the cockpit, I swear I'll -"

"Ah! Cheese and crackers, my favourite," Bentley exclaimed in an overloud voice and perching on the arm of the sofa. He peered through the hole in the wall as if he too was checking on Cohn's position and then leaned closer and said in a whisper; "Kimi, remember that pointy thing that went in the General's ear?"

Kimi nodded.

"It must be some sort of piloting device - like a driver - you know - it reads his thoughts and takes the ship to wherever he's thinking of."

Kimi shrugged, "Suppose."

"Well," Bentley continued, lowering his voice even further. "I didn't get a great deal, but I did pick up some of those thoughts - and -" he peered over the sofa again. Cohn had got up and was trailing a reel of cable over to the starburst.

"Ah yes, best pony cheese on the market," Bentley said. "And from the Dank Forest ponies, no less!"

"Scrummy!" Stella said, crunching down on a triple-decker cracker.

Cohn disappeared inside the ship, pulling the cable in with him.

"And listen," Bentley went on in a whisper, "he's after your mojo, Kimbo. I'm certain of it!"

"What do you mean?" Kimi asked. "How can he take anyone's mojo? That's not possible, is it?"

Bentley paused in thought then shrugged. "I don't know to be honest, Kimbo. But with greylian technology - who knows? All I'm saying is, I picked up some snippets, and to me, it didn't sound like he was after knitting you a scarf!"

"You can't nick anyone's mojo," Stella said, brushing crumbs off her new jacket. "You're probably adding two and two and getting six, Mr B."

"And anyway," Kimi said. "Pony cheese?"

"Aye," Stella offered Kimi the plate. "Have another - they're lovely with a bit of piskie polyp pickle!"

"Um, no thanks," Kimi said, just as the hum of the starburst grew louder and sparks flew from the back of the computer where Rehd sat.

"NEGATORY!" Rehd shouted. "OFF! OFF! OFF!" and the hum died.

Cohn's bulbous head appeared from the starburst's cockpit, hissing a string of curses.

"You know," Bentley said, quietly, "I've got a bad feeling about this. I'm thinking we should inform Babb, erm, you-know-who."

"No way!" Kimi cut in. "Babb - you-know-who, said that this was the only way - *and* he had Dad's backing on that. Trust me - Dad would know best."

"Ah, but best for who, Kimbo?" Bentley said meekly.

Kimi stood up and straightened her jacket. "Look," she said, fixing her eyes firmly on Bentley's. "We have to do this."

"I'm only worried about you, Kimbo. That's all." Bentley said. "I think he's up to something, really I do."

"Listen," she said. "Back in the clearing when you left me alone with the General - he - he tested me – he erm, he threw little rocks and I had to show him how accurate I was."

"And you hit them?"

"Course I did," Kimi said, feeling her cheeks warming. "And then I showed him the stretchy Separation thing and he was very impressed - that's when you came

388

back - so if he was going to hurt me or nick my mojo, he had plenty chance then didn't he?"

"Well, I -"

"Give it up, Bentley. I'm going flying. It's my mission, my risk, and I say we follow you-know-who's instructions to the letter. If you don't want to get involved, then - then I'd understand - okay?"

Bentley slipped from the sofa arm, sank into a cushion and took another cracker from the plate. "I was only saying," he said, shoving the whole cracker in his mouth and crunching loudly.

Kimi went to the juke box, feeling quite sick. She was glad that her back was turned to Bentley and Stella. A strange mix of emotions wavered through her. She wanted to be a brave Balancer like she had been when facing the shuck and the gobby-things, but there was obviously something missing. She should have willed the Separation herself to escape the gobby-things but she hadn't thought of that. Her subconscious had done it for her. And maybe that wasn't a bad thing, but still she would prefer to have better control. She ran a trembling finger over the buttons on the jukebox. Then she remembered that Big Sue had opened up the IPC at this very wall by pressing something on the juke box. She took her hand away from the buttons not wanting to set the thing in motion. Despite the revolting strangeness of Babbage, Kimi knew he was on her side, and the thought of going to see him one last time niggled at her. She hated lying to Bentley, but what if he was right? But then again, what would Cohn want with her mojo? But then, the success of this mission was going to be down to her Balancer's purity, so maybe Cohn was picking up on that.

"Are you all right, deary?"

Kimi jumped. Big Sue was at her side grinning from beneath his beard, a tea towel nipped in his fingers - *ready to wipe away tears*, Kimi thought. "I'm fine, thanks. I - I'm just thinking about what I have to do - you know, making sure I've got everything covered and -"

"Oh, I'm sure you will have, dear. You do realise you're in the best hands with the General, don't you? Isn't it exciting having him here all to ourselves?"

"Er, yeah." Kimi gazed at the buttons on the jukebox.

"Can I get you anything? A cup of tea? Pommy juice?"

"No thanks," Kimi said, looking up to Sue's kindly eyes. "There is erm, one thing," she said, quietly. "The IPC thing - how did you get it to appear?"

"Oh," Sue took a step back, his face crumpled. "I - I - must - I, um, I don't remember."

"You're not allowed to tell are you?"

Sue shook his head.

"But why? Bentley thinks there might be a problem,

and I'm wondering whether Charlie should be consulted - that's all. So which buttons do I press?"

Sue came closer and bent to Kimi's ear. "Your father made me promise not to reveal the entrance code to anyone - especially you and especially with greylian presence!"

"But I don't understand," Kimi said. "It seems to me that Charlie's a pretty bright bloke - if we've got concerns, then surely we'd be crazy not to check with him first?"

Sue looked back to Bentley and Stella on the sofa who were still eating and talking quietly between themselves. He reached into his dressing gown pocket and pulled out a piece of folded paper.

"Your father left this," he said, handing it to Kimi. "He said, should the mission fail, or should you be having doubts, then I was to give you this."

Kimi kept her back to the others and unfolded the note.

Kimi, dearest daughter. If you're reading this, then either something has gone wrong or you are experiencing doubts. If something has gone wrong, if the Jiffy didn't work out, or - well, I can't really think so straight right now. Your mum's still hypnotised, Charlie's getting panicky, and as you might imagine, I'm very worried about you. But enough of that. If something hasn't worked, promise me that you won't waste time chasing blame, or worse still, blaming yourself. What

you're being asked to do is no small task - if - no - WHEN
you pull this off and we are reunited, this will go down in
Heart history as not only a discovery that will propel
mankind in great new directions but a momentous feat of
bravery. There is more at stake here than you might realise.
This is not just about the possibility that you might save me
and Mum - mankind is depending on you to make this
happen. If you're having any doubts at all, well there are
certain people you can trust - Sue, Bentley, Stella, and Rehd
- oh and of course, Charlie. All I ask is that you follow
Charlie's instructions and do your best, but whatever you
do, do not divulge Charlie's involvement to anyone,
especially a greylian - his work is too valuable to jeopardise.
You can do this, Kimi. I want you to keep your wits and know
that we are with you every step of the way. I know how brave
you are, how determined you can be. It's time to stand up,
Kimi. Do it for us, do it for good!
Don't forget how much we love you!
Good luck,
Dad & Mum xxx

Kimi swallowed the lump in her throat. Luck? Is that what she needed, just some good luck? She shoved the note in her jacket and slumped against the jukebox. The classical music screeched into silence, replaced seconds later by *The Sun Has Got His Hat On*.

"There now," Sue dabbed at Kimi's cheek with the tea towel. His big arm came around her shoulders and Kimi's head sunk into his stomach.

"You'll be fine, flower - just fine," he said.

Kimi had to sit, had to put some focus to her thoughts. She took the first book from the shelves, *Notorious Carnivorous Plants of Heart,* and while the minutes ticked away to the sounds of Cohn and Rehd cheering and congratulating each other on yet another obstacle passed, she flicked through the pages and thought of the mission ahead. She ran over it many times, and crazy and scary as it sounded, it all seemed so plausible. Plausible enough to let it ride, to go along with, to maybe have some of that good luck with. She could live with that. But all this digging had unearthed something new. Something not so easy to let go.

Wasn't there always a hero who must save the day? And wasn't that hero always in some sort of danger, or required to sacrifice something? Kimi had realised what both the danger and the sacrifice was in her particular mission.

The Doppelganger Paradox.

It was simple really, and at first, Kimi wondered why no one had mentioned it. They might well achieve time travel. After all, Babbage's and her father's experiments had proved that possible, and whoever the murderer was that awaited them, she was sure that between her and Cohn they would have no problem in taking him out and saving Mum and Dad; yet she also knew, that once it was over she would have to stay away from home. Get too close to the original Kimi, and well, she didn't fancy being turned inside out.

There'd be two Kimi Nichols. One of them would have to live in a cave on the moors or something. This was to be her sacrifice. Mum and Dad would visit, bring food and stuff. She remembered the story of the hermit who lived by the sea in Mousehole cave. Maybe he was an outlawed Balancer. Perhaps Mousehole cave would be her new home. That would be her sacrifice - her fate.

She wiped away a tear. Nobody had talked about this because it was bloody bad. This was the unspoken thing. The thing the brave hero did without mentioning. Like Babbage had said; no one likes a bragger. Her eyes watered, her thoughts on those things she'd miss; Julie, school, Mousehole -

Rehd's furious shrieking gave her a start.

"Everybody!" he shouted. "We're all systems go!"

———

23

~ One Death ~

The workshop was stuffy and smelled of hot electricity. Desks, chairs, waste bins and filing cabinets had been piled up the walls and shoved into corners and the gleaming blue starburst filled most of the long room. Its white belly hovered an inch from the floor. Beyond its globular nose, which almost touched the ceiling, Cohn's scrawny grey figure was hunched in a seat at the main computer. To his right, on a computer chair which had obviously been raised to its highest setting, sat Rehd, cross-legged.

With Sue's hands kneading her shoulders, Kimi moved slowly past the starburst, her skin seeming to vibrate along with starburst's ominous hum. She tried to think happy thoughts; like the pink limo she'd get tomorrow if she pulled this off, but the limo wouldn't come to mind, only the image of Mousehole cave and her in rags, eating seagulls. Kimi felt her legs wobble.

If she showed any signs of wavering, she knew Bentley would find that an excuse to delay things, or even worse, involve the Adepts. She told herself there was nothing to fear, that she was only a kid who couldn't do simple maths, adored pink, and wore baggy tops to hide Little Hand. Sue's hands squeezed her shoulders as they arrived at the main computer. The monitor showed the cctv image of the three big cats peering from the bushes at the golf course, and Cohn's bulbous head was fixed on it intently.

"It's certainly a workable plan," Rehd said, swinging his chair from side to side.

Bentley arrived and stood to Kimi's left, but she didn't look at him and tried to close her thoughts to words like doubt and failure.

Stella appeared crunching a cracker. She leant on the end of the desk and smiled. "You okay, Kimi?"

Kimi managed a smile back, then realised her arms were so tightly folded that they might just spring apart and whack Cohn on the head. She had an immediate urge to do so, followed by a stabbing pain in the brow. Big Sue's hands squeezed her shoulders once more and Kimi relaxed a little. She shoved her hands in her pockets, found the grass dolly and held it tight.

Cohn clicked the mouse and the image on the monitor changed to the one showing Mum and Dad on the golf course. They might only be two small, dark, stick-figures stood on a deserted green, but they were still her parents. Kimi closed her eyes and squeezed her dolly.

"So it's going ahead?" Stella said.

"Of coursssssse," hissed Cohn.

Rehd was nodding but not looking too enthusiastic.

"This isn't a jaunt to the seaside you know," Bentley said. "If this plan has the slightest flaw, then it - well - it should be delayed and reconsidered. And perhaps some professional help sought too!" he added.

Cohn turned and glared at him, his black eyes shiny. "Thisssss," Cohn said, turning back to the screen and tapping it, "is the precissse moment we travel back to -"

"Why then?" snapped Bentley. "Why not earlier? We want them alive and not in any danger from a murderer."

"Sssssimple. Travel back too soon and we risssk losing the killer. If there isssss a killer." Cohn turned to Kimi and made his cutesy little smile. "A killer let loossse, will find a way to kill again. Yesss?"

Kimi nodded.

Cohn returned the nod, his ovular eyes narrowed. "Your father - his calculationsss are geniusssss. I have fed them into the starburssst and it seemsss that execution of the Jiffy will bring no problemsss. You will accompany me as firsssssst pilot."

"First pilot?" Kimi said in dry voice.

"The driver thing, Kimbo." Bentley was pointing to his ear.

"Yesssss," Cohn went on. "Being closesssst to the victimssss, makes you the mosssst suitable navigator." He made the sickly smile. "Yesssss?"

"Yes," Kimi said, swallowing hard.

Sue's hand came over her shoulder dangling a tea towel. Kimi took it and wiped her face.

"Okay?" Bentley asked.

"Just a bit warm, thanks," she said, keeping her eyes on the monitor.

"Good!" Cohn tapped the screen. "Thisss is our moment of arrival - precisssely five minutessss before your parentsssss were ssstruck down - thissss will allow me time to drop the starburst, and if there is a killer he will be vapourisssed! If the killer turnsss out to be a bolt of lightning then we will remove your parents from harm'ssss way. The precision of exactly five minutesss - is important, Kimi Nicholssssss. You must begin focusssss immediately, so that once you are wearing the driver, it will have better chance of successss. Five minutesss - precisssely. Yesssss?"

Kimi nodded. "Got it - five minutes."

"Precisssely!"

"I got it. Exactly five minutes."

"Good!" Cohn returned his gaze to the screen. "According to the Jiffy calculationsss – we need two opposing wind travellerssss, accurate in diameter to within five-point-five metresss of each other. The way of achieving such accuracy is thissss -" he clicked the mouse and a plan view of Pommy Wood came on screen. A tiny square in the middle showed the Shed, and the wood's circumference was dotted with small rectangles - the forty-two enormous standing stones.

"You're not thinking what I think you're thinking? Are you?" Bentley said.

Kimi felt him shake.

"I'm afraid so." Rehd sighed. He was shaking his head at the screen.

"What is it?" asked Stella.

"The stonesss," Cohn said, "are perfect. They hold the power required to assure the gauge and stability of the wind travellersss - without the stonesss we have no guarantee of successsss."

Bentley went into a rant about severe punishments all round, while Rehd chattered nervously to himself. Stella was jabbering excitedly about giant twirlies and hell-to-pay and not caring about being expelled, while Big Sue was gripping Kimi's shoulders too hard and asking for silence. But no one seemed to be listening to anyone. And the red hue across the top of Cohn's head had turned an ugly purple.

"QUIET!" Kimi yelled, which even made Cohn jump. There was silence.

"General Cohn," Kimi began, in the calmest voice she could muster. "Thank you for giving up your time and expertise. I really do appreciate it. But are you sure there is no other way? No other stone circle we could use?"

Cohn's purple scalp diffused to red. He smiled. "We could make our own circle in the wildernesssss - bigger than the one containing the Shhhhhed."

"And that would work?" Kimi said. "Making our own circle?"

"Perhapsss, perhapsss not. You sssssee, the circle around Pommy Wood is located in the centre of Middling - it holds more power than anywhere elssse on Heart.
"If it is your wishhh," Cohn continued, "we can try somewhere elssse, but making such a circle will take time, and even then successs is not guaranteed!"

"Sounds a better plan to me," Bentley said. "I'm all for building our own circle."

"That would take too long," Rehd said. "And besides, I think the general's right. Only the stones of Pommy Wood will do." Rehd sighed at the screen. "Even though I'll be demoted to desk duty until I retire." He sighed again. "Ruthie will be happy though."

"Chief Rehd," Kimi said. "You've helped enough. You don't have to get involved with the actual Jiffy."

Cohn swung around. "The sssimian's help is a necesssssity!"

"Guys!" Stella said. "Why not hear the good General out and listen to the whole plan, then we can decide what to do?"

"She's right you know," Sue said. "Please continue, General."

Cohn said to Bentley: "Sssssstage one – you, Tulpa

400

Bentley will send me and Kimi Nicholsss back to the Ring of Truth - yesss?"

"In the starburst?"

"Yesssss in the starburssst!"

"Right," Bentley said.

"Ssstage two – Ssssstella, and the Tulpa Bentley, will hide behind the stonesss of Pommy Wood until the sssimian createsss a diversion."

Rehd scratched nervously at his armpits. "What kind of diversion?"

"You will announce sightingsssss of many shuck clossssse to Middling, enlissst all duty monkeys, and move them out quickly, so the wood is void of fuzzzzzzzzz!"

"Okay," Rehd agreed. "I can do that."

"This meansssss," Cohn continued. "That you will be absssolved of any blame for our mission - no one will doubt the chief of fuzzzzz when he declaresss a possible shuck attack!"

"Good idea." Rehd nodded.

"Ach, this is so cool!" Stella said.

"Seems workable, I suppose," Bentley muttered.

"Ssstage three. Once the fuzz are engaged elsewhere, the sssimian will fire three green flaresss. No more - no lesssss. Anything other than three and the mission abortsss. Everyone clear?"

Murmured yes's came back.

"On the third flare, O'Brien and the Tulpa Bentley will come out from hiding, travel directly to the roof of the Shhhhed and commenccce making wind!"

Stella snorted. "Sorry," she said.

Cohn clicked the mouse and the graphic on screen began to move. Two misty rings appeared, overlaying the circumference of standing stones. Kimi stared at the image and focused her thoughts on the golf course.

"Be warned," Cohn said. "We will have no more than one minute from thisss point to exxxecute the Jiffy. Any longer and the Adeptsssss will put an end to your wind making."

Kimi heard Bentley swallow.

"I will bring the starburssst in at 42,000 feet above the wind-makersss. If all goesss to plan, the opposssing ringsss of wind will be at the perfect weave and ssspeed to exxxecute the Jiffy!"

"But what if they aren't?" Stella asked.

"Sssimple," hissed Cohn. "I retreat and you and the Tulpa Bentley get locked up."

"Charming," Bentley said. "Don't worry, Stella. We can do this."

Kimi smiled a quivering smile at Bentley. His returned smile seemed a little forced. Cohn went on, "Precision is essssssssential." He clicked the mouse and the graphic showed the starburst spiralling downwards into the

402

weaving rings before vanishing from the screen in a flash.

"What about me?" Big Sue asked. "Where do I fit in?"

"In the Rabbit'sss Foot," Cohn said. "Ensure no one gets a sssniff of our planssss!"

"Alright then," Sue said, importantly.

Kimi realised no one had mentioned taking the crow along. She was about to speak up when Bentley grabbed her arm and spun her round. His eyes were wide and his head was shaking.

"Erm, so when do we leave?" Stella asked.

Cohn turned from the monitor. His eyes narrowed a little and the corners of his mouth curled up. "Now!" he said, and Kimi's heart jumped.

"Now?" Bentley said. "Shouldn't we - shouldn't we be practicing those twirlies at least? And, and -"

"And what?" said Cohn.

"Well I - erm - I -"

"No practicccccce," Cohn said, getting to his feet and moving silkily to the starburst. "The hour is late and therefore, perfect. Tulpa Big Sssue - open the Rabbit'sss Foot - apologissse to your customersss and treat them to bigger portionsss."

Cohn pulled the cables from the starburst and threw them across the floor.

"Kimi Nicholsss," he said, gesturing to the starburst.

Kimi's insides began to squirm. She took a faltering step forwards and was accosted in seconds by Stella, Bentley, and Sue all rushing to hug her.

"I'll be fine," she said, feeling a little light-headed while hugging them all back. "Oh, and Bentley, Stella, thanks for doing this - I know you're gonna get in trouble - be careful."

"Good luck, Balancer Nichols," Rehd said.

If only she could hug him. He could be a cheeky monkey but his heart was in the right place. General Cohn was climbing in the cockpit. Bentley pulled Kimi to one side. "Remember the Balancer code," he said, putting an arm around her and leading her to a noticeboard on the wall. He stared up at it then whispered: "The crow – Audrey – she's inside the seat in the back. She insisted Cohn wasn't to know she was hitching a ride. Said it was important. Good luck, Kimi…"

Okay, thanks, Kimi thought.

"And that's about it," Bentley said. "Oh – and watch your back!" He led Kimi to the awaiting ship. Kimi took a deep breath and climbed up and into the cockpit.
"Oh dear," she heard Sue say as she settled on the padded box-seat behind
General Cohn.

Kimi could see Bentley and Stella, both of them wide-eyed. And Rehd, who'd stood up on his chair to see.

404

Cohn's seat moulded itself to his shape and the cockpit began to slide forwards. Bentley rushed over with a handful of sick bags and passed them to Cohn just before the cockpit shut. "Thanksss," he hissed, dropping them to the floor.

"Good luck, Kimbo!" Bentley shouted.

Big Sue rushed forward and began polishing the cockpit furiously.

Kimi managed a small smile at Bentley and had a fleeting image of him appearing all those years ago in the cornfield. If only she hadn't followed the butterfly. But what then? Would she still have become a Balancer? Would her parents still be here?

"Wind!" Cohn bellowed.

Bentley moved to the front of the starburst and started up the twirly. Big Sue stepped back as loose papers began flapping around the glass of the cockpit. Stella's small white hands and Sue's waving tea-towels soon vanished and they were back in the forest clearing, the tall trees a ring of black around them, the stars twinkling above.

"Sssstraight up," Cohn said and the starburst rose quickly, clearing the trees and rising further into the cloudless sky. He punched the panel by his side and the metal cable snaked out, its slender point sniffing at the air.

"Shhhhow it your ear," Cohn said.

The cable weaved gently towards Kimi, its point twitching. Cohn watched as the cable arrived, floating before

Kimi's eyes.

"Hurry," he said.

Kimi took a breath, swept her hair behind her right ear and turned her head to the side. At first it felt like a cotton bud scraping at her earlobe, but then came a warm, sliding sensation. There was no pain, only a feeling of busyness, as if every brain cell was working at once.

"Is it in?"

Kimi nodded and the cable clicked and pulled away, free of its slender point. Then it shrank back into the panel.

"Kimi Nicholsss!"

Kimi stared at him.

"Think of your target…five minutesss before - precisely five minutesss. Yesss?"

"Yes," Kimi said, deciding to put full trust in Cohn now. She had no choice, and no other part to play than concentrate on the time and place. She had to get this right.

"The starburssst will follow your thoughtsss for final delivery. In the meantime I will ssssteer into the opposing wind travellers at the necesssssary ssspeed and precissse angle. You must alwaysss be thinking of the delivery time in order for the driver to do itsss job. Yesss?"

"Yes," Kimi said. "Exactly five minutes." And so she continued, repeating those words over and over in her mind while picturing Mum and Dad on the golf course, and all the while the driver in her ear grew warmer. And then, through the cockpit window over Cohn's shoulder, far in the black distance, a bloom of luminous green exploded - followed seconds later by another.

"That'sss two," Cohn said, and the starburst sailed forward and the seconds seemed to pass into minutes. Kimi focused. Five minutes – exactly five minutes.

And there it was, the third flare. This one went higher, masking the stars for miles around. Kimi felt sick.

"Go, go, go!" Cohn said, and the starburst shot to the stars. Kimi closed her eyes to a pounding brow. She held an image of Mum and Dad laughing and joking as they stepped onto the green. Five minutes exactly… Five minutes exactly…

***

The second flare exploded, illuminating Pommy Wood in an eerie green glow. Stella pulled the teen Bentley behind a standing stone as a dozen or so squad bikes rolled past. Monkeys on foot ran along after them, screaming at everyone to stay indoors. Cries of `shuck alert` echoed around the ring road. Rehd scurried from the thicket, winked and Stella nodded back. He wound his arm and jumped in the air, shooting the third flare up through the trees like a rocket. It exploded in a brilliant flash of luminous green.

"Now!" Stella said, spinning her hands. The leaves around them rose into a vortex and she and Bentley stepped inside, appearing a second later on the roof of the deserted

Shed just as the last flare died and the stars returned. Curious famoose were scuttling along branches all around them. Bentley and Stella stood side by side in the centre of the roof and linked arms, each facing the opposite way. "Ready?" Bentley said.

"Can't wait," Stella replied.

"For Kimi!" Bentley raised an arm.

"For Kimi!" Stella thrust her arm to the air. And so they began, whipping the air while side-stepping in circles. Those famoose that had ventured nearest where sucked from their branches into the swirl, followed by leaves, twigs and pomegranate lanterns as the opposing twirlies grew bigger and bigger.

***

"We have posssition!" Cohn said, tapping at the buttons to his front. All Kimi could see outside were stars, but on screen, a radar image showed the circle of stones around Pommy Wood below. "Focussssed, Kimi Nicholsss?"

"Yeah," Kimi said, breathlessly, "Five minutes exactly - five minutes -"

"Yessss," Cohn said. A small misty ring had appeared in the centre of the screen. It was followed a few seconds later by a second ring which wavered slightly from the first. Both rings grew quickly, spreading outwards to the circle of stones. "Yessss!" Cohn repeated. "Thirty secondssss!"

Kimi stared at the screen with her pulse racing.

Five minutes exactly… Five minutes exactly…

***

"Nearly there!" shouted Stella, but her words were drowned by the deafening roar. Hundreds of pomegranate lanterns clattered through branches. Famoose fought hopelessly against the wind, squealing as they sucked into the swirl. Bentley and Stella stayed linked and continued to side-step as the two twirlies gained momentum, spreading outwards to the standing stones.

"They're here!" Stella yelled as the comet-like flash zipped across the sky. But Bentley's eyes were fixed on the clearing below. Blue light had painted a circle on the grass and a rounded shadow loomed into it.

"Hurry, hurry, hurry!" he yelled, swinging his arm with all his might.

***

"Here goesss," Cohn said. "Focussss, Kimi Nicholsss! Five - four - three -"

The built up tension, the hard throb in Kimi's brow, the queasy unease in her gut, all of it vanished. The driver pulsed in her ear and the realisation that she could soon be seeing her parents came over her in a wave of golden empowerment.

Previous focus was nothing compared to this.

This was tight like a wire, connecting straight to

Mum and Dad.

A connection that can never be broken.

Focus was easy. Focus was natural.

Five minutes exactly, five minutes exactly…

***

"We've got perfection!" Stella shouted, her hair billowing. It looked as if Bentley hadn't heard. He broke away, continued whipping the twirly, and took a staggering step towards the edge of the roof. Below, the round figure of Blavatsky stood illuminated in the blue light from the doorway; her head, contorted with rage, was rising through the air on a spindly neck.

Bentley pulled his free arm to his chest as the howl of the twirlies continued. He was about to unleash mojo at an Adept, and he knew this might be goodbye for him, but there was little choice. Blavatsky's podgy hands slapped down on the roof's edge and her neck was snaking towards him shouting something he couldn't hear. Bentley swung back his hand. He was about to send stunners to paralyse the Adept's fingers, when a small shadow emerged from the thicket below.

Bentley hesitated - it was Rehd, shaking his fist. A stream of silver balls zipped from his outstretched arm, a direct hit to Blavatsky's back. She shrunk wailing to the ground and Rehd darted back into the thicket.

More dark shapes spilled into the clearing - Adepts -

too many to take on. Bentley carried on twirling, breathless now, his aching arm begging to give up. He looked up to the starry sky and saw the smallest blue light. It was growing bigger.

"This is it!" Stella shouted.

***

"- three!" Cohn said, pushing the starburst into a dive.

Kimi stared over his shoulder at the radar and watched Pommy Wood growing quickly closer. Through the cockpit, faint twinkles of swirling lights came into view and Cohn became excited. "Forty-two degreesss - *yesss* - 732 mph - *yesss* - focusss, Kimi Nicholsss, *focusssss*!"

Kimi focused. The approaching twirlies were like a pair of huge sparkly donuts dancing in the night. She felt remarkably calm as the starburst went into a spiralling twist. And as the ship began to straighten into the twirlies and the first pomegranate lanterns started bouncing off the cockpit, she caught a momentary glimpse of the animated figures of Stella and Bentley, winding the air. Famoose, branches, and lanterns stormed the cockpit's glass and banged furiously down the ship's sides - then silence as blue lightning crackled all around.

Five minutes exactly... Five minutes exactly...

***

411

Patina, in a flowing lemon nightdress, came gliding down the narrow passageway, exited onto the balcony and stopped sharply at the railings. She gazed down at the colourful commotion over Pommy Wood and, when the starburst corkscrewed into view and zipped into the wind in a crackling stream of electric blue, she clapped, placed her hands flat to her chest - and sighed.

***

Blinding blue lightning exploded all around Pommy Wood. The accompanying loud bang threw Bentley and Stella flat to the roof and the wind died instantly, followed by an almighty racket as the debris of lanterns, mangled famoose and loose branches clattered through the trees to the ground. The acrid smell of smouldering electricity and burnt famoose hung heavy in the air. Then came the rumbles. The Shed and the trees all around it were trembling. Adepts below in the clearing were shouting to run for cover.

"Did we do it?" Stella panted, crawling to Bentley and grasping his shirt.

"I - I think so," Bentley said, sitting up.

Stella put a hand on his shoulder and went to stand but the Shed was shaking too much. "What's happening?"

"Look!" Bentley pointed through the trees at the point where the starburst had vanished. One of the huge standing stones was glowing orange and rocking from side to side.

"Shit - it's going," Stella said. Then it did, hitting the next stone with a resounding crack. Then another crack as the second stone hit the third followed quickly by the next and like giant dominoes the entire ring of forty-two stones came crashing down.

The ground shook and the timbers of the old Shed collapsed in a rush of dust and Bentley and Stella went thumping to the floor.

***

Five minutes exactly...

The driver in Kimi's ear buzzed like a bee and there was a whistling shriek and a blast of white light followed by enormous calm and a warm blue sky. Kimi darted forward and looked over Cohn's shoulder just as he was sick down his front.

"Have we done it?" she asked ignoring the smell and staring intently at the screen. The radar image of Pommy Wood had gone. The screen was black. Kimi's heart sank.

Cohn spat to the floor and tapped at his console. "Let me sssee - let me sssee -"

The words: `PENZANCE, EARTH` ran along the bottom of the screen followed by a line of coordinates. Kimi gasped. Cohn tapped more buttons and the screen hissed with white noise.

"Did we do it?" Kimi demanded. "Is the time right?"

"Patienccccce!" Cohn said. "It'sss tuning in - we will

pick up the nearest cctv any sssecond."

The noise cleared into a black and white image, and there, walking onto the green in real-time was the greatest sight in the whole world.

"Yes!" Kimi punched the air. "We did it, we did it!"

Cohn turned, gave his toy smile and dribbled vomit. "Yesss, Kimi Nicholsss. Your father is a human geniusss." He hissed into laughter.

"What's so funny?"

Cohn's hands went to his head and his laughter grew into horrible cackles.

"We haven't time for this," Kimi said. "Come on - get us down there - time's wasting!" She felt strong, fired up, ready for action.

But Cohn didn't look at her. He faced the screen, gave a big sigh, and pressed a button which sent the starburst into a slow descent. As swirling white cloud engulfed the ship, Cohn turned. In his hand was a small silver weapon with a globular end, like a mini version of the rocket launchers.

Kimi thought her heart had stopped.

"There'sss sssomeone I'd like you to meet." Cohn's tongue slipped a little way from the corner of his mouth and cleaned up bits of sick from his chin. The ship sank further into darker cloud and rainwater trickled down the cockpit windows. The storm clouds were starting to form. Cohn raised the weapon and Kimi's chest tightened.

"Please - please don't -"

Cohn jerked his head, indicating the window to his left.

Through swirls of black cloud, a sleek blue shape appeared - another starburst.

The ship came closer. Cohn waved at the pilot who pressed his big grey forehead to his cockpit window. He too had the red hue running up his brow. It was Cohn's double - another Cohn - and judging by the wide-eyed look on his face, he was as surprised at seeing his double as Kimi was.

The General gave a thumbs up and the other Cohn's expression altered from puzzlement to one of delight. His mouth gaped to an O, then he threw his head back and his shoulders shuddered.

"Why," said Cohn. "I even surprissse myself at timesss."

"It - it was you all along?" panted Kimi. "You were here. You knew. You killed them! You killed my parents!"

"Yesssss," Cohn hissed. "With residual mojo stolen from the retired slaves of Mercurial Waters used to power my weapons. And now I have a twin to share my busy schedule!" Then he threw back his head just like the other Cohn had and burst into that awful cackle. Kimi almost lunged forward to seize the weapon from his hand, but the other Cohn was now pressed up against his cockpit and

415

staring madly with his tongue hanging out.

The Cohn before her broke from his merriment. His black eyes glared at her. "In one minute, Kimi Nicholsss - one lassst minute, I shall allow you to witnesss the deathsss of your parentssssss."

On screen, the figures of Mum and Dad standing on the green appeared to be in conversation. Cohn gave a little titter as a high-pitched whine started outside accompanied by a smell like matches. The other starburst was firing up. That's what killed them. She had to do something and do it quickly.

Cohn's free hand thrust toward Kimi. She felt a tug inside her chest and dropped to her knees. Cohn beckoned a long curled finger and she slid up the floor towards him. A second later and his knobbled fingers were clasping at her jacket, almost choking her. Cohn dropped his head to hers and the end of his tongue came within an inch of her eyes. It stiffened and released a trickle of slime before retracting with speed.

"Human brainsss," he said. "What better way to cccelebrate."

"Please let me go to them - please - just one last minute with them before you - before you -"

Cohn laughed. "You humans disgussst me."

The whine coming from the other starburst reached a higher pitch. Kimi could barely hear it. She knew what was coming next. "Please," she begged. "I'll give you anything - my mojo - anything!"

"You will give me your mojo? No. I will be taking it, Balancer Kimi Jo Nicholsss. Once you have witnessed the death of your parentssss, I will remove your brain and use it to alter time and forge new worldssssss."

"Bu – but why me? And why do you have to kill my parents? Let them go and you can do what you want with me."

"Such a martyr." Cohn smiled. "Your parents are too clever. Eliminate them and I will be free to do whatever I please with your preciousss brain once I remove it from your pathetic human skull."

Kimi's heart banged against Cohn's fist. There was no way out of this. She was going to die, and, like before, so would her parents. Death was near and Kimi could smell it. Tears ran down her cheeks. She was about to plead with Cohn one last time when he began to shiver. The hue on his chest and forehead paled, and dark threadlike veins spread across his face. He glanced to the other starburst which seemed to be tilting and coming way too close.

There was a bump and a jolt as the ships knocked together. Crackling replaced the whining as the cockpit glass began to disintegrate. Chunks flew away into the clouds as the two ships bumped again. The other Cohn was clawing at his window, shouting something. Cohn let go of Kimi and

417

fell back in his seat. He was vibrating. His rapidly shaking hand brought the weapon up. "What is thisss…" he hissed and his right eye exploded sending black slush bubbling down his chest. Kimi dodged to one side as the other eye popped and bits flew towards her.

"The paradox!" she cried. "The bloody paradox!" The ship lurched, tipped to one side and both starbursts dropped from the clouds with pieces of glass and panelling tearing away.

The weapon fell from Cohn's hand and crumbled into pieces on the floor. At the same time a slicing pain seared through Kimi's ear and she screamed as the driver shot out and disintegrated at her feet. The second starburst turned in the air, its nose came around and the two noses connected with a crack which sent Kimi flying backwards and more debris flew into the clouds. Air rushed inside the starburst along with the other Cohn's scream as both his eyes popped at once, splatting what was left of his cockpit window.

Cohn, still vibrating, stood up and staggered blindly towards Kimi. His hands stiffened into claws searching the air.

"No way, mister," she said, ducking down on her haunches. The ship was breaking up quickly. She had nothing to lose here. "Now it's *my* turn!"

The mojo came sweetly and effortlessly. Little Hand

glowed hot, her outstretched arm solid and powerful, hammered repeatedly at its socket as bullets of orange fire exploded, pulsating a like machinegun. Cohn took the hit straight in his gut. When he dropped to his knees, Kimi could see the floor behind through the large blackened hole she'd made. He was gagging for breath, his chest lurched and his long tongue came reeling from his mouth and dropped to the floor. Cohn's skin was shrinking in on itself, stretching over bones which snapped and splintered and pushed their way through. His gaping stomach gave way and he twisted to the floor, the back of his bulbous head landing with a smack at Kimi's knees. His gaping mouth pleaded for air but not for long. His chest caved inwards followed by his head. He was dead, and Kimi was about to jump over the crumbling remains when she noticed his tongue by his feet. It was still moving, wriggling along the floor towards her. Kimi was about to jump up on the seat she'd previously been sitting on, when the seat opened up and Audrey sprang into action. The crow leapt to the floor, picked up the wriggling tongue in its beak and swallowed it down in three successive gulps.

"Way to go, Audrey," she said, jumping over what remained of the general. She ran into the cockpit and threw her arms around Cohn's chair as the starburst crumbled around her. Outside, the black cloud vanished upwards. Both ships were dropping fast. Shards of metal peeled away

419

furiously and Kimi braced herself, praying for not too many broken bones. Then came the fierce sound of scraping branches and Kimi lost sight of the other ship as lush greenery and the distinct smell of fir tree filled what was left of the cabin. The weight of the starburst lessened as it diminished. Cohn's chair crumbled from her grasp and the floor shattered and scattered all around her. She tumbled down through the whipping branches and landed onto grass with a hard thump that knocked the wind out of her.

She staggered to her knees and slid down into a bunker while the last particles of the starbursts disappeared in a melody of tinkles.

A crow cawed and Kimi looked just in time to see Audrey landing on the flagpole nearby. "One death!" she screeched before bursting into flames.

Of course! Kimi thought.

"Kimi!"

"Dad?"

She crawled from the sandpit, tears streaming down her cheeks, to the sight of Dad sprinting towards her with Mum close on his heels. Then she saw the shuck - three of them tearing out from the bushes behind her running parents. She sprang to her feet and, despite the throb in her shoulder from the earlier mojo blast, she dived into a sideways roll sending three perfect streams of orange fire flying from the fingertips of Little Hand. The three cats where hit in quick succession, twisting into the air one after the other and exploding in orange blooms of fire. Kimi sank back to the ground as Dad arrived. He dropped to his knees and hugged her tight.

"I knew you'd do it," he said, planting a big kiss on her forehead.

Mum arrived breathless. "What the hell were you doing up there? And – is that a field jacket?"

Dad cut in with a raised hand. "There's no time, Val - please - do as I say and do it quickly - Kimi's life depends on it!"

"Right," Mum said, looking totally perplexed.

Kimi smiled up at both of them through teary eyes, barely able to think straight as her father lifted her into his arms and began running across the green. Despite his thudding footfalls, she could really just go to sleep right now.

"What's going on, Jack?" Mum shouted, running alongside.

"We have to get home right now - run ahead and get the car started - quickly!"

Kimi jiggled in his arms. Mum in her purple sweater went flashing by.

"Du - Du - Dad," Kimi said, realising what was happening. "We can't!"

He didn't reply. Before Kimi could think again she

was being pushed into the back seat, doors were slamming and the car was slewing away with screeching tyres.

Mum was sobbing from the passenger seat. "You're scaring me, Jack!"

Kimi pulled herself up and took hold of the headrests on the front seats.

"Dad - we can't go home - the paradox – it'll -"

"Jack!" Mum screamed as he yanked the handbrake and the car spun out of the car park.

"Wiffy!" Dad yelled and Mum went quiet. "Don't worry about your mum," he said. "She's hypnotised."

"But Dad," Kimi pleaded. "If I meet myself - the paradox - my eyes will explode and -" He wasn't listening. She just knew he wasn't listening.

He put his foot down and they hit the main road, speeding up the centre line, overtaking everything and narrowly missing oncoming cars blaring their horns as they shot by.

"Dad!" Kimi screamed. "You don't get it - I'm stuck here, now!"

His knuckles were white on the wheel. They came to a small grassy roundabout, blanketed in lilac flowers. Dad didn't slow down, he just kept going straight ahead, ripping through the flower bed and the car took off and landed with a crunch of metal on the road beyond. The wheels regained traction immediately and the car rocketed forward.

"It's okay, Kimi - just hold on!"

"No!" she screamed. "The paradox thing will kill me!"

"That's in this world, Kimi," he shouted, yanking the handbrake once again and spinning the car onto the Mousehole road. "When the twirly groans, when Earth space hasn't quite settled into Heart space, yes?"

The groaning, yes, Kimi knew the groaning sound well enough.

"Meet yourself in groan time and you're back where you started!"

"What?"

"As one - you meld back as one!"

"But the groaning doesn't last long, Dad -"

"Five seconds," he said, dropping a gear and screaming every ounce of power from the little car. Kimi's heart was racing just as fast. Then suddenly, as he yanked the handbrake once again and the car tore into the narrow streets of Mousehole - realisation came in a glare of shiny brightness and she knew.

"The bins! It was *us – you - we* crashed into the bins!"

"What?" Dad yelled as the car spun around the final corner and the three bins, painted with big number 17's came into view. Kimi laughed and flung herself back into the seat, clapping.

"Wahoooo!" she screamed as Dad stamped on the brakes and the car skidded sideways, thumping into the bins and sending one banging off the front door.

Dad ratcheted the handbrake and both he and Mum opened their doors to get out.

"Wait!" Kimi said, leaping upright.

Mum looked at her blankly.

Sweat ran down Dad's face. "We have to hurry, Kimi."

"Uh-huh," Kimi said, shaking her head. "We have to wait until I jump - Bentley had a hard time persuading me to go."

"So how do we know when?" Dad said, urgently.

"Easy," Kimi said, opening her door in readiness. "Floor it, Dad!"

"What?"

"Rev the engine!"

"And that will?"

"Just do it!"

Jack pressed his foot to the pedal and the engine roared, vibrating the bonnet which was now leaking steam. Kimi put one foot out and cocked her ear. "Any second -"

"NOW!" Bentley's shout came loud and clear from inside.

"That's it!" yelled Kimi and she leapt from the car and went barging through the front door just in time to see

424

the sole of her trainer disappearing into the vortex in the dining room. She ran up the hall towards it.

"Dive Kimi, dive!" Dad shouted from behind and Kimi dived, head-first.

***

Kimi's knees landed on lush green grass. The thud shook her jaw and made her squeal.

"Kimi?" Bentley said.

Kimi looked up through tangles of hair. Bentley was holding out a sick bag. She looked back at the vortex which was not fading like it should be.

"What the?" Bentley said.

"They're coming." Kimi scrambled to her feet.

"Who's coming?"

"I saw the front door open. Someone came inside."

With a crackle of blue sparks, the air all around the vortex seemed to shudder and a figure came diving through headfirst. Kimi screamed at what looked like her double, dressed in a strange red jacket, was coming at her extremely fast.

Bentley was shouting something but fading quickly to blue.

Kimi tried to dodge her oncoming double, but the double had her arms outstretched and was flying towards her with a look of great determination, and the last thing she saw before she got knocked off her feet was her own grinning face right up at her nose.

For a few seconds, there was whiteness and an overpowering feeling of pumped up muscles. As sight and thought returned, Kimi looked around. Bentley was gone and so had the original Kimi. She still wore the jacket that Stella had given her and she could remember absolutely everything. Her trainers were no longer white. She pulled out her necklace and the cross was turquoise again. At least she didn't have that one to explain.

She gazed across the colourful countryside and saw the pond and the familiar trail zigzagging into the distance, and on the horizon; the green mount, and to the west the distant dark mountains. She guessed there was only one thing for it. She would send up a few flares and hopefully attract the attention of the fuzz. As she was about to do so, the wind began to gust and another vortex materialised a little way up the grassy slope. Mum and Dad stepped out and she ran to greet them.

Mum squeezed the life out of her. "Your Dad's told me everything."

"Well done, Kimi," Dad said, hugging her. "Knew you'd make a good Balancer."

Kimi grinned at him. "What happens now?"

"Want to go home? Get some rest?"

"Which home?"

Dad laughed. "Up to you, Balancer Nichols!"

"Well," Kimi said, gazing towards the green mount. "I really would like to go and check on the others." At that moment the ground began to vibrate.

"Brace yourself," Dad said, and they all grabbed hands.

"What is it?" Kimi said as the grassy slope started moving beneath their feet. It was rippling and the ripple was spreading outwards across the fields which soon billowed like shaken blankets.

"It's changing!" Dad said. "Time's catching up. Hold tight!"

He was smiling, so this must be okay.

As the landscape began to settle, a whole army of figures materialised on the field. A hundred or more sparkling chrome Squad bikes with people and monkeys cheering and waving. A great circular stage had appeared with steps leading up to it. Either side of the stage, makeshift seating had been erected from scaffold and hundreds of people and Tulpas were streaming into the seats, all cheering and clapping. There were greylians among them too - and at least fifty of the teardrop-shaped ships hovering in the sky. Kimi knew there'd be trouble of some sort, what with Cohn disappearing, but for now, this was truly a joyous sight. A few barbecues had been set up and smoke curled from them along with mouth-watering aromas. Music played from Barry's organ and people danced on the grass and a whole load of famoose were performing a synchronised lightshow in the air above the stage.

A small group emerged from the crowd. The first she recognised was the old Bentley. He was grinning, red-faced, wearing a striped apron and brandishing a toasting fork with a marshmallow on the end. Then Stella appeared running behind, punching the air and whooping. Monkey Rehd jumped from a squad bike and they all came running to greet her. Camera flashes were going off all over the crowd and when she spotted Perry by the stage with a video camera, Kimi's cheeks set on fire.

"Kimbo!" Bentley cried, throwing his arms around her and lifting her from the ground.

"Hey - watch that fork!"

"Oops - barbecue duty," he said, putting her down.

She landed in front of Rehd and Stella.

Rehd saluted. "Good job!"

"Thanks!" she gave Rehd a hug, relieved that he gave not the slightest of wobbles.

Stella giggled and they slapped a high-five. "Ach, braw job, sister!"

"Thanks, but what the heck's going on?" Kimi was dragged towards the stage, to deafening cheers.

"It's the time diff, Kimi," Dad's hand came on her shoulder. "You might have been back on Earth for only ten minutes or so, but they've been waiting all day. Enjoy it.

You deserve it."

"I see," Kimi said, smiling with twitching cheeks at Perry's video camera. She stumbled up the steps, arriving on the circular stage to thunderous applause. She looked at her shoes and wished for a trapdoor then turned to find the others and beckoned them to join her. "This is for you, too!" she shouted, smiling again at Perry as he moved to the front of the stage right next to her feet. Kimi could see the relief on Perry's face that they were in touching distance and he wasn't wobbling. She offered a hand and he climbed onto the stage.

"Well done, Kimi," he said. "You did a great job. I'm sorry I couldn't come along, what with the crazy wobble situation. But it seems fine now."

He might be a few years older than me, Kimi thought, but now's a good excuse for a hug. She flung her arms around him and loved that he hugged her back.

Dad, Mum, Bentley, Stella, Sue, Rehd, all joined the stage, patting Kimi on the back and applauding while the famoose danced in the air above. Kimi felt better with everyone around her, yet the ships floating above the seating areas and those further away seemed ominous. The few greylians in the crowd were still clapping. Kimi wondered how long it would be before one of them asked where the General was.

Shouts of "Speech - speech!" rang out and Kimi felt

suddenly weak as the crowd settled. The only sound now was the sizzle of meat on the barbecues and the greylian craft humming in the air. She turned to find help and saw Mum hugged into Dad. They were both smiling.

"Come on, Kimbo," Bentley said, pointing his fork at the crowd. "They want to hear what a hero gets up to."

"Nu - ner - ner nuh," Kimi clamped it. She was getting the stutters like she had the time she stood in front of the whole school to recite some daft thing, which now seemed a million years ago. No way could she do this. Murmurs were starting up all around the crowd.

"Listen Kimi," Bentley said. "It's easy. Take a deep -" Then he went absolutely still, his fork balanced in his fingers.

The murmurs stopped.

The meat stopped sizzling.

The ships in the sky went silent.

The famoose froze in the air above her head.

Even the smoke from the barbecues had paused.

Kimi spun round.

Mum, Dad, Stella, Sue, Rehd - everyone was still. Something was coming.

Kimi glanced around, expecting to see a crow, and that's when the sky opened up. A vertical rip in the blue sky revealed darkness behind. The rip grew wider, smouldering at its edges, before lightning erupted in a great web and a

430

burning craft fell through. It looked like a plane of some sort. It swept gently from side to side like a falling feather, the flames burning out before it came to a stop, hovering in the air some fifty feet beyond the crowds.

"You got to be kidding me," Kimi said. She glanced around at her frozen friends but she was the only witness to this. This was totally unreal. A space shuttle. A bloody enormous, real, US of A space shuttle.

The huge shuttle slowly descended. It looked pretty torn up and scorched. Some of its protective tiles fell away and thudded to the grass before the ship settled.

`Discovery` said large blue letters on the nose, and `NASA` in big letters near the tail. Kimi had no idea what was coming next, but guessed it must be something big. Sounds of clanging metal came from the shuttle's hull and the two long doors down its back began to open. Kimi held her breath, then felt the urgent need to run when a greylian ship rose from the hull. The teardrop-shaped craft moved away and stopped over the crowd to her left. A wide beam of blue light snapped on, engulfing a third of the frozen crowd. They were picked up in the beam just like Kimi had been and the opal swung away over the rocky outcrop towards the trail.

There was no time to wonder why before more movement came from the shuttle. Its crane-like arm was emerging and on its end sat a large chrome bell. Kimi recognised it immediately. It was like the scanner at the library. There was no one in it though, only steam coming from the hole in the top. The crane swung around and lowered it to the grass just as the greylian ship returned, picked up another third of the crowd then zipped away again.

"Bravo!" a gruff voice came from inside the scanner. A voice which Kimi thought she recognised. The doors hissed open to a billow of steam.

Kimi jumped down to the grass and watched as the steam cleared.

"Temporal perfection," the voice said, and there, sitting in some kind of adult baby walker, was the barely recognisable face of Babbage. The contraption trundled out onto the grass and made straight for Kimi.

She wanted to say, *crap-a-something*, but just stood there open-mouthed.

Babbage was more deformed than before. One eye was almost engulfed by sagging flesh, the other spread wide by his monocle. His jaw looked totally dislocated and she couldn't see many teeth. Saliva dribbled over his swollen lips. His arms and hands were swollen too, and he wore some sort of white rubber suit which appeared to be holding him together. There were no dangling false legs this time, only a hefty bulge in the seat of the contraption.

"Surprised?" he said.

Despite his horrific appearance and obvious inability

432

to smile, Kimi could still see the kindness in his eyes. "Mr Babbage?"

The grotesque figure nodded and a string of snot fell to the grass.

"What have you done with everybody?"

"They're in a time-spin," Babbage said. "Safe as houses!"

"But what are you doing here? I - I don't get it."

He removed the familiar clicker device from a pocket on his arm. "Hopefully, I'm here to save you, Kimi."

"Save *me*?"

"Yes!" Babbage pressed the clicker and red digits appeared in the air to his right in foot high letters.

06:00

The digits began counting down.

05:59

05:58

"When the clock reaches zero." Babbage nodded to the statuesque Bentley with the toasting fork still balanced in his fingers. "Your Tulpa will cut off your head!"

———

24

~ The Final Secret ~

"He'll do what?"

"Cut off your head!"

Kimi sank to the grass. "With a toasting fork?"

Babbage trundled closer and the digits in the air moved with him. "Don't you want to know *why*?"

Kimi looked up at a smiling Bentley, frozen in time with his chef's apron and the fork with a marshmallow on the end; then at the smoking space shuttle behind Babbage; and the frozen crowds being lifted in the greylian craft's beam; and at Perry, concentrating on the screen of his video camera. She wanted to say how crazy this all was, but what hadn't been crazy about the last two days.

"There's no time for dreaming, Kimi."

"Huh?" she turned back to Babbage.

Babbage sighed. "Time is unfortunately against us!"

05:33

"Right, sorry. Why the heck would Bentley want to kill me?"

"I never said he killed you. I said he cuts off your head."

"But that's got to kill me, right?"

"I'm afraid you were already dead, Kimi. And your

435

brave Tulpa cuts off your head because it is the right thing to do. The proper thing. His last and greatest service to you."

04:59

Time was ticking before Kimi's eyes. Time to die. "I don't want to die. Not now. Not after all -"

"Kimi, please don't," Babbage said softly. "There isn't much time for either of us. Stay with me. Concentrate."

The greylian craft returned and swept over the stage. Its blue beam engaged everyone apart from Kimi. It even took all the famoose.

"Where are they going?" Kimi asked, as Mum, Dad, Rehd, Sue, Bentley, Stella and Perry all floated away beneath the ship.

Babbage groaned and three teeth spilled over his lip and slavered to the grass. He wiped the blood from his mouth. "To the pond," he said.

"You're putting them in the pond?"

"Yes."

The craft returned, lifted higher, positioned itself over a frozen craft, engaged its beam and shot away towards the trail taking the frozen craft with it.

"*And* all the spacecraft?"

"Yes," Babbage said. "Those too." He pressed the clicker and a screen emerged from the back of the walker. "Please watch the screen. This is footage recovered from Perry's video camera." Babbage coughed and another tooth

436

fell out. "Damn and blast. I'm going, Kimi. We haven't long, let's -"

"Going where?"

04:07

"Dying of course. I once told you, many, many years ago, that another jump would see me off."

"Yes, I remember it like it was yesterday." Kimi sniffed and wiped her eyes. "Thank you, Charlie. Thank you for everything. You helped me save Mum and Dad, and now you're saving -"

"Look," Babbage cut in. "Let's speed this up shall we?" He looked embarrassed and a tear ran out from under his monocle. He wiped it away and pressed the clicker. "Here's what happens in exactly four minutes from now."

Kimi appeared on screen, the camera close up on her blushing face. Crowds are cheering. Mum and Dad are clapping behind Kimi. They look proud. Rehd is eating a dodo dog. Bentley is doing a jig. Then the crowd go quiet and Bentley is pointing the toasting fork and saying something to Kimi. She stutters and mumbles at first, but soon starts to thank the people for turning up. Then there's a rumbling sound and the image begins to shake. The camera swings round and zooms in on the dark mountains where great clouds of smoke fill the sky. Gasps are coming from the crowd and shouts of `it's gonna blow!` are followed by panicked screams.

Babbage paused the film. "When you came back, Kimi, when you dived into groan time and melded with your original self in order to prevent the paradox, the resulting resetting of time made great waves through Heart."

He hit the clicker and the image started up again. *Crowds poured from their seats. Then came the biggest set of bangs. The camera swings back to the dark mountains. Fire explodes from the tallest peak and the sky darkens. In seconds, the first smaller stones begin raining down on the fleeing crowds. Squad bikes and people disperse in all directions as the stones grow in size and come smashing down. Perry's voice can be heard, shouting as he runs, capturing the jumpy chaos on screen as people are crushed by flaming boulders and ash begins to fall like grey snow.*

"This is awful - switch it off!"

"Please. It is important you watch, Kimi."

The images were jumpy, people ran and bodies dropped everywhere. One of the flying reptiles came down in flame. Another, on fire, soared by. Boulders were knocking greylian ships from the sky. One spun out of control and crashed into a crowd of people. Then Kimi saw herself get slammed in the back by a flaming boulder. The camera went quickly to the felled Kimi who looked unconscious or dead. Blood was running from her mouth. Bentley arrived, sobbing. He was fading to see-through. His hands went to Kimi's head. Tears streamed down his cheeks and he started making the most awful rasping cries.

Tears spilled and Kimi let them fall. Babbage gave a little nod.

A golden light appeared over Kimi's body, and those that had gathered round stepped back. The light formed into a figure - Patina - in a flowing white dress, her hair all curls and tendrils. She pulled an axe from her dress and passed it to Bentley. `Take it quickly!` she said. Bentley was almost fully transparent. He looked up at Patina through swollen eyes. Her hand touched his brow and he nodded and took the axe. A monkey dropped into shot on his knees. He was holding a plastic box. Bentley kissed Kimi's head, then lifted her ponytail. He touched the axe to her neck and the camera swished away to the sound of another eruption and a swarm of boulders blazed across the sky. The camera followed them and all the while, people are crying, and above this are the sounds of Bentley's distraught sobs. The boulders come down miles away on the horizon - right over Middling and the green mount containing the library. The image shakes along with the rumbling ground and cries and gasps come from those watching and the camera zooms in as the green covering on the mount slides to the floor in a great mushrooming cloud of dust. Then the screen went black.

"No, no, no, no, no!" Kimi said. "How come *she* showed up? And what the hell did Bentley do that for? And what the hell happened to Middling?"

Babbage clicked his clicker and the image returned. The dust was clearing and the green mount was no longer there. In its place stood a golden pyramid.

"What the bloody hell?"

"You'll find out, soon enough."

Kimi stared at the screen. "So I'm going to die after all this? And all those others, too?"

"I hope not," Babbage said. "But let's stick with the present. We haven't got long!"

02:55

The greylian ship returned and picked another craft from the sky. There were only a few left now.

"Only a handful survived," Babbage said.

"But what about the others? Mum, Dad, Stella?"

"Dead."

"And Sue and Rehd and Perry?"

"Dead."

"And Bentley?"

"We built a statue for Bentley. When he performed his final and most sombre duty to his Balancer, his retirement came at the same instant."

"Oh my God."

"The landslide killed the entire stock of dodo and wounded many people."

Kimi couldn't stop the tears. This was all her fault. "I sh - should have just gone to live in a cave," she sobbed.

"No Kimi. Casualties would have been far greater if it weren't for you!"

"Me?"

Babbage nodded. "When you left in the starburst, the stones around the wood collapsed."

"No way."

"Yes. And landing the way they did formed a barricade that saved the Shed from major damage and prevented many deaths. There was however much despair in the months that followed. We'd survive of course, but then something terrible happened."

"What the hell could be more terrible?"

"War! The greylians blamed the Adepts for the death of the General - no one knew what he really did. And your brain, which Patina knew carried great value, was eventually captured by the greylians. They wanted the means to time travel and your brain was the key. A great battle ensued for many years."

"How many?"

"Ten."

"You've come back in time ten years?"

"No Kimi - the war was lost along with many precious lives. It has taken me twenty-five years to reach this momentous point. You see, half of your brain was eventually recovered - I kept it alive, realising that the only way to stop the war was to get back here and prevent your death in the first place. And with a little help from your driving force and our NASA Balancers, here I am!"

"My brain is driving the space shuttle?"

"A quarter of it. The other quarter is operating the greylian ship."

"So what now?"

Babbage coughed and his left eye dropped out but he didn't seem too bothered. Kimi felt very sorry for him. She wasn't quite understanding all the implications, but that clock was ticking down and she knew that Babbage was a hero.

"I can feel it quickening inside me, Kimi. I'm starting to close down. Let me continue. The cleanup took months. We realised there were very few areas where rocks, boulders, lava dumps or reptiles didn't touch down. I had to look for a place that would comfortably hold all these people, and of course the fifty or so greylian ships hanging in the sky - and I found such a place - the pond nearby."

"Why not fly them far away? Or put them in the shuttle?"

"If my calculations are correct, which I believe they are, everything I have brought here will disintegrate once time resets for the second time."

"So you've dumped everyone in the pond?"

"Yes."

"Even the spaceships?"

442

"Especially them! Any more greylian deaths will not go down well. Our actions today must prevent the war from ever starting in the first place - and that means keeping you alive!"

"But Cohn's dead. Why didn't you go back and save him?"

"Oh no. Cohn had to die, Kimi. The quest to recover your brain uncovered many of Cohn's secret plans. Saving Cohn would have brought death to thousands. Cohn's demise was down to his own inept stupidity and that is something we need to convince the greylians of!"

"Bloody hell. So what do I do?"

01:31

"I think you had better run - we have only a minute and a half. You can't go on board the shuttle or be taken to the pond by the greylian ship because you will paradox with the drivers."

"My brain."

Babbage nodded.

Kimi was shaking. "So I run to the pond, then what?"

"The final secret, Kimi. When time resets and the others come around, you must play dumb and tell nothing of my being here."

"So what do I do?"

"The greylians will be looking for you - initially

curious as to where their General is - but soon, curiosity will turn into lust for your purity. You must return to Middling with great haste, come immediately to see me, and explain everything!"

"This is mad!"

"Yes it is. But you must trust me on this Kimi. I want you to tell me something when you get back to Middling."

"Erm, okay," she said as both Babbage's ears slid down his head.

"Tell me it's in the eyes, Kimi...always get the eyes."

00:42

"The eyes?"

"Yes. Run now Kimi. You have a flaming boulder to dodge and a pond to leap into - run!" Babbage's bottom jaw fell off and his face began to dissolve. Kimi jumped back and yelped as his head turned inside out and a red fountain spurted into the air. The walker collapsed and broke into pieces just as the greylian craft returned, settled to the grass and shattered into a million bits. Then the space shuttle started shaking.

That's when Kimi ran. Down the stone steps into the gulley, through the long alleyway in the rock face and out onto the field. As she sprinted, the air wavered dreamily. The trembling ground came up awkwardly to meet her pounding feet and threw her off balance a few times. The bangs went off and the sky darkened as it had done on screen, and the first small stones hailed down.

And there was the pond, its shallows crammed with statuesque people, and in the middle, fifty greylian ships along with many famoose hung still, inches above the surface.

Kimi ran and leapt into the water as the boulders began to rain down and the two flying reptiles soared overhead, their wings on fire. The odd small stone hit the water here and there, but Babbage had been right, none of the big stuff was hitting the pond. Everyone had been saved. Even the famoose.

She spotted Bentley's striped apron and ran splashing through the water to him. She pried the toasting fork from his fingers and threw it in the pond, then tucked under his arm as the next eruption exploded. The resulting swarm of boulders flew across the sky like meteors, raining down on Middling in a shower of flames. The mount rumbled and its green covering slid away right before her eyes.

Then came quiet - only Kimi, panting for breath.

Slowly, voices were breaking the silence as people came unfrozen.

Kimi turned to face them through a curtain of falling ash.

Dusty greylian ships were lifting to the sky.

Famoose coughed and spluttered and threw ash from their wings.

Stella came splashing through the water looking totally perplexed.

"What happened?" Bentley said.

All around were cries of, "How? Why? When?" Mum, Dad and Stella were wading towards her.

"Crap a calamity," Stella said. "How'd we get here?"

"Later," Kimi said. "We've got work to do."

People and Tulpas poured from the pond in droves, all remarking on the golden pyramid in the distance. Kimi stepped to dry land and pulled Stella onto the trail.

"Come on people," she shouted. "We need to be hurrying here!" She set off walking briskly. Stella, Sue and Perry, followed with Mum and Dad at the rear.

"What the hell happened in Middling?" asked Bentley, catching her up. "And how'd we end up in the pond? Am I losing my head?"

"No you're not," Kimi said. "But we have to go and visit an old friend before I lose mine!"

To Be Continued...

www.johnhudspith.co.uk

Thank you...

Massive thanks with oodles of gratitude must be heaped on Matt, Carol and Rebby for being so doggedly ruthless in ensuring that my babies were shaved. Thank you.

To my good friend and fellow author Anne Stormont for her keen eye and the loan of her wonderfully discombobulated pupils at Portree Primary; their constant reading, laughs, groans, crazy pictures and stimulating ideas – I send a zillion thanks!

And to wifey, Ande for her eternal patience and persistent inspiration. Thank you forever.

———————

Lightning Source UK Ltd.
Milton Keynes UK
UKOW051926110713

213646UK00001B/2/P